The Devil's Violin

Myllysilta's History

Also by Roy Blomstrom

Silences: A Novel of the 1918 Finnish Civil War

The Iterations of Caroline

The Devil's Violin

Myllysilta's History

Roy Blomstrom

Issued in print and electronic formats. *July 2024*.

ISBN: 978-1-7750526-6-1

The Devil's Violin: Myllysilta's History is a work of fiction. Any references to real people have been fictionalized.

Cover design: H. Leighton Dickson

Shuniah House Books
www.shuniahhousebooks.com

For Bill and Karen

Modern Finland

CONTENTS

Part III: INNOCENCE AND EXPERIENCE

Part IV: TRIAL

Part V: ACCEPTANCE

PROLOGUE

MELODIES OF
CANADA AND FINLAND

FOR MANY YEARS NOW, he'd rarely thought of his life back in Finland. It seemed more a memory than a real place.

Besides, his time there was decades in the past—a different life, a whole lifetime ago.

A few things he did remember. The weather had always hinted at winter, even in spring, when the fields were set greening once more, and in summer when the land was redolent with sweat and mosquitos, and in autumn as the season traded its green leaves for vistas of golden tamaracks and birches.

Always, winter itself returned, cold and bitter. It was a season that numbed everything but hunger, a hunger that had gnawed at him, challenging him to survive.

Canada, at least, had promised him escape from Finland. And he'd been successful, for a while. Canada was big, and in that expanse, he'd found it easy to disappear and start fresh. But in recent years, memories of his past—his real past, not the one he'd counterfeited— kept breaking through his happiness.

His daughter, when she was a toddler, had run laughing around and around the coffee table, a stray beam from the late-afternoon sun lighting her face and hair. He would stretch his hand toward her to steady her steps and see, in a flash, all the evil that his hand had done. Before.

One day his dutiful young son stood somber and rigid at a graveside, a victim of cataclysmic, incomprehensible loss. In his son's face, he'd recognized his own unsmiling misery—his own stiffness and cowardice, his personal pain and fear—all left behind, he'd thought, in Finland. Foolish thought.

For decades, he'd been able to resist the memories. He loved his children and wanted better for them. He'd wanted them to have the best of everything, especially the knowledge that they were cherished. Their very existence was a miracle to him—a mercy he could never imagine, much less dare ask for.

As always, grace came unmerited. And it was often snatched away quickly and without apparent reason—at least not a reason that he was able to understand.

But, he told himself, *What is, is.* Or, when he sometimes allowed himself to think in Finnish, *Mitä tulee, tulee.* One of the few things he remembered his mother saying. His father, also.

As the decades accumulated, he lost control of his flashes of memory. He tried not to let them linger long enough to intrude. They had become irrelevant books on a library shelf—books he didn't need to read, because he'd read them all before.

Nevertheless, voices from his previous lives began to speak to him. They crowded in, persistent and insistent, warning him to protect his children and to isolate himself from strangers. Those voices promised him neither sanity nor forgiveness in return.

In his very last years, they reminded him often of two memories.

#

The first was from a winter night when Antti Myllysilta was very young, perhaps six or seven.

Antti was asleep in his spot on the floor in the small bedroom he shared with his four brothers, who also slept.

He awoke to his father's bellows.

"This isn't food!" his father yelled. He'd been drinking. Antti could hear it in the thickness of his voice.

Antti ran into the big room—the one with both a stove and a fireplace.

"It's still raw and it's late!" his father shouted, throwing a plate of food at Antti's mother. Then he flung the kitchen table aside, grabbed an andiron from the fireplace, and struck her in the head with it. She fell to the floor, dead. His father howled and dropped the weapon—it was too hot to hold.

The clatter of the andiron on the floor woke the other boys.

Marku, at nineteen the eldest of Antti's brothers, exploded out of the children's bedroom and saw his mother on the floor. He rushed at his father and pushed him into the wall beside the fireplace.

Their father was strong—much stronger than Marku—and he came away from the wall like a bear attacking a deer. He threw his son to the floor and began kicking him. Marku had the sense to stay down and protect his head.

Antti's other brothers did not try to help Marku. Tuomas and Timo, the twins, were fourteen; Seppo just twelve. They watched in silence, knowing they would be next if they intervened.

Antti, however, yelled, "Stop! Stop!" He tried to get between his father and Marku, but his father flicked him aside as he might a clump of mud on his boot, and kept kicking Marku. Antti stayed where flung.

At last, Marku lost consciousness. Then, unopposed, their father stripped their mother's body and dragged her corpse outside to the edge of the forest, where he left it for the animals to dispose of.

When he returned to the house, he beat Antti until the boy had to pretend to be dead, too.

Then, satisfied that no one would cause him more trouble, he got the violin from under their bed and played it for a while before he sank into the chair in the corner, unconscious with sleep and drink.

Antti and Marku remained on the floor until they were sure that their father wouldn't stir. Cautiously, they slipped into their bedroom.

In the morning, Antti's father had Marku and Antti first clean the kitchen floor, and then make breakfast for him and the "good boys." Marku and Antti got nothing to eat or drink at all that day.

In the early afternoon, their father fell asleep. The brothers sneaked out of the house and buried their mother. They had nothing—not even her clothing—to wrap her in.

#

The second memory was from some years later. Antti, aged about twelve, woke from a nightmare. He went outside and got a heavy rock, larger than his fist. He went straight into the bedroom where his father lay sleeping. A wine bottle, the cork now back in its neck, rested on the floor where his father could easily reach it.

Antti slammed the rock down on his father's head—once, twice. His brothers slept on. Antti stood for a while looking at the blood that flowed from the broken skull onto the pillow.

Sometimes, he thought, *you just have to wait. Wait until you're older. Wait until you know more. Then you too can be strong.* He smiled. The words were his mother's.

It took all his strength to drag his father's body out to the barn and put it in a horse stall. Wolf, the feral dog that Antti had adopted the year before, watched. But if his brothers woke, they gave no sign.

Back at the house, Antti saw no bloodstains on the bedding, but he took the pillow, sodden with his father's blood, to the stall and threw it in with the body.

Something else, he thought. He retrieved the wine bottle, the violin, and the bow. He set down the violin and bow, then uncorked the bottle and entered the enclosure, being careful not to agitate the horse, and laid the bottle beside his father.

He considered leaving the violin in the stall, too, to make it look as if the horse had killed his father because it didn't like being serenaded, but that was a stupid idea. He settled for keeping the violin for himself.

A souvenir, he thought. *To remember her by.* Through the years, he found various hiding places to protect the violin from his brothers— high in the barn loft, under the bed. He moved it often.

That night, Wolf watched the boy re-enter the house. The dog waited near the barn, but Antti didn't return with scraps of food for him, so he trotted back into the woods and began the night's hunting.

The horse, after Antti had gone, added marks of its own to the corpse.

#

Antti didn't regret what he'd done. He never felt the need to confess or to boast, never told his brothers that he had taken the violin, never asked them what his mother's name had been, nor his father's. He never felt guilt or shame.

Even decades later, as the voices grew more direct in their accusations—*Liar! Murderer! Evil!*—he did his best to shrug them off. Perhaps they were right. Regardless, he couldn't change his past. However much he changed the stories he told about it.

He'd pick up the violin and play until the voices subsided. But they, like winter, always came back.

And eventually, he could no longer ignore them.

PART I

FAITH UNFAITHFUL: FINLAND, 1918 - 1921

"And thus the whirligig of time brings in his revenges."

Feste (the Clown), *Twelfth Night*, Act V, Scene i
William Shakespeare

1 • BROTHERS

EACH OF THE FIVE Myllysilta brothers, like others of the Red *lentävä osasto*—the flying detachment raiders—wore an improvised blood-red armband over the sleeve of a heavy winter greatcoat.

The armbands marked them as loyal Red Finns already engaged in the Revolution—though the Myllysilta brothers were not especially loyal to anyone but themselves. And, even then, it was a loyalty born of circumstance and opportunity—not circumspection, and certainly not brotherly love.

Marku, the eldest and leader of the siblings, was thirty years old, with some life under his belt. He had visited both Helsinki and Vaasa and he had worked in the factories of both Tampere and Lahti. The bosses, Marku had told his brothers, were White Finns, and Whites thought nothing of working a man to death, and so *they* deserved the same fate.

The next oldest, the twins Tuomas and Timo, were farm boys of little skill except in caring for horses. They hated farming, and would gladly have worked in a factory like Marku, but the recent strikes and firings in Finland, and their own hotheadedness, made it unlikely that anyone would risk hiring them—especially where they lived, in the province of Ostrobothnia.

In Ostrobothnia, most people were Finland-Swedes, not Finns like the Myllysiltas, and spoke Swedish, not Finnish. The Ostrobothnians worried that 1918 would bring full-blown civil war to Finland—a horrific step beyond the current Red Terror. After all, a few months earlier the Bolsheviks had seized control of Petrograd, Russia—and Finland had been a semi-autonomous province of Russia until it declared independence in December of 1917. And that meant—what *did* that mean?

The twins didn't really understand Marku's hatred of White Finns, but they pretended to. They did whatever he told them to do, and did it without complaint because Marku was the eldest and strongest, and

9

he had, after all, been to Tampere and to Lahti, and they had not. There was no reason to doubt what he told them.

Seppo, a little younger than the twins, was the group's provisioner. He hunted and fished expertly, and he robbed and threatened without pang of conscience. It mattered nothing to him if he was shooting at a deer or a man, a White or a Red. What mattered was the thrill of the kill.

Antti was about seventeen. He didn't know his exact birthdate. The youngest of the Myllysilta brothers, he was slight and still small for his age, though growing quickly. Nevertheless, he rode with the skill of a Mongol horseman. He handled his mount—a Don he had stolen from a Cossack mercenary—with understanding and expertise, even better than the twins could have.

The brothers knew that Antti was the smartest of them all. In better times he might have had a future as a factory foreman or even a clergyman. He could organize and plan. And he had the gift of the gab, with just the right mix of cruelty and charm to get ahead in the world.

His brothers envied Antti, and so they scolded and beat him whenever they felt the world owed them something, which was frequently. Consequently, Antti never asked them how old he was and never showed any need to probe the secrets they withheld from him. Wolf adored him, and that was love enough.

And now they rode on a mission that was likely to be as bloody as their red armbands. They were used to that. All of them.

When they reached the intersection where the road from the village of Gamlaby met the road to the Mantere farm, Marku had the group rein in their horses. He took out his pocket watch and squinted to see the numbers. It was close to three o'clock in the afternoon, and because January of 1918 had only one week left in it, a couple of hours from now it would be dark.

They didn't have much time and were already looking forward to what they'd do after they'd killed the family. They'd decided to go back to Gamlaby, maybe get drunk—not Antti, of course, who was always treated as if he were too young. The rest of them, though, yes. Anyway, that was the plan.

"He might not be there," Seppo said. There was already disappointment in his voice. The son was the main target, and if he was not home .... Seppo left the thought incomplete. Nothing ever worked out for him, so why bother thinking about what they would do if the son was absent? That was Marku's job.

"If he's not there, we'll wait," Marku said, as if on cue.

Antti looked back down the dirt road. "He'll see our tracks," he said. The underlying thought he kept to himself: *To know your enemy, you must become your enemy.* Sun Tzu had said it in *The Art of War*—one of the many books that he had read, but his brothers had not.

"He'll still come," Marku said. "And you're *not* coming. I don't want you involved in this. Go back to Gamlaby and stay out of sight."

"Why can't I come?"

"Enough!" Marku turned his horse around in the direction of the farm. "Do as I say. And if someone sees you, don't let him catch you. We'll head through Gamlaby when we finish here. You can join us as we ride through."

Marku and the others made for the farm.

Antti turned his horse around and started slowly down the road, casting occasional glances over his shoulder. *I should have objected more.*

Marku wanted Antti to stay away from the people in Gamlaby because Marku worried that the brothers might be recognized. They'd killed the owner of the general store some months earlier. The raid had been one of Antti's first. Even though Marku had only let him be the lookout, Antti felt entitled to claim partial credit for the raid's success—they'd stolen some much-needed food and sown terror that had spread through the region afterwards.

Antti, alone of his brothers, deeply understood that sometimes, what had happened was less important than the story people told about it.

But Marku had still taunted him. After the raid, Marku tossed Antti some of the candies they'd stolen, calling him "the little boy Gamlaby was afraid of." Although Antti hated the abuse, he was always hungry, so he'd picked up the candies. No sense in wasting anything good.

And since then, he'd grown taller—nearly as tall as Seppo, now.

When his brothers were out of sight, Antti stopped grumbling and turned back toward the farm. At the fork, he made his horse leap the drainage ditch and take a few steps toward the forest's edge. Then he dismounted, left the rifle in its saddle sheath and, leading the horse by the reins, walked into the woods. Once under cover of the trees, he looked back to make sure that no tracks showed between the ditch and the road, then he continued into the forest. The shadows of the trees would help camouflage his path.

If his brothers got into trouble, he'd ride to their rescue. If he obeyed Marku and went to Gamlaby, people would eye him with suspicion. Since they didn't know him, they'd automatically assume that he was what he was: *lentävä osasto*, a raider, part of a terror squad sent to wreak havoc on the Whites before the *real* war started—the war that Marku said should have begun in 1917.

Marku insisted on calling it the *real* war. He maintained that it would free Finland from the capitalists and landowners and from the domination of the Whites. The *real* war was not to be confused with the war in France and Belgium, of course.

Antti smiled grimly. Marku loved to spout the party line. That Antti's brother was officially *lentävä osasto* was true, and he'd brought his brothers along on raids, as long as the brothers were useful. The rest, though, about the *real* war, was Red bullshit. Those greedy Whites would just be replaced by the greedy Reds, among whom Antti included his brothers.

Antti had no illusions about the Revolution. It was coming, yes, but it would be just as much a mess as the bigger war in France and Belgium. The cold fog of war was rolling into Finland now, from both Russia and Germany. The shouting and the shooting had already begun, and Antti didn't give a shit about which side, Red or White, was right. Probably neither side was.

I think too much, Antti thought. *I need to get the horse away from the road.*

It wasn't difficult to lead the horse through the trees. Because the Manteres had cleared away and burned the underbrush as firewood in the winter, a walk in the forest near their home was almost like a walk in a farmer's field, but the sparse ground cover meant that Antti needed to get a long way from the road to be sure that no one coming to visit the Manteres would be able to see the horse. The Don, moreover, tended to snort and whinny, making it a hard horse to hide. "*People look with their ears*," his father used to say, "*as much as with their eyes*." It was the wisdom of a thief.

Antti led the horse deeper into the woods than he would have liked and tied the reins to a branch. The horse tossed its head but settled down and stood silently. Antti walked back toward the road and, at the edge of the forest, lay down behind a fallen tree.

The gunfire began almost as soon as he'd got comfortable. One shot, then another. A short pause and then a third. Antti waited. When nothing more happened, he thought, *It's over.* He decided to let his brothers go past and get well ahead of him, then he'd leave. Better to have them ahead of him than behind him. He lay still, listening for the sound of hooves, but heard nothing. They were taking too long. A fourth shot. A minute passed. A fifth shot.

Antti wasn't sure what to do next. He squirmed around to see how low the sun was. How much time did he have? The sun would set slowly, sliding along the horizon instead of dropping like a dead bird into the pine needles and snow. Still, it was no more than an hour until dark.

He needed to be able to see up the road to the farm.

He crawled through the scrub brush and brown grass at the edge of the forest, then slithered into the shallow ditch. He propped himself up on his elbows and looked up the road. Besides the hoof prints of his brother's horses, fresh tracks from a cart now marked the patches of snow and mud on the road. The tracks had not been there when he and his brothers had arrived.

The son! Antti thought.

The Manteres' son was at the farmhouse. Sometime between the first three shots and the last two, while he'd been deep in the forest and unable to see the road, the son had come home. Now what?

I will wait, Antti thought. *I will wait here. If my brothers come by, that is one thing. If the son comes by, that is another.*

A quarter of an hour passed, then Antti heard the clatter of the cart approaching from the farmhouse. He worked his way out of the ditch and across the dry grass, then crawled back into the safety of the forest. He did not risk looking up when the cart rumbled past. When the sound had nearly died down, he retrieved the Don and led him to the road. He mounted and headed up the hill to the farmhouse.

As he came into the farmyard, he saw no sign of his brothers' horses. Had they run off? Had the son's arrival made them scatter—perhaps even flee? Not likely. But then where were the horses and his brothers? There were, Antti noticed, no boot prints leading away from the house. That was not good.

Antti went in. He found the body of the woman—the mother—but not the bodies of his four brothers, not the body of the woman's husband, either, or of her son.

He looked at the scene carefully, coldly. The woman lay on the floor, a knife some distance away. She had been both shot and stabbed—then slashed repeatedly. Her dress was striped in red along her side; her apron wet with blood.

Antti knew he should feel something for this woman, killed like his mother, but she was not his mother and Antti felt nothing. He had seen dead people before—at funerals where the body was dressed in its Sunday best and lay posed for presentation. This woman's face was slack, her mouth open. Her eyes stared as if she could see through the walls and beyond them, as if she were looking far into the distance for a hint of light in the sudden, puzzling, darkness.

The kitchen table lay on its side between the body and the door. Splashes and streaks of blood smeared the floor a short distance away. A sewing needle, some thread, and a pair of scissors lay there as well. A rifle stood prim and proper by the kitchen door. *What the hell had happened in here?*

Antti kept thinking about his brothers' horses. Where were they? They were worth a lot of money, now. War used up horses the way steamships used up coal, and as sure as hell there was going to be much more war in Finland. But now he couldn't profit from his brothers' horses. Even if he found them, to whom could he sell them? People would recognize the animals and connect him to this murder.

His brothers, Antti knew, would already be suspects—no witnesses required. The Myllysiltas, though not known personally in Gamlaby, had a certain reputation.

But ... but that was of no importance because ... because, Antti realized, *they were likely dead and in the back of the cart that the Manteres' son was driving.*

So. He was free of them. No more having to listen to Marku badger, bully and bitch. A smile flared momentarily on Antti's face, but he immediately extinguished it. He needed to plan. Marku was no longer the leader.

I am, Antti thought. *But of what?*

First, he needed to get away. He'd go to Gamlaby and then ... somewhere else. Somewhere safe. He looked at the woman again. The man in the cart, whoever he was, had not moved her—had refused to put her in the same cart as her murderers.

Antti went outside, mounted his horse and started down the road, enjoying his Don's speed.

After a few kilometers, Antti saw the cart far ahead, bumping and twisting along the road, travelling as fast as the driver could make the horse go. Even from behind, he recognized the Manteres' son. As he got closer, the shapes in the back of the cart became bodies. Antti's brothers were piled up, body upon bloodied body. The pile shifted and shook whenever the cart's wheels hit a hole or became caught in a rut. It was as if the dead were uncomfortable—tossing and turning in their sleep as the cart carrying them to hell sped down the road.

Antti gained rapidly on the cart, weighing and discarding options. Should he kill the driver and bury the bodies? Too dangerous. The son likely had a rifle beside him or at his feet. If he heard the hooves of the Don, he'd look back, see Antti, and then shoot to kill. Even if he could surprise the driver, Antti didn't like his chances.

The cart wheels made a lot of noise, but was it enough to drown out galloping hooves? Perhaps. *If I can get ahead of the cart*, he thought, *I might even be able to make it home.*

So. He'd let the driver take the bodies to Gamlaby, for whatever the driver had in mind.

He leaned forward in the saddle and spoke to his horse. "Run," he said quietly. *He won't hear us until we're beside him*, he thought.

They built up speed, caught up to the cart, and passed it. To keep from being recognized, Antti turned his face away as he went by. There was no time for the driver to reach down for the rifle, aim, and shoot.

#

Soon after, Antti rode into town, his red armband stuffed in his pocket. Gamlaby was a small village, an enclave of the Whites—Finland-Swedes and White Finns. Here, wearing a red armband could get you killed, or so Markku had said. In Gamlaby, people had no sympathy for communists and revolutionaries, and only a little sympathy—salted heavily with disdain—for ordinary Finns.

It was nearing sunset, and no one saw Antti arrive. He tied the Don to a post behind the blacksmith's shop, then moved to a spot where he could keep his eye on the village's main street, especially

Svensson's, the general store Marku had warned him about. He waited.

Fifteen minutes later, the cart came into view. The driver stopped the cart just in front of Svensson's general store. He got down and went around to the back of the cart and pulled one of the bodies off, letting the bloodied body fall to the ground. Antti was close enough to see the driver's face, streaked with tears. A young man ran out of the store to help him.

"They killed my mother," the driver said to the young man, whom Antti recognized from the raid in November as one of Svensson's employees. The young man put his hand on the driver's shoulder to stop him from dumping the bodies into the street.

The driver shook it off and yelled, "No! They killed my mother. They belong in the dirt."

Antti should have felt something. He knew that. But he watched the bodies come off the wagon and fall onto the road, and his eyes stayed dry. The bodies seemed to him like nothing, like bales of hay. There was no catch in his throat, no grief, no wish to have his brothers back. They had been his brothers, but now they were dead, and they were no longer his brothers. They were nothing at all, and that was just as well.

Dust to dust, Antti thought. It seemed to explain everything. He went back to his horse, mounted, and rode away slowly, as if he were someone who had just made a purchase or completed some business in the town. No one took notice of him.

He headed home. Home? Well, where he'd been born, at least.

#

Because there was no safe shelter on the way, Antti did not sleep that night, although, mindful of the Don, he stopped occasionally. Still, by dawn he was in the port of Kokkola, fifty kilometres north of Gamlaby. Half an hour later, he dismounted in front of the log-and-barnboard shack that his parents had built a few kilometres outside of the city.

The shack was a ruin inside and smelled of mould, but the roof had only a few small holes. The woodstove was still in good shape and would keep him warm. The barn was also serviceable, so he walked the horse up the small hill, past his mother's unmarked grave, and put it in a stall, but not the one ... not *that* one.

After brushing and tending the Don, he spent the rest of the day replenishing the small woodpile. He lit a fire and thrust a few potatoes among its coals. He went to sleep, waking before dark to eat and then drifting off again. Twice during the night the fire almost went out, and the cold woke him, but he put more wood on top of the embers, reawakened the flame, and slept. Sometime during the night, Wolf joined him.

In the morning he woke somewhat refreshed. From the hiding place under his old bed, he pulled out the violin case, opened it, took out the violin, tuned it, and rosined up the bow. Then he put everything back again and closed the violin case.

Two days later, in Helsinki, 500 kilometers away on the south coast, a red lantern was lit in the Helsinki Workers' Hall, and all Finland began to burn. The war that everyone, especially Marku, had been expecting had begun.

2 • MYLLYSILTA

THERE WERE, AND HAD BEEN for a long time, two Antti Myllysiltas.

One, fluently bilingual, could speak both Finnish and the Swedish of Gamlaby with equal ease and without any telltale accent.

This Antti was known to only two people: Bertil Granbakken, the bookseller in Kokkola; and the librarian in Nykarleby, a larger village south, near Gamlaby.

Finnish was the mother tongue of the other Antti Myllysilta, and although he could speak some Swedish, he spoke it haltingly and with a heavy accent, and often made mistakes—deliberate ones.

The second Antti was the one his brothers had always seen. From a young age, he'd known it was safer that way. Antti had, as well, never let them hear him play his father's violin.

Bertil Granbakken hadn't heard him play, either, though Bertil knew both Anttis existed.

Years earlier, soon after the death of his father, a much-younger Antti Myllysilta had asked Herr Granbakken if it was hard to learn to speak Swedish.

Bertil had said, "At the beginning, only at the beginning." Then he had pointed at the shelves of books behind him. "Your textbooks."

And the lessons had begun. They had taken turns reading to each other, and word by word Antti became bilingual—even more so than his teacher. The unspoken rules of Swedish grammar and the music of its sounds spoke to Antti. He did not have to learn and memorize. He knew how an unfamiliar word *ought* to sound, and it *did*. After a while, it was Antti who was correcting Bertil's mispronunciations.

#

After his brothers were killed, Antti let another week or so pass—

time enough to get some rest, buy some real food, and put Gamlaby behind him. And time to think about what had happened. He knew he needed to leave Kokkola. For now.

The bell above the door of the bookstore in Kokkola chimed as Antti entered, violin case in hand. Bertil Granbakken looked up from behind the counter and put on his glasses.

"Antti! I haven't seen you for a couple of weeks. Where have you been?"

"Gamlaby," Antti said.

Just as there were two Antti Myllysiltas, there were two Bertil Granbakkens—one who sold books, and one who sold revolution. Antti had come to visit the second.

"Ah, the Manteres. I heard. People have been asking about you." Bertil knew that Antti would know what he meant. Antti was only about seventeen in body, but significantly older in mind.

"It was Marku's idea," Antti said. "He is dead. The Mantere mother got two of my brothers; the son got the other two when he arrived. The father wasn't there."

It was what the table and the footprints at the scene had told him. He said it all matter-of-factly, in the lyrical Swedish of Gamlaby and Jacobstad and Nykarleby, as if the subject were a pocket watch or a favourite hunting knife. As if there might be a punchline coming.

Bertil Granbakken looked at him with concern. "I'm sorry to hear that."

Antti shrugged.

After a moment, Bertil asked, "Did you kill the son?"

"No." Antti did not elaborate or look surprised that Bertil asked—although Bertil must have known the answer already.

Bertil did not ask for details. After a moment, he said, "I may have a job for you. But you'll need to go to Vaasa. Much as I enjoy your company, Kokkola is not a safe place for you now. Lots of talk about that Jussi Mantere and your brothers."

"Vaasa?" Antti repeated, and Bertil nodded.

It was easy enough to guess why Bertil wanted to send him there. Helsinki, in the south, had fallen to the Reds, Antti knew, and now Vaasa, on the Gulf of Bothnia, a hundred and twenty kilometers south of Kokkola, had become the de facto capital of White Finland. Those members of the Senate who had escaped capture in Helsinki had fled to Vaasa and "reestablished" the government. Of *all* of

Finland, they said. They'd be trying to forestall any further movement of Red Finns to the north.

Out of politeness, Antti asked, "Why there?"

"The Whites have begun moving troops from Vaasa east to Vilppula to keep us from getting control of the railway line—the one that runs north from Tampere. We need you in Vilppula."

Us, Antti knew, meant the Red Finns. "As a spy," he said. It was not a question.

"Yes."

"So I'm to enlist with the Whites?"

"That's the idea."

"Where?"

"Not here. Jacobstad. You can go south by rail. And even if you choose to use your stumbling Swedish, you'll easily pass as a White supporter. I'll make you a baptismal certificate so that your age is not a problem. I have a stock of blank ones in back."

Bertil Granbakken made lots of money in falsified documents. Finns wishing to emigrate to America were sorely in need of them.

Bertil cleared his throat, aware he was embarking on a delicate series of questions. "What name would you like?"

"My own is fine. No one knows my name except people here in Kokkola. My brothers weren't carrying any papers. In Gamlaby, no one knew them before, so there's no way they'd be known by name there now. I should be safe among the Whites there."

It was, Antti reflected, a difficult dilemma, to be known or not. In Gamlaby last week, no one knew him so no one would trust him. In Kokkola, many people had met or heard of his brothers—their ruthlessness, their brutality—and had made assumptions about Antti, incorrect ones. He'd taken care to show a face in Kokkola that was more intelligent and less wild than the faces of his brothers.

Sometimes it was less dangerous to be known and trusted, but sometimes it was easier not to be known at all.

Bertil eyed him. "If you want your name, that's what you'll have. What birthdate?"

Antti said nothing.

Bertil understood. "January 23rd, 1900. That makes you 18."

The day my brothers were killed. "It's as good a choice as any."

"What about money?"

"I'll need some."

"I'll give you enough to get from here to Jacobstad, but not so much as to raise suspicion. You can sign up there. Think about what story you'll tell if they ask you why you didn't join up in ... wherever you're going to say you're from. They probably won't turn you down, but—just to be safe—make it a story that doesn't leak. After that, you'll be riding on White money, not Red. They'll send you to Vaasa by way of Seinäjoki, I think. From Vaasa not far, by train, east and south to Vilppula. And once you're there—well, just stay alive and find some way to let us know what's going on. Perhaps through the mail. The mail train still runs, war or no war."

"I will," Antti said. His eyes strayed to the books behind Bertil.

"I have *The Gold Mine*," Bertil said, seeing the familiar hunger in Antti's face. He took the book off a nearby shelf. "Have you read it? It's not really by Lennart Wikström, like it says on the cover. It's actually by Henning Söderhjelm—Wikström is his pen name. Söderhjelm's one of us."

"Is it any good?"

"It's a detective novel, but the detective is a drunken do-nothing who comes alive with the love of a good woman. It has a lot of smartass things to say about both America and Finland, though. You'd like it."

"Add it to my bill." Antti laughed. He'd never paid for a book.

Granbakken took the book from the shelf and pushed it across the counter.

Antti opened it and looked at the first page. "Should I be a Finn or a Finland-Swede on the train?" he asked, as if he were reading a line from the book.

Bertil smiled grimly. "Don't get ahead of yourself. Your Swedish is good—yes, I know, better than mine—but sometimes you slip up trying to mimic the culture. Besides, it's of more use to us if you're a Finn. So be a Finn. Lots of Finns are White, in this part of the country anyway. Don't show how much Swedish you actually understand, so they'll speak more openly among themselves. That can be useful."

Antti nodded. He closed the book and wished he'd be able to read it on the train. He wouldn't, of course. And not in Vilppula, either, unless he was alone. He pushed the book back toward Granbakken. "Keep this for me."

"That's wise. Better to not call attention to yourself. The less people know about you, the better."

"Something else I'd like you to keep safe for me."

"Your horse? What did you do with that Don, anyway?"

"He's with a friend." Antti had sold the horse to a farmer, but he saw no reason for Bertil to know that.

"A friend?" A smile played about Bertil's mouth. "And here I thought I was your only one."

Antti put the violin case on the counter. "This is what you can hold for my return."

"You play?"

"A bit. Just—keep it safe for me. And don't sell it, for Christ's sake—it has *sentimental* value."

Bertil laughed. "First time I've ever heard you use *that* word. First you have a friend I don't know, and now you're sentimental." Antti wasn't laughing, so he added, "I'll just put the book in the case."

#

On February 7th, 1918, the same day that Bertil Granbakken introduced Antti to Henning Söderhjelm's work, the Reds launched a third and what they hoped would be a devastating attack on the White position at Vilppula. At Vilppula, the railway line that ran north from Tampere met the east-west line that led to both Vaasa in the west, and Petrograd far to the east in Russia. The Red force of 1,300 men attacked the much smaller and poorly armed White garrison of 300.

After holding out for as long as they could, the desperate Whites destroyed the Vilppulankoski dams and flooded the countryside. The Reds, as a result, could not get around the White position and attack the defenders from behind, and the Red armoured train that had been brought to the front from Tampere was forced to pull back as the waters rose. It would, however, be only a matter of days before the waters receded. And then the Whites would need to be ready with as many recruits as they could raise before the Reds' armoured train could be used against them.

On the day of the flood, Antti Myllysilta joined the White army. Four days later, he was on the train, heading south toward Vaasa.

3 • TRAIN RIDES

AT GAMLABY, THE TRAIN STOPPED to pick up more passengers, most of them young men. Antti wondered if someone might recognize him from the November raid, or might mention the Mantere killings and the Myllysilta brothers, but no one did.

Two passengers took the seat just ahead of Antti and his seatmate, Erik Andersson. Antti and Erik had been chatting in Finnish since boarding the train at Jacobstad. Now the two listened as the new recruits in front of them spoke to each other in Swedish.

"Well," said the youngest, "that didn't go as smoothly as I would have liked." He was no more than sixteen, possibly fifteen, Antti thought.

"Mother was upset," the older one said.

Brothers? Antti wondered. *Perhaps.*

"Mother was doing her best to hide it." The younger one said. "Now, Viktoria ...."

A sister? The wife or girlfriend of the older one?

The older one shrugged. "Viktoria will have calmed down by the time we get to Vaasa."

"Four hours? I think she'll need more time than that," the younger said. "The wedding may have been last month, but the honeymoon is now officially over, dear brother."

Ah, Antti thought. *The younger brother is the smart one. Viktoria is the wife of the older one. He is ... twenty-five, perhaps?*

The young one surprised Antti by suddenly turning around in his seat. "I'm Ivor Solbakken," he said, still in Swedish. "And this charming fellow is my recently married brother, Karl." Ivor reached over the back of the seat and extended his hand.

"Erik Andersson," Antti's seatmate said. He shook hands with both Ivor and Karl.

Antti shook their hands as well. "Antti Myllysilta," he said. "Sorry,

I poor on Swedish. But understand."

"Milly ... sorry, I did not understand it all."

"Silta. Milly-silta."

"Thank you, Myllysilta." Ivor repeated it carefully. "I know we go to Vaasa first, but then where?"

Ivor had used the Finnish pronunciation of the city—*Vaasa* instead of the Finland-Swede *Vasa*—to be polite. But he'd made a mistake in what he'd said.

Antti shook his head slightly. "First Seinäjoki, then Vaasa. Spend Vaasa training couple days then Vilppula maybe, maybe Ruovesi."

Ivor turned to his brother. "Where? I don't ...."

He's people smart, Antti thought, *but not much of a student.*

Karl came to the rescue of his brother. "Vilppula and Ruovesi are by the big lakes, south and east of here, in the middle of the lake country. The recruiter told me that the front line runs through there now, and what Mannerheim probably wants to do is firm up the front line and then push south to get down to Tammerfors. *Tampere*," he quickly corrected because Antti was obviously a Finn, and Karl worried he'd be offended at the city's Swedish name.

Antti smiled to show that he appreciated Karl's concern. *His voice*, Antti thought. *It is familiar.* And then he knew. *This is the fellow who helped Mantere unload my dead brothers from the cart.* He felt the shopkeeper no ill will.

"I think that's right," Erik said. "And the Russians want to make us go the other way." Erik laughed. He seemed to speak Swedish fluently, as well as Finnish.

"You have gun, Ivor?" Antti asked.

"No. I'm going to be a cook. But my brother does. He's got our older brother's Grafton gun. It still shoots."

Grafton guns, Antti thought. He smiled, as if he only partially understood what Ivor had said.

But he'd heard the story, some summers ago in Kokkola: how the Port Captain, Gustaf Strömbäck, had kept a hoard of Grafton guns hidden beneath the floorboards of his office so the Russians wouldn't find them.

The guns had been dropped off at the port in 1906 by would-be revolutionaries who had smuggled them into Finland aboard the *John Grafton*. The ship had blown up unexpectedly near Jacobstad, just after its visit to Kokkola. After it exploded—likely the victim of a poorly-thrown cigarette butt—the men of Jacobstad had retrieved hundreds of the guns from the shallow sea, storing them in people's barns and granaries and anywhere else the authorities might not look. Karl's gun might have been fished up along with the boxes of unexploded ammunition. Strömbäck's guns, however, were pre-explosion—payment, some in Kokkola believed, for Strömbäck turning a blind eye to the smuggling of just about anything.

And because Finland was poor and unrest was widespread, the guns had been put to use, however antique. *They are desperate for guns. Bertil should know this,* Antti thought.

"I have no gun," Antti said. "I hope get one of Vaasa."

"Me, too," his seatmate said. "I'm not much good at throwing stones."

"Throw at armoured trains, I think," Antti said. "Tough nuts to crack."

Ivor looked perplexed. His brother had to explain. "The ... Russians are using *armoured* trains at Vilppula," Karl said. "They have cannon."

"Oh," Ivor said. He did not seem to quite understand what Karl was trying to tell him.

Too young, Antti thought.

There was an exchange of small talk for a few more minutes. Ivor, Antti learned, was always called Rabbit by his friends and family. When Ivor lost interest in the conversation, he sat for a while just looking out the window. Erik fell into a light sleep. Antti pretended to sleep, but he remained wide awake, listening.

"Erik said we're fighting the Russians," Ivor said softly to his brother. "You did, too."

"It's what he's been told," Karl said. He yawned. "It's better that way."

That's something else Bertil needs to know, Antti thought. *The Whites, most of them anyway, think they're fighting Russians—not Finns. If they find out, what then?* He wondered if there was some way he could use the information to sow some discord in the White ranks. No; better to just hold on to it, and not draw attention to himself. Bertil could take care of this. He made a mental note for his next letter to "Bergit," his "girlfriend" in Kokkola, Bertil's alter ego.

Antti kept his eyes closed and tried to visualize the White battle plans. The battle at Vilppula would be do or die for the Whites. If the

Reds captured it, they could reach Vaasa in a few hours and wipe out the White's new government. And that would be that.

That would be that, that would be that, the train wheels sang. Antti wished he had *The Gold Mine* with him so he could lose himself in Henning Söderhjelm's story. But he didn't. And, even if he had it, he shouldn't be seen reading a book in Swedish. And that, too, was that.

When Ivor and Karl finally fell asleep, Antti looked out the window. Nothing but farmland, small lakes, and trees. The clouds might hold snow. He closed his eyes and sleep blanketed him.

He was hiding behind the blacksmith's shop across from Svensson's store in Gamlaby. His brothers were in the store. They .... A voice—Rabbit's voice— yelling as he kneeled beside Marku's body and hit it with a rock. The train brake squealed like a violin string breaking as the heel of a boot crushed the instrument on a hardwood floor.

Antti awoke, fists clenched. The dream became a single image, then a nothingness, *something about* .... He could not retrieve it.

They were pulling into Vaasa. He woke up Erik Andersson and the Solbakken brothers. It was snowing.

#

Antti had expected that he would spend a few days training in Vaasa before being sent wherever men were needed. But there was no time for training. The men were needed everywhere immediately. So instead, he and Erik were given rifles and put on a train heading from Vaasa to Vilppula on Lake Näsijärvi, some two hundred kilometers east.

The fighting until then had set up a row of dominos. At Ruovesi, twenty-five kilometers south-west of Vilppula, a fierce battle raged. If Ruovesi fell, the road to Haapamäki would be open to the Reds that were moving north along the west side of the lake. If Haapamäki fell to the Reds, they'd capture the east-west railway line, opening Vaasa to attack. So Haapamäki could not be allowed to fall. And, therefore, Ruovesi, the first domino in the line, must not fall either.

So Erik and Antti would go by train to Vilppula, and from there they would be marched to Ruovesi.

Erik, Antti deduced, had been talking to one of the officers before they boarded the train.

Antti asked Erik in Swedish, "What you know this?"

Erik explained in Finnish. The fighting had begun in the morning with an attack by Red volunteer soldiers and some Russian troops, plus anarchist sailors—the Black Guard—from Helsinki.

"Over six hundred men," he said. "The White defenders included the White Guard from Lapua and some NCO trainees from the Vöyri military school. I don't know exactly how many—far fewer than the Reds, though."

Antti knew of the Black Guard and its flag—a white skull and crossbones set against a black background. The men of the Black Guard drank too much liquor, never drank water, never cried mercy. They attacked and attacked and attacked, again and again, and they never retreated. It was, he considered, a stupid strategy, but one that Henning Söderhjelm might have approved of.

He asked in Swedish, "Red maybe win?"

"We'll know when we get there," Erik said.

They arrived just before dusk on the thirteenth of February. The next day would be *ystävänpäivä*—Friends Day. Ironically, on Finland's Friends Day, Russia would abandon its use of the old Julian calendar in favour of the Gregorian calendar used in Finland. In Russia, February 4th would magically become February 17th. Time flies when you're having fun.

The Black Guard, those still left alive, had fled the battlefield and were already back in Helsinki—drinking to celebrate both their luck in not having been killed, and the fact that they were getting out of Finland alive and going home. Their suicidal attacks had not gone as expected. At Pekkala and Ylä-Pohja south of Ruovesi, the Black Guard had pushed the Whites to the Whites' only line of retreat, an open area with no effective cover. Then, expecting little opposition, the Black Guard had charged across the open snowy field, and the Whites had opened fire on them with a machine gun that had been kept in reserve. When the first wave of the Guards fell, cut down by the machine gun, the Whites counterattacked.

For the Black Guard, that was that. Whatever day it was, it was certainly not Friends Day. It was time to go home. This was not their fight, after all, and battle survivors opted to leave Finland entirely. Home was St. Petersburg in Russia. So home they went.

With the recent victory, Antti and Erik entered a Ruovesi that, though it was still breathing heavily, was breathing more easily.

A week later, the Red Colonel Mikhail Svetchnikov adopted a

strategy that allowed the men of Ruovesi to relax even more. Foolishly, he ordered the bulk of his troops to advance toward Kankanpää, a hundred and ten kilometers west of Ruovesi, to take on the White forces led by Colonel Ernst Linder. Reinforcements from Swedish-speaking Åland, the large island just off the southern tip of Finland, had joined Linder's troops. Svetchnikov's advance had failed, and Kankanpää had stayed in White hands.

As the pressure on the White troops at Ruovesi diminished, pressure on the Red troops began to increase along their northern front. On February 18th, the first contingent of German-trained Jägers—eighty-five men—arrived in Vaasa along with a shipment of machine guns. On the twenty-second, King Gustav V of Sweden gave permission for a volunteer Swedish brigade to be formed to assist the Whites in Finland. On the twenty-fifth, the main force of the Jägers, 950 trained men, arrived at Vaasa.

On the western front, Svetchnikov's offensive stuttered and stalled, and on the twenty-seventh, he called it off.

On the twenty-eighth, White Finland and Germany began peace talks—bad news for the Reds. Antti, still in Ruovesi, kept track of events as best he could.

He had only to look at a map to know what the peace talks meant. They meant that it didn't matter whether he was shooting at the Reds—something which bothered him not at all—or helping them by sending back information that was coded in his letters to Bertil Granbakken in Kokkola.

Antti knew the Whites would win. They had real generals. The Reds—who elected their generals—did not. The Reds' make-believe leaders would not emerge triumphant.

On March 3rd, Germany and Russia—neither of them much interested in what was actually happening in Finland—signed the Treaty of Brest-Litovsk. Russia lost control of Estonia, Latvia, Lithuania, Poland—almost a quarter of the Russian empire's population—and it agreed to withdraw all its troops from Finland. The eastern front was no more. On March 7th, the White Vaasa Senate signed a formal peace treaty with Germany, and that was that.

But the treaty didn't mend matters between the White and Red Finns. Fighting for control of Finland continued.

#

As one day became the next, Antti's sense of comradeship with Erik Andersson changed. Erik talked less, and when he did, he could not keep the sadness out of his voice. He stopped telling funny stories. He lost his interest in little things. His eyes lost their life—he stopped examining what he looked at.

Antti didn't like these changes. But there was nothing he could do. *What is, is.*

"Why are there no Russians fighting anymore?" Erik asked Antti one day.

"Because there *are* no Russians," Antti replied. "There never were. Just Finns. Now that there is a treaty with the Germans, the Russians just sit on their asses, or they go home. They see no sense in hanging around."

Erik paused. "So what are we doing? Fighting ourselves?"

Yes, Antti thought. *Ourselves, and we are always fighting.* Aloud, he said only, "We are fighting."

The next day, during a small skirmish, Erik and Antti sheltered behind a large boulder. Without warning, Erik put his rifle on the ground and stood up.

"Get down!" Antti yelled at him. Erik, however, remained standing. Waiting. "Get down! Goddamn it, get down!"

Erik did nothing. And two minutes later, Erik was dead.

What a waste, Antti thought. *A cowardly fucking waste.*

#

A little over a week later, Ivor Solbakken, the boy from the train to Vaasa, showed up in Ruovesi. It was after dark and the sledges that had come from Vilppula were being unloaded. Antti recognized Ivor at once and in his theatrical Swedish yelled, "Ivor! Is you?"

"Antti! Antti Myllysilta!" Ivor called back.

Antti walked toward the sledge. "Yes! You remember! I hear someone comes from Vilppula so I want to hear news. I never think he will be you." Antti smiled, and the smile was genuine.

"Erik?" Ivor asked. "Is Erik here, too?"

For a moment Antti was at a loss, then he said simply, "He is dead. Almost a week ago. There has been much fighting."

"I'm so sorry."

"He was friend," Antti said. "And brave man." *And a broken man.* That, Antti thought, was not something he should say. There was something about the words ... a poison of sorts. Such words could change a person, start a man dying, just from hearing them or saying them. So Antti would not let himself say them.

He changed the subject. "You are delivery boy now," he said. "Groceries." He made himself say it lightly. "I am put in Ylihärmä Company. Everyone is speaking Finnish language. No Swedish." He wished he could allow himself to speak fluently.

Ivor did not let the conversation be about groceries and the Finnish company. "How did Erik die?" he asked.

So, Antti thought. *There it is.* He did not want to answer the question.

Finally, he said, "He stop shooting." He looked down at the snow where the lights of the camp and a slight wind in the trees made shadows dance. "We are being attacked. Reds come at us, yelling. And Erik, he just stop pulling trigger. I don't know why. He just watch the Reds coming, and he is killed."

It was close enough to the truth for Ivor to believe him.

When Ivor didn't say anything, Antti filled the silence with more words. "And yesterday, when Reds come again, we lose battle and have to retreat. But when we are fighting, I see how thin, how skinny, Reds are. And that they are farmers like us. Jäger who leads us, he tell us all the time that we are fighting Russians from Tampere, from barracks there, but he is lying. We are killing only Finns. Everybody sees this. Now all of Ylihärmä Company want to go home. This is not what they sign paper for."

"Will they try to do that?" Ivor asked.

"Maybe, but I think we won't be let home. Jäger puts machine guns behind *us*. We do like Erik and die, or we shoot to stay alive." *Shot from behind by our own "leaders," or from the front by enemies. Either way, dead is dead.* He chose not to say that either.

Antti took off a mitt and searched in his pocket for a cigarette.

"*Saatana,*" he said. "No cigarette." As he reached into the other pocket he said, "Be careful of this Jäger. I point him out to you tomorrow. He is not good man. He is liar." *And he attacks young boys, the younger the better,* he left unsaid. "Reds have lots of liars, too, but this one is our liar and all liars are dangerous."

Even me, Antti thought.

4 • THE ART OF WAR

ANTTI WAS BILLETED in a farmhouse at Ruovesi with five other men. Two of them—veterans of the battles at Ruovesi since the beginning of the war—had been assigned the beds set up in the kitchen, close to the stove that heated the room at night. Two others slept on the floor in the living room, close to the door to the kitchen. Antti and the last man, both relative newcomers, had the cold beds, the ones set up in the living room but near the door that led into the small porch. Antti slept with his winter coat on.

The veterans, Sami and Misha, often talked with the junior officers. Sometimes they talked about women, and about their past exploits. But sometimes they talked about the war, and Antti learned that sometimes gossip was, in fact, fact. At night he liked to eavesdrop as they spoke Swedish to each other, sure that the rest of the company spoke only Finnish. They talked loudly, though they thought they were whispering softly. The constant gunfire had dulled their hearing and replaced silence with a sound like the whining of a wind that rose and fell in pitch. On this night, they were talking about the battle with Sorin's forces on the tenth of March.

"So Salmela, the Red general, knows he has to capture Haapamäki," Misha was saying, "and he has to get through Vilppula and Ruovesi. But the planning that needs to be done has to include all the commanders that will be involved." Misha stopped to light a cigarette, then he gave a bit of a laugh to introduce his punch line. "Here's the catch: because the commanders are all so far away from each other, they have to telephone their plans and orders."

"And the calls," Sami said, anticipating, "have to go through the long-distance operators."

"And they're all White." Misha began to laugh. "And can place calls of their own."

"God in Heaven," Sami said. "The Reds fight and die like

31

madmen, and their leaders are all clowns."

More laughter, more talk, but Antti had stopped listening. *This is something that Bertil needs to know*, he thought. Bertil would know whom to contact. Antti would write him, or rather, "Bergit," tomorrow. He was gaining skill in sending information that would seem innocuous to anyone who opened the letter enroute. But Bertil would have no difficulty reading between the lines.

Sami is right, Antti thought, *the Reds are led by clowns*. And now, while he hated the Whites, he hated the Reds just as fiercely—the leaders for their incompetence, the soldiers for their blind obedience. He hated the whole country, including his dead brothers and Erik Andersson. *But that is no reason for not sleeping*, he told himself. He closed his eyes and slept like an innocent child.

#

On March 13th, General Mannerheim gave the orders to start the battle that everyone had been expecting.

On multiple fronts, twelve thousand Whites began to move south toward Tampere. A thousand more were dispatched from Happamäki to Ruovesi. On the Ides of March, the Red attack on Ruovesi faltered and failed.

The Whites kept moving. At Vilppula, they started to push the front line of the Reds back, and the Reds, fearful of entrapment, began to run away from the White "butchers." They ran through their own lines, infecting with panic those who watched them approach. What had been a small group of frightened men became a large mob stampeding madly through and over their own comrades, fleeing south to Tampere where there might be safety.

People in the villages through which the Reds ran joined them, abandoning their homes, rightfully fearful that if they stayed behind, they'd be massacred by the Whites. They'd heard about the seventy citizens of Länkipohja, executed the day before. The killing of the civilians had begun immediately after the village was taken, after the Red soldiers defending it had run for their lives. For Red soldiers, running took precedence over dying. Civilians weren't so lucky.

On the eighteenth of March, Antti had had enough. The Reds were going to lose. He decided it was high time to desert. The soldiers in his unit had been given two days' leave.

Antti spent part of the first day writing a letter to "Bergit." Bergit was to begin pulling together Antti's belongings since Antti expected that the war would end soon, and they would be able to marry and to move to better lodgings in Vaasa. Antti did not mention that his "belongings" included a large amount of cash and a small collection of blank official documents—all of which he had acquired on raids with his brothers and which were stowed inside the violin case, along with a few other keepsakes.

Antti's letter concluded: "Say hello to Lennart Wikström. Tell him that I look forward to meeting him in person." Bertil would know that Antti meant he would head to America.

#

Antti thought desertion would be easy, and he'd be gone in a day or two. Instead, the war dragged him with it down the road to the battle for Tampere.

He tried to stay toward the back, which made him among the last to storm the Kalevankangas Cemetery in the battle of Bloody Maundy Thursday. Near the broken statue of a black angel, he recognized the dead body of Ivor's brother, Karl Solbakken.

Antti "fell" beside Karl, played dead, and let the soldiers close behind him pass by. He waited—for what, he did not know, exactly.

When he judged it was safe, he got up and stood looking down at Karl's body.

More waste, more stupidity. No son of mine will ever go to war.

He stopped himself from promising more. Then he smiled grimly at all the improbable, impossible events contained in that one sentence. To have a son? He'd need to find a woman suitable to be a mother and willing to marry him. Then they'd have to raise a son to adulthood. To prevent someone from going to war? Next to impossible. Even Ivor, this poor bastard's gentle brother Rabbit, had enlisted voluntarily.

Thinking of Rabbit made him wince.

Just for the hell of it, he shot Karl's body twice in the back. Then he stole one of Karl's boots.

He wasn't taking revenge for anything. He felt neither jealousy nor animosity. Karl, Antti thought, was likely a good man, one who was close to Ivor. But now? The man who lay on the ground beside the statue was just as dead as all who lay beneath the ground, his skull taken apart by the bullet that had killed him.

As dead as Antti's own brothers, as dead as Mantere's mother. As dead as Erik Andersson and everyone I've killed without even knowing it.

Karl, Antti thought, would not be upset by being shot again. Others might label it as defilement. But Antti did not, and neither, he felt, would Karl.

The dead are dead. They feel nothing, see nothing, think nothing.

Solbakken, Antti thought. *"Sunny hillside,"* his name means. Karl was certainly on the hillside. But he was not lying in the sun, and even if he were, he would not be able to see it.

Antti, boot in hand, rejoined the rest of the Whites. The boot? A souvenir, he told them when he'd caught up. He'd taken it off a Red he'd killed, he said—something to remind him of the battle.

And how stupid it all was, he added, but only to himself.

#

On the third of April the German Baltic Division, sent to help the Whites, landed at Hanko about 125 kilometers west of Helsinki. However, the Reds announced that no such landing had occurred. They claimed it was just some fishermen, or, if you preferred, a few Whites who had disguised themselves as Germans and come ashore.

Tampere fell on April 5th, after fierce fighting. The last battles in the city occurred at the Town Hall and the Market Place. The only Reds left fighting were a few Russian troops and some of the Finnish women's units of the Red Guard. Many of the regular troops sought safety in basements and broken buildings. The formal surrender took place at 9 a.m. on April 6th.

Despite Mannerheim's directives to hold trials, the executions began immediately. First the Whites killed 200 Russian soldiers who had assisted the Reds, then 150 Red prisoners. Then everyone: women who had participated in women's Guard units, all commanders at any level, agitators real or imagined, and anyone mistakenly or deliberately identified by anyone as any of the above.

The railway station's warehouses filled with the condemned, and the footbridge over the tracks was crowded with people who came to watch and applaud the "victors" as the prisoners were lined up against the outside walls of the station and shot. Some of the audience wore their Sunday best and brought their children along.

It was, Antti decided, time to leave Tampere. But it was Sunday, and Antti wanted to be a tourist in this city, just for a while—albeit a tourist with a gun. In the afternoon he went for a walk to see what was left of the buildings. Artillery barrages had destroyed much of Tampere. Wood structures had burned to soot and ashes; brick and mortar buildings had been blasted apart to become gaunt grey and red headstones made of fireplaces and chimneys.

The Theatre, however, had survived almost intact, Antti had heard. He wanted to see this place that he had only read about—this monument to drama and music and the arts. In the basement, at the foot of the stairs that led up to the theatre proper, he found two bodies. One of them, slightly smaller, was about the same height and weight as he was. He wore a red armband on the sleeve of his greatcoat.

It was getting late. The sun had already touched the horizon. Antti rolled the body over and shot it twice in the face to make it unrecognizable.

It mattered not at all if anyone heard the shots—people were smart enough to stay away from gunfire. Even if someone came to investigate, all Antti would need to do is to say that he had shot the Red in the face. There would be no need to provide a plausible or even a probable reason.

Madness was the norm now. In wartime, madness is excusable.

No one came.

Antti stripped off the man's clothing and laid it to the side, took off his own and put on the dead man's garments. Then he dressed the corpse in his uniform. He made sure that his own identification papers would be in the dead man's pockets when the "White" soldier was found.

"Well, my friend," he said to the body when the costume change was complete, "at least you'll be buried in the Kalevankangas Cemetery in a nice grave—not in an unmarked pit with forty-nine other Reds. I gave you that much, at least. Sorry about your face."

He removed the red armband from the corpse's sleeve and, when he was outside once more, threw it into the street. His metamorphosis complete, Antti was now just one more citizen in the fallen city.

And his name was ... what? He took out the man's papers. His name was Riku Saarinen. Three times he said the name softly, committing it to memory. And now he absolutely must leave Tampere. It would not do to run into someone who knew the real Riku. Tonight, he needed a place to sleep—someplace far away from the Theatre.

#

The plan, as Antti had conceived it the next day, was to steal a horse and then travel southeast for a day or two to put some distance between himself and Tampere, where the hunt for Reds was now in full swing. He would head north when he'd found a road that looked like it would take him up to Lahti. From Lahti he would travel north and west in order to get to Kokkola.

Unfortunately, horses were now hard to come by, so he walked for a day or two before finding a horse to steal at last. It was no Don, but better than nothing.

Then, in his haste, he started north too soon. He crested a small hill and could see that his path to Lahti was blocked by a vast river of thousands—perhaps tens of thousands—of people flowing east. He could either wait for the caravan to pass through, or he could cut through it.

This was the great migration that had been urged by Red leaders. Starting on April 10th, to get Red troops to head east, the revolutionary command had announced that in Russia, in Olonetz in Western Siberia, people were to establish colonies and make of them a workers' paradise. Families were told to leave at once for Olonetz, bringing what animals, tools, furnishings, and pots and pans they could. They were to burn everything that could be of use to the Whites. Burn crops, homes, and outbuildings; kill what animals they could not take along.

And this mass of people was the result.

Antti dismounted and got his binoculars out of the saddle bag. He couldn't help but stare. *Fools*, he thought, scanning the parade of the defeated. *They think they're going to make it all the way to the workers' paradise in Olonetz though there's nothing there.* Idly, he focused on faces here and there. A woman carrying a bundle tied with string and leading an old man. Two young girls, each carrying an infant in a sling on their backs.

Antti focused on a family, a man and woman and a young boy, no horse, no cart—just the three of them carrying everything they now owned in a couple of battered suitcases and a burlap bag. They caught up to another youth, somewhere between a boy and a man, and he joined the family, quickening his pace a bit to keep up.

Rabbit? Was it really Rabbit? Antti adjusted the binoculars to bring the scene perfectly into focus. It was Rabbit, all right, but he had looked different. He seemed expressionless—not at all like the boy Antti had met on the train. *That pedophile bastard in Ruovesi got him*, Antti decided. He watched until Rabbit was out of sight in the crowd. He then mounted his horse and, once he had reached the slow-moving river of the homeless, cut through its human waters.

No one cared who he was, where he had come from, where he was going, or why.

All the rest of that day, Antti passed abandoned farms, their outbuildings burned to the ground—their store of seeds now ash, their cattle left to fend for themselves, their owners either part of the grim parade or imprisoned or dying or dead. Here and there a woman, sometimes with her children nearby, waited for her husband to return, waited as she had for days now—days that would turn into weeks, and weeks that would become always.

5 • VEGETABLES

THOUGH MIDSUMMER was still weeks away, the sun was beginning to peek above the horizon soon after 3:30 in the morning. The sun wouldn't set for another twenty hours. Even then there would be no real darkness—just four hours of twilight.

All the light made it hard, but not impossible, for Antti to enter Kokkola unnoticed. He rode a Don, and beside them trotted a grey and white dog—picked up when Antti had offered it a bite of a sandwich.

Luckily, the city of Kokkola was not yet awake. Travelling along its empty streets, the trio headed for its downtown. In front of the bookseller's, Antti dismounted, led the Don around back of the store, and looped the reins over a hitching post. No one would see the horse there—and he wasn't staying long. The dog left to explore the surroundings. It would be back, Antti knew.

At the front of the store, Antti pulled on the cord to ring the bell upstairs in Bertil Granbakken's apartment. Bertil let him in a few minutes later.

"Antti," Bertil said, yawning. "I was asleep. And you're dead, aren't you? Or am I having a really bad dream? And where's the dog? The one you picked up—the one you mentioned in your last letter."

"Good to see you, too, you miserable son-of-a-bitch," Antti said. "Dog's hunting."

"Come inside. How many dogs have you had?"

Antti entered the store. "Not counting you? This Wolf's number three. The one back at home, at the house north of town, that's Wolf number two."

"They're all named Wolf?"

"It's as good a name as any. Easy to remember."

"Upstairs," Bertil ordered. "Let's get you out of the display area." As they headed for the stairs, he asked, "Who are you now?"

"Riku Saarinen," Antti said. "Not as easy to remember as Wolf."

"You have papers?"

"Yes."

"Good. Nice meeting you, Riku. Saarinen is a common name and so is Riku, but I don't know of any Riku Saarinens in Kokkola, or any Saarinens in Kokkola who have a relative named Riku. The name will work."

Bertil led the way up the narrow staircase. "How'd you get back?"

"I did a lot of walking," Antti said. "Also bummed rides, took a train. At last, I stole back my own horse. Well, you could say I traded a lesser one for it."

"You've got the Don?" Bertil shook his head. "I've never understood why you needed a horse that called so much attention to itself."

"Because it's the best."

"Ah," was Bertil's response. He motioned to the small kitchen with its smaller table. They sat, and Bertil said, "When did you leave?"

"I've been on the road since early April. Saw Tampere fall and decided to get the hell out. But I've been looking around, too."

"So what now?"

"As soon as I can, I'm going to America—or Canada if the Yanks don't let me in."

"And you need documents."

"I have documents. Some blank baptismal certificates. When my brothers were alive, we collected a lot of paper from churches and offices. What I need is money. Do you still have my violin?"

"It's in the bedroom closet." Bertil flicked a thumb toward the bedroom door. "It'll cost you, though. How does twenty percent sound?"

Antti waited a beat. Bertil must have looked in the violin case and discovered what he and his brothers had looted. "It sounds fine. How soon can I go?"

"A while. The war's over, but times are hard and getting harder. The gold jewelry will be easy enough to sell. It can be melted down. The gems will have to be pried out of their settings and they'll still be hard to get rid of. The other things—the personal belongings—that's going to take some work. And even then, there won't be enough for passage and living expenses and maybe a bribe or two."

"So how long total to turn what I have into cash?" Antti asked.

"A couple of months, maybe more. We need to be prudent."

"I'll have to get work."

"But not here. Everyone knows you, and they know you're dead."

"So where?"

Bertil considered. "In the south." He paused. "If I were you, I'd go into business there—something to do with food. We're fine in the north. But the south's going to be starving, come winter. Last year's seed grains went up in flames, and you can be damned sure that Russia's not going to be in any position to send wheat this way. They don't even have pots to piss in anymore. The big war is still going, and no help will come from any country that's involved in it. And what country isn't? So, yes, the food business. The suppliers are the Ostrobothnian farmers, the customers are the merchants in the south, and you, my friend, are the delivery man."

Antti considered. Bertil was right that Kokkola would never be a safe place for him. And that the farms to the south had been destroyed. People would have more money than things to buy with it—they'd look at starvation for several years.

"How about we go into the business together?" Antti asked. "I make the contacts in the south, where the need is. You arrange the shipments from here. I already know who grows what up here, so I can write you about what people you should see. Then we'll get it to the guys in the south who have little to eat and nothing yet to sell. You keep books, write letters, and make sure everything gets done."

He pointed at himself. "Contact," he said, then pointed at Bertil. "Connection."

"All right," Bertil said, smiling. "Your box can be turned into enough money to at least start the business. It won't take long to find out if we're going to do well or fall flat on our greedy faces." He paused for a moment. "What are we going to call the company?"

"Gold Mine," Antti said.

Bertil laughed. "Good name. Lennart Wikström would like it. Now, I'm going back to bed. Remember to take care of your Don before you turn in. Make it disappear for a while." He stood up and stretched. "There are blankets in the closet there—you get to sleep on the floor tonight. And I never want you to write the name *Bergit* again."

"Speaking of writing," Antti said without moving, "I've never thanked you for teaching me to read and write. So, thank you."

"I enjoyed it. It wasn't fair for your father to try to keep you and your brothers ignorant. That's not what we're about. The working man needs an education just as much as his boss does."

"My father never went to school," Antti said, "but even if he had learned to read and write—even if he could do mathematics—he would not have been a good man. A good musician, maybe. But a good man? No."

"Education doesn't cure everything," Bertil said.

"True. Lots of the men I fought with—and against—had no education. Doesn't matter which side. They fought without being able to think. When a man can't read, he does what he's told. But when he can, he can choose what he wants to try to be."

"Too bad I didn't teach you mathematics," Granbakken mused.

"No need. Once I'd learned to read a bit, well, math is words, too, you know. I taught myself enough to get by." He laughed. "And now I'm going to be a businessman! What could be better than that?"

"Certainly not your violin playing."

Antti let Granbakken's comment go unacknowledged. "I have a favour to ask," Antti said.

"So ask."

"When I'm gone south, look after my dog, will you? Both of them, I mean. The one I brought today, and the one at home—at the family house, I mean. They don't need anything except a bowl of water. Finding food is their specialty."

"And how will I know this dog out in the country is your dog and not someone else's?"

"I'll introduce you to him before I go. He's grey and white, older than Adam, looks a little like me, and answers to Wolf—as long as you've got food in your hand."

Granbakken laughed. "Sounds like he does resemble you. Does he also never turn down a bribe, if offered?"

"Nobody owns a dog," Antti said. "Dogs aren't property." He said nothing about the bribe.

"Touché," Bertil said.

6 • GOLD MINE

FOR BERTIL GRANBAKKEN, post-war Ostrobothnia really did have the potential to be a gold mine.

"In 1917, before the revolution began," he'd say to anyone who cared to listen, "Finland was right on the threshold of becoming a modern industrialized country—like Russia."

When the revolution failed, however, most of the formerly well-tended farms in the south of Finland had been razed and ruined as part of the great migration to Olonetz in Russia, a mythical workers' paradise. Most of the workers who left, starving, had to turn back. Many of them had died along the way. Russia, ravaged by war, and faced with a famine of its own, stopped exporting food to Finland.

But in Ostrobothnia, the farmers, most of whom were White, had *not* burned their crops and killed their cattle; had *not* turned their backs on their homes and walked east. There was still grain aplenty in Ostrobothnia. Access to that grain and to other food crops, Bertil knew, would allow him and "Riku Saarinen" to prosper.

And so they went to work. Bertil was right, and Gold Mine made them rich. Wealthy, even. At least for a while.

At first, Bertil and "Riku" just arranged rail transport of feed grain for cattle. But soon they were sending wheat, oats, and barley down the line. Then, because the government began to encourage people to eat vegetables to stave off hunger and starvation, they had the farmers of Kokkola and the region grow lettuce, spinach, onions, potatoes, turnips, cabbage, rowanberries, juniper berries, beets—even mushrooms—in addition to the grain. Formerly uncultivated land suddenly had a use.

Bertil Granbakken did the legwork around Kokkola and the smaller villages and towns; "Riku Saarinen" established the contacts in the south and kept the buyers happy. And the money poured in. By the fall of 1919, they felt as rich as kings.

Antti again had occasion to contemplate the trade-offs of being "known" and "unknown." His role in the company required him to work well with all manner of shopkeepers, but as Riku Saarinen, he never had to fear that someone would judge him as a "coarse Myllysilta," like his brothers and father. He learned to be pleasant company, an honest and a fair businessman—and also, a driver of tough bargains, but bargains nonetheless. This was the Riku Saarinen he became.

As it happened, many of the shopkeepers and farm-owners that Riku Saarinen dealt with were women. In many cases, their husbands had been killed. Sometimes their husbands were alive, but broken— too old or too injured to do the hard work required of farming and storekeeping. Frequently, mothers began to rely on daughters to fill in. And their daughters, seeing that functional husband-material was scarce, pitched in.

Riku Saarinen, the successful businessman with contacts in both north and south, held an unexpected form of currency—an aura of mystery. He was not like any of the men the shopkeepers had known. He had travelled. And he was unbroken.

He wasn't like anyone else the women had known, either. They asked Riku about his travels in the country. What were people like in the far north? Were the girls prettier here or there? And what were they like in the south?

The women hung on his every word. The men around them— even the healthy ones, even the younger ones, the ones who had survived the war—were far less interesting to them than Riku was.

But Riku was cautious. He stayed aloof, not becoming too well known, too entangled with any one community, shop, or woman.

One important benefit from his work with food and his subsequent financial wealth was that as Riku, Antti at last had enough to eat. He would never be a tall man, but he was strong, though still slim. As he neared what might have been his twentieth birthday, he still looked younger than his years, but no longer like a child.

Prosperity for Bertil and Riku, however, proved transient. And that, Antti believed, was because Finland had gone mad.

As the Great War drew to a close, Finland had made of the madness of war a madness of politics, and picked itself a king—a German one, of course.

Finland approached the German prince Frederick, whose wife was the granddaughter of Queen Victoria and whose first cousin was an empress of Russia. Since this prince had an acceptable pedigree, Finland offered him the job of king. Frederick, who forthwith called himself Väinö, was solemnly proclaimed king-elect. Unfortunately, his brother-in-law, the then-current German Emperor Wilhelm II, turned out to be on the losing side of the war in Europe, and "chose" to abdicate in December of 1918. Frederick, who had not yet been formally crowned King of Finland, was politely asked to follow suit and abdicate before the day of his coronation arrived—which he did. And all without ever setting foot in Finland.

In the spring of 1919, however, Finland began to look, if not better, at least a little more sane, a little less desperate. With the end of the war, the farms in the south—those that had not been utterly destroyed by their owners—could once again try to grow things. They were closer than Kokkola and Gamlaby to the country's main centres of population—Pori, Turku, Hanko, Helsinki, Loviisa, Lahti, Viipuri, even Tampere. It took a couple of years, but they could ship their foodstuffs to the market more cheaply than could the farmers of Ostrobothnia.

As well, when Europe began to recover from the Great War, trade resumed in earnest. All the little temporary monopolies (and monarchies) began to die. And so did Ostrobothnia, itself. Even Wolf the second, Antti's dog who had lived through so much, died as 1919 turned into 1920.

In post-war Finland, the Reds—though militarily defeated—still outnumbered the Whites. Finnish-speakers outnumbered the Swedish-speaking Finns. And Ostrobothnia's people began to emigrate from Finland to Sweden, the United States, Canada, Australia, and other countries.

\#

Early in 1921, both partners agreed that Gold Mine, though still marginally profitable, should cease to exist.

At their final meeting, Bertil set two small shot glasses onto the counter of what had been his bookstore but had lately served as an office, when he wasn't meeting with farmers. Then he went into his back room for a bottle, and through the open door, Antti noticed several empties stacked on a table and on the floor underneath.

Bertil poured vodka for each of them. They raised their glasses, and Bertil seemed to expect Riku Saarinen to say something. Antti just shrugged. So without speaking, without giving a formal farewell toast, they downed the vodka.

"What's next for you?" Bertil asked. He refilled his glass and held the bottle toward Riku, who shook his head.

Riku Saarinen, when he thought as Antti, had recognized that wealth—or at least prosperity—gave planning for the future less urgency. He spoke slowly. "Emigrate, as I—or Antti—always wanted." He smiled conspiratorially.

"A popular activity nowadays." Bertil downed another shot and licked his lips. "I've heard plenty of talk of emigrating. Last time I was down near Nykarleby—in Gamlaby, in fact—the Solbakkens and Lassilas were having a farewell party for a young woman. She was wearing black. It looked like others might be emigrating as well. At least one other woman."

Solbakkens? Karl's widow? Ivor? Antti kept his face neutral. "Oh? Where were they going, do you know?"

"Canada. To Port Arthur, in Ontario. She has family already in the area. Lots of Finns and Finland-Swedes are there—both colours and both sides."

Antti nodded, storing away the place name. He put his shot glass down on the counter. When he picked it up, it left a wet circle. Bertil had been his friend—his only friend, really—for so many years that Antti had long been able to predict what Bertil would want to talk about. And Antti, at the moment, had no more interest in hearing about Red Finns and White Finns, slaughter and executions and prisoners. Not working men, comrades, owners taking advantage, Russia, or gossip about people he'd never really known. *The past,* he thought, *is past.*

But he remembered the expansiveness and friendly manner he'd developed, with great success, as Riku Saarinen. Antti did not really care, but Riku would ask to be polite.

"And what are you doing next, Bertil?"

Bertil waved at the store around them. "I'll go back to selling books, I suppose. Or reading them. For a few years, at any rate."

"That sounds like a life that would suit you." *As long as you don't keep drinking like that,* Antti thought. Riku's tact prevented him from saying it. They parted friends. Or perhaps friendly acquaintances.

The more Antti thought about Canada, the better he liked it as a destination. Some discreet inquiries confirmed what Bertil had said— the streets of Port Arthur, Ontario, were filling with Finns. Red Finns, White Finns. Swedish-speaking Finns, the Finland-Svensk. Where emigrants had gone before, an immigrant could build a home.

In Canada he wouldn't need to be Riku Saarinen. He could be Antti Myllysilta again, if that's what he wanted. Or he could erase Antti Myllysilta and become someone else—though whoever he was, he owed part of his success to Bertil Granbakken, and in Antti's experience, such debts sometimes came due.

Antti gathered suitable documents from his emergency stash, then travelled to Copenhagen, where he boarded the Oscar II and sailed for Halifax.

PART II

THE SUBSTANCE
OF THINGS HOPED FOR

Love bade me welcome; yet my soul drew back,
　　　Guilty of dust and sin.

"Love"
George Herbert

1 • TO PORT ARTHUR

THE OSCAR II, ANTTI DECIDED, was quite a nice ship. However, half-way across the Atlantic, the storm began, and the boat began to rock and pitch, lean and shudder, like a drunken farmhand on a Saturday night.

Antti left the Second Cabin Dining Room on the saloon deck and headed, as best he could, for the Smoking Room. Everywhere, even on the saloon and upper decks where the Second Cabin rooms were located, the ship boasted polished oak handrails and panels. Today, the handrails were a necessity.

Antti considered making a stop at a lavatory but decided that he was not that ill. Not yet.

When he got to the Smoking Room, he found himself the only one there. Just as well. He didn't feel like talking. He wondered what the upper promenade and the forward part of the saloon promenade deck were like. They were for First Cabin passengers only, but the aft part of the saloon promenade deck could be used by the Second Cabin passengers, too.

Antti didn't want to go outside to watch the waves trying to tip over the Oscar II. And he certainly didn't want to weave and stagger like a drunk, daring the promenade to pitch him into the sea. Instead, he sat down on a comfortable couch and enjoyed his cigarette.

When he was done, he got up, then zigzagged and caromed his way to the Second Cabin stateroom on the upper deck. His cabin mate sat in the lower berth, balancing a basin on his knees. The liquid in it sloshed back and forth, dribbled on the man's shoes—and stank.

Antti stood at the door of the stateroom for a moment or two but did not bother to enter. He went, instead, back to the Smoking Room and lit another cigarette. When he was done, he fished out a small notebook and pencil from his jacket pocket.

So. In Canada, he'd heard, a male teacher could make almost $1,700 a year—a woman about half that. Antti had almost three times that amount in an account at the Imperial Bank. He could live well

49

for three years in Canada—or he could go into business again. He did not, of course, want to become a teacher—just live like one.

He put the notebook and pencil back into his pocket. *A man who risks nothing is worth nothing,* he thought.

His cigarette had begun to taste like bile. He walked unsteadily back to the stateroom, entered, and spat the cigarette onto the floor. Then he took the basin from his cabin mate, threw up in it, and handed it back to him.

Business, he decided. It was in his blood. He would go into business.

Furthermore, he was never again going to have a cigarette or set foot on a ship. It was a vow. He threw up once more, on the floor this time. *So help me, God.*

#

The Oscar II docked in Halifax on the sixth of May, 1921, and by the middle of the month, Antti lived in Port Arthur, Ontario. On Machar Avenue, near the thriving Bay-Algoma intersection, he bought a small house for a few hundred dollars from the family of a soldier who had died a year after returning from Europe.

The family had removed everything from the house except a framed document hanging on the living room wall. "We the Citizens of Port Arthur," it began, "desire to cordially welcome you back home to our fair Dominion of Canada." It ended with "After your strenuous efforts on behalf of Truth, Freedom, Home, and Native Land, we wish you health, long life and happiness: and when life's battles are all over we pray that we all may meet in the Heavenly Home for which these brave soldiers who have heroically fought and nobly died that we and our Empire might live." It was signed by the mayor, Edward Blaquier.

Antti left the document in place. And thanks to Antti's *Engelsk Och Svensk Hand-Ordbok* it became the first English document he translated into Swedish. Whoever wrote it, Antti thought, had never been to war—or received much of an education. He wondered why the soldier's family had left the document behind. *Maybe because the war was over,* he decided. *Time to move on, time to forget. Or maybe because the soldier killed himself.*

Each morning Antti left his house and went to breakfast at the

Hoito, with its real Finnish food and its communal tables that seated a dozen men. When he talked with the other customers—gossip, news of work, politics—he spoke only Finnish. If not everyone's friend, he was at least their friendly acquaintance.

And his name was now Andrew Millbridge—changed, as if by magic, on entry into Canada, sharing a birthdate with Riku Saarinen. A surprising number of the Finns who ate breakfast with him also had English-sounding names, and stories to go with them.

On weekends, Mrs. Stone from Immanuel Lutheran Church—a strange-looking building that was just a roofed basement at the top of the Pearl Street hill—taught Andrew English, for a small fee. To Mrs. Stone, a middle-aged former schoolteacher who was English and spoke no Swedish, and furthermore never went to the Hoito, Andrew was a Swede.

At night, because there was no Finnish/English dictionary that he could find anywhere, Andrew used his *Engelsk Och Svensk Hand-Ordbok* to take him from Swedish to English and back again. He took English articles from the *Port Arthur News Chronicle* and re-wrote them in Swedish.

Even if he had been able to buy a Finnish/English dictionary, he was beginning to understand that Finnish and English were so different in the way they strung ideas together to make sentences that the dictionary would have been worse than useless. It would have given him words but not grammar, and spelling but not usage. English grammar was, on the other hand, very much like Swedish grammar. As he learned to turn his Swedish *words* into English, he was, at the same time, learning how to turn his Finnish *ideas* into English.

But Andrew didn't spend all his spare time studying. He walked all over Port Arthur, heading toward the lake to look at the railroad tracks and examine the lakeside hotels, sometimes stopping in for a drink or two before heading uphill along Arthur Street and back to the Finnish part of town.

Once in a while he walked all the way to the John Street gravel pit, then followed the trail through the bush to bachelor hell—a collection of tarpaper shacks just outside Port Arthur's city limits, near the McIntyre River. In the shacks half a dozen recently-arrived Reds—remnants of the war—slept and drank their summers away.

Andrew had learned of the spot from one of the Finns, Kari

Petterson, at the Mariaggi Hotel down near the railroad tracks. In the bar one afternoon, Kari had become his spur-of-the-moment drinking buddy. And in a moment of too much to drink, Andrew Millbridge had let slip the name Antti Myllysilta.

After that, it annoyed Andrew that Petterson called him "Millie" whenever he felt like it, but he drank with Petterson anyway. Through Kari, he learned a few details of the lives that were wasting away, back in the bush.

In early August, Andrew walked out to the shacks and found Kari dead on the floor, an empty bottle beside him. *Dead soldier*, Andrew thought, but he meant the bottle, not the body. And since nobody was around, Antti Myllysilta—or rather, the dark remnant of him that still lived in Andrew Millbridge—left Kari lying on the floor and set fire to the man's shack, thereby destroying, he imagined, the remains of the one person in North America who'd known that Antti Myllysilta had ever existed.

On his walk back home, he thought, *Let them try to figure that out.* And so began the story that Kari's friend, that guy over there—Kari used to call him Millie-something—had killed him and then set fire to the body.

He doesn't drink now*, you know*, the storyteller would add.

2 • ANNIE

AUGUST OF 1921 CONTINUED, ITS DAYS WARM though visibly shortening. Antti saw no reason to change his routine.

It was Mrs. Stone, who of course knew nothing of Andrew's life outside their weekly sessions, who suggested a diversion.

Not long after the mysterious fire among the shacks at the edge of the city, they worked through an English lesson at a table at the back of the sanctuary at Immanuel Lutheran Church.

As they finished, Mrs. Stone said, "You're doing quite well, Andrew. What you really need, though, is practice. And I know someone who wants to learn about teaching. Are you willing to let her learn to teach at the same time you learn English?"

Andrew searched for the word, although he didn't need to search as much as he pretended he did. "I ... suppose."

Mrs. Stone nodded. "Her name is Annie Crawford. Her dream is to become a teacher, but she needs experience. She'll meet with us a time or two, and then I'll let her take over." She looked at Andrew appraisingly. "You can learn far more from her than you can from me," she said cryptically.

The next Saturday Mrs. Stone brought Annie to Andrew's English lesson. Mrs. Stone paid as much attention to Annie as Andrew. Annie was quick to see not only what Mrs. Stone wanted Andrew to learn, but *why* she did *what* she did *when* she did it. Annie laughed easily, but Andrew suspected that nothing escaped her bright eyes.

At the end of the following Saturday, Mrs. Stone said, "Well done, both of you. Annie, I believe you know now how to proceed with Mr. Millbridge's lessons." She turned to Andrew. "If you're comfortable, that is."

Andrew was more than comfortable. "Of course," he said.

To Annie, Mrs. Stone said, "Would you please wait for me outside? I'd like to say goodbye to Andrew." She waited until Annie closed the door then said, "Annie works long days, Monday through

Thursday every week, as a housekeeper for four different families. She's willing to spend her Fridays teaching you. Would you mind paying Annie a bit more than you had been paying me?"

"Not at all," Andrew said. He enjoyed being so agreeable.

And thus he came to know Annie. Her Fridays became his, and his Fridays became hers.

From their first week, she suggested a change to their routine. "It's a beautiful day. Why don't we walk to a park and have lunch?" She held up a basket with a smile. "I brought sandwiches and lemonade. And we can chat. As a way to work on conversation, you know."

Andrew smiled back. "Yes, I would like that."

So, seated on the edges of a blanket in Waverley Park, they exchanged information between bites of turkey sandwiches. Andrew learned that Annie was a year younger than his papers said he was. She had been born in Canada, in southern Ontario. Her parents were no longer living—she did not divulge details, and neither did Andrew, when his turn came. It was not uncommon, after the Great War, to have lost family members. Not speaking of them felt natural.

Their lunch gone, Annie folded the paper sandwich wrappers and put them in her basket. Andrew watched to see if this meant their lesson was finished, but it seemed it was not. He was in no hurry.

"If you don't mind," Annie began. "May I ask—how did you learn about the English lessons arranged through Immanuel Lutheran? Mrs. Stone said you just appeared one day, earlier this summer."

"Yes, that is true how it happened," Andrew answered. "Maybe you do not know? Immigrants, we sit for meals at long tables, we share news. Sometimes gossip, sometimes better. I heard at a table."

"So you're—your background, I mean—is Swedish? That's what Mrs. Stone said. But you're from Finland?"

Andrew was pleased to share something Annie didn't know, but cautious about telling too much. "Yes, I am from Finland. I grew up a Finnish speaker. But I also learned Swedish. Some. A little. Because in the west of Finland, they speak mostly Swedish, or sometimes both."

"So you're bilingual? Both languages?"

Andrew laughed the question away. "No, no. Not really. Mostly Finnish. And now, may I ask? How did you find Immanuel Lutheran, since you are English?"

She blushed and said, almost as a confession, "I don't really go to church anymore. My parents raised me as a Presbyterian, though I kept getting into trouble. After they died, the Presbyterian Church sponsored my move here from southern Ontario. In exchange, I was to work for the church, six days every week, for one year. I worked hard—but mostly to find another way to live." She laughed. "On one year plus one day, I was already set up with families to keep house for. One family was from the Presbyterian congregation, and I answered ads in the newspaper. And then one of the families knew Mrs. Stone, who helped with the teaching experience."

"Keeping house. Sounds like hard work," Andrew said. "It's good to work if you get what you want."

Over the next few weeks, their Fridays became more informal conversations, and less about formal English.

One Friday they walked through the neighbourhoods near Immanuel Lutheran Church. September's sun felt faded—summer was over, but autumn not yet here. The birch leaves were just beginning to turn gold.

They had reviewed colours and moved on to nouns. Annie asked Andrew to name the parts of trees.

"Barks, branch, leafs," he began, hiding a smile.

"Andrew! We went over this last week. *Bark*, same in the plural. *Branches*, plural. And *leaves*, remember? Not leafs!" At his laugh, she said, "Oh, you're teasing me."

"Only a little. I apologize. Bark, branches, leaves."

"Very good. But I'm afraid people will think I'm not good teacher material if you keep teasing me that way." She talked often about being a *real* teacher in a *real* school.

"You are a good teacher," Andrew said. *Almost too good—I hardly need you anymore.* He didn't like that thought.

"Students like you let me dream of more. I have enough money already saved up for almost half a year of school in Stratford, in Southern Ontario. Then I could get my First-Class Certificate."

"You would come back, though?" Andrew said. He was pleased at her blush.

"Of course. This is my home now! And we need more certified teachers up here. With a First-Class Certificate, I could teach in an elementary school and save more money. Maybe I could even go to university and graduate and then get an Ordinary or even a

Specialized High School Certificate!"

Andrew walked in silence for a moment, as she stared ahead, dreamily. Then he said, "Good. I am glad to know you would come back." *But I wish you would not go.* He caught himself in time to keep from saying anything aloud—he hardly knew this woman.

He made a show of looking at his pocket watch. "I believe we should head back. A teacher must rest and enjoy herself as well as work." *And I must stop and think about what I am doing.* Though he found himself, more often, thinking simply of Annie.

#

The following Friday, they reviewed names of family members. *Mother, father, sister, brother.* Andrew quickly skipped through those without comment. *Children, grandchildren, aunts, uncles.*

Then Annie said, "Here's another word: *ancestors.* The ones who came before you. And *descendants.* The ones who will come after you."

"These are general words—ideas, are they not? Not specific people?"

"That's right. They're ideas that let us be connected to the past and future. We *inherit* from our *ancestors.* We leave a *legacy* to our *descendants.*"

"I understand. We take, we live, and then we give." Andrew mimed it, closing his left fist in the air for "take," and opening his right fist down by his side for "give."

"That's right." Annie was pleased. "When you leave your homeland, what kinds of things do you bring with you from your ancestors?"

Andrew hesitated. "You mean, money and things from the house? Like a gun, or a dish, or maybe a little portrait of Mama?" He, of course, had nothing like this. But people he ate with at the Hoito talked about their keepsakes from home.

"Of course," Annie said. "Some people bring many things—household goods and money. But you can bring other things." They were walking past the Presbyterian Church on Waverley, approaching the Methodist church. Across the park sat the Baptist church. She pointed at the church. "Religion. Food traditions. Holidays."

"I see." Andrew thought, grasping for the word. "Culture, you mean. Not just *how* you live or teach, but *what* you teach. Or learn.

What you expect life to be like."

"Yes. Language, even. Your Finnish and the Swedish you speak, which I'm sure is better than you tell me."

Andrew shrugged, and Annie continued.

"Which reminds me. I have a question and I don't know who else I can ask. I hope it doesn't offend you. I'm curious: a lot of the Finnish children—even the ones born and raised here—don't speak English. Why is that?"

Andrew considered. "Could be many reasons. Maybe there is no way to learn. Maybe their parents don't know English well enough to pass it on. The father might have come from Finland and when he got here, he went straight into a job—maybe a lumber camp—where only Finnish is spoken. Then after he's saved money, he might buy some land—in an area where there are other Finns as neighbours—and farm it. The mother, before she married, might have worked with other Finnish girls in a bakery, say. Or maybe she had a job at home."

"Like a housekeeper," Annie said. "Oh, I see—the family leaves the house, and the woman cleans it. So there's no conversation outside the family, and no real chance to learn English."

"That's right. So the language in the home, the one that a lot of the parents pass on to the children, is Finnish only. Sometimes Finnish kids go to school for the first time, knowing almost no English at all. It's because they live on islands of Finnish in an ocean of English."

"I see," Annie said, her eyes dancing. "I thought … I thought maybe it was because all Finns are stubborn, like you. And it's *children*, not *kids*. *Kids* are baby goats."

Andrew laughed. He found he could not take his eyes off Annie when she talked, and instead of fighting it, he gave himself over to the intoxication of it.

With each week, they relaxed. Their conversation became easier, and the awkwardness less. Annie exploded with interest in everything. She talked as much with her hands as she did with her mouth—her hands danced and tumbled over each other in conversation. Even her arms went wide when she talked of how big something was. Her fingers pointed *here* or *over there* when she wanted Andrew to imagine what something must have been like.

Slowly and then quickly, Andrew felt something in him change. Something deep and bad went away to hide in a closet in his mind. It was replaced by something good ... or if not *good*, exactly, then *calm*.

It was as if the part of him that was Antti Myllysilta released the part that was Andrew Millbridge and gave him permission to be his own, complete person.

The waters in him stilled, the howling winds stopped their loud and cruel declaiming. Inside him, contrary to the seasons of the external world, winter lessened and spring arrived. Andrew Millbridge fell in love. It was a thing that Antti Myllysilta would never have been able to do, and never did.

3 • ANCESTORS AND DESCENDANTS

As Andrew's proficiency in English grew, Annie noticed that he didn't like to show how well he knew the language. In their "classes," which grew from only an hour on Fridays to as much of the weekend as possible (while maintaining Annie's reputation as a "nice girl"), Andrew had almost no accent.

But when he was out in public, even with Annie—especially among Finns—Andrew's speech was different, more accented.

That year, Thanksgiving was celebrated the Monday in November of the same week in which Armistice Day occurred. Mrs. Stone invited Andrew and Annie, in what was a near-command, to a late-afternoon Thanksgiving meal at Immanuel Lutheran Church.

To Andrew, she said, "This is your first official Thanksgiving holiday in your new country, a real feast. Everyone taking English lessons is invited. And I saw you at the church picnic. For such a compact man, you—well, let's just say that you enjoy a feast."

In the early evening, when dinner was over, Andrew walked with Annie up Dufferin Street to the small house where she rented a room.

As they walked, their breath visible in the gathering darkness, she said, "Andrew, may I ask a question?"

"Of course," Andrew replied. "Is it how I am able to eat so much, for being so small a man?"

Annie laughed. "Compact, Andrew. Compact. But no, that's not the question." She fell silent for a few steps, then said, "I've noticed—that is, it seems—well, sometimes your accent comes and goes. With me, now, you speak English flawlessly. But even this afternoon, with all the others also learning English, you sounded more … foreign. Even more so than you did when I first began teaching." At his silence, she added, "Oh dear. I hope I haven't offended you."

In answer, he drew her mittened hand under his arm. "Of course not. You could never offend me. I am just thinking how to explain it. In Port Arthur, among the Scandinavians, there is a moral *precept*."

"That's what I mean! *Precept*—where did you learn such a word? I didn't teach it to you. You used it beautifully, of course."

"I learned *precept* when I learned what it is I am telling you about. This *precept* is a common concept we use in Swedish—both in Finland and in Sweden. For that matter, it's characteristic in all of Scandinavia. I looked it up, because … because I needed to know it, I suppose."

"That makes sense. I'm sorry for interrupting. What is the precept?"

"That people should never act *högmodig*."

"I beg your pardon, *hoog* what?"

Andrew repeated it for her and laughed at her attempts to say it.

"*Hoog-modey*? Is that closer? But what does it even mean?"

"It is very close. And in Swedish, it means *proud*, in a bad way— too much pride and no reason. Literally, *high-minded, arrogant*."

"Haughty? To put on airs?"

"Perhaps. I don't know *hotty* or *put on airs*. The dictionary suggested *snob*, but *högmodig* is a … harder word, related to class. A *högmodig* person thinks he's better than another. When a worker, someone of the working class, calls another person *högmodig*, it's almost angry."

"My goodness. I see. And speaking languages perfectly would be *hoog-modey*?"

"Possibly. I keep my English accented on purpose, to fit in." He didn't add, "To fit in everywhere, even with you." And he didn't explain more, even though he was in love with Annie, even though he hoped—believed—she loved him.

Although Antti Myllysilta was dormant, Andrew Millbridge had not forgotten the need to walk the line between being known and remaining unknown. He wanted to reap the benefits of both circumstances. Even here, in Canada, where he had ensured he was not known as an unprincipled Myllysilta, Andrew Millbridge must maintain some privacy.

"You," she told him, "are a natural polyglot."

"Ah," Andrew said. "But without the feathers."

Annie looked at him in surprise, and then they both laughed.

Yes, she believed him. She believed him for a long time. When, at last, she didn't believe him anymore, she had no truths with which to replace the falsehood, so she let it be—because she loved him.

And the concept of being *högmodig* was one they retained as they became a family, which happened quickly. At Christmas he proposed to her, and she accepted.

There was no reason to wait, so early in 1922, Andrew Millbridge married Annie Crawford in the basement of the Immanuel Evangelical Lutheran Church. Normally, Zion Lutheran Church in Fort William hosted Immanuel's weddings in their manse. A really fancy wedding would be held in Zion's nave and sanctuary. Zion was, after all, a *real* church, not just a roofed basement like Immanuel.

But this wedding was not fancy. Mrs. Stone was the only attendant, and there was no best man. The minister, Holger Pearson, made the wedding a bilingual affair—the Swedish sections for Andrew and the English ones for Annie. For reasons Holger Peterson couldn't—or didn't—name, Andrew Millbridge made him uneasy. However, he was always happy to bless a wedding.

After the ceremony, Mrs. Stone handed Annie a note. "Take this to the photography studio on Algoma. I've arranged a gift. Go now—both of you—while you look so beautiful."

Annie gasped. "Such an extravagance!" She looked down. "And you think I should go wearing this dress? I bought it for practicality, not for a photograph."

"Nevertheless," Mrs. Stone insisted.

So they sat for a portrait and chose one of the poses for a small print. The cap sleeves and modest V-neck on Annie's navy blue dress framed her face beautifully.

Andrew, in his best navy blue suit, managed to look calmer than he felt—he was far more worried about the photograph than the wedding or the marriage to follow. He'd refused to allow any news about their wedding to appear in the newspaper, not even an announcement, and he extracted a promise from Annie that the framed photograph would stand only on the wardrobe in their bedroom.

"Ah, I understand," Annie teased. "The newspaper and a photograph would be *högmodig.*"

They laughed together. Andrew was relieved he didn't need to explain his fear—or rather, his certainty—that someday, his image might somehow be used against him, to identify him in a way that could be inconvenient at best, or even potentially dangerous. Best to be careful. Best not to be known.

Annie moved in with Andrew, adding what she called her "goods and chattels" to the spare furnishings of the house on Machar Avenue.

"Chattels?" Andrew raised an eyebrow.

Annie answered, "Belongings. Things that someone owns that aren't real estate."

"Ah, good. I thought it might be how Canadians say 'cattle,' and we do not have room for those."

"But we do for this." She propped the photograph on their wardrobe.

When Annie asked, somewhat tentatively, about their financial status, Andrew said he had just enough money saved to take more time, looking around, for the right business opportunity. Annie stopped keeping house for the four families, and Mrs. Stone found another young immigrant woman to take Annie's place. Annie still thought of becoming a teacher, but not yet. She had a household to organize and manage. Soon, what had been Andrew's house was theirs, smelling of cinnamon and vanilla and Annie's perfume.

In short, Andrew and Annie were very happy.

Late in September, Holger Pearson performed another office for Annie and Andrew: he baptised their son, Owen.

#

The following summer, Andrew and Annie asked Mrs. Stone to babysit Owen one evening. Arthur Conan Doyle was on a North American lecture tour and would be in Port Arthur on July 15. He would speak on spiritualism at the Colonial Theatre in Port Arthur.

As they began their walk home from the theatre, Annie asked, "So what did you think?"

"Very comfortable seats," Andrew said. Annie gave him a poke in the ribs. "The lecture was interesting," Andrew said. "And ouch."

"But?" Annie prompted.

"But the slides he had—the ones of spirits—didn't look real to me. And he didn't say a word about the photograph of the fairies in the garden. He didn't even show it."

"The one everyone says is a fake?"

"Yes. I think he's a very good writer, but easy to take advantage of. And I think he knows now, or he believes now, that the picture is a fake, but he can't say it yet."

"That's what I think, too." After a pause, she added, "I can see why he'd *want* to believe in spirits, though."

"Can you?" Andrew let his surprise show.

"Of course. Haven't you ever experienced something you couldn't exactly explain? Something that seemed—I don't know—bigger than yourself? Not religion, or not exactly like that, anyway." They walked in silence for a moment. "Something surprising."

Antti, who had been silent in Andrew for many years, whispered, *No son of mine will ever go to war.* Andrew nearly stumbled, but caught himself in time. Because now, of course, he did have a son. And who knew what new wars the future would bring?

Andrew said only, "Perhaps."

They walked without speaking until at last, Annie said, "I have. I've seen—felt, perhaps—something very surprising." She squeezed his hand. "It was when I met you."

Andrew smiled and squeezed back but didn't answer. They walked the rest of the way in silence. When they were outside their home, he said, "I love you, Annie."

"I know you do. And I know it's hard for you to say."

"Not so hard. And getting easier every day. That's the most surprising thing of all." Andrew kissed her as they stood at the foot of the steps, then they went inside to look at the sleeping Owen and tell Mrs. Stone about the lecture.

The next evening, Andrew played the violin. It was the first time since coming to Canada that he'd taken it out of its case. He played a polka. It was a tune, Andrew felt, that the violin enjoyed.

#

In May of 1924, Annie and Andrew had a daughter.

"Named May, for the month I arrived in Canada," Andrew said.

"For the month that has a Maypole in it," Annie countered.

The summer days were beautiful. Annie was beautiful. May was beautiful. Each day was golden and full of life, with Owen chattering and May soon responsive and smiling. Even autumn that year was especially warm and beautiful—not always in the weather, but inside Andrew. The bleak, frigid days of his childhood in Finland seemed so very far away.

But the cold came back. It always came back.

4 • LUMBER AND NAILS

AFTER OWEN WAS BORN, Andrew had taken a part-time job selling lumber at the Black Bay Lumber Company. They didn't exactly need the money, a fact he knew but Annie did not.

When May—the month and the daughter—arrived, Andrew invested two thousand dollars in Black Bay, keeping the exact amount from Annie, and becoming a minor shareholder in the process. He was glad of a more-prestigious job and higher salary. He didn't need either one, but he liked how they looked. He liked how Annie looked at him and how she thought of him—how she understood his role in the world.

He also took it on himself to learn more about the lumber business, mostly the relationships and contacts—the role he had taken in his partnership with Bertil, back in Finland.

In her turn, Annie decided that since Andrew was now part owner of a lumber company, she should learn something about bookkeeping—conveniently, the part of the business Bertil had handled, and Antti had not seen.

In just a few months, Annie learned enough to teach Andrew how to read and manage the company's books. When Owen and May were asleep, their parents sat side by side at the kitchen table and played with trial balances.

However, with Owen's delight in running around the house and the addition of May, their home on Machar Avenue was no longer big enough. They sold it, and Andrew bought a bigger house on Algoma Street.

They took the framed document from the wall to the new house and hung it so that the dead soldier could still have a home. And in this new house, their wedding photograph sat on a small table beside their bed.

If Annie thought it odd that Andrew had offered no keepsakes from his home in Finland—at least for display—she didn't mention

65

it. She knew only about the violin. His other boxes moved silently, invisibly, from the basement at Machar Avenue to the basement on Algoma Street.

#

A few weeks after the move to Algoma Street, Andrew came home from the lumberyard, as usual. But instead of just walking into the house, he knocked on the door. When Annie opened it, Andrew pointed to the curb, where a new car sat gleaming.

He said, "May I take you for a ride, *milady?*"

"You bought a car? But the money!"

Andrew waved it away. "Bonus from the boss. It's a Willys Overland 91—lots of room for the kids. And no need anymore to phone for a taxi. No more riding the trolley. See the split windscreen? You can either flip it up to bring in fresh air, or put it down to keep the rain out."

"But Andy, you don't know how to drive!"

"And yet the car is here—and I appear to have driven it." He laughed. "I learned this morning. Come on, we'll go for a little ride."

"What about the children?"

"They'll be fine for a few minutes. Come on. We'll go once around the block, only that."

Annie came down the steps and got into the car.

"Okay," Andrew said. "First, I turn the key which is on the dash. Then I put my left foot on the clutch—which is the left pedal. Then, using my right foot, I press the starter button which is on the floor between the pedals. Then set the idle speed—this lever on the steering column. Next, I move the other lever to 'advance.' And then I give it some gas by pushing down on the gas button which is that other thing between the two pedals. Hmm."

The car edged forward, then leaped ahead, slowed, and leaped again.

Annie said, "Oh dear! That's a trifle, uh, herky-jerky."

"It will go more smoothly as I learn more."

She put her hands on the dashboard to steady herself as the car sped up. "What's the other pedal for, the one on the right?"

"The brake."

"Oh, thank God. I hoped there was one of those."

They went around the block with growing smoothness, and Andrew parked the car in front of the house.

On their way up the front walk, Annie said, "Andy, are you sure you just learned to drive today? You're actually quite good at it."

"I'm still learning. It reminds me of my horse, back in Finland. A beautiful way to get around." He looked back at the car. "It's the best of its kind."

"And are you going to teach me to drive sometime?"

"Maybe. But this is something that a lot of women just can't do."

"Well," Annie said, "I'm pretty sure that this woman can learn how." And she did.

#

In mid-April, 1925, Annie was happy to see the end of winter, although she was superstitious enough not to say those words aloud: "the end of winter." She allowed herself only one quiet moment of joy—no gloating—when she saw the first of the crocus leaves pushing through the thin layer of remaining snow on the sunny side of the house.

She had begun, about mid-March, to feel the stirrings of spring. Time to hunt out May's oldest clothing, from infancy, and pass it along. She didn't know anyone personally who would need it, but she felt sure Mrs. Stone would know someone, or would at least know where she could donate it.

She went down into the basement of the house on Algoma Street to bring up the few boxes in which she'd stored Owen's castoff clothing and toys. Might as well go through them too.

Looking around to be sure she had them all, she noticed a small cardboard box on a shelf behind the coal furnace. Judging by the layer of dust on the top, the box hadn't been opened the previous summer, when they'd moved. She took it down from the shelf, blew off the dust, and opened it.

Inside, there was a boot and a shoe—and nothing else. She took the box upstairs so that Andy could tell her if she should get rid of it or if it was a keeper.

When Andrew saw the box, he snorted dismissively. Then he said, "This is from the war." Annie knew which war he meant—he'd told her the broad outlines of the civil war in Finland, but no details. "Just souvenirs. You can throw it away if you want."

Annie considered. "No," she said finally. "They were important to you once and may become important to you again. I'll put them back." She went down to the basement, lifted the box onto the shelf, and pushed it into place.

She thought nothing of the box, the basement, the dust.

Instead, she thought of May's first birthday and how they might celebrate. May was growing fast—she'd gone from taking cautious steps on her own to running in just the past few days—but she was still too young even to understand what a birthday was. Owen, however, wasn't. He liked cake, and birthdays, and celebrations. Perhaps she could make small cakes, like those cupcakes she'd seen in a magazine advertisement from an American company, Hostess. But made at home.

Two weeks flew by, with Annie adjusting to two young and mobile little ones.

One day, Annie felt oddly ill. Her jaw was sore, but the feeling passed quickly. *I have a toothache*, she thought. *Too many sweets. Maybe we'll skip even the cupcakes.*

That night, the soreness returned. She could feel the muscles of her jaw contract painfully. Sometimes she could make them relax. Other times the contractions were prolonged. She could feel them spreading to her neck. *An infection,* she thought. *I'll make an appointment with a dentist. Tomorrow.*

But tomorrow passed, full of children and house responsibilities, with no time to make a dentist appointment. That night, as she lay in bed beside Andrew, she woke up sweating. The spasms were excruciating.

"Andy," she tried to say. "Andy, I don't feel well." But she found she could only drool. She poked him to wake him up.

"Annie? What's wrong?"

"Sick," she tried to say. It came out "ihck." She squeezed his arm.

Andrew turned on the light. "Oh, God."

Annie was grinning—an unnatural grin, as if someone was pulling on her face to make her grin. Her eyebrows were raised, her eyes round and staring.

"Oh Annie, we need to go to the hospital. Right now." He pulled on slacks and a shirt. "Did you get a scratch recently, maybe scrape yourself somewhere?"

Though she was lying on her side, her head was tilted toward her back. When she tried to answer, the single word that came out could have been *yes* or *kiss* or *kids*.

Andrew forced himself to calmness. "I'll call Mrs. Stone. We have to get you to a doctor. You might have lockjaw." In the kitchen, he phoned for an ambulance, and then for Mrs. Stone. It took the operator a long time to connect the calls. Mrs. Stone knocked on the door ten minutes later, just as the ambulance arrived.

The doctors sedated her, but the sedation could do nothing to stop the spread of the bacteria and their poison.

Four days later, Annie died.

#

Owen and May sat with their father at the short funeral service at Immanuel Lutheran.

"*Must* the children be there?" Mrs. Stone had asked. "May, especially, won't understand." And Owen, she added privately, might understand too well, and feel it too deeply.

"It is better," Andrew said. "Better that they know."

Mrs. Stone didn't ask, "Better than what?" or "Know what?" Given Andrew's stony face, she decided she didn't want to know either answer.

She came to the house the morning of the funeral and found the new dress Annie had bought for May's birthday. The box was unopened. Andrew had, understandably, not remembered—either the dress or the birthday.

In the church, Mrs. Stone sat in the pew behind the children, ready to sweep them out of the church if they grew restive.

They did not. May fell asleep, but Owen gazed at Holger Pearson with round eyes.

Although Owen was precocious, he still didn't understand everything. He had heard the word "dead" and knew it was about his mother: His mother was dead. He didn't know what "dead" was, exactly, never mind "forever" or "gone to be with Jesus" or many of the other things people said, but he dimly knew that his mother was gone and not coming back.

May did not understand at all the word "dead." In the days between Annie's death and the funeral, she often asked for

"Mumma." No matter how often or how softly Mrs. Stone tried to explain, she saw the effect of May's constant confusion on Andrew.

At last, Mrs. Stone said, "May, she is gone, she is not coming back, and you are not to ask about her again." That, May had accepted. Some of the household tension had eased, though its full complement of sorrow remained.

When the funeral service was over, they all went to the interment at Riverside Cemetery.

Owen didn't know why so many people were at the cemetery—he knew none of them except Mrs. Stone. She stood between them, holding each child's hand, tears streaming down her cheeks.

Their father did not cry.

When the graveside service was over, Andrew drove the family home. Mrs. Stone sat in the back seat with May; Owen rode in the front with his father.

The next morning, Andrew called Mrs. Stone and asked if she could stay with the children for part of that afternoon. When he saw her coming along Algoma Street, he went outside to meet her.

"I would like to visit the grave," Andrew said, "without the children."

"I understand."

"They are inside." Andrew began the walk to the cemetery. He did not want to take the car. It would *dishonour* her, he thought.

His tears began and ended at the gravesite. He left them there when he started the walk home.

Myllysilta sneered, *I knew she would make you soft.*

Millbridge answered, *She did not. She let me live, and happily.* After a moment: *How can I live now, without her?*

See? Myllysilta scoffed. *Soft.* Then Myllysilta raged, vowing vengeance on Death itself for stealing *his* wife, the woman *he* had chosen. But the emotion didn't last long. It never did.

Still walking, Millbridge said, *I don't want to live without her.*

Myllysilta, switching tactics, wheedled. *You must live. You must care for your children. They are what remains of her in the world, are they not? They deserve at least a father, and a home. That will be the start of the vengeance against Death for taking her from you. Later, after they are grown ... well, let that come as it comes. Tulee mitä tulee.*

What is, is. Something his mother had said. Millbridge acquiesced, dully. And thus it was Andrew again, not Antti, who climbed the front steps and walked into his house. It was Andrew who hid the framed wedding photo in the drawer of the bedside table, on top of the headscarf and hairpins Annie kept there.

It was Andrew, not Antti, who decided that the children would never meet Myllysilta.

Two days later, he asked Mrs. Stone if she could look after the children for a while, during the days. He needed—wanted—to get back to the lumberyard. Or so he thought. He hoped.

A week after that, he traded in the Willys Overland 91 for another one—one that had no trace of Annie's perfume.

5 • LIMBO

IN LATER YEARS, THE SUMMER OF 1925 became the summer that Andrew could not remember, no matter how hard he tried.

Oh, he had some of the broad strokes.

For instance, he made solid decisions about the children. Mrs. Stone had looked after Owen and May for a week or two, but they were active and "a little much for her," she said. She recommended finding someone new to Canada to take her place, so Andrew hired a young Finnish woman, a recent immigrant, to care for them and the house. When Andrew had to go out of town to labour camps, the children's nanny stayed over until he returned.

He knew all this, but never really remembered it. He couldn't remember what that first nanny had looked like, or even her name. Nor did he remember any of the two or three who replaced her during the next year.

Andrew was grateful to be able to throw himself into the lumber business—Annie had never been a real part of his work life, aside from bookkeeping—and Black Bay Lumber prospered.

A month before Annie's death, Andrew had shifted from sales to keeping the company's books, putting to use what Annie taught him. His duties revealed an ability to look at numbers and know what they meant and what they heralded.

Near the end of the summer after her death, he helped re-organize the company's operations. As the autumn arrived, he invested another portion of his savings into the company and became one of its managers, albeit not one of its principals.

Andrew was proud that he could function so well. Starting that summer, so much of his life, the one with Annie, now felt far beyond his reach. Each day it dwindled a little farther, and the memory of pain became a little less.

As long as he remained vigilant.

He tried not to think of Annie. Of her hopes for their lives together. Of her own future. Even after the children were born, she'd still wanted to teach someday. She'd found many ways to teach at home. Owen already knew the names of colours and animals, and he could hum along with Annie the lullabies she sang while putting May to sleep.

Andrew could not let himself think about what sort of teacher she might have become, or even what she might have taught Owen next. In that direction lay despair.

He pushed aside the thoughts, ideas, musings, enthusiasms, and voice that had been part of his life with Annie, that every day had filled their home.

As fire and hammer can harden a blade, he hardened himself. Because God had not cared for Annie—and He had not, or Annie would not have died, not so horribly, not now, not ever—then he would not care for God. Let God, Himself, hammer on him; it would only make him better able to hold an edge.

Despite Andrew's efforts to be gentle with the children, Owen felt some of this—some of the hardness, the sharpness, the resolve. May, though younger, felt it all, and it frightened her. The nannies who came and went could offer little comfort, though they tried.

Andrew was not cruel, as his own father had been. He was never angry; he never thundered at them when they misbehaved. He remained quiet and calm, and merely held or soothed them until they were good-tempered again.

He came home at night from work, always in time to eat with them the supper the nanny had prepared. They talked about the weather, about what they'd played that day. In the evenings, he sat in their bedroom with them while they went to sleep.

But sometimes he caught Owen looking at him, eyebrows drawn together. Sometimes, May put her finger in her mouth and cried for no real reason.

At those times, Andrew made an effort to coax Antti from his own forehead.

#

After that first summer without Annie, in the autumn of 1925, Andrew spent more time than usual at the various lumber camps—both those in and around Port Arthur, and others farther north of the city, in the old growth forests.

The men knew that when Andrew showed up, some of them would be fired and some would end up with jobs that might be better, or might just be different. When word went around that Millbridge was coming to do an inspection, the men would say, "The executioner's coming. Sharpen your axe—he's sharpening his."

After the leaves had fallen but before the nights grew much longer and the temperature dropped below freezing, Andrew made yet another trip to yet another logging camp. This time, it was far to the west of the city, near the small community of Sunshine.

The men assembled so that Andrew, now considered one of the "big bosses," could speak to them. They formed a group outside the cookhouse. Andrew, standing on a tree stump beside the foreman, looked them over, readying himself for the speech he was about to deliver.

In the middle of the assembly he saw someone he thought he knew. It took him a moment to place the face—it was not someone he'd met in Canada. A mental photograph came into focus, and he remembered. He felt a shock, though he didn't show it. The face belonged to the man who had shot his brothers and dumped their bodies into the street, back in Gamlaby. Something in him reignited, though he hid it well.

He leaned down to speak to the foreman beside him. "That man, the one halfway back with the cigarette in his mouth. What is his name?"

The foreman squinted into the sun. "Mantere," he said at last. "Jussi Mantere. He is new. Good worker."

Andrew showed no emotion when he said, "Keep an eye on him."

"I will, Mr. Millbridge."

Then Antti Myllysilta elbowed Andrew Millbridge aside. "Good, good. And your name?"

"Rufus Karialainen."

"Rufus? What the hell kind of name is that? What do the men call you? I know damn well it isn't Rufus."

"Rough-house," Rufus said.

"Much better." Myllysilta laughed. "Well, Rough-house, I want a word with you before you leave. Hang around." He faded to let Millbridge do his work.

Millbridge took another look at the men and then raised his voice in the familiar speech. He'd given it half a dozen times now—the one about an honest day's hard work and the duty owed to other workers and to the IWW, the Industrial Workers of the World.

When he finished, he accepted the men's applause, and as the men dispersed, he shook hands with the camp's managers.

At last, Myllysilta, voice low, turned to Rough-house. "I want to know everything you can find out about Jussi Mantere. Everything."

"Yes, sir."

Myllysilta said, "Do this well, and I will have other work for you. Let's just say there will be rewards."

"Yes, sir. Thank you, sir."

It was clear to Rufus—Rough-house—that that he had been chosen to become Millbridge's man. Others might be daunted by the responsibilities, to say nothing of their vagueness, but Rough-house was not. He was clever—perhaps, he thought, as clever as Millbridge. He was sure that Millbridge already knew everything about him, including his given name, and had known it for a while. So. Millbridge wanted him to be more than just a foreman. But what?

I'll need to be careful. Andrew Millbridge was one of those men who are dead inside. Rough-house could feel it. It was something they had in common.

6 • HEMMETS AND HOITOS

IN 1925, JUST BEFORE CHRISTMAS, the Hemmet—a building that was the gathering-place of the Swedish-speaking Finns and other members of the Scandinavian Home Society—closed up shop on Secord Street. The landlord wanted more rent, and the building itself needed work.

The Society, therefore, moved its headquarters to Bay Street—only four blocks from the Hoito, where the Red Finns gathered. In the spring of the following year the Society bought a lot on Algoma Street—within earshot of the Finn Hall—and began building a new Hemmet, a combination meeting house and café. The café and kitchen would be on the main floor, washrooms in the basement. An office, a library, and an all-purpose meeting room would occupy the second floor.

Mag Mathews, the Lakehead's most well-known madam, contributed twenty-five dollars to the building fund. The Society blushed, but took the cash.

Port Arthur had what amounted to two downtowns—one for the English-speaking population and another for the immigrants, primarily Finns, Swedes, Finland-Swedes, Poles, and Italians.

The "real" downtown, the one acknowledged by mayors and city councillors, held the theatres, stores, and proper hotels. Andrew had often walked these streets in his early days in town, stretching his legs and learning English.

The other downtown, less than a mile away, was Little Finland, centered on the intersection of Bay and Algoma streets. If you thought of yourself as both a Finn and a working man, you ate your lunch or breakfast at the Hoito (the word meant *care*), the restaurant in the basement of the Finnish Labour Temple on Bay Street.

If you felt you were a Scandinavian, you went to the new place—the Hemmet on Algoma Street—and ate at the small café in the new Scandinavian Home Society building. The café, of course did not have a name. Giving it a name would have been a bit *högmodig*—too snobbish.

Andrew Millbridge was at home in both the Hoito and the Hemmet. Both served Finnish pancakes—though in the Hoito they were eaten mostly by Socialists or Red Finns and old-country, Finnish-speaking Whites, some of whom had a Temperance background. The Finland-Swedes, almost uniformly White, ate their pancakes in the Hemmet instead.

At the Hoito, Mr. Millbridge sat with the Finnish workers and talked unions and socialism, but never communism. When he went to the Hemmet, he sat by himself at the lunch counter, thought about Annie, wondered who was living in their old home on Machar Avenue only a block or two away, and spoke to almost no one.

Beside the "Big Finn Hall" at 314 Bay Street, there was a "Little Finn Hall" at 316 Bay Street—the headquarters of Local #2 of the Finnish Organization of Canada. The Local was very Red. It had established a number of People's Co-operative stores, a co-op dairy, and a co-op restaurant called Tarmo—the Finnish word for *vigour*.

It was with vigour that the Finnish-speaking population of the Lakehead was growing rapidly. The Americans had decided that only about five hundred Finns would be allowed into the United States in any given year, and so the Finns, in their turn, had decided that Canada, for now, was an attractive enough alternative to the USA.

The Finns, whether they lived in Finland or in Canada, were always picking sides, always on the lookout for something to attach themselves to or get away from.

Millbridge had chosen the kind of Finn he wanted to be—and, since a communist-by-association was not on his menu, he avoided contact with the people at 316 Bay Street. He almost never ate at the Tarmo. As time passed, he ate mostly with the capitalist Finns.

Sometimes, Millbridge drove to Fort William, the other of The Lakehead's two cities, and ate his pancakes at The Workman's Co-operative Association Restaurant—which was also called the Hoito and, though it catered primarily to the Red Finns, welcomed Red Ukrainians as well, along with a sprinkling of socialist and communist Greeks and Italians. The language of that Hoito was more often a broken English—a courtesy, in part, to the Greeks and Italians—than either Finnish or Ukrainian. And, since the Port Arthur Hoito or Tarmo customers hardly ever ate there, Millbridge felt free to do so.

The two Hoitos had one thing in common—they were both sources of information. Men heard about jobs there, learned about rallies or meetings, kept up to date on who was hiring and who was not. And they shared information about themselves. "That guy over there" became Fred, the carpenter, and he worked for a guy who paid fair wages. "That other one, Fred's buddy, is a scab. You can't trust anything he says."

But Millbridge rarely went to Fort William on business, beyond meals. He preferred to send Rough-house to sample the business waters of Fort William, if not the pancakes. The Ukrainians, many of whom were communists, were useful when protest and muscle and banners were needed. They lived on the south side of Fort William, on streets that had no fire hydrants because, the Finns said, the mayor and the councillors didn't like Ukrainians.

The Italians, who couldn't care less about politics, knew how to make wine and how to reward those who sent them customers. So the Italians had more hydrants on their streets than the Ukrainians did.

As for the Greeks—well, Millbridge had no idea what form of sinning they might prefer, but he was confident that if necessary, he could figure out a way to use them, too.

#

As Port Arthur and Fort William grew, Millbridge paid attention to what was going on—as did the part of him that was Myllysilta, but for different reasons. Both of them saw clearly that Port Arthur and Fort William, the twin cities, were prospering. The prosperity wouldn't last, of course. *Nothing lasts forever*, Millbridge knew. But for now, and likely for the next few years, things looked good.

Therefore, it was time for businesses large and small, legitimate or not, to branch out, to diversify. And since it seemed as if the grain trade was becoming more and more lucrative, and new grain elevators were being built, it might be a good time to invest in the things that the average working man might buy.

Millbridge stepped back from his day-to-day involvement in Black Bay Lumber's operations, though he retained his financial interest. It freed him to try new ventures.

Rough-house had proved to be exactly the kind of person that

Myllysilta had been looking for, in much the same way Bertil had been an ideal business partner back in Finland. In the blink of an eye, Rough-house could go from being the articulate and convincing advocate of a particular strategy at a union meeting, to being a ruthless exploiter of anyone whose objectives were not the same as his, or the same as Millbridge's.

In his turn, Rough-house knew that his boss had two definite sides, though he didn't know Myllysilta's name. When he spoke to Andrew Millbridge, he knew both sides listened.

Always, Rough-house was careful in his choice of words. Offending the "spooky" side of Millbridge could be fatal.

Their conversations usually occurred in neutral territory, at the Mariaggi Hotel on the Port Arthur waterfront. The hotel was more Millbridge than Myllysilta. It had large rooms, a first-class view of Lake Superior, a regal front reception area with brass spittoons arranged elegantly and strategically on the floor, and a fine restaurant. That elegance appealed to Millbridge. Because Annie had enjoyed its ambience, they'd dined there a time or two, but not often enough to make Millbridge avoid it after her death. Myllysilta, meanwhile, appreciated that its normal clientele neither knew nor cared who he was, and therefore, they would not eavesdrop.

One afternoon, as Rough-house and Millbridge were finishing up their midday meal there, Rough-house put down his fork. "Did you know that a tunnel runs under Water Street? It starts in the basement here, and it comes out at the boat launch—under the roof of that shed that runs along the shore."

He pointed, and Millbridge looked out the window. Rough-house continued, "In the tunnel, there's a pulley and pipe system for smuggling liquor from the hotel to the lake. But from here, from Water Street, you can't see a thing. The liquor is put on skiffs and then transferred to the lake freighters or—if the client prefers—it's hidden in railway boxcars, the ones that carry grain. All the liquor work gets done at night, of course."

"Bullshit," Millbridge said. *Maybe, maybe not,* Myllysilta thought.

Rough-house laughed. "The thing is, tunnel or no tunnel, bullshit or not, everything is being done small potatoes right now. I've been thinking—together, you and me, we could do better. For instance: we could contact potential clients in the south—Southern Ontario, northern USA. We'd arrange the means of transportation to the market, and we'd provide the labour."

He paused to gauge Millbridge's interest and saw enough to keep talking. "The selling points are that the means of delivery are damn near undetectable, the labour is reliable, and every part of the operation is one step removed from the big boys—and you know who I mean. The clients pay us a share of the profits."

He cleared his throat and launched into specifics. "I'd be their Port Arthur contact, the one who sets up the shipping deals in Port Arthur. I supervise the labour and arrange the transportation. You set up the deals with the producers and the buyers down south—Duluth, Detroit, Chicago, Southern Ontario—and work out the financial stuff. It'll mean some travel for you early on, but once things are in place, we'd be set."

He waited.

Millbridge was quiet for a moment. "You think prohibition's going to become a permanent thing?" Myllysilta knew it would not and was curious what Rough-house would say.

"Not in Canada. Not in the States, either, but they'll hold on to it longer than we will—more Christians down there." He laughed again. "What do you say?"

"You think this could work?"

"I do. It's working small-scale right now. We'll go bigger—but not so big that we catch the eyes of the liquor lords." Rough-house leaned forward. "I know some people who can probably bring the big distillers into this thing, though—as long as we can provide a solid business model."

"This is the truth? No bullshit?"

"Swear to God." Rough-house held up his right hand.

"I'll look into it." Millbridge considered. It would mean leaving the children for travel again, and possibly for longer trips than when he worked for Black Bay. But, as Rough-house said, the travel would be necessary only in the beginning. It seemed a good next step.

Millbridge said, "I have some experience in this—from a similar situation in Finland." He paused. "But if you're lying, Mr. Karialainen, I'll kill you." He smiled a threat.

"Deal." Rough-house, unperturbed, drew the ashtray toward him. "Cigarette?" He reached into his vest pocket.

"I don't smoke," Millbridge said. "Or drink, or gamble. Ever."

"I'll try to remember that." Rough-house flicked the top of the wooden matchstick with his thumb and lit his cigarette. "To us," he said, and drew the smoke deep into his lungs.

#

Myllysilta knew that Rough-house was right—booze, bootlegging, and smuggling were good bets, at least for now. So Andrew Millbridge invested in all three, while making sure both that they were protected as much as possible from the police, and that his involvement went unremarked.

Millbridge's public face—the side of him he presented to Owen and May—was always that of a fundamentally good man who dealt in timber, transportation, and pulp and paper. And, in fact, he worked seriously at making money from these legitimate businesses, while making the illegal ones, the real money-makers, thrive.

To his children, he was "Father" sometimes, but mostly just "Dad." He liked that.

On Sundays he took his children to church—though never to Immanuel Lutheran, which was full of anti-Red-Finns, Swedes and Finland-Swedes, Norwegians, Danes and a few "other." Instead, he alternated between a small Lutheran church in Fort William and a small Presbyterian church. They even visited an Anglican church or two. Baptist churches, he thought, were a little too radical.

But no matter which church they went to—and they attended several semi-regularly through the years—he never sang the hymns. And when the congregation prayed, he always kept his eyes open. A lot of men did. Some, Millbridge thought, were thereby satisfying a streak of matrimonial rebellion.

Millbridge himself had no appetite for anything remotely resembling love, beyond caring for the children—Annie's legacy.

Myllysilta had plenty of appetites, but he was too wary of entanglements to indulge them. Like Millbridge in church, he kept his eyes open. Always.

7 • MYLLYSILTA AND MILLBRIDGE

IN THE SUMMER OF 1928—Owen Millbridge would turn six in the fall—his father bought a house on Prospect Avenue, and the family moved to higher ground. The upstairs rooms had an unobstructed view of Lake Superior. Each morning, the sun rose out of the Sleeping Giant that lay across the mouth of Thunder Bay.

Again, Andrew moved the soldier's framed certificate, the one from Machar Avenue. The soldier felt like part of their family. Andrew mostly thought of it as a good luck charm, but a reminder, too, that all good luck is ruled by Time, and is inherently capricious.

He'd chosen the house on Prospect Avenue for many reasons. The school was close enough that Owen could walk there in the morning and come back home for lunch, no matter the weather.

And the house had four bedrooms. Andrew hired a live-in housekeeper, Mrs. Vogel, to prepare meals, look after the children, and keep the house clean.

Mrs. Vogel was German—practical, precise, and proper. When she had occasion to speak to Millbridge, she always addressed him in the third person. "Is Mr. Millbridge going to be back in time for lunch? Would Mr. Millbridge allow the children to have some friends over after supper?" He said "yes" almost always to lunch, but only rarely to friends, and only when they could play together outdoors. The interior of the home was for family only.

The house also had a driveway, rare on Prospect Avenue, and Millbridge could park the car on his own property now, off the street and out of harm's way.

Both the new Technical School and the Port Arthur Collegiate Institute were within easy walking distance—and, for Owen, about nine years in the future anyway.

In the fall, Andrew enrolled Owen in Prospect Avenue School. On the first day of school, Millbridge had breakfast with the children, walked Owen to school, and made sure that Owen settled in properly. He then came home, said goodbye to May, and drove to work.

"Work," now that he wasn't at the lumberyard, happened in several locations—sometimes at the Mariaggi Hotel and often at the Scandinavian Home.

But the first stop was the Finnish Labour Temple for a second breakfast at the Hoito. His habit was to sit at the counter and start a conversation with whoever sat next to him. Lately, he had been hearing a lot about the way the stock markets were rising and that it was becoming easy to borrow money to start a business. Prices were falling—especially in food—but trade with Europe was slowing down as America's influence over the markets grew larger.

Behind Andrew Millbridge's smiling face, Myllysilta furrowed his brows, and pretended to think.

On that first day of school for Owen, Andrew sat down beside someone—he couldn't remember the man's name, but no matter—from the crew that had included Jussi Mantere.

"Seen Jussi lately?" Millbridge asked.

"Been a while," the man said. "He's with 'Pappi' Maki now. Up at Onion Lake, I think. I'm Pentti Jokkola, by the way. Friends call me Joke-alot."

"No surprise there. I'm Andrew Millbridge. People call me *sir*. Good to meet you, Pentti Joke-alot." Andrew took a sip of his coffee. "Pappi's an odd name," he said. He didn't want his breakfast companion to think that he was digging for information about Mantere, or Maki for that matter.

"Used to be a clergyman—one of those that doesn't have a church over here. He's kind of a religious free-lancer. His real job is running a gang of pulp-cutters."

"Pigeon River Timber guys, right?"

His companion nodded. "They're part of Eddie Johnson's operation. And if you ask me, those buggers are the ones responsible for the wage cuts this year. Last year we were making five bucks a cord, fifty bucks guaranteed minimum per month, plus free board. Now it's down to four bucks a double cord, minus a buck a day for board, minus the ten bucks we used to get for travel, and we still have to spend cash on clothes, boots—all that shit. Pappi's gang is strictly anti-strike. And you know what that means—no strike, no leverage. No leverage, and wages drop through the floor."

"Listen to him," Myllysilta whispered to Millbridge. *"He's telling you about tomorrow. There's* money *in his words."*

Andrew took another sip of his coffee. "Doesn't look good," he said in an off-hand manner.

"Damn right."

Later, when Andrew was driving to the next stop on his list, he started to think about the conversation. *Pentti Jokkola is talking about things in general. He just doesn't know it. The good times are almost over.*

In response, Myllysilta whispered, *Get ready then. The bottom of the tree is starting to rot. It's time to start thinking about what still makes money after the tree falls, because you can't make money from a rotten tree.*

Millbridge laughed, then shook his head in mock resignation.

#

The tree fell, mostly of its own accord, at the end of October the following year. On Black Tuesday, October 29th, 1929, the stock buyers stopped buying.

Andrew Millbridge, however, continued to prosper. He already had a solid income from bootlegging and prostitution, and to these investments he had added shares in shoe stores, laundries, hardware stores, repair and housekeeping services, and black-market cigarettes—all of which did well as stock prices fell and factory jobs vanished.

His customers were the lost, the job-seekers, the men and women with time on their hands and not much food in their bellies. In all his dealings, he was careful to avoid looking too successful, and so most of his investments, meticulously researched and closely managed, were made in towns and cities outside the Lakehead—places he had visited many times in the course of the liquor trade.

At home he advocated for unions and their socialist causes. And when, from time to time, the Finnish Labour Temple turned into a hostel for the unemployed, Millbridge provided some of the beds on which the workers slept. He was, to all who thought they knew him, a good man, a union man.

All but Rough-house. To Rough-house he was a good boss perhaps, undoubtedly a good father to Owen and May, but .... Rough-house, wisely, never let himself finish the thought.

#

Early in November, union matters came to a head. The IWW—the Industrial Workers of the World—which had once been part of the One Big Union, began to lose its power struggle with the Lumber Workers Industrial Union of Canada. The LWIUC—also once part of the One Big Union—had called for a strike. However, for the strike to succeed, it needed the IWW's help.

But Pappi Maki's men refused to join the strike. So Pappi's employer, the Pigeon River Timber Company, hired strike-breakers from Winnipeg to do the work that the LWIUC was refusing to do.

Some of the strike-breakers stayed at the Mariaggi Hotel. Millbridge and Rough-house were there, talking business in the bar, when a fight began between a union man and one of the recently-arrived strike-breakers.

Millbridge said, "Go take care of that, why don't you." Rough-house went, and in seconds the fight was over.

"That was fun," Rough-house said as he returned to the table. He blew on the knuckles of his right hand.

"Lucky for you they were both skinny," Millbridge said. He turned to the table where the union bush worker now sat with two other union men. "Buy you a drink?" he asked. "Cops are coming, I think. You might as well have a drink before they get here."

The man got up and came over. "Bertil Salmi," he said, introducing himself.

"How about that! I have a friend named Bertil. He's got a bookstore in Kokkola." *I've said too much,* Millbridge thought. *Oh well.* "What are you drinking?"

"Just beer. How do you know about the cops?"

"I saw the bartender go to the phone when your little scuffle started. He must know you." Millbridge grinned. "And that guy you were beating the shit out of is standing on the sidewalk out front. So what's the story?"

"I got into some trouble at one of Don Clark's camps a couple of days ago—a few of us tried to get the scabs to go home. Bit of a fight. Some of Clark's guys know me—told the bartender, I guess."

"You know anything about the LWIUC planning to send someone up to Pappi's camp on Onion Lake? I was at the Hoito and—."

"Yeah, two guys," Salmi interrupted. "Maybe Viljo Rosvall and Janne Voutilainen. What's today's date?"

"November 10th."

"There's supposed to be a big meeting on the 17th to finalize plans. The LWIUC wants Pappi's crew to join the strike. From what I hear, Rosvall and Voutilainen are the missionaries. There's going to be a meeting early in the day, and the two will leave right after it's over. It's a long walk, and they'll be loaded down."

"I know a bit about Rosvall. He used to organize the railway guys. Fought in the civil war in Finland—losing side. He picked Red instead of White. What about Voutilainen?"

"Trapper," Salmi said. "Red as hell, but a nice guy. Got some traplines up at Onion Lake, so he knows the territory."

Rough-house, who had been keeping an eye on the street outside, said to Salmi, "Your ride's here." He pointed out the window—the police had arrived. "You want the back entrance?"

"Nah. I can use the rest." Salmi returned to his table.

"Nice fellow," Rough-house said, keeping his voice low. "We could use him."

"Yes," Millbridge said quietly. "He's one of those guys who doesn't mind giving his knuckles a workout. Otherwise, a very sociable fellow—most of the time. Knows what's going on. We'll have to see if anything suitable for him comes up."

They watched as the police came into the room and took Bertil Salmi away. A minute later, they heard the car door slam.

"Oh," Rough-house said, "I almost forgot. Mantere's moved again. Bought himself a house up on Montgomery Street. When he's not working for Pappi, he's fixing it up. He's tacked on a long porch, the whole width of the house, facing the street. Back yard faces south. Got a big garden. Nice place."

"Basement?"

"Not yet—just a dugout. He's waiting a while before he puts a full basement in, I guess. He's married, you know, and wives hate dugouts." Rough-house laughed.

"Finn girl?"

"Finland-Swede. They have a kid about Owen's age—maybe a little older."

"Interesting." Millbridge pushed his ginger ale glass away and reached into his wallet. "Next drink's on me." He put a dollar on the table. "If you learn anything more about Mantere, let me know."

Rough-house nodded. He watched as Millbridge left, then went to the bar.

#

On November 17th, the LWIUC met and voted that Rosvall and Voutilainen head up to Onion Lake. Everyone knew that their prospects for successfully convincing the IWW to strike were poor at best. Voutilainen wasn't present for the meeting—he was already at Tarmola, a little village just south of Onion Lake. Rosvall was to meet him there, spend the night, and the next morning the two would set off together on the long walk to Pappi Maki's logging camp at the north end of the lake.

They never arrived.

On the 24th it was clear that something had happened to the two men, and on the 27th, the local newspaper, the *Port Arthur News Chronicle*, broke the story of their disappearance.

For the next four months, searchers combed the Onion Lake area. No bodies were found.

On April 19th, 1930, trappers discovered Janne Voutilainen's body in shallow water a few feet from shore at the north end of Onion Lake. His packsack was still slung over his shoulders. An autopsy performed three days later determined that there had been no foul play, and the inquest, the day after, confirmed the finding. Case closed, and Voutilainen was buried. The same day, Rosvall's body turned up just half a mile from where Voutilainen had been found.

Again, there was no evidence of foul play.

"No evidence?" the men at the Hoito said. "Bullshit! Contract killing! Fucking Whites."

#

A few days after Rosvall's body was discovered, Bertil Salmi showed up at the Hoito. Andrew Millbridge sat at the counter, having morning coffee with Rough-house.

Rough-house saw Salmi first and waved him over. "Thought your ass was still in jail," Rough-house said. "Sit it down here, beside me."

Bertil perched on the counter stool. "Union lawyer got me out after a couple of days. Told me to play nice for a while, so I did."

"Breakfast's on me—whatever you'd like," Millbridge said. "What's the news on the Onion Lake boys?"

"Just the funeral. The committee's been going back and forth on that—some want it to be on Saturday, some say Sunday. Right now, they're thinking they'll have it on Saturday, the 26th. Damndest thing, though. Because Voutilainen's already in the ground, they're going to have some kind of symbolic black casket in the procession. I don't know if they want people to think it's Rosvall's, or Voutilainen's, or some kind of symbolic thing. Anyway, nobody's supposed to talk about the fact that Voutilainen's funeral has already been held."

"April 26th," Millbridge said thoughtfully. He leaned forward a bit so he could see past Rough-house. "You know anyone on the planning committee?" he asked Salmi.

"I know a few. Why?"

"Tell them—no, ask them—if they can hold the funeral, the interment—you know, the *burial*—on Monday the 28th, starting around noon. Not on the 27th."

"Why?"

Millbridge momentarily ignored the question. He sipped his coffee. "And make sure that when they talk about it—especially with anyone from the *News Chronicle* or the *Times News*—they call it a *joint* funeral. Nobody's to say that Voutilainen's already six feet under."

He took another sip and put his cup down. "There's going to be a solar eclipse on the 28th. It was in the *News Chronicle* a week ago, but damn few bush workers can read English, and the few who can, can't afford to buy a paper. It'll catch most people off guard—give them something to talk about for the rest of their lives."

Millbridge smiled. "When it comes to religious experiences, eclipses trump sermons. If they hold the funeral on the 28th, people will never forget it. If it's on the 26th? Eh." He shrugged.

"Son of a bitch." Salmi shook his head. "I'll pass it along." He waved a waitress over. "Bacon and eggs," he said, "and keep the coffee coming."

#

On April 28th the funeral procession, led by a brass band, wound its way downhill from the funeral chapel on Arthur Street, east to

Cumberland Street then south, before turning back to the west on Bay Street. Eventually it snaked uphill, past the Finnish Labour Temple, where onlookers crowded the balconies and stairs. Once past the hall, it headed south on Secord Street to Oliver Road, then west once more—this time, up a steep hill to Riverside Cemetery.

Halfway along the route, the eclipse dimmed the sky and turned the world grey. Almost everyone—the people in the parade and those at the side of the street, watching—looked up to where a dark mask was being placed upon the sun.

At the graveside, later, Alf Hautamaki, Communist, loyal member and organizer of the Lumber Workers International Union of Canada, and a devout atheist, told the surrounding crowd that God Himself was displeased by what had happened to Rosvall and Voutilainen. The proof? The eclipse, of course. And the cover-up. God wanted everyone to know that the two had been murdered.

Andrew Millbridge marched in the procession, but Rough-house did not. At the end of the service, Millbridge waited inside the cemetery gates. As per instructions, Rough-house came by car to pick him up.

"Well?" Millbridge asked as he got in the back seat.

Without starting the car, Rough-house said, "You were right. Mantere was there with some other guys from the IWW."

"The ones that were part of the brass band?"

"No. Another group—farther back in the procession. He was walking beside that friend of his—the one with shell shock."

"Ivor Solbakken." Myllysilta thought, *Karl's brother. Rabbit.*

"Yeah."

"I'm surprised," Millbridge said after a short pause. "Mantere doesn't like parades." When Rough-house didn't ask why, Millbridge asked, "Is Solbakken still staying at one of the apartments in that building beside the Hemmet?"

"Far as I know."

"I'll see you tomorrow," Millbridge said. "I've changed my mind about getting you to drive me home. Going to walk back—it'll do me good." He got out of the car.

After Rough-house drove off, Andrew walked over to Annie's grave. He stood in front of it for a minute or two.

"I'm sorry," he said at last. He shrugged, turned away, and began the walk home.

• 8 MYTHOLOGY

"DID YOU EVER MEET MAG MATTHEWS?" Millbridge asked casually. It was 1931, just over a year after the funeral and eclipse, and he and Rough-house were having breakfast in the Hoito. Millbridge caught the eye of a waitress and then tapped the side of his cup. She came over with a pot of coffee and gave him a refill.

"The hooker? Sorry, *madam*. Heard stories about her," Rough-house said. "Never met her, though." Without being asked, the waitress filled his cup as well, then walked away. At the Hoito, service was always prompt, and the staff knew not to listen to private conversations. "Don't know much about her, though. She still alive?"

"Far as I know."

"So ... what's on your mind?"

"When I first came to Canada she was running a house down on Williams Avenue—on the south side of the Neebing River."

"Mag's Buffet," Rough-house said. "The cops would raid it when they were on duty and visit it when they weren't. They'd drink her liquor when they were off duty, and charge her for possession when she *said* they could." He laughed. "Cop, one time, asked her if she served *hors d'oeuvres* at her buffet, and she said, 'Whore doers? Sure do! You're welcome anytime.'"

Millbridge smiled wryly. "She had a couple more places on the river," he said. "Same area. One she called the Little Brown Cottage. Another was The Shambles. Good name for it. She even had a place on Machar Avenue, just a few houses down from my old place."

Rough-house was accustomed to the fact that Millbridge never used his wife's name—never said "Annie and I."

"Okay," Rough-house said. "And your point?"

"What I'm getting at is that she isn't—or wasn't—a typical madam. She treated her girls fairly, gave them summer vacations down in Owen Sound. She's got a place there, a big Victorian house called Branningham Grove. She donated money to her parish church, took care of the down-and-out, had lots of friends both high places and low. Hell, when the Scandinavian Home was being built in '26, on Algoma Street, just a block from her Machar Avenue bordello, she coughed up twenty-five dollars for the building fund."

"Business expense." Rough-house laughed.

Millbridge ignored him. "She invested her money, too. She opened up places south of the border, put money into the Port Arthur Duluth and Western Railway—you know, the PeeDee line. There was always one of her houses at the end of the tracks. Hell, without her money, the Fort William Street Railway would never have been built. She even bought a big chunk of swampland across the river from her 'buffet.' I have no idea what she thinks that's ever going to be good for—it's between the two cities, in the middle of nowhere, just a piece of low flat land that dreams of being a swamp. At one point she even owned a stable of racehorses. What kind of investment is that?" He paused. "Money-losers with hooves."

"She still married?" Rough-house asked. "I'm single, you know."

Millbridge didn't even smile. "She'd be, what, in her mid-sixties now. The point is, she knows how to recognize opportunities that no one else can see. If she buys swampland, it's because she knows that someone, some day, is going to build on it. If she buys racehorses, maybe it's because she knows how to fix the race."

"Or maybe she just likes horses."

Millbridge ignored him. "In tough times, like the war years, you can make money as easily as you can when times are good. She saw that as long as you diversify, and know how to fill the needs that are there—not the needs you *wish* were there—you can turn a profit."

Rough-house nodded but didn't interrupt.

"The other thing she saw," Millbridge continued, "was that to stay in business you need to have friends. She gave away tons of money to people who needed it, and they told their friends how kind she was. Even the cops thought she was a good person. And maybe she is."

"And now?" Rough-house asked. "What's she doing? What's she got on the go?"

"I don't know. Some people say she's rich; some say she's poor now. She's healthy, she's ill. She'll die rich, she'll die a pauper. The point is, she's become invisible. She's taken herself out of the public eye."

"Retired?"

"Maybe, maybe not. Dollars to doughnuts, though, I'd bet she's still working in some way." Millbridge stared at his coffee cup.

The silence made Rough-house uneasy, but he did not prompt him or ask him again to explain why he had brought up Old Mag.

At length, Millbridge emptied his cup and broke the silence. "Rough-house, it's time for *me* to become invisible." He leaned forward. "The kids are getting older. May's in Grade One. Pretty soon they'll be old enough to put two and two together. So. I want you to take over the operations—run the business, the part that's at street level. I'll run what's legit. You game?"

Instead of saying *yes* or *no*, Rough-house asked, "Why now? Why me?"

"It's the kids," Millbridge repeated patiently. "I owe them a father, the kind other kids have—not one who's likely to end up in jail or dead in the street. It's time for me to get out of the spotlight. And why you?" He paused. "I *know* you."

Rough-house considered saying something about the kids, then changed his mind. *Leave it alone,* he thought. "I don't know if I can do what you do, boss. I don't even know half the things you're involved in." He looked away, then back at Millbridge. "You trust me to take over?"

"Are you asking if I'll always have my eye on what you're doing? If I'll move in and kick you in the ass if you screw up or try to take what isn't yours?"

"Yes."

"Rough-house, here's the thing about business. Control is everything—especially self-control. As soon as you lose control of what you're doing, as soon as you start consoling yourself with 'If only I had' or 'If only I wasn't,' you're finished. So, yeah, damn right I will. If you try to get in my way, or try to take what's mine, I'll put on my ass-kicking cleats, and you'd better have a good-sized pillow tucked into the back of your pants." Millbridge paused, then smiled.

Rough-house considered. "How are we going to separate everything?"

"It'll take some work. Some figuring. Research, even. And time." He paused. "Years, perhaps, even a decade. You still game?"

"I'm in," Rough-house said. "Boss."

"Good. You buy breakfast this time, then."

#

In the afternoon, Millbridge went to the Scandinavian Home. He sat by himself at a booth and ordered a sandwich and coffee. *Time passes, everything changes*, he thought.

This new Scand—the one built after the move from Secord Street to Bay Street—had become Millbridge's point of contact with the Swedes, Finland-Swedes, Norwegians and Danes. They were a stolid and quiet bunch, which made the Scand a good place to work.

From his briefcase, he took out a black and white marbled composition book that he had bought at Woolworth's, and in pencil on the first page he wrote *Family History*, then underlined the words. *My father was born*, he began, and paused. He needed a name. Toivo Niemi, he decided. *My father was born in Karelia, in a small fishing village on Lake Ladoga.* He smiled.

When Owen and May were older and began to ask questions, he would show them the book. He could, if he wanted, make them a family history that went back as many generations as he cared to invent.

But for now, a page or two of—what was the fancy word for such a statement? *Prevarication.*

He thought briefly of Annie and his English lessons. *Prevarication.* Something you say that comes before you check facts, or perhaps devise some. A lie that buys you time to get your story straight. It wasn't a definition that one might find in a dictionary, perhaps, but it was a definition that Millbridge liked. And so did Myllysilta.

The section on Annie, he thought, would have to be truthful. It could not be else. All the rest could be whatever it became. And it would help keep him from telling conflicting stories about his past, if anyone asked. Which was unlikely.

At 3:30 Millbridge left the Scand and drove to Owen's school. He parked on the street and waited until Owen came out at a little after 4:00. Owen walked right past the car, so Millbridge honked. Owen turned around and ran to the side door.

"You didn't see me?" Millbridge asked.

"I was thinking about sums," Owen said.

"Sums? I thought you knew those already."

"This is harder. We're learning how to add big numbers."

"Are there rules for that?"

"Yes," Owen said.

"What's the most important rule?"

"Keep the numbers in a straight line down the page. If the lines are crooked you might add the wrong numbers, so you have to be sure that the, uh," he wiggled his fingers, "*digits* on the right-hand side are all one under the other—and straight. If the lines get squiggly, you'll make a mistake."

"Squiggly?"

"You know—like a snake. And you have to make teeny-tiny numbers above the bottom line to keep track of what's in your head."

"I see."

"Otherwise, the numbers can lie. My teacher says all numbers want to lie, and our job is to keep them from being able to do it."

"She sounds like she's teaching you something good."

In this new, legit future, I'll need an accountant, Millbridge thought. *Plus a fortune teller. Maybe I'm raising one—or the other.* He laughed, then started the car, and they drove the short distance home.

Owen was pleased that he had made his father laugh.

9 • THE DEPRESSION

IN THE AUTUMN OF 1931, May started Grade Two and Owen began Grade Four. Andrew walked both of them to school on the first day, then he waited until the teachers had lined up all their students by grade and had marched them into the building and to their rooms.

When he turned around to start the short walk home, he saw Rough-house's LaSalle roadster parked across the street. Rough-house was early. The top was down, and a woman sat beside him.

Millbridge crossed the street. "Mag," he said, "good to see you. I gave the housekeeper the morning off. I hope you don't mind meeting at my place."

"Not at all," the woman said.

Millbridge waved them to go on. "I'll walk. See you in a couple of minutes."

Millbridge watched Rough-house do a U-turn and drive off before starting his walk home. He loved walking. For some reason, it always reminded him of the trip from Tampere to Kokkola—even though he rode the last part on his Don.

He had thought, off and on, of getting a Don. *For Owen*, he told himself. Owen was now nine years old, and at ten, Antti Myllysilta had ridden horses, cared for horses, even helped steal one or two. *And at ten, or soon thereafter, he'd also—*

Andrew Millbridge stopped the thought. Yes, he wanted Owen to have the things he didn't have. He wanted, as he and Annie had agreed, "the best" for their children. But Owen wasn't Andrew, or Annie, or even Antti. He was … himself, and Andrew wasn't sure he'd ever be able to handle a Don.

With some regret, Andrew set aside the thought of buying a Don—either "for Owen" or for himself. For now, at least. But he'd still have Rough-house spread a story: that he'd bought Owen a Don, a real one, imported from Russia and kept in the country. They rode it, the two of them. He and Owen had bonded over it. It would be a good story, both about him and about Owen. Perhaps useful someday.

Perhaps, Myllysilta echoed softly.

Andrew took a breath.

The air here has the smell of the air in Finland, he thought. *Or maybe it's just the smell of the stables down on Machar Avenue.*

#

"You're looking good, Mag," Millbridge said, once all three were seated around the kitchen table.

"I'm sixty-six years old." Mag Matthews laughed. "For a hooker, sixty-six is like a hundred. What's on your mind, Mr. Myllysilta?"

Millbridge tried not to show his surprise. "You know my name? My Finnish name?"

"I keep tabs. And no, I won't spill your secret." She pointed at Rough-house. "*He* didn't know, I see."

"I do now," Rough-house said.

Millbridge ignored him. "Mag—is it okay if I call you Mag? The papers always use Meg."

"That's because I *prefer* Mag."

"Mag it is then. You have quite a reputation for looking ahead. So what do you see happening in the next, say, half dozen years or so?"

Mag laughed. "I die. Maybe a little sooner; maybe a little later. We all die. It's no big deal."

"We may hope so." Millbridge paused. "I meant, what's going to happen in the world?"

Mag smiled. "I knew what you meant. You meant, what can you invest in?" At Millbridge's nod, she said, "I have no idea. Personally, I'm going to give away my stuff. I intend to die poor."

Millbridge was curious, not shocked. "Why?"

"Because, when I die, I want to die without baggage. Lots of people—better people than me—can use a little help. Money's not going to buy me a cooler flame in hell or a softer cloud in heaven, so why not give it away?"

Rough-house shifted uneasily but stayed silent.

Andrew said, "Seriously."

"I *am* being serious. Death is a serious thing—the *only* serious thing, really. You'll see that when it gets closer. We don't die rich, and we don't die poor. When we die, we aren't *anything* anymore. We die and we're dead."

See? She's smart, Myllysilta whispered to Andrew. Andrew said nothing.

Rough-house decided it was time to intervene. "Mag, Andrew wants to do what you're doing, kind of. He wants to blend into the background."

"Retire early, you mean?"

"Something like that," Millbridge said. "Go more straight, be less crooked. I don't want my kids to find out … this." He waved a hand.

Mag smiled. "That takes money." She was silent for a moment. "Okay, here's what I think. There's going to be a war—and sooner than I'm going to die. The treaty of Versailles won't hold up. Too punishing. Hitler, he's started to stir people up already. I don't think he'll be the one who starts it, but maybe. And the Japanese, they've started chewing away at China. Now, if they're all really serious?" She shrugged. "It's game over, war for sure. The Americans made a lot of money selling arms in the old war—they'll think they can make just as much in a new one. So, they'll let it get started, wait a few years to let everyone get the hell beat out of them, then *really* get into it."

Mag Matthews suddenly stopped talking and sat looking at her hands resting on the table. No one broke the silence.

"That's a stretch," Millbridge said at last, with more doubt than he felt.

"Is it, now?" Mag asked. "The bottom's fallen out of the economy. There's a hobo jungle, for God's sake, set up near the Pool 6 elevator. Guys are living in shacks just outside town because they can't afford rent. Both the Red Finns and the White ones have started turning the Finn Hall into a dormitory for unemployed bush workers—nothing but cots and beds and sleeping bags in there now. The good times are over. And that means what it always means—that the crazies are getting ready to rule the world again. That's what history is all about."

She sighed. Rough-house started to say something, but Millbridge raised an eyebrow at him, and he subsided.

At last, Mag spoke again. "Look. When you're hungry and out of a job, you'll listen to anyone who tells you that he knows how to make things right." She leaned forward. "My girls tell me that lots of Finns, especially the ones that live outside the cities, and the ones that have pulp sticks for brains, are packing up and leaving for Karelia—wherever *that* is—because they've been told it's a workers' paradise. The little local Finn farming communities are losing men left, right, and centre. Some of the guys are even making plans to go fight in the Spanish Civil War if they can't make it to Karelia. Can you believe it? They'll die—poof! Gone! Never come back."

Millbridge remembered the caravan of the naïve and the helpless—and Rabbit—headed for Olonetz in 1918, where nothing awaited them.

"The point is this. If you want to make money now, invest it in all the stuff that makes money in hard times, but be ready to re-invest it when the war breaks out—because a war means jobs, always. The cash you'll need to finance it will come flowing out of every asshole in Ottawa."

She turned to Rough-house. "And you, Mr. Fancy Pants, with your LaSalle roadster—the average guy who owns a car, a *real* one with rust on its doors and a hole in the floor—has to work two full days to pay for one new tire now. You think many honest guys are going to buy a car in the next few years? Their wives will kill them if they do. And the cops will pay attention to every person within a mile of where you park that thing, and that means they'll connect you to Mr. Myllysilta-Saarinen-Millbridge, here."

Millbridge willed himself not to flinch. *She knows about my days as Riku Saarinen, too.*

Mag, wound up, pointed at Rough-house. "Damn LaSalle is the rum-runners' favourite in the States, and here, too. So sell this goddamned piece of billboard advertising. Buy yourself a bit of cheap four-wheeled camouflage, Mr. Fancy Pants—it'll make you less attractive, and your boss here less vulnerable."

#

When Rough-house returned after driving Mag Matthews home, Millbridge was still sitting at the kitchen table. Rough-house took the chair opposite him.

"Meg—*Mag*—knows a lot about me," Millbridge said. "Including the name I used in Finland at the end of the war. How is that?"

"Don't know, boss. She didn't get it from me. You know you've never told me you even *had* another name. Never mind two."

"Really?" Millbridge studied Rough-house. "So, how then?"

Rough-house shook his head. "Boss, I've never asked you a thing about your past. And if I knew it, I wouldn't tell anyone. She didn't get the information from me. She talks to everyone, she knows everyone."

"I know that. I was just pulling your leg."

Rough-house let out a long breath. "The Lakehead got damn near five thousand Finns after the Finnish war. Lots of Whites, lots of Reds, lots of people from everywhere in Finland. One of them probably gave her the information—someone who knew you, or had run into you, or, I don't know, could be anyone. Could be someone who bumped into someone who had heard something. You know. Rumours."

"So what should I do about her?" Millbridge asked.

"Nothing. No need. Mag doesn't talk."

"You're sure about that?"

"Absolutely. Why do you think her girls have so many customers? Mag knows the dollar value of silence, and her girls do, too. You can bet that she told her source to keep his damn mouth shut. And if he knows what's good for him, he will."

Millbridge didn't say anything for a minute. Then, "It's time for you to get back to work."

Rough-house got up from the table.

"One last thing," Millbridge said, "don't park the LaSalle in front of my house anymore. I don't want my kids to know that you work for me. I don't want them to know that I even know you. And if they see the car—even hear about it...." He let the sentence dangle.

"Understood."

#

Half an hour after Rough-house had left, Owen and May showed up for lunch. After they had eaten and started back to school, Millbridge waited until Mrs. Vogel, the housekeeper, returned.

"Take the day," he'd told her the night before. "Yes, I'll do lunch and take them to school. You can be here to meet them after school, if you like."

"If that's what Mr. Millbridge prefers," Mrs. Vogel had answered.

As he'd expected, she returned soon after 1 p.m. and was surprised to see him there. She said, "I just—the ironing. Am I too early? Or late?"

"No, not at all." He hadn't meant to test Mrs. Vogel's dedication to the family—he'd only wanted the privacy to talk with Mag. "Thank you for coming. I'll be home at the usual time."

At the Scand, he sat down in an empty booth, opened his briefcase, and took out the composition book. He didn't open it immediately.

Bertil Granbakken, he thought. *My partner from Finland. It has to be Bertil. That's who Mag spoke to, somehow, in some way. He told Mag my story—enough of it, anyway, for her to put two and two together. But why hasn't Bertil tried to find me?*

Because, Myllysilta offered, *maybe he's not planning to come here, or maybe he just hasn't arrived yet. Maybe he won't. In any case, he probably doesn't know that you call yourself Andrew Millbridge now.*

Millbridge looked around the room. No one looked back with curiosity. In spite of his self-consciousness, no one in the restaurant knew. Yet.

But if Bertil Granbakken was, indeed, in Port Arthur, sooner or later he would show up at either the Scand or the Hoito. Until the problem was taken care of, Andrew decided, he would keep clear of both places. He'd let Rough-house play detective.

That was that. Millbridge waved the waitress over and ordered a cup of coffee, drumming his fingers on the notebook as he drank. When he finished his coffee, he put away the unopened composition book and left.

All the way home, Millbridge considered possibilities—information Rough-house might need. Would Bertil change his name? No, he'd stick with Bertil Granbakken. Although he might go for something literary, like Lennart Wikström. Bertil might ask Mag about Riku Saarinen, but—because her principles wouldn't let her—she wouldn't tell him to look for Andrew Millbridge. What else? Bertil would have money and he'd still have a taste for nice things. If Rough-house parked the LaSalle outside the Hoito, Bertil would ask who owned it. And Rough-house would find a way to strike up a conversation with the man who asked about his car.

And after that? Myllysilta asked. *We will take care of the problem.*

Millbridge nodded. Rough-house had solid connections. He'd be able to find out information about Bertil Granbakken.

And with that, Millbridge decided, he could let the matter rest. At home, he went in and asked Owen and May about their days at school, fully Andrew Millbridge again.

10 • CRASHES, KILLINGS, AND COOKIES

AUTUMN ARRIVED IN EARNEST, and Owen and May settled into their school routines. And Millbridge decided he and the children no longer required a live-in housekeeper.

To Mrs. Vogel, he said, "I'll still need you to be here and prepare a lunch and supper for the family, and do the grocery shopping. And the laundry." He considered. "And, perhaps, look after the children on special occasions. Do you mind this change in responsibilities?"

Mrs. Vogel looked at the carpet. "Of course not, if that's what Mr. Millbridge prefers." She looked up as if to speak, but hesitated.

Andrew guessed at her concern. "I'll help you find another place to stay, and I'll still pay you enough to cover rent and other expenses."

Relief spread across her face. "Thank you, Mr. Millbridge, that's very kind."

It *was* very kind, as he well knew. It was certainly better for Mrs. Vogel than nothing, which is what many other household workers were facing. The stock market kept sliding downhill, and jobs of any sort were either shrinking or disappearing entirely.

Because he had decided to absent himself from both the Hoito and the Scand until the Bertil Granbakken issue was resolved, Millbridge needed an office. A real one. Mrs. Vogel's residence elsewhere let him commandeer her room, upstairs with the family bedrooms. He bought a lockable filing cabinet, a typewriter, a pair of bookcases, a desk, and a chair. Each day, he locked the door behind him after he'd taken care of the day's business, which involved more intensive newspaper reading, bookkeeping, and paper shuffling than he was used to.

He established some rules: neither Mrs. Vogel nor the children were allowed into Daddy's office. No one was to disturb him when he was working. And no one was to knock on the door when he was playing the violin.

Whenever he was asked about the violin, Millbridge's story was always the same. The violin had been a spur-of-the-moment purchase. He had driven past a pawn shop and seen it hanging in the window. *I can learn to play that*, he'd thought, and bought it. The pawn shop's owner had thrown in the black wooden case, the bow, the rosin, and a pitch pipe.

Millbridge wondered whether Owen would remember him playing the violin, once or twice, when Annie was still alive. But Owen didn't seem to—he didn't question Andrew's story, at any rate—and May would have been far too young. No one else would have any way of knowing about the violin.

"What the hell made you take up fiddling?" Rough-house asked when Millbridge told him the pawnshop story. "I've never taken you for one of those artsy-fartsy types. Drums, maybe, but a violin?"

"Well," Millbridge said, "it's neither a rock nor a horse's hooves."

Rough-house let the answer be. His boss sometimes gave people crazy answers when he was well and truly pissed off with them—and, other times, even when he was not.

Near the end of October, Rough-house showed up unexpectedly at Millbridge's house. He'd parked the LaSalle in front of a mom-and-pop store on a nearby street. He knocked several times before Millbridge came to the door, holding the violin bow.

"That guy," Rough-house said without any preamble. "Bertil, but not Salmi. The other guy, Bertil Granbakken. He's in town. He's got a room at the Mariaggi—and not just one of their dollar-a-night rooms, either. He took one of the two-dollar ones that come with a free mineral bath tablet."

Millbridge rolled his eyes. "We need to talk about this, so don't just stand there, come on in." He waved Rough-house to a chair at the kitchen table. "How long has he been in town?"

"Couple of days, I think. He came up by boat—the *Hamonic*."

"You're sure the name was Granbakken?"

"Positive. He asked the clerk about the LaSalle parked outside, clerk pointed me out, we had a drink together. Just like you said." Rough-house grinned. "He's taken a room for the month. Not too clear on what his plans are—he spent a couple of months in Owen Sound before coming to the Lakehead, apparently. Clerk told me."

Rough-house raised his eyebrows, tilted his head to the right, and gave Millbridge a *look*.

"Ah," Millbridge said. "Mag's summer home. So *he's* not clear about his plans, or *you* aren't clear?"

"Him. He was talking a bit about starting a business, maybe. I don't know how good his English is—we stuck to Finnish, and my Finnish is not even close to first-rate." Rough-house paused, but Millbridge said nothing to fill the silence. "So, what do you want me to do? Of course I didn't mention you."

"I should hope not," Millbridge said, but he kept his voice unthreatening. "You do nothing. I'll take care of it. Do you know what room he's in?"

"211."

"Tomorrow afternoon, between, let's say 1:30 and 2:30, I want you to be at the Mariaggi, having a drink at the bar. Don't get drunk, but drink enough to get friendly with whoever's there. Say hello, strike up a conversation, introduce yourself. Get noticed."

Millbridge stopped talking and let the silence build.

"That's it?" Rough-house asked when the silence had begun to gnaw at him. "That's all you want me to do?" *I'm not implicating myself, right? I'm keeping my nose clean, right?* He could say neither one.

"That's all."

Rough-house could do that. To show he understood, he changed the subject. "I heard a song you should practice on the violin. 'Hälsa Dem Därhemma.' You know it? Real sentimental—a guy separated from his family back home. *Tell my mother, tell my little brother I miss home.* They must have translated it into a million languages. Every Scandihooligan I know can sing it, but none without bawling their eyes out."

Millbridge looked at him. "I have heard it." He said nothing else.

"Okay, then." Rough-house got up. "That's that."

#

At eleven a.m. the next day, Millbridge left his house and drove to the waterfront. It was Myllysilta, though, who parked the car a few blocks away from the Mariaggi and walked to the hotel. He went in without causing anyone to pay attention to him—not that it would have mattered if anyone did—and walked up the stairs to the second floor.

In the deserted hallway he took a carpenter's hammer from inside his coat, wiped the handle vigorously with his handkerchief, put on a pair of leather gloves, and knocked softly on the door of Room 211.

At noon, an hour later, Millbridge was home when the children showed up for lunch. At two o'clock he was having coffee with some of the regulars at the Hoito. For the first time in a while, he knew he could safely pass time there. The conversation was lively and loud— full of laughter—and he was there for quite a while longer.

Later, just after four in the afternoon, the maid tapped on Granbakken's door. When he did not open it, she used her key to enter, and found him dead on the floor. His pocket watch, now broken, had stopped at just after two. The murder weapon, a carpenter's hammer, was on the floor beside him, and his wallet, emptied of its cash, lay discarded by the door.

At the same time the maid knocked on Granbakken's door, Andrew Millbridge waited in his office for his children to come home from school. The watch, Myllysilta whispered to him, had been a really good idea—just re-set the time, break the watch, go out the door. It gave both Rough-house and Millbridge an alibi. Andrew smiled and went downstairs to meet the children.

He could hear Mrs. Vogel cleaning the sink in the main floor bathroom. He opened the front door as his children came up the porch steps and into the house.

"Well," Millbridge said, "what did you learn in school today?"

Owen, of course, answered first. "More stuff about numbers, but you should hear what May learned!"

"May," Andrew said, then with exaggerated seriousness, "what did *you* learn in school today?"

May smiled, and Owen gave her a light poke in the ribs. "Aaah buh cuh," she began to chant, "duh, eh, fah, guh, huh, ih, jih, kuh, el, mmm, nnn, oh!, puh, qwa, err, sss, tuh, uh, vuh, wuh, kss, yuh or ee, zzzzzzzz."

"It's the sounds of the letters," Owen said.

"Oh, good. I'm glad it wasn't a seizure." Millbridge smiled, and the children ignored him. Even a groan, they knew, would have been too much of a reward for showing off.

"I can look up some words now, little ones, in the dictionary," May said. "Did you know that some letters change what they sound like depending on where they are in the word, like the *i* in *fit* and *fright*? And sometimes they change just because they're at the beginning or at the end of a word, like the *y* in *yellow* and *jelly*." Her hands flew as she spoke. "Can we have a cookie? Each?"

May reminded Andrew of Annie—not in appearance, but in mannerisms. She had *his* face, not Annie's. But Annie's gestures were all in May's hands. He pushed the thought aside, and Myllysilta snickered.

"One each," Millbridge said, smiling. "Mrs. Vogel made some this afternoon."

"And they are very goot," Mrs. Vogel said, as she came into the kitchen.

"You don't say the words right," May said.

"May," Millbridge said, "you don't correct your elders. Got it?"

May looked at the floor. "Sorry."

"German language has little bit different sounds," Mrs. Vogel said. "Maybe someday you learn German, eh?" She took the lid off the cookie jar and extracted two cookies. "This we call *der Keks*," she said, "or sometimes *Plätzchen*."

"*Keks* sounds a little like *cakes*," Owen said.

"It is newer word. We borrow word *cakes* from English and change it little to give German sound. *Plätzchen* is word that was name for a company make cookies."

"You know a lot, don't you?" Owen asked.

"I know some things. Some are very important to know, some are not."

May, recovered from her embarrassment by time and cookies, said, "Tell us something really important."

"Really important?" Mrs. Vogel thought for a moment. "It is this," she said. "Always make your bed in the morning."

Millbridge smiled.

"This is not easy to do," Mrs. Vogel said. "Because it is easier to *not* make the bed. But to be able to do it, *every day*, makes you strong. Every day you leave your bedroom and you know that you can do impossible things—things almost no one else can do. Every day you walk the steps downstairs and you know that you have strength of character, *charakterstärke*—power over yourself."

"In Germany you were a teacher, weren't you?" Millbridge asked.

"In Germany, yes, but war, you know—"

"I understand," Millbridge interrupted. He didn't want her to say anything about war in front of the children. "Before I came to

Canada, I was in the food business in Finland. Staple foods, though—not cookies. There, we have something in common."

Mrs. Vogel did not reply to Millbridge's comment. She believed in being polite—and careful. And she always let him have the last word. Always.

She also paid attention to news reports. In Germany, something awful was beginning. And her parents were Jews. Andrew Millbridge was not a German, but he was also not Jewish.

11 • GOING STRAIGHT

AS TIME PASSED, MILLBRIDGE began to see that Mag Matthews had been right about many things. In 1932, the world was thrown into a cauldron and began to boil in war, the depression pushed men into despair and stocks into oblivion, and Andrew Millbridge began to make his fortune. Like Mag, he diversified.

In September, the first day of school, Millbridge walked the children to school, as always. Back home, he played the violin. Just before Rough-house was due to arrive, he put the instrument back in its case and leaned it up against a wall. When Rough-house knocked, Millbridge had him bring one of the kitchen chairs up to the office and set it by the desk.

"I want you to look at something," Millbridge began when they were both seated. He pushed a piece of paper toward Rough-house. "It's a list."

"Ah," Rough-house said. He nodded at the violin case. "The handle looks a bit loose on that thing, by the way, but I'm not to be trusted with tools. Is it old?"

"Yes," Millbridge said. Normally he ignored Rough-house's attempts to poke holes in his story about the violin, but this time, he added, "It's older than I am." He pushed the piece of paper again and Rough-house moved his chair closer to the desk.

"Shoes and shoe repair, coal delivery, food and groceries, stores that run tabs. What the hell is this?" Rough-house asked.

"Money. Investments, maybe. Things that make money in bad times."

"Like now?"

"Exactly."

Rough-house went back to reading. "OK, so. Produce stand, cigarettes, household products—soap, solvents, diapers—candy, liquor, haircuts, repair services (vehicles, home repairs, work boots), repo services, work clothes, security services, empty lots, bulk food sales, prostitution, debt collection services, how to fill out job applications, laundries, advertising billboards, insurance, cheap living quarters, junk removal, work clothes."

He looked up from the list. "You forgot the butcher, the baker, and the candlestick maker," he said, allowing himself a smile. When Millbridge did not react, he put the list back on the desk and turned to him. "So, what the hell? We getting into *all* of this?"

"No. We get into what we can manage, no more. We get into what we can *own*, of course, but also what we can *provide*. Services, for instance."

"Like debt collection," Rough-house said. "I wouldn't mind being part of that."

"Yes. And we partner with people who already do some of these things—especially with those who can obviously do things better than we can, and who know how to make money at it."

"And what makes you think that they'll let us in?"

"Money," Millbridge said. "We have a fair amount of money and, likewise, muscle. Or we will have, once you round up a few unemployed strongmen who don't mind getting their knuckles dirty."

Rough-house smiled again. "I know a few," he said. He picked up the list once more. "Can I take this with me?"

"Copy it before you go. Leave the original with me." Millbridge pushed a blank sheet toward him, then passed him a pencil. "Mrs. Vogel will be here soon, so write fast and get the hell out. You parked down the street?"

"Two streets over." He began to copy the list. "Can I add things?"

"By all means. Put them on the original, too."

Rough-house nodded. Then he said, "Couple nights ago I went to a movie—one of those with John Wayne and Tim McCoy. Walter what's-his-name was in it, too."

"Brennan," Millbridge offered.

"Yeah. Cowboy flick. You know the kind where, if there's a chase, the camera guys speed up the film to make it look like the horses are going faster. One of those where the cowboys wear these really tall hats?"

"Yes. And the point is?"

"In hard times everybody wants some entertainment. Can I add some fun things to your list? Not movie theatres, maybe. But you know, bars, what passes for nightclubs, pay-as-you-go saunas, dance halls—stuff like that. I'd get your approval on all that stuff, of course."

"Live it up, Rough-house. Be as creative as you want. And don't censor yourself."

#

After Rough-house left, Millbridge worked for a half hour, then carried the kitchen chair back down the stairs. Mrs. Vogel knocked, entering just as Millbridge was slipping the chair back under the table.

"You had a guest?" Mrs. Vogel asked. "A lady-friend, I hope?"

"Business," Millbridge said, smiling. Then, "I have a question for you."

"Yes?" There was a touch of apprehension in Mrs. Vogel's voice.

"How many housemaids, cleaning ladies—how many women like you are there working in the Lakehead? Any idea?"

She paused before answering. "A few hundred, maybe. It is a guess, Mr. Millbridge."

Andrew nodded. "Do they make good money?"

"Most paid by hour. Fifty cents, maybe. Sometimes women they work for—their bosses—they test workers. They leaving little change in ashtray. Ten cents, five cents. Try to catch thieves. Not many women work full time—maybe get three hours a day, if two customers that day. Everybody want to work their own homes. Nobody want to hire except wives of doctors and lawyers. Too expensive."

"Would you take on a housekeeping job if I were to offer you one that paid you by the hour and guaranteed you maybe six hours a day, maybe more?"

Her eyes widened. "I enjoy working here, Mr. Millbridge. I hope I have not—that is, I would not want to disappoint you."

Millbridge shook his head. "No, no, I'm not thinking of firing you, Mrs. Vogel. And I'm not suggesting you quit and go to work for someone else." He paused. "I'm thinking of *hiring* you to manage a cleaning service. I'd provide a car and the cleaning equipment. Four women would work on one job, then drive to another place. Homes, offices, other buildings. For the homeowner, there would be some muss and fuss for about an hour, then everything would be finished. What do you think?"

"Would you really hire me to do this?" She clasped her hands in front of her. At his nod, she asked, "How long it takes to learn to drive a car?"

"That, Mrs. Vogel, would not be part of your job. You'd find the workers, make the appointments, and write the cheques on an account we'd set up for the business."

"You are serious?"

"I am."

"Thank you, Mr. Millbridge. I would be happy to do this."

"We'll talk more about this after the children have had their lunch."

"Yes, sir."

"And Mrs. Vogel—" He found he didn't know how to ask basic questions of this woman who'd been part of his family wallpaper for years. "I've never asked about your husband."

"He died. 1918. He was just twenty-one. We had been married only half the year." She did not tell Millbridge that he had been part of the German troops that came to the aid of the Whites in Finland, nor that he had been killed at Lahti during the Finnish Civil War.

"You have no children?" Millbridge asked.

She shook her head, and he went on in a rush, "I'm only asking because—"

She broke in, "Yes, I understand. This work needs a single person. Not someone with … what is the word … *obligations*."

"Exactly. Mrs. Vogel, you're perfect for this."

The next day, Millbridge hung around the Hoito in the morning, talking to the taxi drivers who worked along Bay Street. Mrs. Vogel spent the morning in Millbridge's office. By noon she had her first four girls lined up and had scheduled their first three workdays. When Millbridge returned to the house at lunch, he brought a driver with him. A month later, Home and Office Cleaners had a staff of thirty and was turning a significant profit.

#

Within a year, Millbridge had created half a dozen profitable small businesses. Because people either wear out their shoes and boots or grow out of them, Mr. Shoe was located on Oliver Road, conveniently near the centre of a cluster of elementary schools, in a working-class neighborhood. Beautiful U, a hair salon for the kinds of women who made sure their hair was perfect for church, was downtown on the main bus line. Millbridge had, as well, acquired a small insurance agency and created both a repossession franchise and a debt collection agency.

Mrs. Vogel managed them all; Rough-house's men collected the rent and made sure the businesses did not get behind on their "security" payments.

Millbridge almost never visited his holdings, and on those rare occasions when he did, he never introduced himself. When, from time to time, the curious asked him what business he was in, he always said, "Franchising. The future's in franchising, you know."

He scrupulously kept Mrs. Vogel ignorant of the illegal and quasi-legal businesses that he and Rough-house set up. Rough-house managed those. He, too, was good at it.

#

Two years later, in 1934, it was obvious to almost everyone that the world was headed for war again, and that this war would be global, too.

Everyone had begun to fight everyone else. Columbia and Peru had gone to war in 1932, as had Bolivia and Paraguay. The Chinese Civil War, which had started in 1927, was mirroring the Finnish Civil War of 1918, though on a much larger scale. The Long March was still underway as the Chinese Nationalist army, led by Chiang Kai-shek, chased Mao T'se-tung's Reds, much as the Whites had pursued the Finnish Reds.

In Germany, Adolf Hitler rose to power in 1933. He pulled the country out of the League of Nations, then made himself *Führer* and *Reichskanzler* in 1934. The persecution of the Jews, which had been going on for years in one place or another, began in earnest and on an industrial scale.

When Mrs. Vogel wrote her parents, they did not write back. Nor did anyone else she had known in Germany. Sometimes the letters came back with *Address Unknown* written in German on the envelope. Most of the time, the letters were simply swallowed up.

The Saudis and the Yemeni, both friends of Britain, went at each other in a three-month-long war, starting in March of 1934, over some differences of opinion about territory. The war ended with a "ticking clock" treaty limited to twenty years, as if treaties, like everything else, had a short but measurable lifespan.

In the United States, Franklin Delano Roosevelt implemented the New Deal and stepped into the mire of government-led economic reforms. The Dust Bowl, which had begun in 1930, continued to swallow North American crops and topsoil in big gulps and to blow it all away. In 1934, Congress was told that some American industrialists had urged Marine Corps General Smedley Butler to help them overthrow Roosevelt and establish a fascist regime—one like, perhaps, what the Spanish or the Italians had. But better—something that would *really work*, you know?

In Russia, a government-mandated agricultural collectivization and industrialization program, started in 1933, led to the deaths of millions of Ukrainians in the *Holodomor*—the plague of hunger.

The Japanese, having captured Manchuria in 1931, were eagerly looking forward to expanding their empire, and the war with China, still raging in 1934, was very popular in Japan. In turn, in Manchuria, the Chinese population swore unremitting and unrelenting war against the Japanese.

The world had gone mad.

#

On Maundy Thursday of 1934, Andrew Millbridge decided it was time to begin investing once more in the stock market. The prices of stocks, he reasoned, were as low as they would ever get.

His first purchases, when the stock market opened after Easter, were shares in Canadian Car and Foundry, and the Port Arthur Shipbuilding Company.

"Why?" Rough-house asked him over breakfast one morning.

"Because disarmament isn't working, never mind the Geneva Conference. Germany has withdrawn from the Conference, both England and France have unstable governments, the Nazis have Hitler who is more unstable all by himself than England and France put together, Italy has Mussolini—who thinks he can recreate the Roman Empire—and the US has dropped the gold standard and is so deep in this economic grave it's dug for itself that it thinks if it just keeps shoveling it will soon get to the other side of the Earth. And, by the way, there's what feels like a never-ending world-wide depression going on. So I've decided to put my faith in war, warships, and fighter aircraft."

"Oh," Rough-house said. "I'm sorry I asked." Then, he smiled like a mischievous child. "Does this mean I can get that new LaSalle?"

Millbridge sighed theatrically. "No, but I've got a proposal for you. Let's go back to the house."

12 • BREAD BOMBS

"IVOR SOLBAKKEN," MILLBRIDGE SAID. "You know who I mean?" He sat at the kitchen table and motioned to the chair across.

Rough-house sat. "Jussi Mantere's friend—the crazy guy." He popped a sugar lump into his mouth and sipped his coffee through it the way his boss did. He did not, however, pour the coffee from the cup into the saucer and sip it, like a *real* Finn. "He goes by Mantere now, too. He was working for Mantere for a while, some kind of construction stuff—raising houses and giving them basements, I think—but then he had a breakdown or something. Something about gravedigging." Rough-house laughed. "Don't know what it was. He quit, anyway. Lives in that apartment building beside the Hemmet 'til summer, then he lives in a shack somewhere. Pass the cookies?"

"I want you to keep an eye on him, this Ivor *Solbakken,*" Millbridge said. As he emphasized *Solbakken,* he pushed the plate toward Rough-house. "Just you. Don't involve anyone else in this. Understand? Don't ask about him, don't try to dig up information on him, just keep your eyes open and everyone else's eyes closed."

"Understood. Can I ask why? Should I be looking for something specific?"

"No and no." Millbridge took a sip of his coffee, then slowly put the cup down on the saucer. "Solbakken's shack is in the bush across the McIntyre River. You know the place—the clearing past the power lines. He's made friends with his neighbour—a guy they call 'the bear'. You know who I mean?"

Rough-house nodded. "Vilho ... something. I'll get to know him a little better if you like. Buy him a beer when he's at the Mariaggi, or maybe a coffee when he's at the Hoito, let him talk a bit. I'll listen—but I won't ask him anything about *Solbakken.*" He leaned on the name, too, to show he'd heard Millbridge. "He'll bring up a few things as time goes by. He likes to gossip."

"Good plan." Millbridge paused for a second, then said, "There's another thing I want you to do."

His mouth full of cookie, Rough-house cocked his head.

"You like Mrs. Vogel?"

Rough-house swallowed. "Sure," he said guardedly. "Works hard, keeps her mouth shut, gets along with the kids, makes these hellishly good cookies. And, no, I won't marry her so you can consolidate your empire. Why?"

Millbridge laughed. "Think you can work with her?"

"Work with her how?

"I want to move more of the business crap out of the house and set up a *real* office someplace downtown." He looked at Rough-house. "The Finnish and Scandinavian downtown, not the English one. And incorporate it—Millbridge Enterprises, Inc. Understand? You'd be the boss, but she'd manage the day-to-day duties. I'd spend more time with the kids, maybe get involved in the community."

"Whoa," Rough-house said. "I don't mind filling in for you as Mrs. Vogel's boss—for short periods, only. But the big boss stays you. I suggest you let Mrs. Vogel continue to run the office. She can do that perfectly well without either of us."

Millbridge considered. "You're right."

They sat in silence for a moment, then Rough-house asked, "Boss, how would you like to sell *me* this house? You should move someplace a little more upscale, improve your image, you know?"

Millbridge smiled. "I didn't say I'd give you a raise." He took another sip of his coffee. "What upscale place do you have in mind?"

"High Street, other side of Arthur, just up from Waverley Park, across from that new park on the crest of the hill. Good view of the harbour, lots of rooms, garage, big lot, well-built. It's even got a milk-door in the back porch." He stopped talking.

Millbridge looked at him closely for a minute too long. "I know the place," he said at last. "Been inside it, too. Mag owned it, didn't she? Rented it out, though. But you *know* that, don't you?"

"Maybe. I didn't mean to be forward. I just thought, looking ahead...." Rough-house trailed off.

"Deal," Millbridge said. "You handle both the seller and the salesman, I'll sign the cheque. Get me a fair price for that place, and I'll pay you a little commission. But first find us a *real* office. After that, I'll talk to Mrs. Vogel. I'll give her a bit of a raise, too. Oh, one other thing. No phone in the new house. If there's a phone already installed, have it removed. I want that home to be a *home*—not an extension of the office. The office, by the way, needs to be fairly good-sized, two or three rooms. Not far from Bay and Algoma. Not a hole in the wall, but still reasonably small—something with space for about five workers and their desks. Understand?"

"Phone?"

"Phone at the office—but *no phone* in the new house."

"Understood." Although Rough-house didn't, really. But after all these years, he knew he didn't need to understand. He just needed to produce results. And that, he could do.

#

The new house on High Street became a home—of a sort. As real a home as Andrew could make it, at least.

One June day, late in the school year, Andrew and the kids set off for school, as usual, and on foot, as usual. Their walk was only a few blocks farther than from the house on Algoma, but they had to cross two busier streets, High Street and Arthur Street, to get there.

"Father?" May had recently turned ten and no longer held Andrew's hand as she walked along beside him, but sometimes it seemed as if she wanted to.

"May?" Andrew mimicked her tone, adding a touch of humour.

"I'm glad we got the new house. But I'm really glad we didn't have to change schools. Mrs. Barret would have been sad."

"Would *she*? Or would *you* have been sad?"

May considered, then grinned. "Yes?"

"That's not how you answer an either/or question." They both laughed. Andrew looked at Owen, who wasn't laughing. "Something on your mind?"

Owen slowed his steps and glanced at May.

Andrew stopped and said to May, "We're nearly there. You go on ahead, yes?"

Owen kept his eyes on May, getting smaller and smaller as she approached the school.

Andrew kept his voice gentle. "What is it?"

"It's just—Father, I'm going to be twelve soon. And—"

Andrew waited. At last, he prompted, "And?"

It came out in a rush. "You don't need to walk us to school

anymore. We can cross the streets okay without you." Owen looked up, his face red as he searched for the words. "And we're—or—I am, I'm—too old—that is, I'm old enough. To be responsible."

Andrew pursed his lips for a moment. "You are, indeed, a responsible and careful young man. And so you shall walk on your own, starting this very afternoon." He held out his hand as if to a man, and Owen, surprised, shook it. Andrew couldn't resist adding, "Be careful," before he turned and walked toward home.

That afternoon, he waited for them in the kitchen with a plate of Mrs. Vogel's cookies ready on the table.

May burst in first. "Father! Owen says we can walk to and from school by ourselves! Is that true?"

"It is indeed. Owen knows how to read the traffic." He suddenly remembered the day when Antti Myllysilta, some sixteen years ago, had cut across the river of the living dead that was bound for Olonetz. He blinked and May came back into focus. "You, however, sometimes don't pay attention, so his job is to keep an eye on you and teach you." He looked up at Owen, who nodded solemnly—suddenly older this afternoon than he had been in the morning.

May's sweet smile showed a hint of mischief. If she erred, she reasoned, Owen would have to take the blame. She liked that.

Her father, however, did not smile back. His expression was suddenly indecipherable, and she wondered what she had done.

She didn't know that another memory had suddenly flooded the room, a memory of the night that Myllysilta had killed her grandfather. Myllysilta had remembered the relief in his brothers' faces when, the next morning, he had shown them the body. The youngest had solved the problem for all of them. He'd seen a flash of respect from Marku. It didn't last long, but it had been there.

After a moment, when Millbridge at last returned his daughter's smile, she relaxed. But she learned, always, to be cautious.

And after a couple of years, when it was time for Owen to walk downhill to Port Arthur Collegiate Institute, she walked alone to grammar school, as careful of traffic and mistakes as Owen had been.

#

In August of 1937, Rough-house paid Millbridge a visit at what they all still thought of as the "new house." He showed up early in the afternoon. Owen and May had gone to Boulevard Lake with some of their school friends. Millbridge answered the door, violin in hand. "Practicing," he said.

"I heard you when I was coming up the street. And yes, I parked two blocks away. You're pretty good with that thing."

"Not yet. I know where the notes are, but the vibrato—well, gotta work on that."

"You read music?"

"No, but I like to read *about* music. Does that count?" Millbridge was silent for a moment. "Look, I'll tell you a bit about this violin. First of all, it isn't from a pawn shop or music store—it was made by my father many years before he became a drunken bastard, and he built it the way that people did in those days in Finland. I've read up on what the Finns thought a violin should look like."

Millbridge turned the violin over. "See how it bulges out at the back? People thought that you'd get a fuller tone if you carved the back of the violin to look a bit like a woman's ass—minus the you-know-what, of course. The tone would be sexy instead of just squeaky. It wasn't true, but it was fun to believe."

"Had a girlfriend like that once." Rough-house pointed at the strings. "What the hell are those made of—some kind of leather?"

"Gut—not catgut, though. That's a misconception." Millbridge plucked the bass string. "It comes from the intestines of bigger animals. The skinny ones are best. The workers get rid of any fat and then they put the guts in water. There's a skin—a membrane—that they get rid of, and then they put the intestines in potassium hydroxide. Later, they pull them out of the water, stretch them—they can be forty or fifty feet long at this point—then twist them and let them dry. The thicker strings, like this one—" he plucked the string once more "—are for the low notes, and the thin ones are for the high notes."

Rough-house pretended to stifle a yawn. Millbridge ignored him. "Most of the G-strings now are wound with metal wire. It gives the string a louder, more resonant sound. In just a few years, they'll probably have new materials to make strings from."

"Progress," Rough-house said. He hoped that the lesson was over and kept his mouth shut.

"Another thing they believed," Millbridge said, seeing that Rough-house was beginning to suffer, and taking advantage of his discomfort, "was that the violin was the devil's instrument—the violin didn't belong to the man who had made it or bought it. *He* belonged to *it*. And the violin was seductive, you know—to both the violinist and the person who listened to him play. That made it a good instrument for a dance or a wedding, both of which could ultimately lead to a person going to hell."

Rough-house asked, "And if the guy who was building, or carving, the violin made a mistake? What would he do? Just start all over?" *Damn*, Rough-house thought. *Mistake. I asked him a question.*

"No—he'd look for a way to solve the problem. If the back started to develop a crack, he might take the violin apart, find a few toothpicks and glue them across the crack—inside the violin, not outside—and maybe fill the crack with a bit of glue for good measure. Violins got put together and taken apart lots of times to fix mistakes."

Suddenly, Millbridge had to stop talking. The memory of Annie and the first time he played the violin for her was overwhelming him. He could smell her perfume. He turned his back to Rough-house and put the violin back in its black wooden case, taking his time. As he latched the case, he found his voice. He turned back to say, "Time to talk business."

What the hell was that all about? Rough-house thought. "Sure. Before we do, though, I've got some news for you."

"Good news?"

"No." Rough-house paused. "Mag's dead. August 12th, 1937, paper said. This past Thursday. Didn't say how old she was."

Millbridge was silent for a moment. He stood the violin case up against the living room wall. "Did she die rich or poor?" he asked.

"Who knows? Doesn't matter, does it? We're neither one when we're dead." He paused. "She had a lake named after her. Did you know that? Mag Matthews Lake. It's right in the middle of nowhere on a canoe route in the boonies. Some prospector named it after her, I heard. A customer, I'd bet." He smiled.

Millbridge nodded. "Or maybe a friend," he said. "Back to business. What *really* brings you here? Are you thinking we should take over some of Mag's territory?"

"Yes."

"I've already started. I heard about Mag's death yesterday. So what else? What's on the shopping list?"

"Pool halls."

"Okay, tell me why we should invest in pool halls," Millbridge said, and they stopped jousting to talk business for a while.

As Rough-house got up to go, Millbridge stood as well. Casually, he asked, "Why do I never see Mantere anywhere? Not the Scandinavian Home, not the Hoito. He wouldn't go to Fort William, surely?"

Rough-house considered, jingling coins in his pocket. "He's got a wife to keep house and cook for him, a kid in school at home. What's he want to eat in a restaurant for?"

"For business?"

Rough-house shrugged and headed out the door. "Doesn't need to. He already knows plenty of people. He works, then he goes home." He didn't add, *Like a regular person.* "See ya, boss." He escaped with relief.

Rough-house knew his boss wasn't a regular person. But he couldn't swear that Jussi Mantere was, either. Something had happened to both of them—maybe together, back in Finland, maybe since then, maybe both.

But he knew better than to check into it. Rough-house didn't want to know what it could be dangerous to know.

\#

On September 1st, 1939, the day that Germany invaded Poland, Owen Millbridge was almost seventeen and about to begin his next-to-last year of high school. At breakfast a few days later, he asked his father about the invasion.

Andrew said, "It's going to get bigger. The English and the French haven't strapped on their balls yet, and Hitler's boys are armed and god-damned ready."

It was the first time that Owen had heard his father swear. "The war will get bigger?"

"Much. And soon."

"When?"

"Poland will be overrun in less than a month, and you can bet that Russia will want in on the action, too," Millbridge said. "They'll ask for a piece of Poland, and if Germany gives it to them—and it will— Russia will invade Finland."

Owen was quiet for a moment. Then he said, "Finland? Why Finland?"

"It's a long story." And he did not tell it.

#

For the Hoito's breakfast regulars, the *real* long story began almost two months later, on November 30th, 1939.

"Son of a bitch!" Rough-house said when he joined Millbridge at the table. "You hear the news this morning? Molotov's claiming it was Finland that shelled that border post someplace, Mainila, I think, a couple of days ago. So Stalin jumps in and says no more non-aggression pact. Damn Russians have invaded Finland! They've bombed Helsinki! And Molotov's started lying through his ass again, claiming that they haven't—the planes were just dropping off food, loaves of bread, bread-bombs for the poor starving Finns!"

Andrew put down his cup. "And you know this how?" he asked. "BBC."

"If it's from the BBC, it's likely true. The Brits demand that their news be facts. The Americans like their *stories* to be facts." Andrew allowed himself a grim smile.

"Another thing," Rough-house said. "You remember Bertil Salmi—the guy in the fight at the Mariaggi? God, years ago now. I saw him on the street yesterday, and he told me he's signed up."

"Military? Why the hell would he do that?"

"The rumour is that the Lakehead Scottish Regiment's going to be sent to Europe sometime. Lots of guys are volunteering."

"Jesus. They have no idea what they're getting into. No idea."

In the restaurant everyone, it seemed, had been eavesdropping. Few of the men in the Hoito owned a radio; almost none could read the newspaper. The Hoito was a place where news could flow from man to man in rivulets and rivers of sound, no literacy required.

There was a second or two of absolute silence, and then the room erupted in noise. Andrew drained his coffee and left Rough-house to handle the bill and the shouted questions.

#

At the Hoito, the Russian invasion of Finland quickly became stale news as fresh stories grabbed the headlines. No one offered the Finns any significant help. After all, the odds, based on population, were 60 to 1 that Finland would lose the war with Russia, and it would likely take bits and pieces of their allies with them.

The world took to listening to shortwave radio broadcasts and waited for the United States to step in and spank somebody. But it didn't, and the League of Nations also didn't—though it did expel the USSR, voted to send non-military assistance to the Finns, and then went back to sleep.

The Mannerheim Line, built to hold off a ground attack but not an air war, collapsed. In March of 1940, Finland signed a peace treaty with Russia. The Winter War was over. Lost was a huge chunk of Karelia and all of the northern coastline. *Too bad. No Arctic ports for Finland.* Russia promptly leased one of Finland's air bases, insisted on a trade treaty, and told the Finns to build Russia a railroad line that would give it commercial access to Sweden.

At the Hoito, the passion for all things socialist started to wane. Young men began to think of signing up to go to war. And old men, remembering the bloodshed during and after Finland's Civil War, shook their heads and stared into their coffee cups.

#

After school one day early in April of 1940, Owen found his father sitting at the kitchen table with the ever-present plate of cookies. A newspaper sat on the table, and Andrew's eyes rested on it, but Owen somehow felt he wasn't reading. He took a deep breath.

"Father?" He cleared his throat. "I am asking your permission to join the Lakehead Scottish Regiment. My friends are signing up, and it's the right—"

"Stop!" Millbridge shouted. "You will *not* do any such thing. I don't care how many *idiots* are signing up. You will *not* join them!"

"Father," Owen said again. "Dad." He kept his voice as neutral as he could manage. "I know you think I'm too young. But I can come back for Grade 13 later." He cleared his throat again. "I'm going to do this. It's my choice—not yours. The Lake Superior Regiment is being mobilized, and it's my duty—my responsibility. I want to be part of it."

"No." For a long time, Millbridge said nothing, *no son of mine* ringing in his ears.

Owen waited, still standing.

When Millbridge finally spoke, his voice was calm, unemotional.

"Owen, of course I'm terrified you'll be killed. But it isn't just that. If you try to sign up, you'll just be turned down. There's something you don't know about yourself, and I'm sorry I've waited this long to tell you. You have only one kidney, and ever since you were young, that kidney has never been very healthy. If you try to sign up, there's a medical examination. You'll be rejected." *Would Owen believe him?*

"What? I don't—" Owen began.

"Son. Before you head for the Armouries, please do one thing for me. Go see our doctor. Ask him about your kidney. And tell him it's because you want to join the armed forces—that's important. Okay?"

"Kidney?"

His father nodded, but said nothing.

Owen was silent for some time, then reluctantly he said, "Okay." There was no point in arguing.

"Tell him that you're considering signing up with that goddamned Scottish Regiment," Millbridge said. "I'll stay completely out of this. You know where Dr. Wainwright's office is?"

"Across from the Collegiate," Owen answered. "On the hill that overlooks that little church, the one you and mom were married in. And, yes, I'll tell him it's because I want to sign up."

"Right. Tomorrow, you go there after school, introduce yourself, and when he's finished with the exam, you tell him that, and you ask him whatever else you think you need to ask—including if he thinks they'll take you into the military."

"All right, I'll go."

"You'll go tomorrow. I'll call him to let him know you're coming. And you'll listen to what he says, okay?"

"Okay."

"Tomorrow," Millbridge said again, tapping the table with his finger. "Tomorrow, you and the doctor can set the date and time of the next appointment, if one is needed. And be sure to tell him that you promise to show up on time. For a doctor, time is money."

"I will."

"He'll probably make you have an x-ray at the Clinic. If he gives you a clean bill of health, well." Millbridge paused, then began again. "If he gives you a clean bill of health, you have my permission to sign up. But you have to understand—" He broke off.

"Father, I understand, okay? I won't try to enlist if I fail." Owen went upstairs to his room.

Later, after Owen and May had both gone to sleep, Millbridge left the house and drove to the office to phone Rough-house.

"I know it's late. Listen. I need you to pay that visit to Dr. Wainwright," Millbridge said. "About Owen. You know what to do. Yes—single kidney and not healthy."

After signing off the call, Millbridge sat in the office. Rough-house would show up at the doctor's house within the next half hour. Wainwright would put the night's morphine addicts on hold for a few minutes and add Owen to his list of after-school patients.

In his mind, Millbridge watched it play out. In a few days, after the appointment and phony lab test results were in, Owen would learn that the x-ray had shown that his only kidney was in a little worse shape than when he had been a child. He needed to take some pills to keep his disease at bay. If he took one of the pills each day, there would be nothing to worry about, but no, the army would not—could not—accept him. He wouldn't pass their rigorous physical, and that was just as well. There were other ways to serve one's country—less dangerous ways and just as important to the war effort. Blah, blah, blah.

Annie, Andrew Millbridge knew, would not want Owen to die. As well, she would not want Andrew to live the life he was now living, to tell the lies he was now telling.

But, Myllysilta whispered to him, *she is dead, and the dead cannot judge us.*

Because the dead are truly dead, Millbridge responded, as if reciting from a catechism.

He broke off the thought. Though Rough-house had said goodbye and hung up a full minute ago, Millbridge still held the receiver. He stared at it for a moment, then returned it to its cradle in the office, walked back to his car, and drove home.

At home, he went down into the basement where, beside the book and the boot, he now kept the violin. Softly, so that he wouldn't wake May and Owen, he played some of the old tunes, but they couldn't push aside his thoughts of Annie and their life together. When he'd used up the old tunes he remembered, he tried Rough-house's suggestion, that sentimental "Hälsa Dem Därhemma," but abandoned it after the first line of the chorus.

He never understood nostalgia for a "homeland," or wanted to go back to one.

Instead, he went upstairs and got ready for bed.

His dreams were full of ration cards for sugar, meat, and gas. A taxi driver tried to charge him too much. Men wearing large red circles on their backs strolled outside on the streets and looked threateningly at him. Kids kept knocking on the door and asking for donations of aluminum, cooking fat, scrap iron, lead foil. He was, for a time, on his horse as the caravan of the hopeless staggered by him. Ivor Solbakken—Rabbit—was with them. When he woke in the morning, his pillow was drenched with sweat.

#

In April of 1940, a week or so after Owen saw Dr. Wainwright, Germany invaded Denmark unopposed, then took Norway by ousting the British forces trying to defend it. Germany needed Denmark and Norway as buffers—both to keep the Russians at bay and to deprive the Allies of northern naval bases.

In September, the streets of London became the target of the *blitzkrieg*. The German daylight bombings turned, over time, into night-time horrors—sudden blinding explosions, bright lights, smoke, dust, cries, falling bricks—horrors that, as soon as the warnings sounded, sent the population scrambling into basements and subway tunnels, anywhere that might tonight be safe in a world that had no refuge from the sky. Parents sent their children out of London into the countryside, anywhere that seemed an unlikely target.

On the 10th of October, the Lake Superior Regiment marched down to the CPR railway station on Water Street—now a street of tears—and boarded the waiting train. Owen was part of the crowd that had come to the station to watch, although Millbridge was not. As the train pulled out, Owen felt everyone looking at him.

13 • WAR

THE SECOND OF THE GREAT WARS of the twentieth century did not, for the United States, follow the pattern of the first, but that didn't become apparent for some time.

As in the early days of the Great War, America avoided becoming directly involved in Europe in 1939 and 1940, but immediately began to assemble a strong defense force, just in case. It also sold war materiel to the Allied, but not the Axis, powers, and started planning for the peace that would inevitably come, one way or another.

Because the United States had become truly rich during the Great War by taking advantage of its distance from the war zone, it had learned that war's early stages can be a godsend for business. As long as you stay out of the shooting.

So, while the combatants slugged it out, America developed strong economic ties and friendships with the countries of South America, then sat back for a few years to wait for peace. The strategy had been successful in the previous war. So why not this one?

On December 7th, 1941, the Japanese attacked Pearl Harbor.

Andrew Millbridge, when he heard, remembered the day in 1918 that the Germans had come ashore at Hanko, Finland's all-season port. "Just some fishermen," the Red leadership had said then. "Definitely not Germans."

Now *that* was a lie of the sort that made his embellished family history seem the gospel truth.

#

Military advice that has become folk wisdom: wars are won not with soldiers, but with factories.

In World War II, American and Canadian factories remained intact and highly productive—unlike the factories of most of the combatants, both Allied and Axis, because North America was generally out of range of the enemy. As Europe and Asia exploded in fire, America exploded in the production of everything that could be used in war—aircraft, warships, commercial vessels, tanks and artillery, all manner of equipment, and even a couple of atomic bombs. The United States produced more war materiel than all other nations combined—or so it seemed.

Although Canada sent thousands of young men into harm's way, it suffered comparatively little, in economic terms, from the war. At the Lakehead, Port Arthur built ships; Fort William built aircraft. Port Arthur's Shipbuilding Company built nine Corvettes and a dozen and a half minesweepers—in addition to barges, parts for aircraft, and engines of various kinds. The Fort William Canada Car plant made Helldiver aircraft. In 1940 the Canada Car plant had employed just over six hundred men. By year's end it had almost six thousand employees, two thousand of them women. The shipyards in Port Arthur grew to over two thousand workers by 1944.

All over the world, military innovation created new tools of war—radar, armour-piercing shells, flame-throwers, incendiary bombs, flying fortresses, cruise missiles.

On the day that the Allies landed at Dieppe, four thousand ships backed by eleven thousand aircraft transported the soldiers across the English Channel. The soldiers—the ones who didn't drown when the landing craft dumped them into the sea—got help from fighters and bombers as they fought their way across the beaches.

Still, on that day, they died and died and died.

Soldiers kept dying for three years after Dieppe, and for eleven months after D-Day, where Canadian forces fought at Juno Beach.

But in the long term, their mission was a grand success. Eleven months after D-Day, the Germans formally surrendered.

All the fighting and dying had made Andrew Millbridge rich. You wouldn't have known by looking, though.

#

In August of 1945, Andrew Millbridge was having coffee at the Hoito when Ivor Solbakken's friend, Vilho, showed up. Millbridge waved him over. Vilho came over immediately. Millbridge, he knew, was not a person to ignore.

"Vilho, right? Ivor's friend," Millbridge said. "Have a seat.

Coffee's on me." Because it was Millbridge who asked, Vilho did as he was told. Out of the blue, Millbridge said, "Tell me about Raimo, Jussi Mantere's kid." He caught the eye of the waitress.

"Raimo?"

"Yes, Raimo. He married that girl that works at Bridal ... something or other. They had a kid."

The waitress came over to fill Millbridge's cup and looked inquiringly at Vilho, who said, "Just coffee, please."

A minute later she was back with a cup for him. She poured the coffee into the cup and set it down on the table. They sat in silence.

When she was out of earshot behind the counter again, Vilho asked, "What do you want to know? I don't know very much about him—Raimo."

"But Ivor told you what happened, right? So what's the story." It was a command, not a question.

Vilho did not hesitate. "Not much to it, really. Raimo and Marilyn were in high school when the bombs hit Pearl Harbour, and just after they'd graduated, Raimo signed up at the Armouries."

"With the blessing of his parents?"

"Not exactly. Jussi—Jussi Mantere is ... was, you know, Ray's, *Raimo's*, father." Vilho nervously took a sip of coffee.

"I know who's who," Millbridge said. He leaned forward. "You got the story from Ivor, and I'm getting the story from you, so get on with it."

"So Viktoria, she's—"

"Jussi's wife, Raimo's mother. I *know* who the characters are, goddammit."

Vilho glanced nervously at Millbridge and tried to calm himself. "So." He gathered his thoughts and spilled them out in a rush. "So Viktoria wasn't going to let her son fight in the war. She was afraid he'd be killed. Very afraid. It turned into a big argument between her and Jussi. Viktoria thought Raimo was too young and too inexperienced to understand what a war really is. And—"

Millbridge interrupted. "And Jussi argued that Raimo wasn't as naïve as Viktoria believed. Same conversation in houses all over Canada. So go on. Let's get to the *end* of the story."

"Jussi wasn't as afraid as Viktoria but they still both thought Raimo shouldn't enlist," Vilho said. "So ... and this was pretty stupid. Both of them, they thought that Marilyn would be able to stop him. She couldn't." He paused.

"That's not the end of the story."

"No."

"And it's not the whole story, either."

Vilho sighed. "Jussi—he figures that the war's going to end in a year or two—he bets on the war being over before his son is trained and sent to Europe. Viktoria, she's more pessimistic. She keeps thinking about how her parents just *disappeared* in the Finnish Civil War—no bodies, no gravesite, no *nothing*. And she argues that the only thing she has left of her parents is what's in Raimo—her father's eyes, her mother's wit. That kind of thing."

"You know this from Rabbit, from Ivor?"

"Yes. It's what Jussi told him, later."

Myllysilta wondered if Vilho knew exactly how anguished those conversations must have been, if he knew that Ivor himself had fought, that his brother Karl, Viktoria's first husband, had been killed. He doubted it.

"Go on. What was Marilyn supposed to do?"

Vilho paused, drinking coffee, before he continued. "I don't know. Jussi tells Viktoria to talk to Marilyn, see if she can think of something to keep Raimo from signing up."

"And that's when the idea of the two—Raimo and Marilyn—getting married comes up?"

"It was pretty obvious that they wanted to get married, so Viktoria and Jussi just let them do it. Her parents too. Her father was heading to Winnipeg for a new job, and Marilyn, if she stayed in Port Arthur, would need someplace to live."

"Did the Manteres encourage this?"

"Not really. They didn't like the timing, though they like Marilyn fine and were happy enough for a wedding—but someday, not yet. But ... remember that all I know about this is what Rabbit—Ivor—told me, and his stories are sometimes just stories."

"So Raimo marries Marilyn last autumn, and Marilyn gets pregnant."

Vilho added, "And Raimo gets sent overseas and is killed. She had a boy last month. A son."

In the silence that followed, Vilho's perpetual look of worry increased.

Myllysilta released him. "Thanks, Vilho. Another coffee?"

"No thanks, Mr. Millbridge. I have to—"

Myllysilta waved him away. "Good talking to you," he said. As Vilho got off the stool, Myllysilta put his hand on Vilho's arm. "One more thing. That business of Kari Petterson. Was it really *you* who set fire to his shack?"

"No!" Vilho said forcefully. "That wasn't me!" Some of the customers in the restaurant looked up from their meals.

"Was it Ivor?" Softer. "Was it Rabbit?"

Everyone seemed to be listening.

"I don't think so." Vilho cleared his throat. "It—it had to be someone else."

Myllysilta let Vilho leave.

When he had gone, Millbridge lingered at the counter for a while. He remembered the train ride with Karl Solbakken, and Rabbit. And that other fellow—Erik something.

Who had let himself be killed at Ruovesi. Welcomed it, even.

And Rabbit, who had been so full of joy and humour and idealism, had been turned by the war into a haunted and guilt-ridden drunk.

And I'm coming out of yet another war with one of Karl's boots in my basement and a knack for business in my head, Millbridge thought. *We're all more than just a little crazy.*

#

At the Hoito two weeks later, summer was blazing into autumn, and Millbridge and Rough-house were, as usual, talking business. But Millbridge's mind kept wandering from the job at hand.

The trouble with Owen, Millbridge thought, *is that he's turning into a man—a bit late, perhaps, since he's nearly twenty-three, and finally has a university degree. But men ask questions—good ones—and Owen is starting to ask them. I need to give him some real work to do.*

Rough-house put his empty coffee cup on the table and waved for the waitress to come over and fill it up. "Penny for your thoughts," he said to Millbridge.

"Owen." Millbridge took a long drink to empty his cup, and when the waitress finally came over, she filled it along with Rough-house's. "He's starting to ask questions—not directly, you know, but casually Off-hand, like, well, 'How did you meet Mr. Karialainen?'"

"He knows my name?" Rough-house laughed, perhaps a little too long. "What about the *Rufus* part?"

"That, too. What he doesn't know is what we do—apart from the visible businesses. And I'm not sure he's ever really paid attention to *them*, even."

"So send him back to university. Isn't he already enrolled for this term? Why did you ever let him come back up here after he graduated from Queens? Didn't he like southern Ontario? There's no girl up *here* to come home to, surely?"

Millbridge shrugged. "Not that I'm aware of. Or in Southern Ontario, either." At Rough-house's raised eyebrow, he clarified, "Not *just* one. Not one *particular* one. I'm sure there are many girls who'd be interested in him."

Rough-house let it go. He knew a few things about Owen that his boss did not. "Well. He's good at that deep learning stuff. Tell him this time, he needs to focus—get a PhD in whatever. Fill his head up with study or something. What does he want to be?"

"I don't have any idea." For a time, Millbridge said nothing. Then, "I know he likes studying history. Basic sciences, no. He failed those courses, had to re-take them. Political geography too. But sure, religious art in Europe 200 years ago, that sort of thing, high marks. Enough to get into another degree program." He grimaced. "What good is it?"

Myllysilta, deep inside Millbridge, snorted in agreement. *Recent history, maybe. This century, it has shown us a lot—people never change. They want things, they fight, and they get them or they don't. And if they don't, they raise the stakes and try to kill each other.*

Rough-house recalled Millbridge to the conversation. "That's the kind of thing they teach them at Queen's. Which you had to know—you're the one who sent him there."

"Yes. Because it is the best." Millbridge said. *Like a Don,* Myllysilta reminded him. *But you knew he wouldn't have been able to handle a Don.*

Rough-house shrugged. "So, their students learn things like art and history." He refrained from saying, *What did you expect?* "Maybe he could teach something. He might like it, teaching. You should ask."

Teaching. Like his mother. Millbridge kept the thought just below the surface. "I guess I have to."

"You could always put him in charge of the legit businesses—if he can't come up with something better." Rough-house paused. "Ah, that's what you were thinking already."

"Perhaps. It would be a challenge for him. Like a PhD in bookkeeping."

Rough-house laughed. "They need two kidneys for that? Drink your coffee and let's get the hell out of here. Time's a-wasting."

Millbridge left a dime on the table.

14 • MARILYN

JUST AS THERE WERE TWO SIDES to Andrew Millbridge, there were two non-competing "corporations" that he owned and operated. One—the illegal one, with no name—was run by Rough-house. The other—scrupulously "by the book"—was headed by Millbridge himself.

Millbridge Enterprises paid its taxes on time each year and gave its employees the occasional raise in pay. Millbridge Enterprises even tolerated union workers. The corporation contributed to charities and a surprising number of churches, though Millbridge never attended fund-raising events. There was never a photo of him in any of the newspapers.

Rough-house's half of the business, meanwhile, didn't leave a paper trail. It had always been part of the vast underground economy of North America's Great Depression—the Dirty Thirties. However, as the Depression morphed into the booming economy of the war years, and Millbridge Enterprises prospered, the underground economy shrank. When the days of prohibition vanished in the United States, the big money stopped flowing in rivers from the illicit liquor trade and other questionable enterprises. It became a small creek.

Andrew Millbridge collected his profits and sent them to the financial institutions on various islands in the Gulf of Mexico. The "sand banks," as he called them, prospered. He paid himself a substantial salary, declared a far smaller one on his taxes, and drove a much humbler car than Rough-house's LaSalle, though sometimes he dreamed of something fancier—not to be *högmodig*, but because he wanted the best.

In Port Arthur he was, outwardly, the President of Millbridge Enterprises Inc. Not especially friendly—essentially distant. To the Caribbean islanders he was just another rich man who sent money, a faceless sum in an account that built and built. To the patrons of the various restaurants he frequented, he was that man whom few discussed in public. He was, it was whispered, a *dangerous* man.

The Myllysilta in Andrew Millbridge fancied himself a berserker— the roaring and violent drunk, dressed in a bear's skin, whose place was at the front of a Viking raiding vessel. In battle, the berserker's job was to be the first man off the longboat. He was the harbinger of havoc, the tip of the spear that pierced the enemy's defences and made it possible for his fellow seafarers—both drunk and sober—to get off the ship intact and do some *real* fighting.

The Millbridge half of the duo saw himself as the steersman—the man at the *back* of the boat, its sometimes navigator, sometimes pilot, and *always* the smartest man in the crew.

All Myllysilta and Millbridge had in common was the metaphor— each a soul with whom they shared the boat.

Neither being recognized the importance of either captain or crew.

#

As Myllysilta had learned from Vilho, for the Manteres—Jussi and his wife Viktoria, and their son Raimo's wife Marilyn—the summer of 1945 ripped all metaphors to pieces.

On May 4th, Germany surrendered, ending the war in Europe.

In July, Marilyn gave birth to James (Jimmy) Mantere.

Two days later, Jussi and Viktoria received the information that Raimo had been killed when he stepped on a landmine as he was crossing a farmer's field outside Longueur in France.

About two weeks later, the first of the atomic bombs was dropped on Hiroshima. On the same day, in Port Arthur, the Pool 5 elevator suffered a grain dust explosion that blew the elevator's workhouse apart. Some of the casualties were men that Jussi had worked with in the lumber camps of the 1930s.

A few days later, a second atomic bomb turned Nagasaki into ashes and rubble. And on August 14th, the Japanese surrendered, ending the war in the Pacific.

Forever after, summer for Jussi and Viktoria and Marilyn became a season of terrible darkness and blinding light—a blitz. It was a season when they never asked each other, "What are you thinking about?"

#

What Rough-house knew about Owen, but Millbridge and Myllysilta did not, was that there was, in fact, a girl in Owen's life—beyond his sister May, of course. The girl lived mostly in Owen's fantasy life, but still, the situation was more ... delicate than Rough-house would have liked.

How he was in a position to know this had come about years before, when girls, sisterly or otherwise, were not an "of course" part of Owen's world beyond the classroom.

It started, in fact, soon after May's tenth birthday—after May and Owen had been allowed to walk to school by themselves.

One morning May said, "You know Hanna, in my class? Her big sister—not Zofia, the oldest one, Alina. She has to leave school, without even a Grade 10, and go away for a long time. Maybe forever. Hanna says she's in trouble. She let herself get in I don't know what *kind* of trouble, Hanna says it's about birds and bees. I don't think she's telling the truth. Do you?"

At Owen's shrug, May persisted. "What is she talking about, then? Wings? Honey? I don't know."

Owen did know. Conversations among his friends, with whom he usually remained quiet, had shed some light. A dictionary and furtive reading in the school library had filled in other blanks. But he knew he didn't know everything, and he wouldn't—he couldn't—explain it. Least of all to a girl—and *especially* not to his sister.

They were near the playground at that point, and May dropped the subject. She didn't bring it up again on their way home.

Fortune smiled on Owen Millbridge that day. As they arrived home at "the new house," they met Mrs. Vogel, who was leaving with some papers their father had signed. After she hugged May, she turned to Owen and offered her hand for him to shake. He shook it, half-watching to be sure May ran into the house. Then he screwed up his courage.

"Mrs. Vogel, I have a favour to ask. I can't—it's impossible—to ask my—anyone else."

He took a breath and stood straight, as his father always insisted. Still, the words were hard to find.

"Could you, please—with May—there's been talk at school, a friend, about—about birds and bees." He felt his face heat up, and he looked at the space between Mrs. Vogel's eyes, unable to meet them directly.

"Ah." She nodded once. "Ah. Ah, I see. I see how it is. Yes, Owen, I will be happy to do this, at some time. Not today, but soon."

She paused. "Owen, I am honoured that you asked me. And now I need to ask you something in return."

She, too, seemed to find words difficult. "Do you know? About men, I mean?"

At his shrug, she cleared her throat. "Well, I will say only this, and forgive me for speaking so blunt. You must not get a girl … pregnant." She took another breath. "And now, I will ask someone suitable to speak with you. Rufus Karialainen. He is an associate, or I should say an employee, of your father's. You do not know him? Never mind. He knows your father. He will speak frankly."

She paused. "Does that suit you?"

Owen nodded, grateful underneath several layers of newborn misery and embarrassment.

Later that afternoon, when Mrs. Vogel approached Rough-house, he guffawed only briefly before agreeing to have the conversation. "And maybe a follow-up or two," he added. "Make sure *he* stays out of trouble as much as any girl he might know."

Mrs. Vogel said firmly, "I thank you. And now we need never speak of it again."

Rough-house, still smirking, waved a hand in agreement.

It occurred to none of them that Andrew Millbridge could, should, or would speak to his own children. It didn't occur to Andrew that he needed to, either. He'd learned what *he* knew from growing up on a farm, then from having older brothers, and then from his earliest days as a traveling salesman. If he'd ever thought about it, which he didn't, he would have assumed that May and Owen would learn through osmosis as well.

Rough-house's job, at least after that first conversation, had turned out to be an easy one. Through the years, Owen had gone to a few school dances with a group of friends, boys and girls together. He mentioned specific girls only a few times, and only in passing, even during his Queen's years.

But in the summers, Owen came back to Port Arthur, and in Port Arthur, he went to dances at the Finn Hall. And in both 1943 and 1944, Owen had danced with a girl, a nice girl named Marilyn—a girl he mentioned to Rough-house, adding that although she danced with several people, she seemed to like him and danced with him often.

Rough-house kept his questions casual. "Do you know any more about her?"

Owen did not, and he seemed not to want to learn. Marilyn, however, became the girl to whom he compared all the girls he met at Queens. None of them measured up.

Rough-house, of course, unearthed who Marilyn was. He also soon knew that she was not available to Owen for several reasons, no matter how kind she seemed.

Which is why, in the late summer of 1945, Rough-house suggested that Millbridge send Owen back to southern Ontario, to Queen's University, for more degrees. Even a widowed Marilyn would remain off-limits for some time, and the more distance between Owen and Marilyn, the better, Rough-house hoped.

#

When she was younger, Marilyn Jeanette Doucette—in 1945 the widow of Raimo Mantere and mother of the infant Jimmy—had been headstrong and voluble, a good-enough student with many friends. When her schooldays ended, she worked diligently as a salesperson at Big Day Bridal along with her friend, Laura.

At Big Day, Marilyn sold dresses and accessories. Laura also sold dresses but mostly did odd jobs, kept the books for the store's owner, and tracked the inventory. On Wednesday and Friday nights throughout the war, the two of them sometimes went to the dances at the Finn Hall.

There, in 1943, Marilyn met Owen who, as she later put it, danced like a billiard ball—all spins and caroming.

Owen had learned to "dance" as he had learned most social things—by watching. He had a natural reserve that, coupled with an outsider's perceptiveness, made him seem self-confident. He saw through Marilyn's carefree persona to see the kindness and intelligence underneath, and he liked what he saw.

In turn, what Marilyn saw was a shy young man who was also solid—he would likely become a *good* man. Too bad she was head-over-heels in love with Raimo Mantere. Her affection for Owen extended only to learning his last name, Millbridge, and to dancing with him. If she had ever thought of him before or after marrying Raimo, it was in a vague way, with a sincere wish for his happiness.

Then Raimo died just as Marilyn had to learn to mother an infant. With the help of Raimo's parents, luckily.

Although she liked the little apartment where she and Raimo had been briefly happy, soon her in-laws invited her to live with them. She knew it was a wise decision. She enjoyed being with other people who missed Raimo, even if Jussi and Viktoria rarely spoke of him.

Marilyn's friend Laura, though a less successful salesperson than Marilyn, had a knack for "straightening out" things—making things work. To her, Marilyn was more than just a co-worker, more than just a friend—she was a project.

As early as August of 1945, when Jimmy was just one month old, Laura decided that Marilyn would not become one of those perpetually weeping war brides. She, Laura, would simply not allow it. So what if Marilyn was a widow with an infant son? Time doesn't stop. The present morphs into the future, and infant sons grow into children, and children become adults. *So get on with it.* Let a decent amount of time pass—six months, a year at most—and go back to work. Let yourself go dancing at the Finn Hall.

In the summer of 1946, Laura began her campaign. That spring, Marilyn had begun working again at Big Day Bridal. Again she showed sensitivity and real skill in outfitting brides and their attendants, though sometimes she took refuge in the back to shed tears for Raimo. And she enjoyed the work, most of the time. She very much liked helping the household finances, and Jussi and Viktoria appreciated her contribution. They also seemed to expect that she might someday move beyond Raimo, although she would never forget him.

And Viktoria, Laura argued, would want Marilyn to relax. Marilyn needed some hours free from responsibility. Not only that, Jimmy was, for Viktoria, a joy. He was part of the son that she had lost to the war. He was the part of Raimo that didn't die.

Marilyn knew that Laura was right. She knew that Viktoria, too, had lost family in a war, though she was unclear on the details.

Viktoria, for her part, held Jimmy up to the window on Marilyn's first day back at the store. "Wave good-bye to your mother," she said softly, lifting his chubby arm for him.

And on a late-spring Saturday evening, both she and Jussi watched

Marilyn leave with Laura, heading for the Finn Hall. Jussi put his arm around Viktoria, who said, "Jussi Mantere, you are a good man."

"Perhaps." He swallowed. "We have a good life."

Upstairs, Jimmy began to fuss, protesting life in a crib, wanting out so he could practice walking again.

"We do," Viktoria answered, and went to pat Jimmy back to sleep.

15 • MAY

FOR ANDREW MILLBRIDGE, SUMMER always seemed a circus. As the summer of 1945 approached, he felt that the war's end in Europe and in the Pacific had left their world a House of Mirrors, with distortions in every direction.

But in a House of Mirrors, he thought, a few customers learn, eventually, to find their way out of the maze. They ignore the lights and the reflections. They look only at the floor. Most customers don't learn and, consequently, never escape. Even after the circus tents have been torn down, the "captured" never stop wandering around, completely lost, fooled by all the mirrors in their minds.

Andrew Millbridge was always leery of mirrors. Early in 1945, months before V-E Day, he had begun to adjust his portfolio of investments to reflect the realities of the present and the probabilities of the future.

What would people want? He bought land and lumber and labour because after a war, he knew, people want to build nice houses, live in the suburbs, and buy themselves a better life.

Most of his money flowed out of the Lakehead toward Toronto and other cities of Southern Ontario.

He invested in shopping centres and golf courses and companies that made appliances—refrigerators, electric stoves, radios—and, of course, automobiles. He bought stock in big companies that ate little companies, and he paid cash for tasty little companies that could be sold to bigger, hungrier ones.

Socially, he became the model *communitarian*, but he never described himself that way—too *högmodig*. He let others do that, and he profited from it.

He chose not to confide in Rough-house about this diversification. Because really, the conversation he should have with Rough-house should be a different one. One he kept postponing.

#

In May of 1945, May turned twenty-one. She was slim and strong, and had long ago taken to heart Mrs. Vogel's enlightening explanations about birds and bees, along with their implicit warnings.

Further, Mrs. Vogel had made sure she knew how to type and file—"they are good, solid skills," she had said to May—before May left Port Arthur to attend the University of Toronto. Andrew had decreed that she, like Owen, would seek some post-secondary education, but he wasn't as adamant that she attend "the best." U of T was plenty good—some would say better than Queen's.

And anyway, May wanted to go her own way, free from being the daughter of Andrew Millbridge and the sister of Owen Millbridge. She wanted to be unknown.

Once she'd descended from the train in Toronto, May had embraced anonymity without looking back. She returned to Port Arthur mostly for brief summer visits and a few days at Christmas.

In Toronto, she usually worked full-time as a salesclerk—sometimes at a pharmacy, even for a hardware store, but most of the time at a bookstore. Home was a small apartment above a Chinese restaurant on Bloor Street in Toronto.

She accepted the monthly cheque her father sent to pay her room and board, and the larger occasional cheques, which he intended for tuition. Sometimes she even *used* the money for tuition for a few courses—but mostly she saved it instead. Not for any particular purpose—she had no overarching drive or interest. If pressed, she'd have said she saved money for emergencies, but no one ever asked, and she never had to enumerate, even to herself, what those emergencies might be.

Officially, she studied history at the U of T—mostly because she'd always enjoyed the stories Owen had told her about days long past. She did well enough in classes, and beyond enjoying history's stories, she believed in the power of research and logic to solve mysteries and to offer consolation when things went wrong.

She did not, however, altogether discount luck. After all, her brother, because of his kidney disease, had dodged a bullet. And, somehow, responsibility. Because he hadn't served in the war, he hadn't found what he wanted to do with his life. *As if a life's purpose were a treasure, hidden someplace, instead of something he could find by trying harder to look*, May thought but never expressed to him.

Though Owen had earned an undergraduate degree in history and had enjoyed his studies at Queen's, May knew he thought little about "what's next." He didn't want to teach in a public school. He wasn't driven by an interest in any particular historical era—no research project called to him. Beyond classes, he had few serious interests. He could play the piano, but not well enough to study it seriously, and he certainly didn't have the personality to earn a living as a musician playing in night clubs.

Owen was ... *feckless*, May decided. *A nice guy, but* .... She left the thought unfinished.

Meanwhile, she wasn't pulled to anything particular, either. Life was, for her, just life. Throughout the war, she hadn't tried to follow the ebb and flow of fighting. The events of 1945, like those of the earlier years of the war, were neither completely unpredictable—wars began and ended, the world changed—nor tragic and traumatic. She didn't see how *she* was involved, or anyone she needed to care about, since Owen wasn't able to fight.

May wasn't superstitious, nor did she look for meaning in matters of human nature and behavior. She looked *at* life, not *into* life. Events were what they were. In all this, she was much like her father.

"What is," she told herself, "is. That's all." Her father had said it. She had listened, and learned.

#

May had no memories of her mother, and only dim memories of a few visits to the cemetery to look at a gravestone—usually on a Sunday about the time of her birthday. At school, she eventually associated the phrase "Mother's Day" with those spring Sundays, though they'd stopped visiting after only a few times, about the time she'd started school.

One afternoon when she was nearing her ninth birthday and Mrs. Vogel was with them after school, May risked a question that had been on her mind for a few weeks.

"What did my mother look like?"

Mrs. Vogel glanced around before answering. May knew why. Mrs. Vogel was cautious. May understood caution. She herself had known to wait for a moment when her father was out before asking anything about her mother.

Owen, of course, had already disappeared upstairs with a book.

Eventually, Mrs. Vogel said, "I did not meet your mother. Mrs. Stone connected me with your father, after—after your mother died."

She looked at May, considering. "When I first began living with your family, and I first cleaned your father's bedroom, I found—that is to say, I *saw*, in the drawer of a table beside the bed—a photograph. Your father had left coins on the table, and I was looking for a dish or someplace to leave them." She shook her head.

May didn't know enough to care about coins or theft, and even as a child she never doubted Mrs. Vogel's sense of duty and ethics—if Mrs. Vogel needed to open any drawer in the house, she had good reason. "A photograph? Of my mother?"

"Both of your parents. On their wedding day. You have not seen it? Ah, too bad. Your mother was radiant that day." Mrs. Vogel studied May's face. "No, Owen has more of her look—around her eyes, especially. You look more like your father, or the two of them together. But Mrs. Stone told me, when I first met you, that you laugh like her."

May enjoyed hearing that.

Mrs. Vogel said, "Perhaps someday—or I could ask, I suppose." She sighed. "No, I think it would be wiser for *you* to ask. Perhaps someday *you* could ask your father about the photograph."

"Are you worried that he might get mad?"

"A little, just a little worried," Mrs. Vogel said. "Angry, perhaps, yes. But more *hurt* than angry. And we do not like to hurt Mr. Millbridge, do we?"

"No," May answered. "We do not." So she didn't ask.

And she became even more careful, through the years, not to ask difficult questions. She watched, she listened, and she stayed out of trouble. By the time she walked to grammar school alone while Owen went to the high school down the hill, she was known for being pleasant, friendly, but essentially distant. She had no close friends but enjoyed reading and spending time alone, staring out the window. She was a diligent student, if not a brilliant one.

When Owen went off to Queen's, May was in high school. She had more freedom in general and was alone in the house fairly often. She began opening closet doors that had been closed, telling herself she wasn't looking for anything in particular. She was doing it just because.

In the basement, she noticed first that all the boxes seemed scrupulously clean. Apparently Mrs. Vogel, or someone, continued to dust down here. And at last, she found a very small box that held the photo of her parents that Mrs. Vogel had mentioned, along with a few scarves and a small wristwatch.

The photograph prompted her to study her own face in the mirror—not unusual for a high school girl—and, reluctantly, she agreed with Mrs. Vogel. She looked more like her father, and Owen resembled her mother. They had the same serious eyes.

As she moved through high school, May felt restless and uncomfortable in Port Arthur. She didn't understand the other girls at school. She half-heartedly wanted to escape somewhere.

She didn't like feeling that her mother, in the photograph, looked into her and perhaps found her wanting. So she didn't ask her father about her mother or the photograph. She didn't surreptitiously take her mother's likeness to her own bedroom, hide it in her dresser drawer, and pull it out to gaze at it wistfully, although she knew from movies that other girls would.

When alone, she often went for walks, often on Sunday afternoons. If those walks sometimes took her to the cemetery, to her mother's grave, especially on Mother's Day Sunday, well, that was between her and her mother.

If Andrew knew she went—and there was little he did *not* know—he said nothing. Neither did Mrs. Vogel, though she had remained May's sounding board for fashion and etiquette advice for years, long after their "birds and bees" conversation.

In Toronto, May at last felt free of those eyes. Her friends—friendly acquaintances, really—knew that her mother had died years earlier, yet they seemed incurious about her. When they asked May about her father, she'd reply that he was, to her, "a bit of a cipher." But she didn't spend her life trying to figure him out. When she thought of him at all, she pictured him in the basement, sawing away on that infernal violin.

She wrote a few letters home—mostly thank-you notes for the cheques, with a little local colour for her father to share with Mrs. Vogel—and a few to Owen, when he was in Kingston. But otherwise, she lived firmly in the present and where she was. The years of her life in Port Arthur took on a hazy quality. They seemed less to her like life she'd experienced than dreams she'd had.

Although Toronto was a big, bustling city, she remained apart from it in many ways, too. In this, she was also much like her father.

For instance, her apartment had no telephone. Every telephone, she had learned from her father, came with the obligation to answer it when it rang. She rarely called home, and when she did, she couldn't dial the phone-free house, so she dialed Millbridge Enterprises. Her father, when he answered—something he rarely did—would say a few words, ask a small and safe question or two, and then find an excuse to get off the line.

May constantly felt that her family was a little askew, but it had its own rules-driven version of normalcy. The more she saw of students and coworkers and even people unknown to her, eating in Toronto restaurants and going to museums, the more she assumed that all families operated by habits unknowable to others.

Those with large families complained at having to leave Toronto to see family for holidays—Thanksgiving and Christmas, sometimes Easter.

Those who ate, solo, on holidays at the Chinese restaurant where she sometimes waited tables—they were the only people she understood. She felt a distant kinship with them, even. She saw them as solitary—not lonely—strangers.

It was odd, though, that of the people whom she, her brother, and her father knew, none had families. Not Mr. Karialainen, not Mrs. Vogel, not even Dr. What's-his-name, the one up the hill from the high school. Not a family member among them. Outside their own little household, her father had no living family members, not even cousins. There were, apparently, none on her mother's side, either. How do such things happen?

Her father wasn't old—certainly not old enough to have out-lived any brothers or sisters or even cousins. But he *never* wrote to relatives in Finland. Hell, he didn't even seem to *know* any people in Finland— no old friends, no former neighbours, no co-workers, no whomever.

May realized she didn't even know what her father had *been* in Finland—a farmer? a teacher? a soldier? One guess was as good as any other. He never talked about Finland or things Finnish, except to say that the Hoito had good coffee.

Thinking about the family—all the dead people—was downright

depressing. But sometimes, perhaps after a conversation with her father or when she received a letter from Mrs. Vogel with many expressions of goodwill but little news, she allowed herself to wonder.

What the hell was with the box in the basement of their house? One boot and one shoe? Who keeps shit like that? Whose were they? The boot size and the shoe size weren't even the same. Did her father imagine that he'd find the other shoe or the other boot, someday, and it would still be exactly the right size? And what kind of crazy thought would that be?

She decided she'd ask him about the box. Someday. Probably in a phone call; that would be safe even if he did become angry. But she'd ask nicely. Casually. If she remembered.

#

Although May refused to own a telephone, she needed one sometimes. So she had an arrangement with the couple who owned the Chinese restaurant below her apartment. They would take calls for her, and she would wait tables at special events, beyond serving the occasional shifts for which she was paid. Special events were a rarity, as were her phone calls, so it was an equitable arrangement.

One special occasion occurred in mid-August of 1945, after the war had ended.

May took the call in the restaurant's kitchen.

"Got a favour to ask you," her father said.

"Shoot," May said.

"I'm retiring. Not immediately, but soon. Going to take some time to enjoy life."

"Oh?" *And do what? Do you need more time to play that violin?*

"I'm going to ask Owen to run the business for me."

"Owen? Really? He's, hmm." She wasn't sure how to say "not up to it" without being mean.

"I know, but he's teachable," her father said. "He's plenty smart enough. He just doesn't have much confidence in himself. And he sure as hell doesn't have any kind of commitment to finding work in academia. When you get a chance—he'll likely give you a call about this—encourage him to take me up on it. I haven't talked to him yet—thought it better to talk to you, first."

"You'll ask him to give me a call?"

"That's the idea."

This might be a difficult conversation, she thought. "Dad?"

"Yes?"

"Owen doesn't want to be a businessman. He likes learning. He really is best-suited to being an academic." There was silence for a moment at the other end of the line. *He thinks I'm lying,* May thought. *Maybe I am. Maybe Owen wouldn't thank me for this after all.*

"Academic?" Millbridge said. "Owen?"

"Yes. Maybe a history prof. Doing something where he can read and spend time in libraries, mostly. Although he's talked about becoming a clergyman." He'd mentioned it once, so this was, technically, not a lie, she reasoned.

"Owen? A preacher? That's crazy talk. We don't even go to church, not really."

"Owen's nearly twenty-three, Dad. He's wasted some time—I know that. He isn't graduating at the top of his class or in record time. But Dad, he says he really wants to keep going—get a Master's degree, then try for a PhD, maybe. He's not sure. And he doesn't *know* what's next. He's just not a money and cars sort of guy." May was positive that the last sentence, at least, was true.

"Oh," Millbridge said. "I—I thought he—"

May interrupted. "He's not *you,* Dad. He's … he's still looking for something he can want to become."

She ran out of words, spoken and unspoken. For a moment there was silence, then Millbridge said, "Yes. You're right. He's not me. He has a right to his own life."

May waited for him to continue, but he did not.

After a moment, she thought, *I'm already uncomfortable; might as well keep going.*

She said, "Dad, on a completely different matter, I've got a question for you. I know it's silly, but it's been in the back of my mind for a while. Down in the basement of the house, there's a box that has a boot and a shoe in it. What's that all about?" She held her breath.

Her father's voice was casual. "That? Nothing much. Souvenirs. From when Finland had its civil war. I spent a few months fighting for the Whites in that. Picked them up on the battlefield—thought I'd keep them just to remind me how stupid wars are."

"I didn't know you'd been in a war."

"It was more like a squabble. The guys at the Hoito still like to talk about it, though."

"Ah. I was just wondering."

"Nothing wrong with that." Millbridge paused. "I expect Owen's going to call you sometime this coming week. If he does—"

"Yes, I'll tell him what we talked about," May said, fairly certain she wouldn't. "Love you." It was her signal that the call was over.

She wanted to get off the phone before he could ask how she was and how her classes were going (especially tricky since she wasn't planning to take any this term), what she was studying, was she coming to Port Arthur before the end of summer or for Thanksgiving. Luckily, it was too early for him to think of Christmas.

"Love you, too," Millbridge said mechanically.

"Whew," May said aloud when he'd hung up. *That was a little weird. Owen as a businessman? It might do him good. But he'd have to learn everything, from the ground up, and then figure out how to do it all his own way. And would Dad allow that?*

She wasn't sure. But that would be Owen's problem, not hers. Maybe she'd mention the business idea to Owen after all.

16 • MRS. VOGEL

"WAR'S OVER," ROUGH-HOUSE SAID. "Owen's back in Kingston." He caught the eye of the Hoito's waitress, and she promptly came over with the coffee pot.

After she'd filled both his cup and Millbridge's, Rough-house asked, "So what's the plan? Same old same old?"

Instead of answering, Millbridge said, "Look around. What do you see?"

"Women," Rough-house offered, then he laughed. "Used to be that women hardly ever came here. Used to be full of out-of-work timber cutters and scruffy guys who had no jobs and just enough money to pay for a cup of coffee. The only women here were the waitresses and the cook."

"That was in the Depression," Millbridge said. "That's history. Last few years, the war—what's different now?"

"Like I said—women. More of them. Lots of chitter-chatter and chirping. Lots of talk about children, churches, schools ... all that stuff. Used to be working men bitching about wages and working conditions. Now there's guys in suits come in here."

Millbridge smiled. "And why is that?"

"Why? I dunno—more money floating around, I guess. More women thinking they can do whatever a man can do—which they can't. More men coming in to talk business. Not as many *real* workers as there used to be."

"And what do these men and women have in common?"

Rough-house nearly choked on his coffee. "The men are turning into women? What is this—a sex quiz?"

Millbridge laughed. "Jesus. You and your women. No ... here's what I see." He leaned forward. "Times are good. People are thinking about the future—planning it, figuring out how long it will take to save enough money to buy a lot and build a house, wondering if they'll own a car someday, thinking about making sure that their kids

150

get an education and maybe land a good job. They're trying, all of them, men and women, to figure out what kind of future they want for their kids—and for themselves."

"Well, sure," Rough-house said. "But so what?"

"Well, for one thing, it means that women feel more relaxed, more comfortable in a place like this. Times are changing—things aren't so threatening. So, we have to change from businesses that worked well in hard times to businesses that work well in good times."

"Like?"

"For instance, to raise a family and build a house, you need a lot for the house to sit on. So we buy lots, hold them for a while, sell them at a profit. We go into the construction business—not as a contractor, but as the financier for the guy who wants to *be* a contractor."

Millbridge took a sip of coffee. Rough-house knew to wait. "We sell house insurance, health insurance. We go into businesses that provide entertainment, or appliances, or car parts—businesses that make life easier for people."

Rough-house stared into his half-empty coffee mug.

"You know what I think?" Millbridge said after a moment.

"I'm afraid to ask."

"I think that people are going to want to have a batch of kids— four or five to a family—because they can, because they think that their kids will have an honest-to-God chance at having long and happy lives. No war, no hunger, no need to scrimp and save. I think that in the next few years there'll be a whole new bunch of schools built—not just elementary schools, but high schools and maybe, in time, even a college or a university, here, in the Lakehead." He paused for a moment. "You think I'm crazy?"

Rough-house considered. "No. I think you're mostly right. Mostly. Don't know about that college stuff, though."

Millbridge said nothing. He let the silence build.

"You remind me of Old Mag," Rough-house said at last. "Always looking around, always thinking." He wondered, briefly, if Mag had been paranoid, too.

"Nicest thing you've ever said to me."

Rough-house raised his cup. "Here's to you." He drained what little remained in it.

"There's something else," Millbridge said. "I want to retire. And to do that, we need to go legit."

"Legit." Rough-house repeated it without expression, without saying, "This again?" or "I thought you already were." He simply waited for Millbridge to explain.

"Or at least *I* do. I mean, *really* legit," Millbridge said at last. "No separate operations. No ties between the old and new businesses, between mine and yours—no ties at all. I want you to take over, completely, everything that *isn't* legit."

"Because…" Rough-house prompted in the slow and dragging voice he might use when talking to a child who hasn't quite figured something out.

Millbridge had his eye on the waitress who was again scanning the room for empty cups. He waved her over.

The waitress returned, coffee pot in hand. As she filled Rough-house's cup, Millbridge looked up at her. "I predict that someday people are going to drink out of mugs—more coffee for the customer, longer time between refills for you."

The waitress smiled. "Can't come soon enough for me."

When she left, Millbridge turned back to Rough-house once more. "Because? Because Owen is taken care of for now, but someday, he and May will find out about me if I stay in the business."

"And the money?" Rough-house prompted.

"It's yours—not every penny, mind. I keep what the legit businesses make. What you control, you own, though. I've got enough, thank you."

Rough-house smiled. "And you and me? No more coffee at the Hoito? No more conversations about the world to come? No time for scoundrels?"

"'Fraid not."

A silence grew between them.

Rough-house looked down, then up at Millbridge's face. It was cold as stone. *Well, then,* he thought.

"Deal," Rough-house got up to leave. "One thing, though. I get to have breakfast here. You get the Hemmet—this place is mine."

"Done." *I'm going to need to replace Rough-house,* Millbridge thought, *with someone who is as honest as they come—someone who can look after the "clean" investments, full-time and without supervision, as if they were his own.*

Rough-house was at the steps, now, and heading for the door. Millbridge watched him leave.

There goes a person who knows a lot about me, Myllysilta hissed. *I hope not too much. And another thing: Don't be a fool picking the person who's going to replace you. What you want is a Paul—not a Peter, not a Jesus. This is business. You need to find someone who is a bit brash—idealistic, sure, but no dummy. A salesman, maybe—one with a sprinkling of guilt but also the gift of the gab.*

Millbridge smiled sardonically. *Damn,* he thought. He should have asked Rough-house if he knew someone who might make a good replacement. But the front door had closed. Rough-house was gone.

#

The next day, Millbridge considered Myllysilta's advice. Some of it, he wasn't so sure of. Brash? Gift of gab?

In the end, Millbridge decided that of all the people he knew, the best person to replace Rough-house and manage the "clean" businesses was right under his nose—Mrs. Vogel. *Neither Jesus nor Peter,* he thought, *and not even Paul. But she's smart as hell. And times have changed. Paul's become Pauline, and she has different skills with people.* He suspected that Rough-house would approve.

Up to this point, he'd never involved Mrs. Vogel in any of his less appealing business deals, but he figured she probably knew at least that they existed. She had never asked about them, never made any effort to delve into his personal affairs. Gossip was not coinage to her; it was not legal tender—and it was not to be used for buying either attention or respect. And, Millbridge knew, Mrs. Vogel was close to Owen and May, in different ways.

More importantly, Mrs. Vogel's feet were always planted solidly on the ground. She had a life outside the office. She had real friends, too—utterly normal folk who laughed and cried and complained and boasted and told her what things they liked and what things they didn't. *And that,* Millbridge thought, *was what made her so valuable.* If Mrs. Vogel thought something was important, it was. If she thought something was bound to happen, it did. She not only had a knack for business, she had an ear for it. And she knew it. *And, if and when the day comes, she can wrap Owen around her little finger.*

A day later, Millbridge approached Mrs. Vogel with his offer. She agreed to take it—on condition that he provide her with a secretary and a new office, preferably in the same neighborhood as the one they were in. Not in the "other" downtown where the Scandinavians were scarce, and certainly not in the Whalen building where the monied lawyers with their stinky cigars had their offices.

They shook hands, and a week later, Millbridge Enterprises hung out its new shingle on Bay Street, close to the old office.

Mrs. Vogel began by buying property in both Port Arthur and Fort William, and even in the no-man's land between. There, she picked up empty lots, sections of subdivisions that were in the planning phase, buildings that were owned by merchants who were in the wrong place for what they sold, but in the right place for something else.

In the next few months, she travelled frequently to Toronto, Windsor, Kitchener, London—cities that seemed to her to be on the verge of population explosion, cities attractive to companies who saw them as places to build factories. She invested in places regular people went every day, from diners to department stores.

She also found occasional oddball, one-of-a-kind companies like Bombardier, run by a brilliant man who did not yet have a brilliant product—just a big box that could be driven over snow.

Some of Mrs. Vogel's bets did not turn out well in the short term, but most of them proved profitable in the long run and, over time, a few of them made Andrew Millbridge even richer than before.

PART III

INNOCENCE AND EXPERIENCE

A truth that's told with bad intent
Beats all the lies you can invent.

"Auguries of Innocence"
William Blake

1 • CHRISTMAS, 1948

FOR THE NEXT TWO OR THREE YEARS, Millbridge felt that although many parts of the world had changed when he wasn't looking, a few things remained the same.

The Kellogg's Dairy milkman still showed up with his horse-drawn wagon, and he still delivered two bottles of milk to the house's rear entrance, where its two little milk doors were built into the outside wall. The milkman carefully pushed the bottles through the inner door all the way into the house so that the milk wouldn't freeze solid. He always made sure that the outside door was closed.

Mostly, though, as Millbridge had predicted, the world had sped up. During the war, new highways had linked little towns in northwestern Ontario, like Hearst and Geraldton. Every car on a cross-Canada journey passed through them.

Railway buffs could ride a summertime "tourist train" now—one with a dome car where passengers could better see the scenery on both sides of the train.

Beacon's Bread and Cakes delivered their baked goods with an English Thames panel truck.

An international flight, operated by Trans-Canada Air Lines, connected the Lakehead to Duluth-Superior in the United States.

Even the streetcars in the Lakehead had been pulled out of service, and most of the old rails had been torn out of the streets. Brill buses with electric motors and rubber tires now used the old overhead wires. An Intercity trolley coach line linked Port Arthur and Fort William.

Canada Car had laid off thousands of workers at the end of the war, and now those who remained made the trolleys and diesel buses; the Shipyards built tugs and barges.

But no matter how quickly the world was changing, it was not changing as quickly as Millbridge was changing his past.

The "history" of the Niemi family, begun in 1930 when Millbridge had selected "Toivo Niemi" as his father's name, had acquired new relatives, interesting anecdotes, colourful characters with their own stories to tell, and, unfortunately, many, many inconsistencies in the storyline.

Millbridge's solution was to engage his penknife in the storytelling. Once in a while he would take the knife out of his pocket and use it to cut loose a page or two that he knew belonged in the garbage can or, perhaps, somewhere else in the narrative. If it managed to escape the can, he would flip to the location (Karelia, perhaps?), insert the material, and carry on.

If he thought of something that might improve the storyline, but didn't know quite how to write it, he scribbled a note to himself so that he could flesh out the idea later. Such notes were often filed away in the rosin compartment of the violin case, because the ideas frequently came to him while he played.

When Millbridge felt like writing in the black and white composition book, he first opened the violin case to look through his notes. If he found something of interest there, he'd spend a bit of time putting it into words, and then slip the new pages into the family history.

The book itself he kept in the basement, under the box that held Karl Solbakken's boot and his own brother's shoe—one of the pair of shoes his brother Marku had worn the day Antti Myllysilta's brothers had killed Fredric Svensson, the owner of the hardware store in Gamlaby. A few days after that, Marku had flung the orphaned shoe at a terrified shoemaker in Narpes who insisted that he couldn't just make another one like it because "all leather is different" and "the colour and, of course, the stitching would not match." After Marku had left the store, Antti had picked it up, already conscious of never leaving traces behind.

That raid was just before mid-November in 1917, Myllysilta remembered. Some two months later, his brothers were all dead. And somehow, he'd kept the shoe through the years. Not as a keepsake. There was nothing sentimental about it, neither for Myllysilta nor for Millbridge.

So why had he kept it? Millbridge wasn't sure. But somewhere deep down, Myllysilta recognized that the shoe wasn't simply a shoe. *Just in case. Might come in handy.* Millbridge was glad that Annie, all those years ago, hadn't thrown it away.

Millbridge actually hadn't thought about the box for years, not until May had asked about it, just after the war. He'd given the stock answer he'd practiced ever since her mother's death: *Just souvenirs.* It was as reasonable an answer as any.

Now, thinking of the shoe, Millbridge chuckled. Jussi Mantere, for all his brilliance, had never thought to match the shoe he and Karl Solbakken had to the size of any of the Myllysilta brothers' feet.

Mantere is no Sherlock Holmes, Myllysilta reminded him. *He's smart, but....* He left the thought unfinished.

#

As Christmas of 1948 approached, Andrew Millbridge mailed his children invitations to come home for Christmas. Owen was twenty-six; May, twenty-four. Issuing a formal invitation seemed an odd thing for their father to do, but they made the plans as requested. The two of them met in Toronto, then took the train to Port Arthur. Andrew met them at the station on Friday, the 24th.

At breakfast on Christmas morning, Andrew said, "There's something I'd like to ask you."

"Oh?" May said. "Is it what we'd like to name this dog you've somehow acquired?" She leaned down to scratch the head of a nondescript mutt—a knee-height mess of panting gratitude—who sat watchfully at her side, hoping for treats. Her hand came up covered in hair. "Perhaps *Sheddy*?"

Owen laughed. "Oh, I have a question! 'What's for Christmas dinner?' Because I've been wondering about that myself."

Over their laughter, Millbridge said, "The dog's name is Wolf. He fends for himself." The dog looked at him briefly but returned his adoring gaze to May as a likelier source of bacon. "And about dinner, Mrs. Vogel is coming. And bringing it. She should be here soon, in fact. Which is why I wanted to ask you something. Special."

They quieted quickly, sober now. "No, it's nothing to do with business or my health." He paused for a moment. "You may not know this, but every Christmas morning since your mother died, I've paid a visit to her grave at Riverside Cemetery." He laughed lightly but warmly in the self-mocking tone May remembered from her childhood. "When you were little, I used to sneak off before you kids woke up, and even when you weren't little anymore, I'd cook up an excuse for leaving the house. I'm sure you noticed. You must have. No? That's surprising."

He turned serious again. "I always walk there and walk back and—well, it's going to be cold. When I got up this morning it was 20 below, and it's only going up to maybe 10 below or so this afternoon. I thought this year we could all walk there, leaving sometime around one or two in the afternoon. It'll be warmer, and it's not that far—maybe a mile and a half."

It wasn't exactly a question. Millbridge looked first at May and then at Owen.

"Yes, of course. I'd like to go with you," May said.

"Me, too," Owen added. "I brought along my Port Arthur winter clothes."

"So did I," May said. "We'll be plenty warm, Dad."

"Good! Your presents are under the tree. I snuck them there very early this morning."

"So are yours, Dad," May said. "*Sneaking* is one of the things we're all good at—except maybe Owen."

They adjourned to the living room and opened their presents. Late morning, Mrs. Vogel came by with gifts, a turkey to roast, and two pumpkin pies. May and Owen helped peel the potatoes and carrots.

At two o'clock, the family left Mrs. Vogel still tending their Christmas dinner and began their walk to the cemetery. Instead of going downhill along High Street to Oliver Road and then following Oliver Road uphill to the graveyard, Andrew led them west along Beresford Street.

"You can have a look at the new houses," Millbridge said.

Owen and May glanced at each other. "Good idea," Owen said. "That'll be interesting."

May raised an eyebrow, and Owen nodded. What their father really wanted to do was keep out of the wind and, also, to avoid climbing the hill on Oliver Road.

After a few blocks along Beresford, they cut down to John Street. At the Y-intersection where McBean Street and Montgomery Street met, they went down McBean. Montgomery Street was populated by Finns and Finland-Swedes. Some of the residents on Montgomery might recognize him, and neither Millbridge nor Myllysilta wanted that. It was, in fact, the street where Jussi Mantere lived with his wife and daughter-in-law and grandson.

At Oliver Road they turned right, and a few minutes later they came to the two cemeteries: first Saint Anthony's, the Roman Catholic cemetery; then Riverside, for Protestants. Annie's grave was in Riverside, not far from the main gates.

They assembled in a row in front of the headstone.

"I remember being here after mom died," Owen said.

"Hmph," Andrew said. "How can you remember that? You were not even three. May was just one."

Owen said, "I do, though."

May recognized Owen's tone—stubborn—and chose to keep the peace. "I don't. I never really knew Mom. But I still miss her." She didn't mention her own graveside visits, during high school. They were private, between her and her mother.

Millbridge's throat tightened, and he found he could not look at the headstone anymore. He turned away.

Three rows east of where they stood, he saw another family—husband, wife, a young woman—bundled against the cold. A daughter? And, presumably, the woman's child, a boy of two or three. The child held his mother's hand.

The child saw Millbridge looking at him and smiled. Millbridge smiled back, then looked more closely at the father—no, the grandfather. Jesus, was it Mantere? He examined the man's face, which was partly hidden by a scarf. But yes, it was Jussi Mantere.

Millbridge turned quickly away and fixed his gaze on Annie's gravestone, trying to tune in to the chat between Owen and May.

"Whew, it's cold," May said at last. "Can we leave soon?"

"Of course," Millbridge answered. He glanced with apprehension toward the other family—he did not want to acknowledge them. Luckily, they were getting into their car in the parking lot.

He walked slowly, leading Owen and May past the grave where the Manteres had stood. It was marked with a grey military headstone, one of many standing in a row, most serving merely as markers for young men whose bodies were buried in Europe. *Raimo Mantere.* They kept walking.

A few graves away, *Bertil Salmi.* Millbridge recognized the name, but it took him a few steps to place Salmi—the man, in and out of jail, who'd been involved in the deaths of Rosvall and that other Finn. Union matters. So, Salmi had signed up, but apparently hadn't made it home alive.

Poor unlucky bastard, Millbridge thought. *Stupid war.*

Like all of them, Myllysilta added.

The walk home felt longer. The wind had picked up, and it drove the cold into Andrew's lungs. He fought off the need to cough and tried to pick up the pace, but was soon forced to slow down again. It took almost an hour to get back to the house.

He was grateful for a house warmed by Christmas and dinner and oil heating. As they sat at a table heaped with food, he knew he would warm up again. Sometime.

#

On New Year's Day, the Millbridge children took the train back, riding together as far as Toronto.

A half-hour out of Port Arthur, May turned from the window and elbowed Owen awake. "What was that about?"

"What was what about?" He stifled a yawn.

May waved her hand. "Everything. The whole thing. I mean, I got a nice warm scarf from Dad. And thank *you* for the books. It was nice to see Mrs. Vogel again. But this whole thing seemed like an invitation to an event that somehow didn't happen. Unless we were invited mostly to meet Wolf."

"We did go to the cemetery. That seemed important to Dad."

"It did. But why? And I'm not sure I buy his whole claim of an annual pilgrimage. Did he really go all alone, every single year, even when we were kids? Before we woke up?"

Owen shrugged. "Maybe. I can't remember him being gone, but why would I? It never occurred to me to wonder where he went or what he did."

"No, and it still doesn't pay to wonder about Dad. Though sometimes I'm curious about what he does with himself, other than play the violin and seek out stray dogs."

She kept her voice casual. She'd never bothered to mention her father's hopes for the family business, and to her knowledge, her father hadn't mentioned it to Owen, either. More important, Owen apparently hadn't snooped in the basement, and therefore didn't know about the boot and shoes, or any of the papers she'd come across. He might not have any cause to wonder just who or what their father actually was.

"Well, however much he plays that violin, he could stand to practice more. Did you hear his attempt at 'Back in the Saddle Again'?"

"Hoo-ee. Painful. Do you think Dad's ever ridden a horse?"

Owen pondered. "Surely he must have. Back in Finland, at least. Cars weren't common."

"Hmm," was May's only answer, and Owen closed his eyes again. May, however, kept looking out at the vast Canadian landscape—the lake frozen over in smaller bays, trees and rocks hiding under snow. Shouldn't she know more about her father—at least some basic information?

Ah, well. He was a businessman. He'd have a will, at minimum. Probably other official paperwork. If anything terrible happened— and "anything terrible" was as close as she allowed herself to think about death or illness—he'd probably be fine. Besides, Mrs. Vogel was around. She'd take care of things.

By the time they parted in Toronto, after May saw Owen onto the train to Kingston, her curiosity about her father had abated. Her life in Toronto felt comfortable and familiar. No sense in stirring up anything in Port Arthur, or as far back in time as Finland, to rock the boat. Thoughts of her father surfaced only occasionally after that.

But on the train heading to Toronto, Owen had been only pretending to sleep, part of the time. He kept his eyes closed so May would leave him alone while he tried to figure out what was different about being at home this year. Other than the weird invitation from their father, of course.

During the week, he'd attended a dance, hoping to see Marilyn, but she hadn't been there. He'd danced anyway. It was nice to get away from the house, with its stuffiness and oppressive feeling— "secrets behind every door," as May had said.

Mostly, though, Owen wondered about Rough-house. When his father had invited Owen and May for Christmas, Owen had dropped a note to Rough-house—perhaps they could see each other, maybe for lunch. He'd heard nothing in response. That was definitely unusual.

He hadn't seen Rough-house for several years. In fact, not since 1945—but then, he hadn't been back to Port Arthur since.

And there was no one he could ask about Rough-house, even Mrs. Vogel. Through the years, beginning with their first conversations,

Rough-house had always insisted that they keep their occasional discussions and get-togethers private.

"Not secret, mind," he'd said with a smile and a wagging finger. "Just private. Between men. No apron strings, you know?"

Owen had understood—no idle chatter with Mrs. Vogel.

And early on, Owen had loved that sense of being a man—his own person, beyond his father's orbit.

But it also meant that, over the years, he'd never been sure how friendly his father and Rough-house were. They knew each other, and he felt sure they had some business interactions. Mrs. Vogel had said Rough-house worked for his father, but their relationship seemed different, he wasn't sure how. For years, he'd kept any questions he'd asked about Rough-house very casual, and his father had replied with equally casual words that answered nothing.

The motion of trains always carried Owen toward sleep. But before he gave into it, he recognized that the various libraries at Queen's probably subscribed to newspapers from across Canada. One of them would likely receive at least one of the four published in the Lakehead. He could search the obituaries to see if one Rufus Karialainen appeared—he could even read the news to see if Rough-house was ever mentioned.

He pictured himself walking into the library's quiet room, current newspapers lined up on wooden hanging racks, deep leather chairs. He settled into one and knew nothing else until they arrived in Toronto.

#

Had his children stayed to the end of January, Millbridge might have taken them to the Fort William Carnival parade. But they hadn't, so he bundled into his heavy coat and drove by himself. He had no interest in the parade *per se*, but he took his Brownie Six-20 camera along so that he could take some shots of the floats and send copies to Owen and May. As soon as he had taken the pictures, he left. The car took a long time to warm up, and Andrew was glad to get home, where Wolf waited patiently in the kitchen.

When the pictures came back from the camera shop, four of the eight prints were of the parade: Shaw's Bread Man lounging on a loaf of bread, the competing Parnell's Bread Man (Mr. Butternut, "The

Best Loafer in Town"), the Great Lakes Paper Company giant bull, and a float featuring a Scot (with a tam on his head, of course) proclaiming Fort William a Year-Round Vacationland.

Millbridge's body remembered the cold. He shivered as he had on the day the pictures were taken. As he looked at the photos, he knew he should feel something more than just the memory of the cold morning. Affection for tradition, perhaps? Sentiment? Some *plus ça change, plus c'est la même chose* insight? But he did not.

Instead, he decided that Owen would get the Shaw's Bread Man and the Scot. That left the other bread man and the bull for May. The remaining four photos, taken at Christmas, were blurry and not especially flattering, so he put them into the kitchen garbage can. Then he decided he'd write notes to Owen and May later.

He went down to the basement to get the composition book. Everything there was just as he had left it. *Something about my mother and father.*

Back upstairs, he sat at the kitchen table and took out his pen. It was a banker's pen—black with a solid gold cap that protected the nib. He took off the cap and then unscrewed the ink bottle's lid and laid the lid carefully upside down on the table. Then he loosened the pen's plunger and pulled it part way out of the top of the pen. When he pushed the plunger back down, the pen's ink reservoir slowly filled, and as it filled, he counted to ten as per the manufacturer's instructions. Then, satisfied that the pen had fully sipped its measure of ink, he tightened the top and wiped off the tip with a scrap of toilet paper.

It was a routine that he followed religiously, taking great pleasure in caring for a fine-quality writing instrument. He opened the black-and-white notebook and smoothed the pages.

My father, he wrote, *was a soft-spoken man who had an interest in music. After the day's fishing was over, he would play the violin while my mother made supper. Because I was an only child, he would often finish playing, then hand the violin to me so that I could learn. I was not much of a student, but I loved the sound of the instrument.*

Millbridge wrote for a while and then, with his penknife, cut the sheet out of the book and slipped it in among the first pages of the family history.

"You loved the sound of the violin, did you?" Myllysilta asked him. They laughed together, but the laughter was bitter. It tasted of lies and cheap wine. It smelled of a horse's stall. It sounded like a fireplace andiron, dropped on the floor.

Millbridge got up, put the pen in his shirt pocket, and went down to the basement once more. He slipped the book under the cardboard box that held the boot and the shoe, then headed upstairs. He took the steps slowly and grasped the banister with care. In the kitchen he sat down at the table once more. *I'm getting old*, he thought. *Old and sleepy.* He leaned forward, crossed his arms on the table, and laid his head down.

After a short rest, he got to his feet and started up the stairs to the top floor. On his bed lay the book he'd been reading occasionally, just to refresh his Swedish—Lennart Wikström's *The Gold Mine*. He set it carefully on the floor. A minute or two later, his clothes still on, he was asleep on his bed.

As usual, he slept through the night without dreaming.

2 • A FAMILY HISTORY

MAY KNEW IT WOULD TAKE OWEN some time to get to the phone, so she let it ring until he picked up.

"Hey, brother," she said, "Happy Valentine's Day. I've got a question for you. Have you ever looked at that book Dad's got socked away in the basement?"

"What book?"

"It's black and white—lots of pages stuck in among other pages. That one."

"Ah, the family history," Owen said.

"Yes. What do you know about it?"

"Not much. Dad said he writes in it from time to time—when he's not still tied up in company stuff. It's a work in progress. He remembers something, and then he writes it down, and then puts the pages where he thinks they should go in the final copy. That help?"

May sighed. "Yes, except that he's retired now, remember? Mrs. Vogel's in charge. So he's got more time to work on it. I read some of it at Christmas when we were there." She paused. "Dad doesn't know that."

"Your secret's safe with me. So, what about the book?"

"It's odd. I noticed parts that all seemed to be about the same thing, but they were all really different—not just in little ways, but completely."

"He's getting old," Owen said. "Maybe his memory's going. He probably doesn't remember stuff exactly as it happened anymore."

"He's only ... what? Maybe fifty-five, sixty?"

"Maybe. Maybe not that old. I don't know," Owen said. "We don't know his birthday, remember? He never talks about it and never mentions his parents or family."

"Yes, I remember his weirdness around his birthday, but mostly how disappointed you used to be to miss out on another occasion for a cake!" She laughed before becoming serious again. "But why?"

"Why what? The secrecy? I don't know why. Because he's Dad!"

"Nope, I think it's something else. I think he doesn't know when he was born. I don't think he knows for sure how old he is."

"That's crazy. First of all, his parents would have told him when he was born. That's what parents do. And besides, he would have had to show the immigration people paperwork or something when he came to Canada."

"Okay, that's true," May conceded. "But who knows where those dates would have come from. Have you seen a birth certificate? A confirmation record, even? And the book, what I read anyway, sounds completely made up. Like he's trying out different versions of the past."

"Oh, I doubt it," Owen said. "He's just trying to remember things. I do that, too. For instance, I remember Mom, but I can never remember what colour her hair was. Sometimes I picture her with dark brown hair, and sometimes it's more blonde. There's no picture of her—never has been, I think—so the picture in my head keeps changing. I think it's like that for Dad. He puts down the possibilities so that sometime, when he's sure he really remembers, he can pick out the right version, or one that's close."

"She wasn't blonde," May said. She'd never told Owen about the wedding photograph, and apparently, Mrs. Vogel hadn't either.

"You remember her?" Owen couldn't keep the disbelief out of his voice.

"Not exactly. I just know she wasn't a blonde. But maybe you're right about Dad."

"Dad says you look like her."

May had no response.

"Can we change the subject?" Owen asked after a second or two. "Seeing as how I don't seem to know what I'm talking about."

"Deal," May said.

Owen said carefully, "I think Dad's sick. Remember the way he walked back from the cemetery? I didn't think he'd make it. I thought we'd have to knock on someone's door and ask if we could call a cab from their place. He kept slowing down."

"I know, but we got home fine, eventually." May paused. "And he's the one who wanted to walk."

"Which is another mystery. Why didn't we just drive?"

May considered. "Maybe it makes a better pilgrimage if it's on foot? If that's what we were doing. Or maybe he's usually stronger. That's probably it—his cough was just the start of a cold, catching him by surprise. Maybe he walks fine, and this was an anomaly."

"Maybe. But it sounds like he's tired all the time now. He just covers it up. Are you going to call him this week?"

"Next week, maybe. And, yes, I'll ask him how he's feeling."

"He'll lie," Owen said. "Ask him something about what he's been doing, where he's been, what he's been up to—other than practicing the violin. We know he's lying about that." They both laughed. "Maybe ask if he's gone for a drive in the country or something. But not like some kind of detective. Pretend you're his daughter. And remember, you have to call when he's most likely to be at the office. Since that's not so often anymore you might have to fall back on a letter."

May laughed. "Okay, smartass. But then it's your turn next, Sherlock."

"Done."

"And Owen, since we're asking questions. Did Dad ever ask you to help him run the business?"

"No, was he going to?" Owen let surprise show in his voice.

"Couple of years ago. I just wondered."

"Hasn't yet." He wasn't sure how he felt about it. Insulted? Hopeful? Resigned?

"Well, he still might. Be ready with an answer, brother. Anyway, I gotta go. And don't worry. I won't bring up anything about that to Dad." She hung up.

So like May, Owen thought. *End with a mystery.*

#

Winter turned to spring and spring to summer. In the summer of 1949, Andrew Millbridge, at May's urging, went to the doctor. He chose to go to the one he knew best and who, he knew, would tell him the truth. Dr. Wainwright knew that lying *for* Mr. Millbridge was a necessity, but lying *to* Mr. Millbridge was dangerous.

"You've got a bug, I think," Wainwright said to Millbridge. "Throat's red. Trouble breathing?"

"Yes, when I've been doing something strenuous, like walking up three sets of stairs."

"What about in cold weather?"

"Yes. Air always feels too dry."

"Show me your hands."

"My hands?"

"Play nice."

Millbridge held out his hands, palms up.

"Other side," Dr. Wainwright said.

He turned them over.

"They look okay. You smoke?"

"Never."

"Ever?"

"Not for years, not since 1921, when I came to Canada."

"Were you a heavy smoker before then?"

"Not heavy, no. Cigarettes were expensive." Millbridge allowed himself a smile.

"Okay. What you probably have is just the usual leftover effects of the winter's dry weather—plus a touch of time passing." He checked Millbridge's chart. "Not that you're old, but you're getting older, and your lungs—since you once smoked—are even older now than the rest of you. We're going to have to keep an eye on them."

"So?"

"So start doing some exercises—simple stretches, walking up stairs, that sort of thing. Nothing overly strenuous. Try to build up to more. Other than that, do what you usually do, and see me in a year."

Millbridge got up from the chair and left. Back at the house, he fixed himself a cup of coffee.

I should tell the kids about this, he thought. *May, anyway. She can pass it on to Owen.*

"No," Myllysilta said. *"This you keep to yourself."*

"Why?"

"Because I say so." It was his father's voice.

#

One afternoon in August of 1949, Millbridge felt himself at loose ends. The trouble with living a normal life, he decided, was that it was boring. Same thing, day after day—that's what a "legit" life had turned out to be. Slowly, every day became a day much like the one before and the one that would come after. There was no point, on a normal day, to look forward to what was coming, nor was there any reason to examine the previous day for what it had been.

He found ways to pass the time—more easily in the summer. On occasion, he drove into the countryside, as if he were a tourist. He'd spent so much time in the area decades earlier, mostly visiting bush camps but also checking on various investments, that he could feel his way around without worrying about signs and highways. Eventually, he'd find his way home.

He'd stop at the hamlet of Kakabeka, twenty-ish miles west of town. In June, the spring snowmelt streamed over Kakabeka Falls in a mesmerising torrent that he could watch for an hour. From there, he'd drive along winding roads, watching farmers' fields in various stages of cultivation and harvest.

Once he passed a farm with horses standing near the fence along the road, and he stopped to look at them. He got out and leaned against his car.

The horses eyed him calmly.

Sturdy, he thought. *Probably good enough horses for the farm.*

He approached the fence, but they backed up, out of reach of any attempts at a friendly pat. Briefly, he remembered riding his Don— the sense of unity with another creature larger than himself, potentially dangerous, but in an alliance. No fear.

That night, he dreamed of riding not his Don, but a Pegasus— flying high and light over his life, the lake, the earth. As he drifted toward wakefulness, a heaviness descended on him again, and he felt crushed inside his body, the very act of breathing a continual nuisance.

Once fully awake, he wondered where that farm was—he hadn't been paying attention. He could probably find it again, though, and maybe even ask the owner for a ride. He imagined himself astride a common farm horse, but he knew the feeling wouldn't be what he wanted.

So he thought no more about actually riding, and instead, turned over and over in his mind that feeling of lightness. So different from living every day.

He had decided, after all, to tell May about his appointment with the doctor. She would not let the matter rest until he did. But he said nothing specific. Just that he had been examined and nothing seemed to be wrong. And that was that.

See? he told Myllysilta. *I can seem forthright without actually being forthright. It's one of my specialties.*

He smiled ruefully. It was a practiced smile—but, for him, a normal smile. Now.

When Millbridge tired of country drives, the only part of "legit" life that interested him at all was the time he spent with the Book. Occasionally, he thought of this time as an opportunity to reflect on what had been or could have been. Other times, he felt it was a cancer—one that lived in his basement, feeding on dust, waiting for him to quench its thirst with some of the black ink in his pen.

And then, on an otherwise normal day in mid-August, as Millbridge stood gazing out the living room window, thinking about the Book, Rabbit walked past.

Rabbit? Ivor Solbakken, Jussi Mantere's friend? Is that Rabbit?

It was, at least, someone who reminded him of Rabbit. The man was middle-aged, looked like hell, could be fifty, could be younger. Millbridge stepped back from the window so that Rabbit wouldn't see him.

Where was he going? Coming from what? Why did the Manteres keep appearing in his life? Some feeling for Jussi Mantere—not quite resentment, not quite hatred, but something—flashed again.

Focus, he thought. *Rabbit. Where is Rabbit coming from, and where is he going?*

Slowly, he followed the logic. *He's coming from downtown, the one on Arthur Street. Not the apartments in that building beside the Hemmet—those are his winter lodgings. He's going to Mantere's place, or maybe the shacks past Nahjus Park, across the creek, past the city limits.*

He went into the kitchen, where he pulled a pad of paper from a drawer and wrote: *Aug. 18, 1949, Rabbit on High Street going south.* He tore off the sheet and slipped the pad back into the drawer. He put the sheet into his violin case.

While he had the case open, he played a few tunes, to keep himself company. Maybe, some day, he'd put the incident to use in The Book, devote a few lines to it, make it a moment of incitement or realization. Rabbit hadn't looked in the window, but that was no problem. In the Book, perhaps he did—he looked, saw Millbridge, and began to run down the street. Or not.

#

The next day was a Friday. In Kingston, Owen waited until 7 p.m. before he called May. It took her five minutes to pick up. Meanwhile, Owen was treated to noise from the restaurant kitchen.

"Sorry, I was washing my hair when Mrs. Chi came up to say I had a call—from a man, wink, wink. What's new?"

"Convince me to stay the course," Owen said. "I'm thinking about not finishing the PhD. I like the learning and the knowing, but I don't think I want to spend the rest of my life teaching and doing research."

"Therefore?" May asked.

Owen knew exactly what she meant: *Do something else, then.* "I was thinking about giving Dad a call and finding out if he'd offer me that job, finally."

"I thought you hated the business. I even told Dad that. You're not much of a people person, you know. And what would you do, exactly? What Mrs. Vogel does? That sort of stuff?"

"That's what I was thinking."

"As Mrs. Vogel's boss, or as her apprentice?"

"Apprentice. Definitely apprentice." He laughed. "Can you see me trying to boss her around?"

"Is hell freezing over?"

Owen waited and when he spoke again, his voice was serious. "What would Dad say?"

"He'd say, 'You're hired.' But don't kid yourself—you'd have to do some honest-to-God work or he'd say, 'You're fired.' He'd see through you in a second if you started to drift, or even if it turns out you're not temperamentally suited for the work. And the other thing—remember, he's not particularly well. That lung stuff."

She paused. "Huh. Well, if you want to do it, he'd probably be happy. You know Dad. He's always wanted you to be the one who ultimately takes over the business. God knows I don't want to do it."

"So he'd hire me? For sure?"

"For sure. Call him."

#

Less than a month later, Owen got off the Trans-Canada Airlines plane at the Fort William municipal airport. He still was unsure whether his father considered him to be returning to Port Arthur in triumph or disgrace. As for himself, he felt only relief.

His father met him inside the terminal.

"North Star?" his father asked, as a greeting. He pointed at the plane.

Ah. Apparently, neither a triumph nor a failure, but merely a fact.

Owen answered, "Uh, yes. A Skyliner model—noisy as hell. Bumpy ride, too. But I brought you a present." He handed over a blue matchbook.

"Well, that's something," his father said. "Courtesy of TCA, I suppose."

"Nothing but the best."

"Luggage, belongings?"

"For now, just what's in the suitcase. The rest's being shipped up—should be here in a week or two. Greyhound."

"Good. The car's in the parking lot. I guess we can just pick up your bag—if they can find it—and go."

"I'm glad to be home again, Dad."

"Mrs. Vogel's looking forward to seeing you. But don't expect mercy if you screw up the job. She's already looking ahead to retiring, and if you don't learn your stuff, she'll kill you. Unless I kill you first."

"Point taken."

In the car on the way home, Millbridge said, "By the way, you've rented a house from me—thirty bucks a month."

"A house? I thought we'd—"

"I need my privacy. And, therefore, you need yours. The place is near the top of the Dufferin Street hill, practically within spitting distance of my place. I can see your house from mine. The rent is income for me, and any costs of upkeep are deductible. The place is a good investment—nice view, good location. Just needs a few updates and some clearing out."

"But—"

"Look, once you get immersed in the work, you're going to be up till all hours, and I need my sleep. I also don't need to be getting in the way of whatever Mrs. Vogel gives you to do. If you were hanging around here, I don't think I'd be able to keep from looking over your shoulder. Also, don't forget that I like to play the violin, and you have neither taste nor stomach for good late-night music." He laughed.

"Are you sure about this?" Owen asked.

"Dead sure. Tonight, you'll stay at my place. Probably for a week or so, till the carpenters, electricians, and cleaners can finish. When they're done, you'll have your own home sweet home. And I'll have mine back. Oh, by the way, remember that there's no phone at my place. When I need one I just go down to the office. Mrs. Vogel knows all about this."

"Yes, Dad, I know about the phone, and what's more, I know how inconvenient it is when May and I can't get in touch with you. What if you need to call for help or talk with someone outside office hours? May's often said she wishes you'd get a phone."

It was only a small lie.

"Fine, get a phone for *your* new place. If I need one, I'll use yours." He wagged a mocking finger at Owen. "And don't lie. May has *never* wanted to call me."

It was Owen's turn to laugh, though he didn't tell his father why it was funny that he, a grown man nearing thirty, found his father impossible to fool. He wasn't sure himself.

For the rest of the trip to Millbridge's house, father and son said little.

The next morning, Andrew sent Owen into the basement to hunt up an electrical cord. Remembering May's questions, Owen looked, but both the family history book and the box with the boot and shoe were missing. His father had either squirrelled them away or thrown them out. He made a mental note to report to May.

Back upstairs, Owen handed over the cord. "When do I start?"

"Tomorrow morning," Andrew said. "I'll drop you off. No sense in me hanging around. No, I'll plunk you into Mrs. Vogel's hands— they have talons, you know—and after that, may God have mercy on your soul."

3 • MILLBRIDGE ENTERPRISES

MRS. VOGEL HAD GROWN OLDER. Not slower, though. Her hair was completely white, but she hugged Owen at the office the next morning with strong arms.

Beyond Mrs. Vogel, three young women sat at desks. On each desk sat an enormous mechanical/electrical *something with a keyboard*. A fourth desk was empty except for another of the *somethings*. A fifth desk held only a telephone. In a small room that was, he assumed, Mrs. Vogel's office, Andrew saw only a desk decorated in bills and paperwork—no *something*.

Mrs. Vogel introduced Owen and then asked, "You can type?"

"Yes, in a way. Is that the typewriter?" He pointed to the machine on his desk. All three of the young women laughed; Mrs. Vogel smiled—but the smile was loaded with mischief. Owen remembered it well. And he worried, but only a bit.

He knew how it would go. For the foreseeable future, most of what he'd be given to learn would be incomprehensible. He'd learn to do tasks by rote, not by reason. But he also knew that reason would come eventually. Reason—and a deeper understanding, even—had come partway through every research project he'd ever done, and it would come again. Just not now.

Patience, he counseled himself. *You can do this. Set your mind to it.*

So Owen stared at the machine. It was, he estimated, almost a yard wide and another yard long. It occupied not just some of his desk, but all of it except for a narrow strip on the right side.

"Barbara?" Mrs. Vogel said. "Your turn. Would you explain to Mr. Millbridge what he's looking at?"

"It's a National Multiple-Duty Accounting System. The part that juts out at the front is an electric typewriter. On the far left are the function keys and bars. In the middle, ten columns of digits and four columns for dates and types of transactions. Do you have a pen?"

"What?"

"A pen. Shiny thing, cylindrical—ends in a point. You might want to write some of this down. Paper's just outside Mrs. Vogel's office. Small table, by the door."

"Office?"

Barbara pointed. "It's that room over there. The door is that wooden slab with a doorknob in it. It has *Office* written on it. Mrs. Vogel's desk is in there, and the office phone."

All the girls began to laugh. Mrs. Vogel permitted herself a smile.

"The unattended desk—the one with the NMAS on it—is yours," Barbara continued.

"And the fifth desk? That other one, with the phone?"

"Your father's. He's the only one who's allowed to answer that phone, or to place a call from it. When it rings, if it rings, ignore it."

So, Owen, thought. *My father claims to be retired. He also insists he wants no part of training me. Yet he has a desk, and a phone here reserved for his own private use.*

But after a moment, he set aside his puzzlement—add it all to the list of his father's idiosyncrasies. Best for him to focus on things he could, eventually, figure out.

#

On his second day at work, Owen was tutored by Mrs. Vogel in office routine. The fifth desk, besides having the telephone no one except his father was to use, had another function. When work was completed, it went on that desk. Once in a while, Mrs. Vogel would leave her office, pick up the completed work, and glance at it. If it was up to snuff, she would take it into her office. If it was not, it would go back for correction to the unlucky person who'd put it on the desk. When complete at last, the work met its end in one of three filing cabinets in the office.

Most days, Owen's coworkers brought a bag lunch. Occasionally, some of them ate at the Hemmet or the Hoito—both were nearby. On special days—birthdays, paydays, holidays—the staff ate at the Prince Arthur Hotel or one of the little, less expensive restaurants on Cumberland Street or Arthur Street. It was not unusual, however, for someone to just use the lunch hour to catch up on work.

When Owen started work, weeks passed between his visits to any of the nearby restaurants. He worked to figure out what everyone did and what his role might be someday. Also, he brought lunch in a paper bag, which he took home at the end of the workday. He made each bag last at least a week—five lunches—and sometimes more.

On an occasional Wednesday or Friday evening, Owen went to the Finn Hall for the music and the dancing. It was a little reward he gave himself for working hard. And for "just because"—a phrase Mrs. Stone, long ago, had told him reminded her of his mother.

It had been at least two decades, now, maybe more, since Mrs. Stone had given him the gift of "just because."

It was several years after his mother had died. The family—his father, May, and himself—had been at church during April, as winter and spring vied for control over the weather. That week, they'd gone to Mrs. Stone's church, and Mrs. Stone had sought them out after the service. Owen had been young—school age, but May wasn't yet in school.

After a few polite nothings, Mrs. Stone had leaned down to Owen. "And what will you do with the rest of this fine day?"

"I hope to take my sled out," Owen said. "If the rain stays away, the snow will be fast. That's when it's the most fun." He laughed, thinking about it.

"So like your mother," Mrs. Stone said. "She knew the value of enjoying the beautiful things in life. 'Just because,' she used to say. And you, young man, have some of her looks, especially about the eyes."

At that point, his father had urged them away, but Owen hadn't forgotten. His mother had liked beautiful things, and he looked like her.

He knew enough never to ask his father about either thing Mrs. Stone had said.

On the Finn Hall evenings that autumn of 1949, Owen always hoped to see Marilyn—she remained his ideal woman, kind as well as pretty. But the thought of seeing her was more a fantasy than any real hope, like perhaps he'd run into Deanna Durbin or one of the nymphs from that Disney movie, *Fantasia.*

Just now, regular life took all his energy. Although he was living in his hometown, he still had much to get used to.

For starters, this house of his was not yet his castle. His father charged him thirty dollars a month rent—a reasonable sum—and

Owen was responsible for the utilities. The house had a coal-fired furnace and a coal bin in the basement. The coal truck came around and dumped coal directly into the bin. But from there, Owen had to shovel the coal into the furnace each day in winter. And he'd never had to consider coal in any form before, shovelled or unshovelled.

Oddly enough, taking on the responsibilities brought great satisfaction. He came to value the contentment of a home he'd warmed himself. The thought of leaving to spend an evening out, even for the joy of a dance, lost some of its allure. Instead, he played LPs on his record player or read.

He also had to figure out what to do about his laundry, after years of first Mrs. Vogel and then his landladies in Kingston handling it all for him. Instead of sending it out, he chose to learn to do it himself. A clothesline stretched across his back yard. A new automatic washing machine sat square and solid in the basement. His hot water tank, however, spat on the basement floor whenever it felt like it. But it didn't spit much.

And slowly, he learned, like Hamlet, when *to be* and when *not to be*. It didn't take long for him to gain skill at finding help for solving problems. He stopped trying to iron and starch (burn and wrinkle) the shirts he wore every day to work. He dropped them off at a laundry near the office, instead, to save them from his despondency and maybe from a fire. He did the same when his suits needed "freshening."

He also recognized that he had much to learn about Port Arthur, and he'd need to find different ways to experience the city. In Kingston, he'd had peers in his classes—ready-made companions, if not exactly friends, with similar interests. As an undergraduate, he'd eagerly sought out lectures and concerts and restaurants. Port Arthur had no university, no college, no debates, and precious few restaurants. But the Lakehead (Port Arthur plus Fort William) had two newspapers apiece, and they seldom agreed with each other about anything. Owen subscribed to them all, and read them.

Eventually, Port Arthur came to feel like a real home.

And with his immersive study, the office routines began to make sense, in a way. Ledgers, journals, accounts payable and receivable, the general journal, chart of accounts, reference numbers—all of these and more became slowly real to Owen. He learned that debits and credits cancel each other out and that it was important to record each transaction in real time. He learned the importance of transferring journal entries to account ledgers regularly and routinely. He mastered the discipline of making an entry in the journal right after making a record in the ledger. And bit by bit he started to like his job.

Slowly, slowly, even the National Multiple-Duty Accounting System began to make sense. His fingers marched north from the typewriter keys up to the function keys and planted a flag.

By December, 1949, Owen had become, in Mrs. Vogel's words, a competent member of the office staff. It no longer mattered who phoned in sick—after three months, Owen could step into that person's job, though not necessarily well.

At last, Mrs. Vogel decided that it was time to begin training Owen to do her own job. If he proved unteachable, she'd have to find someone else. Mr. Millbridge senior would understand.

Mid-December, Mrs. Vogel called Owen into her office. She closed the door, sat down at her chair behind the desk, and had him sit opposite her.

"Your father has asked me to start teaching you the business," she began.

Owen immediately knew that he'd find this conversation intimidating and that he shouldn't interrupt.

Mrs. Vogel eyed him. "Someday—another year or two, maybe—I am going to retire. Your father is of the opinion that you will be able to run the business by then. Not just manage what exists today, mind, but run it for always. I am not so sure a year will be enough. However, I have been wrong before. Are you a fast learner?"

"I ... think so," Owen said, "but surely someone else would be better. Barbara, for example?"

"Barbara is smart; she is personable; she knows what this office requires of the business manager."

"Exactly. Surely she—I don't mind—"

Mrs. Vogel interrupted. "She is the heart of the day-to-day operation of this office and of the business, but to be successful, to *last*, you have to be able to read the future, not just the present. That is what Mr. Millbridge can do, and Barbara cannot. I can, but only a little. Your father is ... prescient. Is that the word? He does things I can't do. He reads the future *accurately*."

Owen nodded.

Mrs. Vogel continued. "Because I know what has been done before and what is happening now, I *try* to see the future—but I'm not particularly good at it. Your father thinks I have foresight, but I really don't. I see only the present and how it came from the past, and when I see something similar happening again, I act on it. But you're different."

"I don't see the future either, Mrs. Vogel," Owen said.

"But you understand history," Mrs. Vogel countered. "That is the same thing. You are your father's son, and you have his gift—some of it, anyway. And *some*, in this crazy world, is good enough. Very well. We will begin in the new year. We will have many conversations about the past, the present, and the future. Be ready."

"I will," Owen said. It was more a hope than a conviction that he could ever be ready, but he meant it.

#

May did not come home for Christmas in 1949, so Owen called her on New Year's Day from his new home.

"Happy 1950!" he chirped. "Busy? Hung over, maybe?"

"Asshole," May said. "Just whisper. You're talking very loud."

"Good thing you've finally got your own phone. It's nice not to have to listen to Mr. Chi trying to make his voice penetrate your living room floor—especially when you're hung over. How's the job?"

"It's Wu now, not Chi anymore—and the job is fine. I spent the whole week switching the bookstore's window display to stacks of new books, interspersed with streamers and champagne bottles. One bottle might have disappeared last night. And yours?"

"Mrs. Vogel's introducing me to tax forms." He didn't mention their conversation about her retirement or that Mrs. Vogel was trying to teach him about the business. Thinking about it intimidated him.

"How exciting. You'll have to introduce them to me sometime. How's Dad?"

"He's, hmm. He's slowing down. Walking's getting harder for him, but he still tries, mostly for the exercise."

"Arthritis? Joints?"

"He runs out of breath. We drove to the cemetery this year."

"You went with him? Did he ask or did you?"

"I did, and I suggested driving his fancy car. We got out at Riverside's parking lot, walked to the grave, stood around for maybe a minute or two, and then walked back to the car. It was relatively warm, too—we hardly needed our hats. But still, he wheezed. I've convinced him to see the doctor as soon as he can get an appointment."

"Think he'll do that?"

"He said, 'Yeah, yeah.' So, no. Maybe in the summer again."

May paused. "Hey, guess who I ran into the other day—Mr. Karialainen!"

"Rough-house?"

"The same. He took me to lunch."

"Ha, imagine you two at a business lunch. I wondered where he'd gone—I never could turn up any news about him. Well, at least he's alive. What's he up to?"

"Furniture business," May said. "He's some kind of wholesaler. His company sells furniture to the big retailers, and they sell it to the public. When I asked him what the job's like, he said he thinks of himself as a fortune-teller. His job is to know what the public is going to want before the public wants it. He said he's mostly in the States trying to figure out what'll become the next big thing in Canada."

"Huh. Sounds like the kind of thing Mrs. Vogel wants me to think about."

"I guess it's par for the course in business. He said he helps retail chains do their staging, which sounded a lot like my display windows, except I guess they put together mock living rooms and bedrooms. He says people will soon have whole rooms for a family to play in. 'Recreation,' he called it. And, of course, he asked about Dad."

"*He* asked *you* about Dad? What did you tell him?"

May paused another beat. "Basically, nothing. I said that Dad's fine. Then, I told him about you and your new job and that you liked working for Mrs. Vogel."

"Good," Owen said. "I always liked Rough-house. Even if he was a little, I don't know—creepy." He felt only slightly disloyal. Rough-house had been good to him, but the unknown parameters of the relationship between Rough-house and his father still made Owen uneasy.

"Only a little creepy." May laughed. She knew there was no real reason to believe the truth of anything Rough-house had told her.

For all she and Owen knew, Rough-house still lived in Port Arthur. He could even live next door to their father, and they'd be none the wiser. She shook off her suspicion. "How's your little doll house?"

"I sure hope you mean my place here on Dufferin. It's not bad. Feels homey. But I'll tell you, after work I try to avoid taking any route home that forces me to walk up the escarpment. Sometimes I just hop on the bus and ride it to the top of the Waverley hill. From there my place is just a couple of flat blocks away."

"Like father, like son," May said.

"I guess. Hey, have you stopped trying to call him at the office?"

"Yes. He's never there. Or at least, he's not supposed to be there, right? Retired, right?"

"God only knows. But listen, this is how it works," Owen said in a conspiratorial tone. "He's told everyone at the office, including me, that no one else is to answer his phone. So the phone rings, no one answers it, but maybe someone tells Dad a few days later that it rang. He asks who it was, and of course they can't tell him, because we've all been told not to answer the phone."

May attempted a laugh. "Ow. My coffee hasn't kicked in yet. But trust me, brother, I'm amused."

"We all are. Also perplexed. Honest to God, it's like working in Alice's Wonderland. It's a system that's designed not to work. And on a completely different matter, remember the box with the boot and the shoe?"

"And the fake family history?"

"We don't know for sure that it's fake," Owen said.

"Okay, let's say it's ambiguous."

"Fair enough. Anyway, the box and the book both went missing for a while, but they're back in the basement again. I haven't the faintest idea why they left or why they're back."

"Dad's a mystery." May slurped coffee. "Think of all the money he makes. Where does it go? He doesn't spend it on himself, as far as I can see and, God knows, he doesn't spend it on you or me. So what does he do with it?"

"He spends a *little* on us," Owen felt compelled to say. "The house I'm renting. Your tuition payments." May said nothing. "But you're right, that's not much, and for the rest, I have no idea. A lot of it—almost all of it—goes into various banks, but I don't know how much, or which ones. Mrs. Vogel probably knows. You think I should ask her?"

"Of course. That's part of the job, now. She'd want you to ask, and so would Dad. After all, that's his retirement we're talking about."

The phone call went on. When Owen had figured that $9 had gone by, he tried to end it. At $12 he succeeded. Gone, he figured, were all his wages for a day and a half—more if he didn't count weekends.

4 • THE BUSINESS OF PROGNOSTICATION

A WEEK LATER, MRS. VOGEL asked Owen to have lunch with her at the Prince Arthur. From this choice of location, Owen knew that whatever their conversations about "the past, present, and future" were to consist of, wherever they were held, they shouldn't be allowed to explode into office gossip.

After the waitress took their order, Mrs. Vogel began speaking, her words as precise as ever.

"Owen, what we do at the office is take care of paperwork. At the basic level, money comes in, we track it for ourselves and for the government, and with the profits, we pay the staff and put money in your father's bank."

She took a sip of water. "That's the visible part of the work. What's invisible—what we really do is this: we find companies, big or small, that are going to be profitable, and we fund them. Some we buy outright; some we buy a share of, but most we just take on as clients. We make it possible for someone with a good idea to turn a dream into a profit—at least in the short term. Before one of those dreams starts to *lose* money, however, we have a system that allows us to analyze it—to see if it can make the grade. If things go sour, we can drop it, sell it, or just chase it away, before the damage gets too bad. Understand?"

"So far, yes. But how do we know for sure they'll fail?"

"We don't. And we don't let go of a company to be mean. Everything we do is to make money and, at the same time, be as merciful as possible. Sometimes, we set things up so that the owner buys us out and does his own damn paperwork if he thinks his business can bloody well survive without us."

Owen smiled. He had never known Mrs. Vogel to use profanity. Not even the day she dropped a dictionary on her foot.

"Other times, we tell the owner that he's on his own. It was nice doing business with him, but…." She paused.

Owen supplied the tactful rejoinder. "But my father can't continue to handle the management of that business."

"Yes. Thankfully, your father—not the office staff—still handles those situations. That's how he uses the phone. He calls the owner in advance and tells him when to call back. It's usually after hours."

"For privacy?"

"Exactly. It lets the other party save face, and it's one way he rewards us. We don't have to make the call or do the explaining. And it is a very small part of his life, now that he's retired."

It made sense. "So besides using the profits to acquire more businesses, what's the plan for the future?"

"That," Mrs. Vogel said, "is something only your father knows, and what he hopes you will learn. Millbridge Enterprises has an accounting firm that looks after taxes and such, and a lawyer who handles leases and, presumably, his will. Your father is the owner, of course, but he's also one of the employees, and as such he draws a salary—bigger than mine, but not by much. And that's all I know."

At Owen's surprised look, she added, "Believe me, it is enough for me to know and coordinate so much."

Absently, she straightened the cutlery on the tablecloth in front of her, then met Owen's eyes. "But it will not be enough for you. You must know more, because you will not have me, and you will someday not have him. Sometime soon, you will need to sit down with your father and really *interrogate* him. You must make yourself the master of his whole situation—and not just the business side. Does he indeed have a will? Who is the executor of his estate? With whom does he make medical decisions? To whom may he owe personal debt, beyond what we know in the business? All those things. I think I know your father well enough to know that he's not going to enjoy that at all. But you still need to do it. Understand?"

Owen nodded. Mrs. Vogel then looked around. "I'm going to miss eating in places like this, but as I said, I need to retire. You think a year or two is a long time, but it is not. And it's time for you to start learning *my* job, so you can learn your father's someday. So. After lunch, there's no need for you to come back to the office. Instead, come into the office tomorrow morning with a list of five possible clients. I'm going to ask you which one you think we should approach with an offer, and I'm going to ask you why. Got it?"

"Yes," Owen said. "Now?"

"No, no," Mrs. Vogel said. "Lunch is not over—we haven't eaten. Never miss an opportunity to eat the food bought for you by a business. This lunch is on me. And now, it's gossip time. So tell me—how *is* May, really?"

#

In the spring of 1950, the Red River devastated Winnipeg after torrential rains. Fifty mile-per-hour winds created waves that broke the dikes, did a hundred million dollars' worth of destruction, and damaged the homes of ten thousand people. The water stayed high for weeks.

"That," Mrs. Vogel told Owen, "was inevitable."

"The flooding?" Owen stood in her office's open doorway, jingling change in his pockets.

"Yes. And what will result from it. Remember, Owen, every investment decision is a bet on what is going to happen sometime in the future. So while one eye should always look forward at the possibilities for investment, the other—*knowing what we know*—should keep looking behind, at the past, just to keep track of what *normally* happens, especially what *bad* things can happen, given enough time."

Later in the day, Barbara, who had overheard this exchange, drew a cartoon of a man standing in neck-deep water. A periscope, pointed backwards, emerged from the top of his head. She left the drawing on Mrs. Vogel's desk. Mrs. Vogel had it framed and hung it on the wall of her office.

In late June, 75,000 North Korean troops attacked South Korea. They breached the 38th parallel and began a drive to Seoul.

Owen read about the attack in the newspapers. When he arrived at work soon after, Mrs. Vogel came out of her office and signaled for Owen to join her. She closed the door behind him and went around to the "business side." It was how they always sat while she taught him about Millbridge Enterprises, unless they left the office.

"Owen," Mrs. Vogel began, "How is Wolf?"

"Wolf? My father's dog? Fine, I suppose. I haven't seen him recently, come to think of it. Why?"

"No reason." Mrs. Vogel said it over-casually. "I have known your father for many many years, but I had not known him to enjoy animal companionship, so Wolf's appearance—two years ago, now?—was an anomaly. And now, Mr. Millbridge buys dog food. And a dog bed."

"Sure. He makes noises about Wolf hunting and sleeping on his own, but he keeps food and a blanket in the kitchen." Owen wasn't sure what she wanted. "And?"

She sighed. "You have an interest in history?"

"Almost a PhD's worth." He frowned. *Now she's asking me questions when she already knows the answers.*

"How do you define history?"

Owen thought for a moment. *What is history?* He decided not to tell her that it was the study of the past. For one thing, she was driving at something else. And for another, history had never been only about the past for him. Instead, he answered, "It's science fiction."

"Oh?" She looked pleased. "In what way?"

"It tells us what we're likely to do in the future." Owen warmed to his analogy. "That's why generals study history, why economists do it. Why merchandizers, even, look to the past to tell them what people *always* want or *always* need, even if some things change." He leaned forward. "My dad thinks that I want to be a history prof—my sister thinks that, too—but I never wanted to lecture in history. I want to live it and work in it."

"I see," Mrs. Vogel said. "So tell me about North Korea. Tell me what North Korea means to us, to the company."

"North Korea?" Owen puzzled for a moment.

"Yes. Did you expect the invasion?"

"Um." Owen said. "No, I didn't. I'm not an expert on Asia; I studied Europe, especially art. The papers—well, I guess …."

Mrs. Vogel let him flounder for a moment longer, then laughed. "No, Owen. You cannot be an expert in everything. You cannot even keep track of everything in the world. It is impossible. Events will always surprise you—big and small, international invasions, local murders. Even an exceptionally hot summer or cold winter. Surprises."

Owen could feel understanding wash over him. "Ah. Anomalies. Wolf was an anomaly, and his presence changed what my father usually buys—but in foreseeable ways. So you think anomalies still hold an element of predictability?"

"Yes. North Korea has invaded the South, and there are opportunities for us—but not in Korea itself. What are they? Take a moment, think about it, then tell me."

"What are they." Owen repeated it slowly. A few second later, he looked up. "Okay. Not in the shipyards or Canada Car—it's unlikely that those businesses will be called on to build war stuff this time."

"War stuff?"

"Planes and ships. Nobody's going to want to change the Korean War into a world war or even just a long war. So, no demand. American medical companies, though—ones that make penicillin and sulfa drugs and whatever other antibiotics they'll figure out—oh, and medical equipment, like sutures and supplies, plus prosthetics. They'll get rich during war. And, uh, 'cheer me up' stuff—clothing, appliances, household goods, furniture, automobiles, etc. They'll pay off in the postwar period. Maybe not immediately. England still has ongoing rations for sugar, even for clothing."

"Yes. And?"

"Assuming South Korea doesn't lose either the war or get bombed to nothingness, people will crave consumer goods—mainly made in the US, mainly advertised on American television. Lumber, west coast lumber companies. The US won't let North Korea win, so South Korea—after the war—will buy all kinds of construction materials, from cement to electrical wiring, because the North might still feel free to bomb the bejeezus out of the South."

He paused. "And ... I'm stuck. No, wait. Baby products—diapers, baby food, blankets, things like that. Every big war ends in babies. Who grow up into children. Bigger families."

Mrs. Vogel smiled. "Very good. Now, what else in Canada? Apart from Korea."

"Television's coming, and fast, and it'll be around forever. We'll see everything American, especially in Southern Ontario, where they can pick up US stations by antenna. So, department stores, shopping centres, everything should look and feel like them. Music, too. Record stores, musical instrument stores, music schools, even printed music books, because every kid wants to be a musician now."

"Change of focus," Mrs. Vogel prompted. "Winnipeg and the floods, as they clean up."

Owen nodded. "We've already seen increases in lumber and

building materials, of course. But also general goods—everything from suitcases and clothing to kitchen appliances. Anything people normally keep tucked away in their basements. We could stock the goods lost and in need of replacing, a place Winnipeg merchants go when they run out. Oh—eventually, house insurance, farm insurance, small construction businesses. Um, camera shops, maybe. You know, take photos and protect your memories in pretty albums on a shelf upstairs, not in the basement. And … I'm getting stuck."

"Not bad," Mrs. Vogel said. "I'm not sure about some of those ideas, but you still have a quick mind. I'm glad to see you haven't stopped thinking as you've aged." She paused momentarily. "I've decided. A year from now, I will retire. You'll be the boss, and I'm not worried. You've come a long way in the last six months. You'll do fine."

"I hope so." Owen paused. Mrs. Vogel could see that he had more to say. "Mrs. Vogel, when television becomes part of everyone's life, the world is going to change. The television networks need to tell a dozen different stories every day, for advertisers, just to keep in business. The stories won't just sell goods, though. They'll change us, women especially, into *consumers*, first of all. They may even create a world in which men and women are more like equals than they are now. Men and women will buy things differently than they do now. Women will buy cars and homes. They may even become doctors and cops."

Mrs. Vogel interrupted. "And business owners."

"Yes! Hairdressers now have women for customers, but someday they may have male customers, too. And they'll own other things. Maybe not tobacco shops, but with women buying anything and everything for the home, maybe department stores."

Mrs. Vogel smiled. "You are more hopeful than I can be about ways working women will find opportunity and be compensated, but optimism is good." She paused. "You know, I asked your father once where he'd learned his business skills. He said it was all in Sun Tzu's *The Art of War.*"

"I've heard of that. Should I read it?"

"Yes. But I trust you to not be ruthless. You've got the same kind of mind as your father. But Mrs. Stone always says you have your mother's heart." She nodded at the door behind him. "And now, back to our regular days."

At his desk, Owen made some notes. His head always spun after conversations with Mrs. Vogel.

After work, he walked to Arthur Street, rode the bus up the hill, and then walked two blocks to his place on Dufferin. He checked his mailbox and found a letter from May. In the kitchen, he opened it.

Dear Owen,

Happy spring! Almost summer now, eh.

I'm concerned about Dad. Yes, again. Or still? He doesn't reply to my letters. Any idea what might be wrong? If anything? Could you check up on him— make sure he's not going goofy?

He hasn't sent pictures in a long time, even weird ones like the clowns from that winter parade. The last letter I got from him was early last fall, just after he bought that house for you. He sent a picture of that. I wrote back, told him there wasn't much room in the driveway for a car, so you'd have to buy a horse. Is there still a horse barn down on Machar Avenue?

Hmm, maybe that's why he hasn't written lately.

Anyway … check on Dad, keep your nose clean, etc. etc.

That's my two cents worth. (No $12 phone call today; I bought a stamp—my treat.)

Love, May

Owen walked the block to his father's house, past the sunken gardens in the park at the top of the hill. He wasn't hungry for supper yet, and though he was lazy about walking up the hill, he enjoyed being outdoors. These long June days, the sun hardly seemed to set. It was what he'd missed most during his years in Kingston—the early sunrises and lingering twilights of a northern summer.

When he knocked, his father opened the door almost immediately.

"I spotted you heading this way," Andrew said. "Problem?" He made no move to invite Owen in.

"No, but May's worried about you. You're not replying to her letters. And you never use the office phone. You said you'd use mine if you needed to."

"But why do I need to?"

Owen waited a beat. "To call your daughter, perhaps?"

"Mmm. In any case, tell Mrs. Vogel she can get rid of the office phone. I don't think I'll need it anymore. I'm pretty busy these days—I don't get down to the office much."

"Dad," Owen said, "you haven't been in the office in months, almost a year. Mrs. Vogel has me making those difficult after-hour phone calls now. And when May writes you, you don't write back. What's the problem?"

At last, Andrew gave up. "Come in."

Owen went up the three front steps and took off his shoes inside the door.

His father, watching, said, "I'm pretty busy, you know. But I spend too much time down in the basement playing the violin, I guess. I like to saw away on that thing after supper."

"Why do you play it in the basement? It's damp down there."

"I don't want to play it upstairs here, because the neighbours might hear it. Or they might walk past the house and sneak a peek through the window. The violin doesn't care where I play it—it just wants to be played. Can I interest you in a cup of coffee? Got fresh-perked in the kitchen."

"Sure."

They sat at the table. After his father had poured the coffee, Owen pointed at the book on the counter behind the kitchen table. "Is that the family history?" he asked.

Andrew turned to look. "That's exactly what it is. I do some writing in it every day or two—whenever I remember something. Sometimes I remember it one way, and sometimes another—so I record both of the 'memories' and when I think I know which one is the right one, I throw the other one out."

"Good system," Owen said. "That's what I told May, in fact."

His father looked at him keenly. "May? She's been asking?"

Owen, aware of some mistake, laughed it off. "Oh, you know, it comes up when we chat. Hey, where's Wolf?"

"In the bedroom. He likes to sleep under the bed during the day. He dreams of being a guard dog, I think. I'll let him out later tonight. He likes to hunt in the dark."

Owen, fairly sure Wolf didn't hunt as much as his father liked to boast about, waited before he next spoke. "Dad, you feeling okay?"

"Sure. Got a bit of a cough. Get tired sometimes when I'm out for a walk. Gotta expect that, I guess—I don't exercise, listen to the radio all the time. And I'm getting older."

"Got an appointment set with Dr. Wainwright yet?"

His father made a noncommittal noise, and Owen dropped it. They were both quiet for a moment, then his father asked, "Do you know that you look a lot like your mother?"

"Mom? Me?"

"May, poor thing, looks more like *me*, but you've got your mother's ... smile and ...." His voice trailed off. "Anyway," he said at last.

Owen rescued him. "How about the fighting in Korea, huh?"

The conversation, now safely impersonal, continued for another half an hour or so, then Owen rose to leave.

"Come over to my house some evening soon. I'll feed you, and we can phone May. Put her mind at ease."

Andrew put an extra touch of Finn into his voice. "Yah, sure, sounds good."

Owen was home by seven. He wondered if his father would ever come by. Maybe he'd have to be more specific, say "Come over tomorrow night." Then he set the thought aside.

"Supper," he said aloud. He got out the bag of potatoes from the lower cupboard. The price tag was still on it. "Jesus, thirty-five cents for a ten-pound bag." A loaf of bread sat on the counter. "Ten cents! For bread! What the hell happened to the Depression?" *Still*, he thought, *Mrs. Vogel's paying me three thousand a year now. The girls are making only half that.* He thought briefly of May and wondered how much she got paid in Toronto. If she worked for him, would he want her to make as much as he did, if she did the same job? Should he do something for his co-workers, get them bigger raises? *Not yet*, he decided. *Maybe when I'm in charge.* At last, something positive about taking that responsibility.

He opened the refrigerator door and took out a tomato and a couple of wieners, then turned on the hot-plate, got out a frying pan, set it on the hot-plate and retrieved a knife to drop butter in the pan and split the wieners. He found mustard in the refrigerator, too.

"Perfect bachelor supper!" *Gotta remember to stop by the People's Co-op tomorrow though—get some lettuce, maybe. Maybe stop talking to myself, too.*

Later that evening, after he had gone to bed, Owen lay awake, thinking about Mrs. Vogel. *There was something she wasn't telling him. Something about his father.* That was as far as he got. He fell asleep.

During the night, Wolf died. Owen's father left a note in Owen's mailbox. At the bottom, he'd added, *And I will see Dr. Wainwright. In September.*

Mid-September, when Owen asked how the appointment had gone, his father merely said, "I went. He said nothing helpful. But I went."

Owen knew to leave it alone for another year.

5 • RETIREMENTS AND COMMENCEMENTS

ON JULY 31ST, 1951, MRS. VOGEL RETIRED with a pension, as planned, and Owen Millbridge became the general manager of Millbridge Enterprises.

Owen had attempted to do what Mrs. Vogel had suggested—pin down more details of the business—and little by little, he'd gained some understanding of his father's holdings, if not his methods. He felt more comfortable that he'd be able at least to assume Mrs. Vogel's role and perhaps even to help the company grow, without making too many mistakes.

On Mrs. Vogel's last day, Owen took her and his coworkers, minus his father, to lunch at the Prince Arthur. They finished with a cake. And Owen had some satisfaction in meeting Mrs. Vogel's eyes when he said, "My treat now," before heading off to pay the tab and leave liberal tips for the manager and staff.

There had, of course, been no such party for his father. No formal leave-taking. Andrew Millbridge had simply stopped coming in and had faded from sight, and possibly from the memories of all but Owen and Mrs. Vogel.

Despite Andrew's direct instruction, neither Mrs. Vogel nor Owen had removed the phone from the office in the intervening year. They didn't even discuss it. Owen knew a phone would be handy, if not required, in a place of business in the future. So he waited. And when Mrs. Vogel retired, he began using the phone at the office to set up appointments. He upgraded the phone lines and hired a receptionist, too, to transfer phone calls to him in the office, and to take messages.

"Like a regular office from the 1930s! Only in the 1950s," May said when Owen told her.

At the beginning of September, Andrew Millbridge paid his annual visit to Dr. Wainwright. The loss of strength and the constant dry cough had not gotten any better. Most days, he felt tired by noon; by suppertime, he was exhausted.

Owen had made the appointment and driven his father the few blocks to the doctor's office, just to make sure he went, but Owen wasn't allowed into the exam room.

Millbridge sat in a chair, not on the examining table, when Dr. Wainwright appeared.

He said gruffly, "Like last year. So, what have I got?"

"Show me your hands," Wainwright said. "Palms down, then palms up."

"Every time I see you, it's the same routine. What's with the hands?"

"You're getting old."

"Older," Millbridge said, "And that's not an answer to the question. It's a deflection. What's with the hands?"

"They tell me about your lungs. You have a cough that isn't getting any better. You get tired easily. But your hands still look normal, and that's good."

"Good because...?"

"Some diseases of the lungs change the look of the hands. It's a way of telling me if what you have is serious—meaning untreatable—or if there are things we can still do for you."

"And?"

"Your hands look like normal hands. So I want you to start exercising more. Go for walks. Get outside—where it's not so stuffy. Hell, unretire yourself if you want. Go back to work. Do what you enjoy doing. I know you don't smoke, so don't take up smoking. And give your lungs a chance to experience even more good air by staying away from places where people *do* smoke. Okay?"

"No pills? No magic tricks?"

"None. You are what you are. You have what you have. I'll know what it is when it gets worse—if it does. For now, get used to it. And if you want a doctor who lies to his patients, go somewhere else."

Millbridge said nothing about the lies he knew Dr. Wainwright had told Owen. "No guesses?"

"Jesus, Millbridge. Do I have to wrap you up in dental floss and throw you out the god-damned window? Get out of here. I've got paying customers that need that chair."

"Damn waste of time," Millbridge muttered as he passed Owen in the waiting room.

"It's not a waste, Dad," Owen protested, following his father to the car. "Now you can tell May you went and it's the truth. We should call her. Come by tonight at 6."

Andrew kept his words short. "No, not tonight. I have something to do."

Owen shook his head, afraid to ask what it might be. He took his father home and returned to work.

Later that day, once Andrew was sure Owen wasn't hanging around to spy on him, he went to the dog pound and picked out a scruffy-looking mixed-breed.

"You," he told the dog as he led him inside, "have a name. It's Wolf, and here's the deal. You get to stay here at night—if that's what you want—but during the day you're on your own. You're responsible for finding your own food. All you get at night from me is water and a place to sleep. Understand? You're not a pet. Pets are for the rich. For a little while, I'll give you something—a dog biscuit or two, maybe, once in a while—but then, you're cut off."

It was a deal that Millbridge once again couldn't make himself enforce. This Wolf became a real pet, although that mostly meant he was fed daily and left to his own devices. He received absolutely no training in social graces. He remained mostly outdoors in summer and indoors in winter. It was all the companionship Millbridge needed.

6 • CHRISTMAS, 1951

DECEMBER 1951 ARRIVED WARM—at or just below freezing—but the warmth was short lived. By the middle of the month the cold arctic winds had brought the temperatures down to ten below zero Fahrenheit, where it stayed for three weeks.

Andrew Millbridge, wary of his lungs, didn't leave his house during the worst of the deep freeze. Owen did the grocery shopping, paid the bills, shoveled the snow, and tried unsuccessfully to convince his father that a telephone at his home was a necessity—not a nuisance. When he asked his father if he would like to see the folks down at the Hoito or at the Hemmet, his father shook his head and said, "I don't go to either place anymore."

Owen and May were now in the habit of calling each other once a week. When May called Owen, the calls were short. When he called her, the two of them could talk for ten minutes or so before Owen began to feel the pinch of his wallet.

Owen paid for May to fly to Port Arthur for Christmas. She arrived late Saturday, three days before the twenty-fifth. Owen picked her up at the airport. They went straight to Owen's house.

"It's small," May said as they pulled into the driveway.

"Yep. Thirty-foot lot," Owen said. "Driveway's about eight feet wide and the house is maybe sixteen feet and a bit—but there's a second storey, as you can see."

"My bedroom?"

"Yes, indeed. At the back of the house is the kitchen and a set of stairs that takes you up to the second floor. The ceiling's pretty low up there—except in the center—so you've got to watch your noggin. The room's drafty, too, but I bought a comforter for the bed."

"Is that my Christmas present?"

"Damn. I didn't think of that."

They got out of the car. "It's about eight below now. The snow's from this past Wednesday. We got maybe four inches. Not too hard to shovel." Owen fetched May's suitcase from the trunk, then climbed the front steps and unlocked the door.

May followed him into the house. "It's cold in here."

"There's not much insulation, and what there is, is just wood chips. The heat is from a coal furnace. Most days when I leave for the office I let the fire die down, then put more coal in when I get home. This week, though, I'm going to let *you* feed the furnace in the afternoon. You'll have as much warmth as you can stand up here. And, I picked up an electric heater for you. You just plug it in and instantly you're in Florida, with the warm sun shining directly onto your feet."

"You're such a gentleman," May said. "Do I get my own special coal shovel since I'm *not* in Florida, or do I have to use your dirty one?"

"I'm afraid there's just the one."

"And if I go over to Dad's place, instead?"

"His place has oil heat. No shoveling. And you're perfectly free to stay there. I've talked to him about that. He's got another new dog, as of the autumn. Did I tell you that?"

"No. Is it stuffed?"

"No, it's real. Name's Wolf."

"Of course," May said. "I wonder why Dad always names them Wolf. Anyway, thanks for the welcome. I think I'll just visit Dad for a few hours, then come back here, if you don't mind. He's...." She didn't quite know how to end the sentence.

"Gloomy? At loose ends? Lost? Yes, he is," Owen said. "I want to talk to you about that. But not now, and not at Dad's place. He's got a cleaning lady now, you know. Comes in a time or two a month, to stay ahead of the dust."

"Has it helped?"

Owen hesitated. "The house *seems* cleaner. Nothing's growing on the baseboards. But I think she spends minimal times in the bedrooms, and I know she stays out of the basement."

May merely nodded, content to see the rest for herself.

#

The talk resumed the next evening, after Owen had stoked the furnace. "So, about Dad," Owen began. "What do you think?"

"I think he's pretending," May said. "I think he's deliberately trying to look needy, or helpless, or maybe a little confused. But I don't believe he's any of those things."

"He does have lung trouble," Owen said. "That's genuine."

"Yes, the lung problems are real. But his sadness? C'mon, Dad's never really needed anything or anyone—not even us. Except, maybe, Mom. But it feels like he's pretending. His imitation of loneliness looks so odd—fake, like that 'family history' he works on. Remember when I read part of it at Christmas a couple of years ago?"

"Yes." Owen had never felt the slightest curiosity to look at it himself.

"When I got home, I started thinking about it. And if I'm remembering things correctly, and I might not be, I think he knew that I'd looked at it. I think he had marked the box somehow, and if it wasn't exactly how he'd left it on the shelf, he'd know."

"That's crazy."

"I hope so, but I don't think so."

"Well, it's been moved all over lately. Every time I stop in over there, he's deep in it. For sure, his lungs are shot. And you're right about the needy bit. He appears needy, but I don't know what he *really* needs. I think he loves us, but he doesn't really *see* us. It's like he tries to look through us because something of Mom isn't dead since we're alive. And...." Owen paused. He did not know how to complete the thought. "I think he wants to be able to look at us and see her," he said at last. "But he can't. Mom's gone, and we're the constant reminder of that. We're her remains."

May shuddered. "Remains." Then she took a deep breath. "Hey, it's Christmas. Let's talk about something else. Maybe more cheerful? How's business?"

"Better. I hardly ever get lost in spreadsheets anymore. I may know something about what I'm doing, even."

"Been on any dates?"

Owen reddened. "Nope. Still no idea what I'm doing there."

They laughed.

#

They did the now-usual Christmas things, with some concessions.

After opening token gifts, they drove to the graveyard for a brief visit. This year, they were alone in the biting cold.

Then they had Christmas dinner with Mrs. Vogel—at the Prince Arthur Hotel.

May surveyed her heaped plate and turned to Mrs. Vogel. "I'm glad you're spared the work of making dinner," she said, "and nobody has to pretend that any of us knows how to cook."

"Hey, I'm a whiz with anything you can fry," Owen said.

Millbridge laughed, which turned into a cough. He waved away their concern.

With tact, Mrs. Vogel asked May about Toronto, and the moment passed.

In the new year, May went back to Toronto, where she felt at home. Owen went back to the office with its routines and its surprises.

Andrew Millbridge went back to creating his genealogy, adding a page or two each day to the increasingly implausible story, and slipping a tiny piece of paper underneath the back of the box so that he could instantly tell if someone had moved it.

The lies and the tell-tale trap made him feel...he didn't quite know. *Good* was not the right word—a little bit *human*, perhaps, or *creative*.

More like the boy who had created the scene in the stable after killing his father.

The boy who had spared both the violin and the dog.

7 • TV DINNERS

For all three of the Millbridges, each day blended seamlessly into all the others. 1952 became 1953, and all that really seemed to change was the weather. Even that was, in the long run, governed by a stuttering repetition of similar days and weeks and months like those that had come in the years before.

Occasionally, Millbridge noticed Rabbit walking in the neighbourhood. He'd make a note. On one July evening, driving past the cemetery after one of his aimless tours of the countryside, he stopped in. From the parking lot, he could see the row of military headstones beyond Annie's stone. As it happened, a woman and young boy stood in front of one. *Mantere's dead son,* he thought. *That's the son's wife, with Mantere's grandson. He's growing up.*

Instead of visiting Annie's grave, he drove home.

For Owen and May, the Christmas visit had become a Christmas tradition just as, for Andrew Millbridge, the yearly visit to the doctor had become just another event in his life—one that helped him keep track of the seasons. The only real change was that the entries into the black and white notebook suddenly caught up to the present, and then died.

On Christmas Day, 1953, before Owen and May showed up with their presents, Millbridge put the notebook into the cardboard box in the basement and slipped the tell-tale scrap of paper underneath the box's rear left corner.

Finished, he told himself. *Requiescat in pace.*

He was tired of it, anyway. He was tired of everything—tired of the truth, tired of the lies, tired of feeling tired all the time.

As he slowly climbed the stairs, he glanced at his hand on the railing. It didn't look right somehow—didn't look familiar—but he could not pin down what was wrong with it. It felt the same as always.

No one tried to see what was in the basement box that year.

#

In early February of 1954, at Owen's insistence, Andrew Millbridge paid a winter visit to Dr. Wainwright.

"Take those gloves off, and get your ass on the table," Doctor Wainwright said. "You know the routine."

Millbridge sat on the table and laid his gloves beside him.

"Tired?" the doctor asked.

Millbridge shrugged. "All the time, but no more than usual. Damn tired of your damn sense of humour, though."

"Hands. Palms up, then turn them over." Millbridge did as he was told, and Wainwright grasped one. "How long have they been like this? Rounded fingertips. Your nails are, too."

A shrug. "Cold weather."

"No, not cold weather. Your son made this appointment for you because you're worse. When did you first notice your fingers?"

"Just before Christmas, maybe." Millbridge said. "May was home."

"That must have been nice. Get yourself out of that sweater and shirt." Wainwright placed his stethoscope on Millbridge's chest. "How's your endurance these days, really."

"A little worse," Millbridge admitted.

"Do you still go for walks?"

"Not so much. I feel chilly all the time, even with the heat turned up in the house."

"Coughing?"

"When I'm outside, mostly. Cold air. Feels dry, makes me cough, makes my throat feel raw."

"Take a deep, deep breath—deep as you can make it, then exhale slowly."

Millbridge inhaled, exhaled, and began coughing.

"Well." Wainwright paused to find the right words. "I'm afraid I've got bad news. You've got something we call idiopathic pulmonary fibrosis—IPF."

"Going to make me take penicillin? I don't like pills."

"No." He paused again. "Andrew, there's no cure for this. We don't even know what causes it. The lungs become scarred, they get stiff, and suddenly it's hard to breathe—all the time."

"Fingers?" Millbridge asked.

"It's how the body reacts to a long-term lack of oxygen. We don't know why. They get round. Fingernails, too. And it's fatal."

"Ah. So how long have I got?" The words were matter-of-fact. Emotionless. Controlled.

"Hard to say. Every person's different. From start to finish for IPF, five years or so. For you, now—maybe a couple of years. An x-ray would tell us more."

Millbridge waved off the x-ray. "What about drugs?"

"No drugs. Nothing seems to work for this. Maybe in a few years there will be something, but there's nothing now."

"Shit," Millbridge said.

"Yeah. Who takes care of your house? Keeping it clean, I mean."

"I have a cleaning lady. She comes in maybe once a week."

"Good. As this disease progresses, it's going to get to the point where it severely limits what you're able to do. Right now, you're probably able to do most things, but in a while you're going to need more help. With cooking, even." He paused. "And, Andrew," he said sympathetically, "you need to put your affairs in order."

Millbridge parodied the doctor's softened voice. "And you, you need to...." He stopped himself. *No anger, no accusations*, he thought. *Let it be. What is, is. Mitä tulee, tulee.*

"Sorry," he said.

Wainwright shook his head. "I know it isn't easy to hear. You should do it, though, if you haven't already. A will, at the very least. You've got a lot of business interests. It's a favour to your kids. You should tell them, too."

"Yes, okay," said Millbridge. But it wasn't his business or his children he was thinking of.

You're a dead man, Myllysilta told him. *It's not all bad, though. You're free to do whatever you want now.* Myllysilta began to laugh at him. Andrew Millbridge let nothing show.

#

Leaving Dr. Wainwright's, Andrew drove downtown to the Woolworth's where, years before, he'd bought the black and white notebook. This time, he bought a binder made of cardboard covered in cloth. Inside it, a steel spine held three rings for the binder paper, and at each end of the spine was a lever for opening the rings. It was not much like his old notebook, but times had changed, and it would suffice.

It might even be better, in some ways. *I can write in whatever order the events come to me, and then just slip the page into the binder in the right spot*, Antti thought.

When he got back home, he put the binder and the package of three-ring lined paper on the kitchen table. He got out the violin and played a few melodies from his standard repertoire, some he recalled dimly from Finland, a few he'd learned in Canada. He hated the look of his fingers on the violin's neck. He hated the fact that this violin's bridge needed to be placed high up the instrument's body, past the point where the scrolled f-holes marked the appropriate place. He wanted the violin to be perfect—not deformed.

"What is, is," he heard, this time in his father's voice. It had been a rare quiet moment after his mother's death, perhaps after a meal. His father had been rosining the bow while Antti looked carefully, without touching it, at how the violin was put together. He'd found a drawing of a violin in a book at school that looked quite different. More symmetrical, flowing. More cohesive. And with the bridge in a slightly different spot.

Antti hadn't had to risk asking about the odd shape and configuration. His father noticed him looking and picked up the violin, nestling it snugly under his stubbled chin. With a flourish, he played a few notes.

Then he looked at Antti, his eyes hard. "This is the way this violin *is*, this is how it does what it *does*. We don't choose. *It* chooses *us*."

Now that Andrew thought about it, he wasn't sure about the memory. He remembered his mother saying, *Mitä tulee, tulee*. But he also remembered it in a male voice. Maybe he'd made up the story about his father—it could, he supposed, have been Bertil Granbakken, or even someone else. A writer, in a book? Lennart Wikström?

The Bible, jeered Myllysilta.

Antti shrugged. He played a few bars of that sentimental Scandinavian favourite, "Hälsa Dem Därhemma," but once again found it too saccharine. Tired of music, he put away the violin.

He sat down and took out his pen. Myllysilta stood behind him, looking over his shoulder. *My earliest memory*, Antti wrote, *is of the night my father murdered my mother*. He chose to write the words in English, not Finnish, not Swedish.

"Yes?" Myllysilta asked. "What was that night like? What do you remember? Tell us. Tell us everything."

Antti wrote slowly, willing his fingers to make the letters smoothly, asking his mind to remember things as they were, not as they might have been. When he was finished with the events of that first memory, he put the cap back on the pen and set it aside. Then he closed the binder and took it to the family room.

The longest wall in the room consisted of built-in bookshelves, most lined with books. Some were books that he had actually read. Most were not—they were for show, purchased at estate sales and auctions for their leather bindings. They looked impressive on the shelves.

But you never have guests, Myllysilta would say. *So who's going to look at them?*

"I will," Millbridge had answered, again and again. *I will.*

Interspersed among the books were small sculptures—an eclectic mix of faux Greco-Roman and Victorian pieces from the previous owner, decades before. There were also chintzware pieces—little bowls and pots and pottery candleholders decorated in various faux Romantic and Victorian styles. They were, like tiny watchdogs, things that would keep a nosey guest from snatching a book from a shelf.

On an adjacent wall hung the framed document commemorating the dead soldier, which had been with the Millbridges for decades now—since the house on Machar Avenue. "Our soldier," May called him. Andrew wondered if she even noticed the document anymore when she came home. It had long been a family artifact, and a witness. Now, it could be a guardian of memories.

Andrew reached up and took down a substantial Finnish book, *Suomalaisen Kulttuurin Historia*. Each page was both longer and wider than a standard sheet of paper. *This will do*, he thought. He put the book down on the couch.

"Straight-edge," he said to himself. From the bathroom, he retrieved his old razor, its blade folded safely into the handle. Then from the kitchen he fetched a wooden ruler—one of those with a steel edge for drawing perfect lines.

He sat down on the couch with the open book on his lap. The first twenty pages or so were on the left, the rest on the right. Placing the ruler along the fold, he carefully made a cut on the right-hand page. The cut began an inch from the top and went down the side, ending exactly an inch from the bottom of the page. Three cuts later, he lifted out a rectangle, leaving a one-inch margin. The hole was just slightly larger than a piece of the binder paper that fit his three-ring binder. He cut three more sheets, creating a well deep enough to hold a few sheets of paper.

Perfect, he thought. *I have a hobby, it seems.* Four cuts each on four pages at a time, he would build a box—a well, really—inside this book to hold his life story, his true history. The first twenty pages, and the edges, would maintain the illusion that this was an ordinary, encyclopedia-type book.

Millbridge looked at his watch. He could expect Owen to stop by in about a half-hour—oh-so-casually, of course, but really to check on the doctor's appointment. Millbridge returned the razor to the bathroom and the ruler to the kitchen, and then threw the scrap paper into the kitchen garbage can.

He sat on the couch again. *It will take a while*, he thought, *but the story will be safe. And I'll be able to see it from here.* He patted the book, still on the couch beside him. Into it he put the first page of his true history.

He put the book onto the second shelf from the top, and then hid the binder under his bed.

Fifteen minutes later, Millbridge sat at the kitchen table with a cup of coffee when Owen came in the back door with a grocery bag.

Wolf greeted him. "Hi, Wolf." Owen set the bag on the kitchen counter carefully, so it wouldn't tip over. Wolf, disappointed, went back to his bed. Andrew raised his coffee mug in greeting.

"And how did your doctor's appointment go?" Owen asked his father.

"Pretty good. Apparently I've got something called 'getting older.' It's almost as common as the common cold."

"Nothing about how much exercise you should be getting?"

"No, he left all that up to me."

"Foods you should eat? Things you should avoid?"

"Nope. Just the usual bit about not smoking."

"Good." Owen reached into the grocery bag and pulled out two boxes. "Ta da! It's a TV dinner."

"I don't have a TV. And since when do TVs need to be fed? Do they snarl and bark if you don't feed them, or does a commercial just come on?"

"Ha, ha," Owen said. "Bad joke, but it doesn't matter—because I'm a good son. Supper will be served exactly twenty-five minutes after I get these things into the oven."

He took the dinners out of their cardboard boxes and set them on the counter, then consulted a box briefly and turned the oven to 425 degrees.

"What the hell's *in* that?" Andrew asked, pointing to the foil-wrapped squares.

"Turkey, stuffing—cornbread, I think—sweet potatoes, gravy, and, let me see—buttered peas. It's a frozen dinner." He picked up the carton and read again. "Okay. I leave the foil on when I put it in the oven, until near the end. You haven't seen these? Apparently people eat these things when they watch TV. Some of them even buy what they call TV tables so they can eat in the living room."

"Not in the kitchen or a real dining room? That's barbaric. How much do they cost?"

"These were $1.29 each."

"Each? Is that what they mean by 'Put your money where your mouth is?'"

Owen laughed. "Oh, that reminds me. May wants to book off holiday time for a summer visit, sometime around the end of June. She didn't tell me the exact dates yet."

"Busy girl," his father said.

"She's the one who told me about TV dinners. Which reminds me, you're getting low on bread for those endless sandwiches you eat. Better put the bread card in the window for the bread man. Get two...no, three loaves, white, sliced. Okay? Last time you forgot to ask for sliced. And don't forget to keep the back door unlocked. The bread man doesn't like to have to knock."

They ate the TV dinners at the kitchen table.

"Interesting, I suppose," said Owen. "Could use something more."

"Bread. You can't have too much bread at a meal. Still, this beats any other turkey dinner you've brought me lately."

He'd eaten it all, Owen noticed. Maybe only because of its novelty, but maybe it wouldn't hurt to bring them again sometime. Maybe soon.

After Owen left, Andrew got a piece of paper and his pen. *Sliced, three, white*, he wrote. In the back porch, he checked that the door was unlocked, and put the note on the floor where the bread man would find it. He weighted it down with coins.

All the while, he was looking forward to tomorrow, when he could make his box a little deeper and add more pages to his true history.

8 • SUOMALAISEN KULTTUURIN HISTORIA

February, 1954, turned into March and March into April. Most mornings, Andrew Millbridge sat at the kitchen table and wrote, sparing nothing. The war, his business arrangement with Bertil Granbakken, the voyage to Canada, Annie, the children, Annie's death—all of these went into the binder and were locked into place in chronological order. The crimes, the murders, the business arrangements with Rough-house—he left out nothing, censored nothing in the Book.

In the living-room-cum-library, the Suomalaisen Kulttuurin Historia grew no larger and no heavier in its transformation into The Book. From a celebration of life, it morphed into a coffin. The photos of Finland's churches and cathedrals, its lakes and forests, its statues and statesmen—all of them ended up in the kitchen garbage can and left the house. Always, the Suomalaisen Kulttuurin Historia, filled with more and more of Andrew's past, went back on its shelf. The binder went under his bed, the straightedge to the bathroom, the ruler to the kitchen.

By the middle of April, Andrew Millbridge had finished his autobiography. Had anyone asked him why he had written it, he could not have given them an answer, *any* answer—even a fabrication.

The day he finished, he put The Book on its shelf, same as always. He felt no need to read it or check it for errors. He had done it, finished it. There was nothing else to write. It was for no one other than himself.

For me, Myllysilta whispered.

At the end of April, May phoned Owen.

"Hello, brother. This is your call reminding you that you'll see me soon."

Owen kept his voice unalarmed. "Soon, as in another month or two."

"Soon, June," she replied cheerfully. "I have to be back at work on the fifth of July, so I'll come June 26th and leave on July 3rd. Can you remember all that? Write it on your kitchen calendar."

Owen rolled his eyes but did as she suggested and then walked over to tell their father. He took along a few new TV dinners to replace the ones he'd previously stashed in his father's freezer.

As promised, May arrived on Saturday, June 26th. Owen picked her up at the airport.

"So," Owen said. "My place first, or Dad's?"

"Yours. Dad's place still gives me the creeps. His cleaning lady never seems to dust, and the house always has that musty smell."

"It does?"

"Eau de socks—the smell from hell. A man-nose can't detect it. It's just another way that Mother Nature demonstrates female superiority."

#

Upstairs, in the attic bedroom at Owen's house, May began unpacking almost as soon as she walked in the door. She noticed that Owen had done some vacuuming. He'd also replaced the old rusting clothes hangers with new ones, bought a new comforter and linens, and added a night table and lamp to the bedroom furnishings.

"It's nice up here," May called down from the bedroom. "Did you give yourself a raise or something?"

"Bonus ... for riding the bus less and walking up the Dufferin hill more."

"So you're an athlete now?"

"I must be. My eyes run, and I'm a good cardboard boxer." May's groan from upstairs was all the applause he needed.

May came down, and Owen, sitting at the small kitchen table, pulled out a chair for her.

May sat. "Speaking of Dad, how is he?"

Owen thought for a second or two. "Preoccupied. Something's on his mind, but you know Dad. He's keeping it all to himself."

"And the family history?"

"Finished, I guess. I don't think he works on it anymore. It's gone, now, from the kitchen counter. I'm not a bona fide sleuth like you, but I've checked the box in the basement a time or two, and nothing seems to have changed in many months."

"Wait—you've read it? Recently?"

"Yeah. Dad said I could, so I did. It was a while ago, maybe March? The maybe-this-happened, maybe-that-happened stuff isn't there. No more this or that, no more multiple possibilities. The book's in the basement still, in the box on top of that other one, with the boot and the shoe. I was down there last week for something, and the box is just gathering dust."

"You don't think it's odd that he said it was okay for you to go through it?

Owen sighed. "It's been a strange few years, entering into the business and taking over. We've had a lot of discussions that weren't easy. So this was just more of the same."

"And what *do* you think?"

"About the history or about Dad?"

"Both."

"Well, Dad's changed. Even since you were here at Christmas. He's less sure of things than he used to be. He forgets stuff from time to time. I think he didn't so much edit the family history as flip a coin to decide what could stay in, and what should be tossed out."

"What about us? Are we in there?"

"Yes, and it all seemed accurate," Owen said. "But odd."

"Odd? Isn't it good that it's accurate?"

"Yes, but it's more than that. It's as if he's saying—no, *suggesting* —that since all the stuff about *us* is true, the stuff about *him* must be true as well."

"You think it's not?"

"I don't know. Frankly, I don't think the truth of what he's written is something we can pursue. I don't know how we might do it, or why."

"You could be right." *But you might be wrong*, May's eyes said.

For a minute or two, neither of them spoke, then May asked, "Any plans for the rest of the day?"

"No, but on Monday I'm taking Dad to the office for an early Dominion Day celebration. I ordered cake. All the office people will be there, and Mrs. Vogel said she'll come, too. You want to come?"

"Thanks, but no. I think I'll just hang around here or maybe at Dad's. An office is an office is an office."

#

On Monday at noon, May walked over to her father's house. The plan was that Owen would show up around one o'clock, after she and her father had eaten lunch, and Andrew and Owen would drive to the office. May would stay behind.

The lunch was uneventful. May had brought a jar of pickles and spread mayonnaise on her sandwich, while her father ate his dry. May opened the kitchen windows to let air in. She laughed at her father's jokes and mimicked one of her co-workers to amuse him. Owen arrived while she was washing their few dishes.

After the car disappeared on its way to the office, May went into the living room with its wall-to-wall bookshelves, and sat down on the chesterfield. She'd spent many high school afternoons nestled there with a book or magazine. Her plan was to fall asleep, but before she did, she took a moment to look over the wall of books. There were the usual encyclopaedias and classical literature offerings, atlases, histories—lots of books with leather covers. All of the shelves, all of the books, were dusty.

Except one. She got up from the chesterfield and walked over.

Almost out of reach, the large tome on the second shelf from the top made her curious. Even up close, she couldn't tell what the title was, and she couldn't reach it. She stood on a chair from the kitchen to see the title better—*Suomalaisen Kulttuurin Historia. Finnish*...cultural history? No dust on it. Probably one of her father's favourite books.

She reached up and took down the volume. Her father wouldn't mind if she looked through it. She didn't read Finnish, of course, but a cultural history should have pictures.

She sat on the chesterfield, the book in her lap. She looked at the first few pages—some drawings, dim photos of old paintings, some maps. She kept turning pages.

#

Owen and his father arrived back at the house an hour and a half after they had left it.

"Where's May?" Andrew asked.

"Probably back at my place," Owen said. "Napping. I'll go wake her up."

"Remember," his father said, "TV dinner tonight."

"I'm bringing buns, from Kivela's bakers," Owen answered. It had become their routine.

When Owen went into his house, however, May was not there. A note on the kitchen table said, "Emergency at work. Catching afternoon flight to T.O. May." After he had read the note, Owen walked back to his father's house.

"A work emergency," Andrew repeated. "Well, I really wish she could have spent more time here. Perhaps later this summer, she can come back to stay her week."

After supper and Owen had gone home, Andrew went back into the living room.

Acting on a hunch, he took the *Suomalaisen Kulttuurin Historia* off the shelf and opened it.

Everything he'd written—all of the pages in the coffin—were gone.

#

It was nearly midnight when Owen's phone rang. As soon as he picked up, the voice on the line said, "Owen, it's May. Don't talk—just listen."

"Okay."

"I need to disappear for a while. I know this sounds crazy, but it's not. I—I have to take care of some business here. I can't stay at my apartment anymore. I have to move, and I can't tell you where I'm moving. I'll give you a call once I'm settled in at the new place—wherever that happens to be. Don't tell Dad anything—that anything's amiss, okay?"

"Okay, but are you in trouble? I could help, you know."

"No. I can take care of this. Just don't—don't say *anything* about this to Dad. Don't even tell him that I called you. Promise me. This is really, *really* important."

"I won't say anything to Dad," Owen said. "I promise."

"If you feel you *must* say something, *invent* something. Don't even give him my phone number. I'm going to have it changed anyway, but don't."

"May, now I'm worried. What's this about?"

"I can't tell you. I'll call you when I'm settled in at the new place.

And Owen?"

"Yes?"

"I'll be okay. I just—" She stopped talking so suddenly that Owen thought she had dropped the phone.

He started, "Good, but—"

She talked over him. "Bye, Owen."

The click of the receiver was followed by the phone's hum. Owen hung up.

"What the hell just happened?" he asked, but the house had no answer. It was not the first time May had left him as perplexed about her as he usually was about his father.

#

Andrew Millbridge sat on the couch in the living room. The *Suomalaisen Kulttuurin Historia* was back on the shelf. Empty.

Now what? Millbridge thought.

She knows. But will she tell Owen? She'll tell him something, but what? And who else might she tell?

Suppose I replace my copy of the book with a copy that hasn't been turned into a box?

Myllysilta snickered. *Doesn't solve a thing,* he said. *May would still have your notes, your "history." And Owen knows your handwriting. You wouldn't be able to pass the work off as being someone else's if she decided to show it to him.*

Millbridge considered the problem. *But I can't send someone to Toronto to kill her. Look, I've done a lot of things, but that I can't do. And even if I could—if I could stand it, my own daughter! It would be far too risky. It would be like giving someone permission to blackmail me for every penny I have.*

Myllysilta laughed. *First of all,* he said, *you don't have many actual pennies. What you've got is a whole tangle of things—properties, stocks, bonds, promissory notes—that would have to be turned into cash before you could "pay" your mythical assassin anything at all. And no right-thinking assassin would ever take you up on that kind of an offer.*

And second, even if you did that, what would it mean? You'd have bought yourself a few months. Of what? This life?

The next morning, Andrew Millbridge watched Owen leave for work. Then he slowly walked over to Owen's house. He let himself in the back door with his key and sat down at the kitchen table to recuperate. The house felt empty. *Owen needs a dog,* he thought.

Then, he placed a call to Toronto. Rough-house answered.

"I've got a job for you," Millbridge said.

"Hello and how are you, too, boss?"

"Fine. You still got that house thief working for you?"

Rough-house laughed. "Yeah. Don't you still have men working for you up there?" A pause. "Oh, you need a burglar down *here*, do you? Are you sure?"

"Positive."

"Give me the address and tell me what's to go missing," Rough-house said. "The usual fee."

"Deal. But listen. Don't phone when the job is completed."

"How could I? I've heard there's a regular phone in the office, like all the other offices. No separate phone for your use only. And there sure as hell isn't one in your house."

Andrew wondered how he'd heard, but let it go. "Well, don't call Owen, either. Write me a letter—something vague. The item is a packet of notes in my handwriting. Send it to me by registered mail, parcel post. First page says 'History' at the top."

"And where will he find this item?"

Myllysilta gave him May's address.

#

A week later, a letter arrived from Rough-house. He apologized for not being able to send the requested item(s). The addressee had moved out on the day that Millbridge had called, and she'd left no forwarding address. Her apartment was currently empty. Her previous employer said she'd quit without notice and hadn't mentioned a new position. Rough-house's man had checked the outside garbage cans—nothing but food scraps and related trash.

Millbridge burned the letter and took stock of his position. Owen, if he knew anything about the history, wouldn't be able to keep secrets from him. He might even ask. And Millbridge could obfuscate. To Owen, managing today's issues was more important than any family history. But he still needed to find May—to explain, to soothe, to ... placate, he supposed. *Now what?*

Nothing, Myllysilta told him. *Absolutely nothing.*

But Millbridge wasn't made to do *absolutely nothing.* Because he knew that Owen's mailman delivered the mail sometime after noon, he began watching Owen's house. When the mailman dropped off something, Millbridge checked it. If anything looked as if it *could* be from May—an envelope without a return address, for instance—he took it to his house. There, he'd shine a strong flashlight from behind the envelope to get a better idea of the contents. If all seemed well, and it always did, he'd return it to Owen's mailbox.

He did this for the rest of the summer before abandoning it. May, obviously, no longer corresponded with Owen by mail.

And if she still talked to him by phone…well, a phone call wasn't something that Millbridge could intercept. Of course, he could hire someone to build a gizmo that would let him do that, but May wasn't stupid. She likely had considered that, so she wouldn't phone.

Once or twice, as the summer passed, he even attempted to get information from Owen, as casually as he could.

"Heard from May lately?"

Owen frowned. "No, in fact. She must be really busy with that work emergency."

His father snorted. "Do you even know where she's working these days?" He'd long ago stopped asking about university studies, degrees, or graduation.

"Well," Owen said. "Not really. There was a bookstore, and a hardware store for a while. But I think she was applying at a department store, to do something. Window displays? Inventory?"

Andrew shook his head. "And people think *I* don't listen." He was careful to let Owen think he was teasing.

Owen, who wondered about May every day, only said, "Let's go to that drive-in for some ice cream before they close for the season."

PART IV

TRIAL

"Madness in great ones must not unwatched go."

King Claudius, *Hamlet*, Act III, Scene i
William Shakespeare

1 • DANCING

AFTER SHE LEFT PORT ARTHUR in July of 1954, May disappeared from her previous life in Toronto as well. After her first call to Owen, she phoned only once more, on Owen's birthday in September, to give him another new phone number.

"Listen, brother," she said softly—as if someone, even at that moment, might be listening to their conversation—"I'm serious. Write down my number, but not in a place anyone would think to look for it. Not in your wallet. Not near the phone. Not in your nightstand drawer. And above all, do *not* give it to Dad. Don't give it to anyone, not Mrs. Vogel, even. And especially, *especially* not to Dad."

Owen sighed. "I heard you the first time. He's still sick, by the way, but no worse, I think." Owen didn't say *Dad misses you.* He couldn't say it—not truthfully—even though he suspected that his father *wanted* to miss her.

He tried to sound rational, to cancel out her fear. "Come on, May, why all this secrecy?"

Weariness etched her voice. "Just trust me. As I am trusting you. Where will you leave my phone number?"

"Taped to the bottom of my underwear drawer."

She laughed briefly. "Good, no one will want to look there." She paused. "Promise me, brother."

"I promise, I promise. But where do you live? What are you doing for work? Are you okay?"

"I'm fine, and beyond that, it's best you don't know. I have to go."

"What if I come to Toronto for Thanksgiving, or even Christmas? Can I at least see you?"

"Absolutely not. You might be followed."

And that had been that. Owen had tried calling the number about once a month since, and more often as Christmas neared, but no one ever answered.

Owen was not a religious man and did not pray, but on Christmas Eve, he went for an evening walk and found himself sitting in the back pew of Trinity United Church. The service, with Bible readings and carols, gave him comfort.

Other people believe in something, he thought. And he allowed himself to hope for a better year for May, and his father, and himself.

Christmas Day followed the usual pattern: breakfast at his father's house, a drive to the cemetery with him, and dinner at the Prince Arthur. Only two of them this year. Mrs. Vogel had claimed another commitment when Owen had asked her, but he wondered if she simply found it awkward to be with them, without May as leaven and entertainment.

Owen spent New Year's Eve at the lookout in the park across the street from his house, watching the fireworks being set off at the Exhibition Grounds a couple of miles away. He was alone, and it was cold, but not bitterly so. He thought of May, wondering idly how she was and how she might be celebrating the coming of the new year. After about half an hour, he walked the few hundred feet back to his house and went to bed.

The next morning, he moped. His life was busy—he enjoyed his work, and sometimes even felt competent—but he was lonely.

He knew what May would say: "And?"

"Okay, okay," he said aloud. *I'll make an effort to go to dances. Maybe,* he thought, *even ask out someone nice. Someone who might not care how weird this family is.*

There *had* been someone he'd liked, long ago—years, now. Owen pondered for a moment, but no specific memory of her arose. The past years were overlaid with layers upon layers of business opportunities, customers, tangled bank accounts, business relationships, and worries about his father—and now, May.

So, he decided that 1955 would be different. Not looking for anyone in particular, Owen went to dances every other week or so and chatted with the women he met. He recognized some of the men from their jobs at insurance companies, hardware stores, high school—even those who worked as clerks or officers at the police station. He learned to talk about cars and movies. He liked everyone well enough—he even took a few of the women out on dinner dates, but only once or twice. Any lingering sense that he'd someday meet an *ideal* woman dissipated. He felt—just a little, though—that he was becoming part of a community. He became more comfortable being the guy from Millbridge Enterprises.

In due course, spring arrived.

On Easter Sunday, April 10th, spring announced its plans for the summer in Northwestern Ontario: just a brief a month and a half more, and the trees would burst into leaf and summer would be allowed to approach. *Be patient*, spring said.

Though it was cool on Easter morning, Owen decided to see what the interior of Immanuel Lutheran Church was like. The church was, after all, only a few blocks from home—and downhill, at that. His father turned down the invitation to come along.

Owen couldn't remember if Immanuel Lutheran had been part of the merry-go-round of churches that the family had attended, decades before. And because Owen, driving past in his car, had never really looked at the church closely, he had never noticed that Immanuel Lutheran had no main floor. The entire church was just a roofed-over basement. It was not, as he had assumed, a bungalow resurrected as a church. *God, I'm unobservant*, he thought as he got out of the car and started to walk toward the building.

When he entered the church via its only door—on the far right of the building—he found that the inside of the church, accessed by the narrow stairs that led down to the basement, was damned cold. Ahead of him as he came down the stairs was a wall, and in the middle of the wall, was an opening—without a door. Owen could hear, from somewhere on the other side of the hallway, a furnace coughing as it tried to warm up the basement sanctuary. Above the open area was a sign that advertised washrooms.

A half-dozen rows of wooden chairs, painted barnyard red and arranged in two banks, made up the seating area. The sanctuary floor was not linoleum. It was concrete, painted red—and peeling.

Owen picked a chair a couple of rows from the back wall of the church. He decided that a speedy exit from the church was more important than easy access to a washroom.

As more and more of the congregation arrived, they, too, headed for a back row—the farther from the pulpit, it seemed, the better. One family in particular seemed bothered by Owen's presence as soon as they came down the stairs. *I'm in their row*, Owen thought. *I'm taking one of their chairs*. But he didn't want to move to the front. He held his ground. After all, the family was made up only of a young woman and her son, and an older lady—probably the grandmother (who gave him a bit of the evil eye when she came down the stairs)— but no husband, no grandfather.

The young woman was likely a war widow, Owen decided. He kept his head down. *I know her from somewhere,* he thought, though he couldn't get a clear view of her face.

The family settled into the row directly in front of him.

At the end of the service, Owen tried to leave as quickly and unobtrusively as possible, but the family he'd displaced tore past him at the final *Amen.* The boy's mother winked briefly at Owen as she beat him out the door. She, the boy, and the grandmother vanished into the car that was parked across the street from the church.

Owen wasn't fully outside, but he caught a glimpse of the driver, who looked Finnish. They probably followed the same routine every Sunday. Drove the family to church, drove back home, drove to the church once more to pick them up. The young woman had looked— at least from the back—English, Owen decided, though he could not pinpoint why. He continued creating her biography: Maybe second- or third-generation Canadian, self-possessed. She doesn't necessarily enjoy going to church, but she does it anyway because she thinks it's good for her son.

Wait. I do know her. Don't I? The girl at the Finn Hall? Owen thought. *Is she the girl at the Finn Hall, comes to dances sometimes? Now, or a long time ago? Oh, God. I can't remember her name!*

Once outside, people in the congregation suddenly stopped moving forward and began chatting with each other. Owen tried to push through them politely, but the small river of people following him up the stairs flowed left and right and cut off his escape route. And because he was now the meat in their open-face sandwich, he put on his office smile, and began to introduce himself.

#

Andrew Millbridge looked at his watch. Though it was just past noon, he was still sitting at the kitchen table and finishing off the last of his breakfast. He was cold. This year, he'd experienced the end of winter not as the time when life returns once more to the frozen earth, but as the beginning of the end of things.

He decided that he could not—would not—endure another winter. He'd had enough.

Enough what? Myllysilta asked. *Living, if you call this a life? I've wondered why you insist on living. For years, I have wondered what you wanted. Acclaim? We chose to stay unknown, you know. Grandchildren? What would we offer them? A Don? For the child of your mealy-mouthed son?*

Millbridge tuned out the jeering voice in his head.

He hated the look of his fingers, wrapped around the morning's cup of coffee. He hated that his body now valued oxygen more than money. He hated that Easter Sunday always brought back memories of the attack on the Kalevankangas cemetery in Tampere, the day he'd put two bullets into the back of the corpse of Karl Solbakken and had stolen one of Karl's boots. The day that was the start of his madness.

Or maybe it wasn't the start. Maybe it was just one of the days that gave Jussi Mantere the right to hunt him, and hunt him not as a man, but as an animal. Someday Mantere would figure out that Andrew Millbridge was Antti Myllysilta, not only the defiler of Karl's body but one of the family who killed his mother. And Mantere would try to kill him.

This, I understand, Myllysilta said. *But I will not allow myself to be killed easily—and somehow, if it comes to that, I will take Mantere with me.*

War never ends, not really. Sun Tzu had taught him that.

#

Two months later, as June faded toward July, Andrew Millbridge carefully descended the stairs to the basement, gripping the railing tightly. He took Karl's boot and his own brother's shoe out of the cardboard box and brought them upstairs. He had to sit in the kitchen for some time to catch his breath. He couldn't pinpoint why, but he had an errand, and it felt urgent.

Once his breathing was normal, he put the shoe and the boot into a paper bag. He drove to the shoemaker's shop on Oliver Road.

A bell rang as he opened the door to the shop. No customers were present. The shoemaker sat behind his sewing machine, carefully sewing the sole of a shoe to the shoe's body. Andrew approached the counter in front of the shoemaker.

"I would like to rent some space in your display window,"

Myllysilta said.

"One moment, I can't quite hear." The shoemaker finished stitching and let the walking-foot sewing machine slow and stop. "Now, how can I help you?" he asked.

"I will pay you ten dollars a month to display these in your window." Antti reached into the paper bag, took the boot out first and then the shoe.

"Oh?"

"If anyone asks, you can say that they are from the time of the Finnish Civil War. Souvenirs, keepsakes. They are decorations, and not for sale."

"And the Finnish Civil War was…?"

"A revolution in Finland in 1918."

"I see."

"No, you don't. And it is *important* that you do not let your curiosity get the best of you. Another thing—the space *between* the boots is mine too, and you are to never, ever touch the items I place on the windowsill. Agreed?"

"Ten dollars?"

"A month."

"You have a deal."

Myllysilta was delighted. "Good. Here is the first month's rent." He extracted a ten-dollar bill from his wallet and put it on the counter. He went to the window and placed the boot and the shoe on the sill. They stood back to back, spine to spine, like duelers in a feud—one a soldier, the other a businessman—ready to begin their paces, before turning to fire.

"Thank you." He waved, the shoemaker waved, and he left.

On the way to the car, Myllysilta laughed. Andrew Millbridge thought, *Rabbit comes by here sometimes. That's why you're doing this, isn't it? You didn't tell the shoemaker that, though, did you? Keepsakes! You're a funny man, Antti Myllysilta. Always were—even as a boy. Remember when you put the pillow in the horse's stall? Now that was really funny.*

A few days later, Owen was looking ahead at July's calendar, wondering idly if May would appear sometime for a summer visit, since the one the previous year had ended so abruptly. He found a note clipped to July's page: "get winter boots repaired."

He found his worn winter boots in the hall closet. The right boot's heel was worn down on the left side; the left boot's heel was worn down on the right. *No wonder I skated on my ankles when I was a kid,* Owen thought.

He left work a little early, and drove with the boots to the shoemaker's shop on Oliver Road.

"Got a pair of boots for you," Owen said as he put the boots on the counter. "The rubber heels are shot. Think you can fix them up sometime? I'm in no hurry. With any luck, it'll be November before I wear them again."

The shoemaker lifted his foot off the treadle of the large sewing machine, and let the machine coast to a stop. Then he got off his stool and came over to the counter. "Nice to see you again, Mr. Millbridge," he said. He picked up one of the boots and examined it. "No problem. You can pick the boots up on Wednesday next week."

"If it's no trouble," Owen said. He barely glanced at the window display.

The shoemaker watched him carefully as Owen went out the door. His walk reminded the shoemaker of another customer—the odd man with the boots on display. But it didn't matter. He went back to his work.

#

Owen left the office around three o'clock on the following Wednesday. He parked in front of the shoe repair shop. The boot and the shoe displayed in the window caught his eye. They looked a lot like the ones in the box in his father's basement.

When he entered, bell ringing, he saw that he was the only customer.

"Be right with you," the shoemaker said. The bell over the store's door rang again, and another customer came into the shop and stood behind Owen.

The shoemaker came around the counter and fetched Owen's boots from a shelf. When he returned, he said to Owen, "It will rain soon. I can feel it in my hands. Rheumatism, I guess." He put Owen's boots down on the counter.

"The Winnipeg Goldeyes are playing the Superior Blues at the Stadium tonight," Owen said, then quickly added, "What do I owe you?"

"On the house, Mr. Millbridge. You're a regular, and it was just a small repair."

"How's your son these days?" Owen asked.

"Passed this year. Plans to go on."

Owen put two dollar bills on the counter. "Take him to the game with you," he said. "Buck and a quarter for you, seventy-five cents for the kid, right?"

"Yes, sir," the shoemaker said. He put the money in his pocket.

Owen picked up his boots and left. Just to satisfy his curiosity, he considered paying a visit to his father's place to see if the boot and shoe were still there. But he decided not to. *It would be safer—was that the right word?—to leave things as they are. There must be a lot of old boots and shoes in the world. And even if they were from his father's basement, perhaps he'd just decided to give them to the shoemaker for use as part of a display.*

He thought of May. She'd probably make a beeline for the basement, try to figure out what was going on. Not that learning about their father seemed to make May happy. He'd tried calling on her birthday in early May, but still, no one answered. Sometimes, Owen decided, it paid—not in money, but in peace—to be incurious.

#

That week, Andrew Millbridge spent part of one morning thinking about writing a letter to Viktoria, Jussi Mantere's wife, formerly wife to Karl Solbakken. This time, he stopped himself before thinking, *The soldier I shot in the back.* This time.

A letter would need to be in the old-style Finnish script, maybe a little wobbly-looking, as if the writer were trying to control a shaky hand. He looked at his left hand with its rounded nails, the calluses from playing the violin more pronounced. The tips of his fingers reminded him of the pads of a frog's front feet.

He'd give the letter the stumbling tone of someone who has been out of school for a long time. A Finn … yes, but not well educated. Someone, though, with a strong need to be understood. *Remember*, he told himself, *both Jussi Mantere and Viktoria are going to read this.*

He thought about it for a day, rehearsing sentences in his head. On Saturday, he got his pen and paper and sat at the kitchen table.

Please forgive my bad English, Millbridge began. Antti Myllysilta shook his head ruefully and took control of the pen. *I do not write well in English. When I need to write I have my son do it for me but this one I have to write it myself.*

The reader might, Myllysilta thought, feel some sympathy here, so the next sentence would need to catch the reader's full attention. *I was with the men who killed Fredric Svensson and I also took your husband's boot at Tampere.* Now that we have your full attention, Myllysilta thought, we scramble the next revelation—just a bit. *Somebody else killed him but I shot your husband in the back when he was dead. I was lentävä osasto.* No explanation of the term. Viktoria would be forced to ask Jussi to explain the expression if she needed one. *I do not ask for your forgiveness, but I am sorry for what I did. I took your husband's boot because for each boot or shoe I was paid.* Good.

Scramble the next sentence a bit. *Your present husband, I was also part of the group that killed his mother, but I was not there when she was killed. To kill a woman is wrong.* Nicely done.

Myllysilta congratulated himself. Mantere and his wife would, without a doubt, read the letter together. Oh, to be a fly on the wall when they did!

Andrew Millbridge folded the letter and put it in an envelope. *Viktoria* he wrote on the outside. He decided that he would not take the car—he would walk to the shoemaker's shop. It was a warm Saturday afternoon, good for his bones. The walk, downhill on High Street all the way, still tired him. His legs had to work hard to keep him from speeding up.

The walk home—uphill—would be harder still.

As he entered the shop, the bell above the door rang. The shoemaker, a notebook in one hand and a pencil in the other, stopped examining his stock of laces and glues and thread and half-soles.

Millbridge handed him the envelope. "Put this in the window. Switch the boot and the shoe around, and put the letter between them—standing up. But do not do it today. Do it Sunday, in the afternoon. Monday, a man will likely come to your shop. He'll ask you about the letter. Even though it's addressed to Viktoria, let him have it. If he asks you anything about the letter, just answer his question truthfully. Got it?"

"Yes."

"Good." Millbridge left the shop and began the long walk up High Street. He tried to walk briskly in case the shoemaker was watching. Soon he had to slow down. Where the road widened at the park, he sat on a bench to catch his breath. He was exhausted when he got home.

Myllysilta, however, couldn't stop laughing. *Mantere thinks he's so smart!* he told Millbridge.

The shoemaker had watched Millbridge start his walk home. Now, sitting at the sewing machine, he thought, *What the hell have I gotten myself into?*

#

On Wednesday after work, Owen showed up at his father's house with two TV dinners.

"What are we celebrating?" Andrew Millbridge asked.

"Nothing in particular. I'm going to the Finn Hall tonight. It's Wednesday. Dancing."

"Just dancing, or have you got your eye on someone in particular?"

"No one in particular. But I thought I'd make sure you were fed before I left. And me, too."

"I see. Well, fire up the oven, then."

While he watched his son, for some reason, he thought of Rough-house, wondering how he fared in southern Ontario, wondering if he'd lied about finding May. He let the thought dissipate.

#

At eight o'clock, Owen paid his fifty cents at the door and entered the main hall. Kurt, one of Owen's acquaintances, stood just inside. "Who's playing?" Owen asked him.

"Al Jason and the Melody Ranch Boys. They've got Buddy Duval with them—you know, the guy who sings 'Are You Mine?'"

"With Myrna Lorrie."

"Right. She's here, too, so you can bet they'll do it."

As his eyes adjusted to the low light of the hall, Owen saw a familiar face. "Damn," he said.

"Problem?"

"There's a girl here. I should know her. At church I accidentally sat in her family's usual spot. I even danced with her a couple of weeks ago. Marilyn? Marilyn something?"

"Doesn't sound like much of a problem—even if you can't remember her full name." He smiled, enjoying Owen's awkwardness and embarrassment.

"She's with her friend," Owen said. "They work at—oh, her friend's leaving."

"Go get her, tiger. She's probably *sent* her friend away, to make room for you."

Owen walked toward Marilyn. He tried to look casual. "Dance?"

"Sure," she said. "Owen, right?"

"Yes. And you're Marilyn … something."

"Mantere."

"Of course," Owen said. "Marilyn Mantere. Good to see you again." The memory of other dances, hoping to see her, long-ago conversations with Rough-house about her kindness and beauty—it all came flooding back to him, colouring his face. "And not just from a couple of weeks ago."

She smiled, beautifully and heart-breakingly. "I wondered if you were the same Owen I knew years back. My son, Jimmy, is nearly ten now."

Owen took her by the hand and they walked out onto the floor.

#

"Her last name's *what?*" May asked. The late-night phone call from Owen had surprised her into answering, at last. Owen had launched into his news, not asking her about her situation, so she hadn't hung up. Yet.

"Mantere," Owen said. "Marilyn Mantere. I used to dance with her a long time ago, ten years or more, and I'd head back to Queens with her on my mind. I think she was in high school about the same time you were—but at Hillcrest, not Port Arthur Collegiate. Mantere's her married name, though."

"Whoa. Marilyn Doucette married Raimo Mantere? Remember the football games between PACI and Hillcrest? Raimo Mantere played for Hillcrest. I had such a crush on him! So what's the story? Are you making out with a married woman?"

"He died," Owen said. "Signed up in his last year at Hillcrest, I think, or soon after, and didn't make it through the war."

May was silent for a moment. "Sorry. I have a big mouth. I don't think before I start talking."

"It happened." Owen's voice held a shrug. "Marilyn has a son," Owen said. "Jimmy."

"Owen," May said, caution darkening her voice, "you don't need to tell me everything—you don't have to tell me *anything*, if you don't feel like it. Sometimes it's safer that way."

"I know *you* think so. But this is important, and I want to tell you. I want *you* to know about *me*."

May was silent, but still did not hang up. "I guess I deserved that. And brother, I'm fine, believe me, and believe me when I say I don't know more." She cleared her throat. "Does Dad know anything about this?"

"No. I haven't told him anything. Nothing at all. But I'm not keeping it a secret, necessarily."

"He probably already knows," May said. "Dad keeps tabs on *everything*."

Owen shrugged, even though May couldn't see. "Do you think Jimmy would … like me?"

May laughed. "Oh Owen, what's not to like? You're a nice enough man. You're successful. But listen, are you and Marilyn that serious already?"

"Already? I've known her for ten years, sort of. I've asked to meet her in-laws, and Jimmy too."

"Her in-laws? You have to get the approval of her late husband's parents?"

"She lives with them. Her parents are gone. They're her family now. She's put me off so far, but she knows I want to."

"I see. Well, this could get complicated before it gets easier, but I'm happy for you, brother. Keep me posted. Love you."

She hung up before Owen could say, "You'll have to keep answering the phone, then."

2 • LETTERS AND LIAISONS

"WELL, WELL," ANDREW MILLBRIDGE SAID aloud as he drove past the shoemaker's shop on Thursday morning. A letter lay propped between the boot and shoe in the window—undoubtedly, Mantere's response. He got out of his car half a block from the shoemaker's place, walked to the shop and entered. The shoemaker looked up as he came in.

"He left something for you," the shoemaker said. "Window."

"Yes, so I see." Millbridge went to the window and picked up the letter. "If he asks," he said, you can tell him I got the letter. Tell him I'll answer it as soon as possible."

"That's all?"

"Yes. Say nothing else about me."

The shoemaker nodded his head. "My lips are sealed," he said.

As soon as Millbridge was home and back in his kitchen, he opened the letter.

"*We need to meet. When and where?*" and it was signed, J. Mantere.

"Got you," Millbridge said out loud. *Time to send you a reply. But not yet*, he thought. *You need to learn patience. I'll drop it off Saturday afternoon, maybe. You'll have to wait until Monday, unless you're lucky. But there's no reason I can't start working on it right now.*

He took out his pen, got the ink well, and went through his discipline of filling the pen's bladder with ink.

Then, *Dear Mr. Mantere*, he wrote. *Forgive, please, my bad handwriting.* That much, at least was honest, he thought. His weakness and his frog fingers made writing difficult now. *I have Parkinson's*, he wrote. *I also have cancer in my stomach.* Too much? No.

But now, make the letter just a touch fake-sounding. Give Mantere a line that will make him think you are lower class, a working man. *The doctor says that I am going to die.* Perfect! *Not right away, but not too long.* Good. Obsequious in its own way, and sufficiently awkward.

233

So. Before I die I need to tell you about what I did. I do not ask you for forgiveness. What I have done I have done and that is that. Tulee mitä tulee.

Even my family does not know what I was so long ago. They would be ashamed of me— Millbridge scratched out the last words. "Too grammatical," he said to himself. *It would make them shame,* he wrote instead, *if they find out.*

Perhaps some time we can meet, but not yet. I would like to hear from you, but if you do not want to write back, I understand. I know about Ivor Solbakken, but I promise you that whatever your decision is, Ivor's story I will not tell.

"No signature," Millbridge said. "That's best. I know Ivor's family name and you don't even know who the hell I am." He took a fresh piece of paper and made a clean copy of the message, then he crumpled up the original and put it in the wastepaper basket.

I have to stop talking to myself, he thought.

On Monday morning he drove past the shoemaker's shop. His letter was there in the window. Just after noon, he drove past again, and the letter was gone. *Got you,* he thought. *You're checking the window every day.*

#

On Wednesday, Owen left work mid-morning and drove to Big Day Bridal. *God, I hope Marilyn's there,* he thought. *It's Wednesday. She should be there until noon, maybe a little after. If she's not, I'm going to look damn silly.* He parked in the small space in front of the store and walked in.

Marilyn was there—as was her friend. For a moment Owen could not remember the friend's name, then it came to him: Laura. Marilyn came around from behind the counter to meet him. "Marriage on your mind?" she asked.

Owen felt his face grow red. "Uh," he said. "No, I mean—are you going to the Finn Hall dance tonight?"

Marilyn smiled wickedly but said nothing.

"She's going," Laura said. "Don't look so worried."

"I'll be there," Marilyn said.

Owen caught a glimpse of Laura rolling her eyes. "Good," he said. "I have a friend. Kurt. More a friend of a friend. He's a good guy, though, and he was wondering ... the last time we were there, if...."

He stalled out.

"If Laura would be going to the dance this evening," Marilyn filled in.

"Yes!"

"And you told him she might."

"I was guessing. But I thought that if she was going, the four of us could—"

Laura interrupted, "Maybe go out for something to eat or drink after. I'll be there. And so will Marilyn. Anything else on your mind?"

"Uh," Owen said. "I better be going. I'll see you later," he said to Marilyn, then he hurried out. As he let the door swing shut, he heard the start of the laughter. *Oh well*, he thought. The laughter did not sound mean. *God, I'm stupid.*

He drove to the office. The rest of the day it was hard, he discovered, to keep his mind on his work, and his eyes off the clock.

#

Andrew Millbridge coughed. He couldn't stop.

The kitchen clock said that it was almost suppertime. Each cough felt as if someone was tearing open his chest.

Cough after cough erupted from his lungs.

He tried to sit as erect as possible in the kitchen chair and breathe deeply. Always before, sitting in that way had helped. Not this time.

Suddenly, still coughing, he felt the warm flow of urine. *Jesus, no*, he thought. *Not this.*

He stood up and was hit by an incredible dizziness that came with a flood of white sprinkled with flecks of light. His legs began to buckle, so he sat down—it was either that or fall on the floor. As the dizziness diminished, he risked leaning forward. *He was tired, really tired, and he needed ... he needed something.* The world went blank.

Sometime later, consciousness returned. He lay sideways on the floor. The kitchen table had been pushed up against the wall as he had fallen out of the chair, and the chair now lay on its side.

Slowly, he got up from the floor and made his way to the bathroom. The crystal of his watch had cracked, he noticed. He remembered Bertil Granbakken. *Damn.*

His thoughts were flitting around in his head like moths around a light. He took off his clothes and left them where they fell. Then, since he no longer felt dizzy, he had a shower.

When he felt he was clean, he got out of the shower and dried off. Then he went to the bedroom closet and got a fresh pair of pants and a clean shirt.

At last, he turned to the mess in the kitchen. He poured a bit of bleach into water and slowly, carefully, mopped the floor from the kitchen to the bathroom with it. He had to rest several times while mopping, but he kept the rest periods brief.

He gathered up his reeking clothes, stuffed them into a paper garbage bag, and put the bag into the garbage can outside the back door. When he re-entered the kitchen, he couldn't smell urine.

Still, after another rest, he refilled the mop bucket with water and more bleach and mopped the kitchen again.

By this time, it was almost eight p.m. He was far too tired to eat, so he went to bed.

The next morning, he watched Owen leave for work and made the slow walk to the Dufferin Street house. Using Owen's phone, he called Dr. Wainwright and made an appointment for the following day. Then he walked back home.

#

"So what happens next?" Andrew asked.

He sat in the chair in front of Wainwright's desk. For no reason, the bronze sign that bore the doctor's name bothered him. Andrew pushed it to one side.

Wainwright put it back where it belonged.

"You sure you want to know?" There was no approbation in the doctor's voice.

"Yes."

"Just from the look of you, I'd say you've got—at most—just a couple of years. If you make it through the winter, you'll be bed-ridden in the summer."

When Millbridge made no comment, Wainwright continued. "Idiopathic Pulmonary Fibrosis. Remember? IPF is a nasty disease. It's like a batch of diseases, a horde of dogs, all taking hold of you at the same time. It's a lung disease, of course, but those lungs move oxygen into the circulatory system, and that system carries blood to every part of your body. Everywhere the oxygen-short blood goes, the body gets damaged because the organs are being starved of something that makes it possible for the organs to use their fuel supply—the food you eat. And it's that lack of oxygen in your blood that ultimately kills you."

Andrew thought of the long line of Red families trying to walk to Olonetz. "How? I mean...."

"It's a completely individual thing. Here's one way. The lungs don't give enough oxygen to your body. You feel breathless and begin to have trouble swallowing. If you can't swallow well, you may eat less. The less you eat, the weaker you get, and the more susceptible you are to conditions that, as they accumulate, can kill you. Another person might notice a completely different symptom first—light headedness, for instance—but what would kill him would be a fall down the stairs."

"So let's say I have trouble swallowing, which I do. Should I eat more, less, different foods? How can I fix this?"

"Well, for a while, you can try eating smarter—not more *or* less. You can eat more small meals—have five or six meals a day, little ones. Your throat won't take such a beating, and your stomach might complain less, too. Loss of appetite, by the way, often occurs with IPF. Another thing you can do is you can throw more sugar and butter and cream on what you eat—to get by on less volume of food per meal, less need to chew and swallow, but more calories."

"I get it." A pause. "I die anyway."

Wainwright hesitated, too. "Yes," he said finally, "you do. You die anyway. But you have an easier time getting to that point."

"And the pissing in my pants?"

"I can give you some diuretics to help you urinate more frequently—on *your* schedule, not your body's. You can learn to watch the clock so that your body doesn't catch you off guard. You can also take cough medicines to help prevent the coughing or, if it can't be prevented, at least lessen it. Sometimes it's the coughing that triggers the urination."

"What else?"

"Andrew, your lungs feed your brain the oxygen it needs. As your brain gets less of it, your ability to think, to plan, and so on, may become more difficult. You may become forgetful, start to feel more anxiety—depression, even. Or, because everyone is different, your mental state may not suffer at all. Everyone really *is* different. I can give you sedatives for depression, even morphine, but....” He shrugged.

Finally, Andrew said, “The end is the end, and I’ve got maybe two years.”

“Yes.”

“And there’s nothing I can do about that.” He felt almost relieved. He remembered his desire, when spring arrived, to never see another winter.

“Nothing. Sometime in the future someone’s going to find a way to pull oxygen out of the air with some kind of personal magical device, and make it possible for you to have oxygen pumped into you whenever you need it. But that time’s not yet. It may be decades away, and you don’t have decades. You’ve got this year and the next—if that.”

#

A full week passed in much the usual way. Owen came by his father’s home once or twice with TV dinners. Andrew hoped that Owen noticed nothing different. He didn’t feel so different—nothing remotely like his previous “fit,” as he thought of it, occurred.

Otherwise, Millbridge brooded. And waited.

On Saturday, the last Saturday of July, Andrew Millbridge could no longer stand it. He drove to the shoemaker’s shop. He parked on Oliver Road, just half a block away, then crossed the street and positioned himself so that he could see the display, but no one inside the shop could see him without standing right at the window and looking up the street.

He wondered momentarily what Owen would think if he saw his father lurking on the street. He wondered when Owen would tell him about Marilyn Mantere. Of course he already knew; he knew most of Owen’s movements. Sometimes it was difficult to wait to be told.

Waiting has always been difficult, whispered Myllysilta. *Although not for Jussi Mantere. Or so it would seem.*

Andrew looked closely at the window, where the shoe and boot were still on display. No reply from Mantere. No reply, and it was two weeks since Andrew had written his note—the one in which he said that he did not want to meet him yet, the one he wrote to make sure that Mantere understood that he still wanted him to write back.

Two weeks! What if Mantere wanted to leave the past in the past? What if he never responded?

He will, Myllysilta assured him. *If he doesn't, we will make him.*

He glanced across the street. *Dammit!* Ivor Solbakken—Rabbit— leaned in a doorway, watching him. There was no chance that Rabbit could recognize him as the boy on the train so long ago, but still. There was also no chance that Rabbit would keep this moment to himself. Jussi Mantere would hear about it the very next time he spoke to Rabbit.

Dammit!

3 • THE CIRCUS

ANDREW MILLBRIDGE KNEW that the Canadian Lakehead Exhibition would begin early in August. His plan was to confront Jussi Mantere at the CLE and insist that Mantere tell him why his letter had been ignored—why Mantere had not contacted him. After that, his plan was far less clear. He'd think of something.

Each day the CLE was on, Millbridge was there, too. Not for the whole day, of course, but for the part of the day that most people were there.

He was partly rewarded on August 10th, when Jimmy Mantere and his friends spent the afternoon hanging around the midway and going on the rides. Millbridge stayed for about an hour, watching them, and then went home. It was Jussi he wanted to confront—not Jimmy.

On Thursday, Millbridge went back. Thursday's car giveaway was a Dodge, and Jussi Mantere, based on what he drove, favoured Chrysler cars, not GM or Nash or Studebaker or Ford.

It was likely that the whole family would come to the Exhibition together. At some point they'd go see the animals in the animal barns at the south end of the Exhibition grounds. Or maybe just Jussi and Jimmy and Ivor would go there. Viktoria—and Marilyn, Owen's girlfriend—might go to one of the buildings where there were women's things. How to cook a frozen TV dinner, for instance.

I guess we are already as smart as a woman, Owen and me, cooking our TV dinners without a lesson. He paused. *I'm getting lost in my own thoughts. I'm having trouble staying focused*, he thought.

Millbridge stationed himself close to the barns. And success! He saw the family come in the main gates and walk past The Bottle, the meeting place at the CLE. The group headed for the demonstration buildings—the ones with prizes for handicrafts, show-and-tell lectures, and displays. After a few minutes, the men emerged from the main demonstration building. They walked toward the Coliseum

Building, which held more-interesting items for sale—everything from bull whips to cosmetic jewellery.

Patience, Myllysilta counselled. Millbridge waited, but he was getting tired. The day was warm.

In a half-hour, Mantere's family regrouped. After some discussion, they separated once more. Jussi and Rabbit went toward the animal barns; Viktoria, Marilyn and Jimmy started to walk up the midway. Millbridge waited for Jussi and Rabbit to enter the cattle barn, then he moved closer—to a spot still outside, but where he could see into the barn.

It was a bad choice. Rabbit spotted him almost immediately and yelled to Jussi, "He's here!" and began to run toward him.

Jussi yelled back, "Ivor, stop! Who's here? Where are you going?" Jussi sprinted to the barn's door, then tried to catch up to Rabbit.

And Millbridge, feeling his chest burning with the exertion, dodged people and ran until he could run no more. Then he stopped to see where he was—the north end of the fairgrounds, the domain of tents holding sideshows. Which one?

Flinging coins at the concessionaire outside, Millbridge ducked into the tent behind him, only briefly seeing the sign: the World's Smallest Horse. Exhausted, he stood doubled over for a minute or two.

When his breath returned enough for him to move, he found a seat in the audience. He stayed in his seat until he felt strong enough to walk again, then left the tent, walked slowly and carefully out of the Exhibition Grounds, got in his car, and drove home.

After he parked in his driveway, he spent a few minutes just resting in the front seat. When he felt he could, he opened the car door, got out, went into the house, lay down on the living room couch, and immediately fell asleep. He dreamed of riding the Don.

#

The next morning, Friday, after breakfast, Millbridge sat with his coffee for a long time.

Mantere hadn't answered. Maybe he *wouldn't* answer. Millbridge must write again. But this time, Millbridge would simply send it to Jussi's house.

Ah, you're edging closer, Myllysilta said. *Well done.*

So Millbridge retrieved his pen and wrote a letter: *Herr Mantere*, it began, *I would like to meet with you soon. There is too much that I want to say to you for a letter.* He paused, then elected to back off just a bit on the proper English. *The time is not enough. Thursday I was very afraid when I saw you and your family at the CLE but I have to talk.* He went on to explain that he had thought it might be fun to go to the fair with his own son, but had felt uneasy about doing it. He wrote a little more, finished the draft of the two-page letter then put it on the kitchen table. He left it unsigned.

I'll mail it this afternoon—that way, Mantere will have it by Monday.

That afternoon, Millbridge started awake from an unexpected nap. He'd opened windows to enjoy the warm weather and slight breeze. But now, the afternoon was draining away. He hurried into the kitchen, addressed an envelope and folded the letter in. Then he drove to a mailbox outside the Post Office downtown to mail it. *Just in time.* He felt elated.

When Millbridge came back into the kitchen, he found the second page under the kitchen table.

"*Dammit!*" he said aloud. "Stupid, stupid, stupid. Now what?" If he went back to the post office and mailed the missing part of the letter, it wouldn't go today, but it would be picked up tomorrow and be in Mantere's hands on Tuesday. That was the best he could do.

A newspaper lay on the table. He tore a small piece and scrawled with a pencil, in block letters, "*SORRY THIS IS REST OF LETTER.*"

He debated for a moment. Should he sign it?

Myllysilta laughed. *What is the point of secrecy now? If Jussi Mantere, with all his brains, sees that Millbridge is a simple translation of Myllysilta, would it matter? Maybe yes, maybe no.*

It doesn't matter to me and it should not matter to you. One way or another you and I, Andrew Millbridge, are going to die soon, anyway.

To the letter's second page he added "A. Myllysilta."

He chose a different mailbox this time, in a different part of town. When he closed it, it clanged. A bell, tolling.

\#

The waiting became a little easier. Andrew imagined a letter arriving at the Mantere home on Monday. Perhaps he and Viktoria—

because Mantere and Viktoria no doubt shared everything, as he and Annie had—would be mystified by the missing second page.

Myllysilta said dryly, *You and Annie did not share everything. But if it comforts you to believe that, go ahead.*

Millbridge ignored him, knowing that on Tuesday—or by Wednesday, for sure—the second page would come. And what would they make of that? He hadn't planned this mystery, but he relished it regardless.

One early afternoon, just after the middle of August, Millbridge drove past the shoemaker's. A letter—Mantere's reply—stood between the shoe and the boot.

When he opened the door, the shoemaker said, without looking up, "He told me you'd be in today." He let the sewing machine glide to a stop, then turned to Millbridge. "When are you going to tell me what all this is about?"

"Never," Millbridge answered. He picked up the letter and left. Only when he was in his car did he even open the letter, but then he read greedily. Mantere had set up a meeting for them tomorrow, Friday, noon, in the Hemmet—in the meeting room.

#

The next morning, a thunderstorm settled in. It brought rain, but no relief from the high temperatures. The air closed in on the city. The temperature was forecast to hit 90 Fahrenheit.

Millbridge carefully selected his clothes for the meeting. Blue dress shirt—light blue, almost the blue of the Finnish flag. Black trousers—business attire, conservative, the crease sharp. Shoes—polished. He chose to wear galoshes over the shoes, against rain. Summer jacket—nylon, light blue, zippered. Cap rather than a hat. Umbrella.

A little before noon, he drove to the Hemmet. Because of the rain, he had to park a distance from the building. Even out of the car, Millbridge felt claustrophobic. *Hellish weather.* He tried to keep his breathing slow and even.

As he entered the café, with its once-familiar long counter, one of the wait staff signaled that he should go up the stairs to his left. Millbridge nodded, then started the climb. He was panting by the time he was on the last step. At the top, he paused several moments to catch his breath. When he felt more in command, he entered the meeting room.

Jussi Mantere sat at the long table, facing the door.

To indicate a bit of deference, Millbridge asked, "Jussi Mantere?"

Mantere nodded, then pointed to the chair opposite his. "Sit."

"Thank you." Millbridge raised his hand to indicate he needed a moment. He leaned his umbrella against the wall behind him, making sure that the wet fabric did not touch the wall. He hung up his jacket on the nearby coatrack, then he took off his galoshes and put them on the black rubber tray beside the door. Jussi Mantere seemed to be watching every movement, as if analyzing him, reading him.

Millbridge pulled the chair out and sat down, but before Mantere could speak he asked, "Do you mind if we speak in Finnish?"

The reply was quick. "Let us speak in English. We are not in Finland."

"Very well."

Mantere seemed to glance at Millbridge's hands. As if to provide an explanation, Millbridge said, "I don't have long to live."

"I can see that." Mantere paused. "But death becomes you. Why did you ask to meet me?"

Andrew had expected the question. He gave a long-considered answer while watching Jussi's face carefully. "I wanted to ask your forgiveness," he said, "but I can see that would be too much."

For a few seconds, Mantere waited. Then, "That is true. I can't give that to you. I couldn't even if I wanted to. It isn't mine to give."

"I didn't kill your mother. I wanted to tell you that." Millbridge folded his hands on the table. Mantere now openly stared at them, examining them with the same expression Wainwright had used when he told Millbridge he was going to die.

The silence grew.

After an eternity had passed, Millbridge offered, "My brothers sent me to the village, instead. Gamlaby." He held back the fact that he had hidden himself in the trees, in the snow, and that he had made sure his horse was hidden, too.

"To set up an alibi, I think," Mantere said.

"Maybe. But you killed them all."

"But not you. You're still alive, if not much alive."

Mantere tipped his chair back—the way a logger might do when he wanted the whole table of men to pay attention to him, to listen to what he had to say. "I could forgive you for the harm you did me. I could do that, but I won't. And, unfortunately for you, no one can forgive the harm done to someone else."

Mantere let his chair come to rest in its normal position. "Even if I wanted to, and I don't, I cannot forgive you the death of my mother. She has to do that, and since she's dead, she can't."

He looked at Millbridge's hands again—the puffy fingertips, the rounded nails. "God perhaps could forgive you, but I doubt it. For my mother's death you'll go to your grave with all your sins intact."

Myllysilta stared down at the table for a moment. "I have a son," he said at last.

Mantere did not reply—nor did his expression soften.

Myllysilta continued, "I have a son and a daughter. My son is a good man. He has no mother—she died many years ago—but he is like her, not like me."

"Owen," Mantere said. "Yes, I know."

Myllysilta did not react. "To him I am both his father and someone he believes is—*was*—an upstanding, honest businessman."

"The sins of the fathers—" Mantere began.

"Do not have to fall on the sons," Myllysilta said angrily and instantly. "God doesn't work like that."

Mantere leaned in. "You believe in God?"

"Sometimes. When it suits me." He tipped his chair back as if mimicking Mantere. "But only if someone asks." He put all four of the chair's feet back on the floor. Myllysilta leaned forward and looked closely at Mantere. *Can I intimidate him?* There was no change in Mantere's expression or demeanor.

"Tell me about your names," Mantere said. "Myllysilta and Millbridge. Which are you?"

"I am Myllysilta in my head, Millbridge everywhere else. I'm Finn most places, of course, but when I was processed at Pier 7 I told them I was a Swede and that I wanted to be Andrew Millbridge. I had stolen a blank baptismal certificate from a church we burned down, and I had filled in the usual stuff, so when I told the officials I wanted my name changed there was no problem. I wasn't Antti Myllysilta on the baptismal certificate I showed them. When I started work in Canada, people called me Andy. Antti is my real first name. I used it even on the train going to Vasa."

He knew he was rambling, but he could not stop himself. He was filling the room with sound—if not with sense.

"I know," Mantere said.

"Ivor remembered me?"

"Yes."

"Antti is dead. I left the name behind when I emigrated. Every time I hear Andy, though, especially when a Finn tries to say it, I think of Antti. It's my ghost name." Myllysilta made himself smile, but he kept his eyes on Jussi's face, watching every expression, however small. Jussi seemed content to let him talk, to let him dig his own grave.

"What does your son call you?"

"Dad. He never says Andy or Andrew."

Mantere's voice was cold when he asked the next question. "I'm curious. When did you come to Canada?"

"About the same as you, I think. I had enough of Finland. The Whites didn't make life easy. Didn't even let us honour our dead, didn't allow us to hold religious services, didn't even let us put up gravestones for a while. And everyone I knew was dead, or in prison, or crippled. Too many other people knew that I was a raider, *lentävä osasto*. Such knowledge could be traded for bread, and everyone was hungry. It wasn't safe for me to stay. And I had—*acquired*, let us say—quite a lot of money during our little war. Do you know, when you came to Canada you worked for me for a short time?"

Myllysilta watched Mantere's facial expression change from analytical to investigative and then to recognition.

"You were the Finnish kid who was part owner of the lumber company. I never knew your name."

"Yes, I was the kid."

For a long moment, Mantere was silent. Then, he suddenly drummed his fingers on the table. "Why did you write the first letter, the one you sent to my wife?"

"I was drunk."

"I don't think so. I don't think you drink at all."

Myllysilta shrugged. *Believe whatever you want*, he thought. For some time, neither man spoke, each waiting for the other to speak first, to make the first serious mistake.

"My son," Myllysilta said to break the tension, "one day he told me that he had met a girl. At a dance. Marilyn Mantere, he said."

"You knew she was my daughter-in-law."

"No. Not then. But later." He paused, and waited for Mantere to speak, but Mantere said nothing. Millbridge gave up. "I had someone find out who she was, then who you were, of course, and I knew that you didn't know me. But I never … investigated you, not until Owen said her name."

Millbridge could feel his right hand twitch. He placed his left hand over it as if he were just getting ready to say something revealing, something serious. *Is he watching? Does he know how much I am lying?* Myllysilta asked.

Mantere spoke slowly. "You haven't come after me. Why? Someone like you could easily find someone to kill someone like me."

He made Mantere wait a moment for his reply. "Did you know," Myllysilta said finally, "when the war started, we were told to kill the smart ones first. Begin with the peacemakers, the reasonable ones—like that storekeeper, Fredric Svensson, for instance—the leaders, the intelligent, the influential. You can't have a revolution if no one wants to fight."

Millbridge paused but he did not avert his eyes, did not look down, did not do anything that would make him seem weak to Jussi Mantere.

Instead, he leaned forward. "Shopkeepers, clergymen, school teachers, anyone who might be able to gather followers, *organize* men, learn *tactics*. My brothers were not at your farm to kill your mother. They were there to kill *you*. But you know that, don't you? You've always known that. Felt guilty about it. But you were not home when we came to your house. And here in Canada … well, there was no hope of revolution. There was no need for war between us."

Mantere leaned forward, too. He glanced first at Myllysilta's hand, then met his eyes. "You were part of the Red Terror. People like you killed hundreds of Whites in the early months of the war. What makes you think that in Canada, even now, you're safe? Do you think the war happened so long ago that no one remembers it?"

"No. But it's different here. This isn't Finland. And, besides, when the war turned in your favour, you took your revenge. We had killed a couple of thousand of you. You killed *five times* as many of us. You *executed* us. You *put us in prisons and starved us*. You broke our families into pieces and *gave away our children*."

"Yes," Mantere said, "we did. You had frightened us. We did what frightened people do." He sat back in his chair.

Myllysilta folded his hands on the table. The trembling was gone. "I think you left Finland because of what you saw happening. You didn't want to be part of the White Terror."

Mantere was silent for a moment, then he said, "In your letter you said that you know about Ivor. You made it sound like a threat. Ivor is family, and I will keep him from harm. So do I need to kill you?" He paused, then, "I *could* make it look as if you killed yourself, you know. It would be easy to do."

"I don't mind," Myllysilta said off-handedly. Mantere's expression did not change at all. *You're a tough son of a bitch*, Myllysilta thought. "Do what you feel you must. My affairs are in order." He weighed his words for a moment, then said, "I know Ivor was in the war, of course. Nothing more. That is all I meant."

Mantere's face reddened. "Oh, you know more, I think. So perhaps I will talk to your son about you. To find out what he knows about you. To let him know the truth about you." He leaned over the table toward Myllysilta. "A son has a *right* to know his father, wouldn't you say? A *good* father would have told him. A good father would have told his *daughter*, too."

Does he know something about May? What does he know? Millbridge thought.

He knows nothing, Myllysilta answered.

Mantere spoke quietly. "You have not told me her name."

A second passed. "May," Millbridge said. "Her name is May. Please, I ask you—*beg* you—leave them out of this. You have no quarrel with them. Your quarrel is with *me*."

Mantere leaned forward as well. "What year was your son born?"

The question caught Millbridge so much by surprise that he could not lie. "1922."

"And his mother—you met her here?"

"Yes." *Make the questions stop*, Millbridge begged Myllysilta. He forced himself to become emotionless, to sit stone-faced.

"A Finnish girl?"

"English."

"What does she know about you?"

The room suddenly became less real than the small house on Machar Avenue, full of cinnamon and vanilla, a framed certificate on the wall, home. Andy Millbridge caught a whiff of Annie's perfume.

The question, asked so quickly, so assumptive of life, so powerful, overwhelmed him.

"She died in 1925." *Could he say more?* "Tetanus," he said. *Keep going.* "May was not yet a year old. Owen not quite three. Before my Annie died I told her nothing but lies. Useful ones—the same ones I tell my son." The room felt cold. Millbridge shivered.

Mantere did not speak for more than a minute.

What is he waiting for? What is going through his mind?

"Your daughter does not live here?" Mantere asked at last.

Millbridge came to himself again. *Now, that wasn't so hard, was it?* Myllysilta asked. *You had him there for a second.*

"Toronto," Millbridge said. "I am a grandfather." *Would Mantere recognize the lie? And if he did, what would he do?*

Mantere leaned in toward him. "And *lentävä osasto*," he said.

He doesn't know everything, Millbridge thought. *Not everything.* "Not anymore. Here I am Andrew Millbridge to everyone." *But not to me*, Myllysilta whispered.

"Except those who speak Finnish."

"To them, too. None of them come from Esse or anywhere close to it. No one knows my real past." *I do*, Myllysilta said. *May does, too. And it terrifies her to know it. She is frozen in her fear, and that keeps her safe. But he cannot know any of this.*

"Not even the man who spies on my grandson?"

How the hell did Mantere know that? "He knows what I want him to know. Nothing more." *Liar*, Myllysilta said. *Liar, liar, pants on fire.*

"So what do you want from me?" Mantere asked after a moment.

"If I cannot have forgiveness, then silence," Myllysilta said. *I will make the bargain*, Myllysilta whispered. *Stay quiet.* "Just silence."

"What do you give in return?" Mantere asked.

"Nothing but silence. I offer silence—the same silence I have kept for over thirty years. The silence that keeps the war at bay."

"And if your son and my daughter-in-law get married?"

"I will not be there to see the wedding. The doctor says I will not need to buy Christmas presents this year. Your silence will be my only gift, my last gift, to my children."

Mantere said nothing for a moment, then "They won't know they have received it."

"Does that matter? It doesn't matter to me," Myllysilta said. *We have him*, Myllysilta told Millbridge. *We have him. He will do what we say.*

And he will be the target of suspicion around what we do. They will think he held a grudge.

"I will give you my answer in the usual way," Mantere said. He got up abruptly and left the room. Myllysilta sat alone.

A few minutes later, Myllysilta rose with difficulty from the chair, collected his jacket and umbrella, and maneuvered himself down the stairs, his grip tight on the handrail. As he passed through the restaurant, he became Millbridge once more, and it was Millbridge who noted that none of the customers were speaking Swedish, or Finnish or Danish or any of the other Scandinavian languages that had been part of their families, back in Europe. It was all English now—not like at the Finn Hall.

#

Millbridge made his way back to the car in the rain and drove carefully home. When he pulled into his driveway, he decided to sit awhile in the warm car before going into the house. He was tired—tired beyond all reason—so he closed his eyes.

He woke in darkness, shivering. Once he realized where he was, he opened the car door and got out. Gingerly, he let his legs take his full weight, then he closed the car door and leaned against it, fighting to get his balance. The sudden coughing made him bend over. His mouth tasted of blood, so he spat on the driveway, then started for the house.

Part way to the door, he remembered that he had left his keys in the car. He turned back, retrieved the keys, and began walking to the front door again. The world lost its hold on him, and he fell into darkness.

Half an hour later, his neighbour heard a dog barking and went to the front door to see whose it was. He saw Millbridge lying in his front yard and called the ambulance.

Millbridge was fully revived by the ambulance's oxygen tank. In fact, he felt more himself than he had in some time. However, he forbade anyone calling his son, and he refused to stay at the hospital. He took a taxi home. The driver helped him up the stairs. Wolf followed him in.

4 • JIMMY

MARILYN AND OWEN SAT ON A BLANKET at a picnic spot near Current River, upstream from Boulevard Lake, in the shade where a breeze reached them. Owen had picked up Marilyn at work at noon, bringing sandwiches and bottles of root beer from Maltese's Grocery. They'd made a tentative plan to go blueberry picking later in the afternoon but were in no hurry to get there.

"Sandwich *du jour* and *crème glacée* for dessert." Owen handed her a turkey sandwich. "Only we'll have to see if the Boulevard Lake concessionaire has the *crème glacée*. I couldn't figure out how to keep it from melting."

"Your French accent is … questionable," Marilyn said. "But you have good ideas." She unwrapped part of her sandwich.

Owen put a paper cone with pickle spears on the blanket where they could both reach. "So, you … do you speak anything other than English? French? Finnish, maybe?"

"Nope. Just English."

There was an awkward silence as they managed bites of the sandwich.

Marilyn came up with something. "Your turn. Tell me about your sister. She's in … Toronto? What's she like?"

"Yes, Toronto." Honesty compelled him to add, "More or less. Somewhere in the area, anyway. May is, let's see. She's very organized, smart but opinionated, kind to a fault, and though I'm a bit older than she is, she's definitely more mature than I am." Owen waited until she stopped chewing. "What's Jimmy like?"

"I'll tell you a story about him." Marilyn set down her sandwich and wiped her hands on a napkin. "A few years ago, the city decided it was time to start work on Francis Street, which runs east-west just one street south of my in-laws' place. Francis Street used to end at Franklin Avenue, which runs north-south.

"The first step for the city was to cut down all the trees so that Francis Street could run from Franklin Avenue west for another block. The city crews came in with their fancy saws, and in the blink of an eye, all the trees were gone, roots and all, the brush picked up like magic and carted off to God knows where.

"Jimmy was devastated, and so were his friends. The bush had been their playground, and now it was gone. He and his friends had made trails that ran all through there. The kids had been able to walk in the bush from Franklin Avenue all the way to the McIntyre River—the creek, they call it—before the city cleared the north section of Balmoral Street. They had built their forts and cabins and tree houses in the bush, and now all those things had vanished with the rest of the trees and brush. Poof! Gone." She waved an arm upward, toward the branches of the birch shading them.

"That's sad," Owen said.

"Yes. The next summer, the street work—turning Francis Street into an actual street—hadn't been started yet, but milkweed had begun to grow where the trees had been, and Jimmy and his friends made trails through the milkweed. The plants were almost taller than the kids. Anyway, their paths led everywhere, and each boy had a place of his own nestled among the weeds, a place that was mostly just a circle of stomped-down milkweed. But each kid could sit down and enjoy the sun, and there was almost no wind. Each spot was a sort of private sanctuary. If you sat down, the milkweed was taller than you, and all the houses disappeared from view. It was magical to them.

"In early summer, the monarch butterflies arrived. Hundreds of them, and they fed on the milkweed, and became almost tame. A child with the right touch could coax a butterfly to sit in his hand."

"And Jimmy had the right touch?" Owen picked up a pickle spear to crunch. He pushed the paper cone toward Marilyn a little.

"He did. And he made it a 'law' that no one could harm a butterfly. Some days, when the other kids weren't around, he would go out to his place and just lie there in the sun, in the warm breeze, content to just enjoy being there—butterflies or no butterflies. He's that kind of kid. Do you know what I mean?"

"I can imagine it. Does that count?" He took another bite of sandwich.

"I never had to worry about him, even as he's gotten older and often on his own during the summers, when school's out. I could go to work and know that at noon my mother-in-law, Viktoria, would make sure he had a sandwich and some milk and maybe an apple for dessert, and that when lunch was over, Jimmy could go outside and play." She paused. "No, not *play*—more like *be*. He didn't need to invent a fantasy in order to be happy. He didn't need to be entertained. Does that make sense?"

Even chewing, Owen was sure he could listen to her talk all day. He nodded and swallowed. "Yes, it does."

"Another thing about Jimmy—well, he doesn't have a father. As you know, Raimo was killed in the war. But Jimmy has two father-figures, now, and they're amazing people."

"Who are they?"

"Jussi, Raimo's father, is one, of course. The other is Ivor. Everyone calls him Rabbit. He's younger than Jussi and Viktoria and not related to Jussi in any way, but they've known each other since they were kids."

They were silent for a moment. Owen said, "Say, you've hardly tried your sandwich. You don't know what you're missing."

Marilyn laughed. "Down the hatch," she said, and took a bite.

A brief pause ensued while they ate and Owen considered. "So back to Jimmy for a sec. Does he have a lot of friends?"

"Not a lot—all his friends are close, though. Three of them, especially, and a couple of others that are around frequently, but not every day."

"And Jimmy's their leader?"

"He doesn't *lead*, exactly—he's more their *idea* guy. He's the one they ask, 'What are we going to do today?' and he comes up with something. He pulls ideas out of the air the way a magician does rabbits.

"He's sensitive, too. He used to hate when the city's street-oiling truck would come along in the summer and spray the sand and gravel with oil. It made the street stink, he'd say, and kept the kids from crossing over to the other side of the street until the oil no longer stuck to the bottoms of their shoes. He knew that some of them would get in trouble at home if they got the soles of their shoes dirty. They had just the one pair."

Owen laughed, but sobered as Marilyn looked at him steadily. She said only, "We are not rich. We are comfortable, but we are better off than many in town, and we are careful with our belongings."

Owen cleared his throat. "I'm sorry for laughing. That was thoughtful of Jimmy. Adult."

"He is thoughtful, when he's not being silly. He likes comic books. He even has one that needs 3-D glasses, which he hides from Viktoria and me."

"Private?"

"Yes, I suppose. But not secretive. He's never mean. Sometimes, the kids have wrestling matches. But they don't hurt each other. They have these elaborate rules—Jimmy's rules—that keep the wrestling fun. And when they go to the creek and race crayfish, he has rules for what you can and can't do with and to a crayfish. When they're done playing with them, they plunk them back into the water for another day."

"He sounds like a nice person. Like you?" Owen risked a sideways compliment.

Marilyn smiled, aware of his strategy. "I don't touch crayfish. And frankly, I'm kind of glad when the streets are oiled, because there's less dust. So yes, he's like me in some ways, but he's more like Jussi, his grandfather, and like Ivor, who is Jussi's brother without being a brother."

There was another brief pause for eating. Owen finished first. He opened his bottle of root beer and stretched out, leaning on his elbow. "And your mother-in-law, Viktoria? What's she like?"

"Oh. She's wonderful. Kind-hearted, smart, and very disciplined."

Owen teased, "Push-ups and sit-ups every day? Rulers on palms for misbehaving?"

"Hardly. But in her own way, she keeps us in order. All of us know that when she's around we mustn't use colloquialisms. We say *why*, not *how come*. And we don't speak in slang, and we don't start our sentences with *and*. And we know the difference between *can* and *may*."

It was Owen's turn to smile. "I like her already."

"She has a lot of friends. She's well known in the neighbourhood, of course, and at Immanuel Lutheran. But she knows many people. Once a month or so she goes to the new Psych hospital to visit a woman she's known for ages. They met when Viktoria first came to Canada."

"Oh?"

"It's funny, and it's sad," Marilyn said. "When this woman's husband left her in the early '30s, she had three kids—the youngest was just a baby. And the woman didn't have a penny to her name, so she tried to feed the baby by putting some water in a milk bottle, and then adding flour to make the water look white. My mother-in-law, whenever she'd visit, would take along a couple of bottles of milk for the baby.

"Those kids are grown now, but their mother is mentally ill. She's convinced that Frank Sinatra is in love with her. I know it sounds funny, but it's really sad. She has a mental illness, or maybe hardening of the arteries. Anyway, Viktoria visits her. Viktoria's like that—she doesn't ever give up on people." Marilyn took a sip of her root beer. "And she's always saying *It is what it is.* What happens, happens."

"I think I've heard my father say that. Maybe it's a Finnish thing. So what's Jussi like?"

"He and Viktoria are a matched pair."

"Oh? How?" Owen thought, *What an interesting way to think about a marriage.*

"Jussi isn't the head of the household, and neither is Viktoria. They have a common understanding of things. Sometimes, like kids, they play with each other—verbally, I mean. And sometimes they discuss things that they believe are important, but they discuss them as equals. They never seem to argue—there's none of that *your job* and *my job* when they talk to each other. And by the way, although I refer to them as Jussi and Viktoria, I call them Mom and Dad. They are like parents to me."

She met Owen's gaze.

This is important to her. He nodded to let her know he understood. "They sound like interesting people. Thank you for telling me about them." He drank root beer, thinking about his father and watching Marilyn eat. He wondered what his parents' marriage had been like, really.

Marilyn swallowed a bite of sandwich. "So, Owen. Are you still serious about meeting them?"

Elated, he said, "Absolutely. I'd enjoy it." He hoped.

"That can be arranged," Marilyn said. "And so can meeting Jimmy. That's obligatory."

"Good. Soon?" He tried not to let his eagerness show.

"I'll check with Viktoria, but perhaps this Wednesday." Marilyn dusted imaginary crumbs off her hands. "And now, I think you're stalling. If we're going to pick berries, we should go. And you'll need to pick clean, because Viktoria doesn't like spending a lot of time chasing down stray stems and leaves." She began retrieving sandwich wrappers and napkins.

Owen said, "I've never picked berries." At Marilyn's look of surprise, he added, "Not to bring home, anyway. I mean, I've picked them. I've just eaten what I picked."

"Well, you may find picking blueberries hot work, and hard work. We don't pick them for fun, though. We need them for food. So come along."

That afternoon, they filled two big baskets. Owen insisted that Marilyn take them all with her. Marilyn insisted on making a small cup from a piece of paper in Owen's car and filling it with berries. Owen had fresh blueberries for a full week.

5 • THE MANTERES

ON TUESDAY, THE TWENTY-THIRD of August, Andrew Millbridge parked his car across from the Finn Hall and walked over to a cab near the entrance. He knocked on the driver's window. The driver unlocked the passenger door and Millbridge got in.

"Well?" he asked the cab driver. "Give me your impressions."

"There's not much to give," the driver said. "I went to the McIntyre River like you asked, and watched what the kids—Jimmy Mantere and a couple of others—were doing. Mantere's definitely the leader, the one in charge. The others do what he says. He's not bossy, though, just smart. He doesn't push the kids around; he doesn't play favourites; he's not a bully." He paused. "What do you want me to tell you about?"

"Suppose … suppose another kid showed up—hell, a gang of kids—and started to pick on Mantere's group. What would he do?"

"Talk to them. Talk first," the driver said, "but if they wanted a fight—the gang, I mean—this Jimmy kid wouldn't back down. He'd try to be reasonable, I think—try to talk them out of it—but then, if it wasn't doing any good, he'd wade in."

Myllysilta did not say anything for a few moments. "Brave?"

"Definitely. The kid's brave as hell. But he's not a chest-beater. If I had a kid, I'd want the kid to be like him."

"Thanks," Myllysilta said. He handed over a ten-dollar bill.

"That's way too much," the driver said.

Myllysilta shook his head and got out. "Fuck," he said as the cab pulled away.

Back in Finland, he and Bertil Granbakken, the shopkeeping communist, had often debated the seemingly paradoxical phrase, *The child is the father of the man*. The nature of the child is the nature of the father. Was it, or was it not, true?

Antti Myllysilta, of course, given the nature and behaviour of his father and brothers, had a personal stake in the discussion. Bertil Granbakken perhaps less so. But on this, they agreed: the answer to the question was, *sometimes.* Sometimes, the son showed how he'd been raised, showed the true nature of one of the primary influences on his life.

"But," Bertil had insisted to Antti, "not always. Not in every way. It is possible to be *from* a place, or a family, but not *of* that place."

For a while, Myllysilta had agreed. He had believed that being *unknown* to be a Myllysilta would make him less like his father. Now he was not so sure.

And in this case, he would be a fool to not believe that the child was the father of the man. Or in this case, the grandfather of the man.

Given what the cabbie had said about Jimmy, Jussi Mantere was, as he suspected, dangerous to predict. Worse to underestimate.

I need to be careful, Myllysilta thought.

He never wondered what Owen's behaviour implied about him. Long ago, Millbridge had come to understand that Owen was like Annie. It was May who still concerned him. She was, he hoped, still frozen. *Let's hope,* whispered Myllysilta, *she does not do anything … foolish.*

#

On Wednesday, Owen Millbridge left work early. At home he changed clothing twice because he didn't feel that business attire— even casual-looking business attire—was appropriate for meeting Marilyn's family.

No suit, he decided. *Dress pants, yes. Or maybe? But no suit. And shine the shoes. Dress pants? Cancel the dress pants—casual pants.* Because it was Wednesday, Marilyn would have had the afternoon to get ready, and *Oh, God,* he thought, *don't let me look like a dink.* He opted for casual slacks, a freshly-pressed light blue shirt, and newly shined shoes. *There!*

At exactly five-thirty, Owen knocked on the Mantere's front door. Marilyn opened the door before he could knock twice. Forewarned, Owen took off his shoes as soon as he entered the house. He stopped himself from just slipping them off his feet, and undid the laces first. Then, inside the front porch, he put them on the mat beside the door, not just on the floor.

"I hope I'm not late," he said.

Jussi Mantere came out of the living room to greet Owen, who stood by the door in his stocking feet.

"Owen," Jussi said, extending his hand. Owen shook it firmly, but not too firmly. "I am Marilyn's father-in-law, Jussi, and this is my wife, Viktoria. My grandson, Jimmy, is upstairs but," he raised his voice so that it would carry, "he will be down soon."

Owen nodded at Viktoria, who tilted her head when she looked at him. *As if I'm a side of pork*, he thought.

Jimmy appeared, and Mantere said, "Mr. Millbridge, my grandson, Jimmy."

Jimmy extended his right hand. "Pleased to meet you, sir," he said. Owen and Jimmy shook hands.

For a second or two longer than Owen found comfortable, the three stood shoeless by the door, Viktoria and Marilyn just beyond.

Then Mantere said, "Come to the living room," and led the way. Millbridge followed; Jimmy, however, went back upstairs to his room.

Viktoria headed for the kitchen and started to take out the good dishes and cutlery.

Marilyn had followed Millbridge into the living room. "Marilyn," Jussi said, "perhaps you could give your mother a hand in the kitchen."

"Yes, of course," Marilyn said. She seemed a bit flustered.

Jussi motioned for Millbridge to sit down. "We have met once before," Jussi said.

"Oh? I don't—"

"It was in July, I think. You were in the shoemaker's shop on Oliver Road. The shoemaker, as I recall, mentioned that your parents were from Finland."

How could he remember that? Owen wondered.

"Just my father," Owen said. "My mother was born here. She died many years ago." He hoped he didn't sound maudlin. He also wondered why Marilyn's father would bring up their meeting —even if he *did* remember it.

"I am sorry to hear that," Jussi said. "Millbridge is an odd name for a Finn. Your father changed it?"

"He was a Niemi. *Niemi*, I understand, means *peninsula* in Finnish, and my father thought that if he called himself Andrew Peninsula—

his name is actually Antti—it would sound silly, especially if some well-meaning people tried to pronounce it as a Finnish name, so he chose Millbridge, instead." *I'm babbling,* Owen thought.

"Ah. That was wise. Where in Finland did his family live?"

"Well," Owen said, "it's not even in Finland now. The family was from Karelia."

"Yes, which is mostly in Russia these days. You have relatives still there?"

Damn, Owen thought, *is part of Karelia in Finland and part of it in Russia? I'm an idiot.*

Before he could start to frame an answer, however, Viktoria called "Supper!" from the kitchen.

Oh, thank God, Owen thought. He had no idea whether or not his relatives—if any even existed—might be living in Karelia. He wasn't even sure where Karelia was, exactly. In spite of his study of history, he remained unclear about boundaries and borders, especially in Europe, especially in the past fifty-plus years. Maps kept changing.

Jimmy reappeared and the family assembled around the kitchen table. When everyone was seated, and the meal began, Jussi shifted the conversation to articles that had recently appeared in the newspaper.

After supper, Viktoria brought dessert—rice pudding with a little cinnamon on top. The conversation around the table continued on non-personal topics: city politics and neighbourhood growth, followed quickly by speculation about how ocean-going ships would change the Lakehead, as they developed the St. Lawrence Seaway.

Owen was careful to say neither too much, nor too little. He hoped.

#

When the meal was over, Viktoria, with a meaningful glance, sent Jussi and Owen into the living room. Marilyn washed the dishes; Jimmy dried them; Viktoria put them away.

"So," Jussi began when he and Owen Millbridge were seated on the living room couch, each at one end. "Your father's family is from Karelia. Your mother's?"

"That's a bit of a mystery. Her father was a trapper, a Scot. She may have told me once or twice what part of Scotland he was from, but I was very young—she died before I turned three—and I really don't have any memories from that time."

"You have a sister, a brother?"

"A sister. May. She lives in Toronto. She's two years younger."

"And your father, he must have come to Canada around the same time I did."

"When was that?"

"1920," Jussi said. "I told them I was a Swede so I could get in."

"My father did the same thing," Owen said, "though I'm not sure what year. Early twenties, though."

"He speaks Swedish?"

"No, just Finnish, and English, of course. He knows a little—what does he call it—kitchen Swedish. Mostly swear words. Enough to have fooled the customs agents." Owen laughed. It was an unforced laugh, a friendly laugh. "He was a bit of a wild man, I understand, before he married my mother. Drank a lot, swore a lot. She tamed him, though."

"Do you live with your father?" Mantere kept the tone light.

"No, I have my own place. He values his privacy."

Jussi paused briefly before he next spoke. "In Finland, was your father Red or White?"

"Sorry?" Owen said. *What an odd question*, he thought.

"When he came to Canada, did he support the Communists or the Socialists?"

Owen spoke uncertainly. "I don't think he was interested in politics at all. In fact, I don't think he ever voted."

Marilyn called from the kitchen, "Hey, Dad, no more grilling. Play nice."

"Okay," Jussi called back. "I'll behave." He laughed. "When I came to Canada, I went to work in the lumber camps."

"My father had invested in a lumber company early on, I think. He was a silent partner. I can't remember the name of the company, though. Later on he went into wholesaling—selling building supplies, furniture. Then real estate."

"Lots of immigrants—Finns, Swedes, Norwegians—worked in the lumber camps. In some of them, if you weren't a Red, the guys who supported the Red side in the war in Finland gave you a hard time."

"There was a war in Finland?" Owen thought: *I don't know*

geography. I know a lot of history, but this is a part of history I don't know. I'm an idiot twice over already, and I've only been here for an hour or so.

"1918," Jussi said.

"I didn't know that," Owen said. "World War One, though, right?"

"It became part of it, I guess," Jussi said. "But it didn't start out that way. Or maybe it did. The Russians—"

"Jussi!" Viktoria's voice this time. She spoke his name as if she were concerned that Jussi would bore Owen with a long and rambling history of the war.

Though Owen would have been interested to hear about the war, he was grateful that Viktoria left him a shred of dignity.

#

When at last, the dishes were done, Owen and Marilyn left to see a movie. In the car Owen said, "Your parents seem like really nice people, and your son is bright as anything."

"They are, and he is," Marilyn said. "So, Owen … your sister. When do I get to meet her?"

Owen was quiet for several seconds. "I don't know," he said, finally.

"Oh?" Marilyn sounded puzzled. "You said she lives in Toronto? Or the area?"

"Yes." Having met Jussi and Viktoria and Jimmy, Owen decided to be honest. "That is, as far as I know."

"As far as you *know?*"

"Yes. She—I don't know—she may have moved. Last summer. We speak on the phone, but rarely." He sighed. "There's a lot I don't know, but …."

"But what? You don't have to tell me, but you can." She meant, she wouldn't tell anyone else.

"I know. I want to."

And then Owen told her as much as he knew. And at some point in his story, Marilyn recognized that many families, not just the Manteres, included stories from the past—stories that they couldn't pass along to a younger generation. Instead, they held those stories in silence.

#

On Thursday after supper Owen's phone rang. He expected—or rather, hoped—it would be Marilyn. He'd been trying to keep himself from phoning her all day.

May began, "I need to tell you something."

"Are you okay?" Owen asked immediately.

"Yes, I'm not sick, I've got a good job, a nice place to stay—at least for now—but I need to talk to you about Dad."

"Okay. Shoot."

There was a moment of dead air, then, "When I came up to visit in June last year...." She stopped talking.

Owen waited.

"When I came up, I found—I read ... I'm sorry, Owen. I can't—I mustn't do this." She hung up.

A minute or two later, she called back. "I have another new number," she said. "Also unlisted. Same rules as last time."

He wrote down the number, and she warned, "Do *not* leave it where Dad can see it."

She paused. "Bye, Owen."

"Goodbye?" He said it to dead air then stared at the phone. *Whatever this is about,* he thought, *I can't ask Dad.*

#

When he drove past the shoemaker's shop on Friday, Andrew Millbridge did not expect to see a note between the boot and the shoe in the display. He circled the block, parked, and a minute or two later, was in the shop.

"Something for you," the shoemaker said, looking up from his work.

"Yes," Millbridge said. "I see that."

"You guys ever going to tell me what the hell's going on?"

"No."

The shoemaker shrugged.

Millbridge fetched the envelope and left the store without saying anything more. In the car he tore the end off the envelope and took out the single piece of paper. *Hemmet. Upstairs. Saturday. Noon* was all it said.

263

6 • ENDGAME

MYLLYSILTA WAS ALREADY SEATED at the table upstairs in the Scandinavian Home when Mantere arrived. Before Jussi even had a chance to sit down, Myllysilta asked him in Finnish, "What have you decided?" Myllysilta didn't want to wait; didn't want to give his foe any opportunity to "read the room" or see what Myllysilta might be thinking.

Mantere pulled out a chair opposite Myllysilta. He took his time sitting down, then folded his hands on the table.

"I have heard a number of things about you," Mantere said in English. "Most of what you have told me is ... what do the English call it? A *fabrication*. A ready-made lie. And I have spoken to your son and asked him about you. He knows almost nothing of your real past. You are a skillful liar. You know how to weave one lie into another and leave no holes. I think he believes everything you have told him."

"I think *you* have spoken to your friend, Ivor," Myllysilta said in English, leaving the bait untouched. He refused to get into a father-son debate; he refused to let Owen be used to entrap or weaken him.

"I think you killed a man and burned his body so that your secrets would not piss out of him when he was drunk," Mantere said.

Myllysilta let a smile play on his face for a second. *How long that story—that fabrication—has lasted*, he thought. "Perhaps," Myllysilta said. The smile returned. "That is something I certainly might have done, before I fully became Millbridge."

Mantere leaned forward, but he kept his hands flat on the table. "I think you bought your young son a Don because you still like to remember the feeling of being an outlaw on a warrior's horse."

Myllysilta did not react, did not acknowledge the assumption— another convenient fabrication still making its rounds—or the incident from the past.

Instead, he said, "A Don is a fine horse. The Cossacks knew how to breed strength and athleticism into both their horses and themselves." Teacher to student.

"Is that what you pretend to be—a Cossack?" Mantere asked. "You are no more a Cossack now than you were the day you rode away from Svensson's murder."

Mantere's evident contempt annoyed Myllysilta. *Get him irritated in return*, Myllysilta whispered. He leaned forward and looked Mantere in the eye. "Was that the storekeeper's name?"

"You know it was," Mantere said evenly. "You said it the last time we met. And it is the name you used in your letter, when you claimed to have killed him. You didn't take part in the killing, though. Except to act as a spy for your brothers, I think. You were the boy who rode away. Weren't you? One of your brothers stole some candies for you, didn't he?"

You're no prosecutor, Millbridge thought. *Oh, yes, he is*, Myllysilta replied.

"If that is what you want to believe," Millbridge said. He leaned back in his chair, then changed his mind and sat up straight. His hands, with their rounded nails and fingertips, had been too much on display. He put them in his lap.

Mantere eyed him. "At the time I thought you had been one of the killers. But you weren't. You were just a boy told to keep your eyes open and not get into trouble."

"I was young."

"Were you also the boy acting as lookout the day my mother was killed?"

Myllysilta shrugged. "Yes." He paused, evaluating Mantere. *He can put two and two together*, Myllysilta thought. "But I had no part in the killing. My brothers would not let me." He smiled ironically. "They thought I would not have killed a woman, but I would have. I *did*. Several." He paused again. "Just not your mother." He put his hands on the table once more. "Are you a member here? A member of the Scandinavian Home Society?"

"I'm not a joiner," Mantere said. He looked straight into Millbridge's eyes.

And you don't like surprises, Myllysilta thought. *Even ugly finger surprises*. Millbridge said mildly, "A legacy of the war, I think. No church, no political party, no fraternal organization—not even Kansallisseura, the Loyal Finns. No boss telling you what to do. Just you, just your decisions. No Red, no White, no visits to 'the old country.' All because of the war."

Mantere did not seem at all fazed by the words. *He was expecting me to say them*, Myllysilta thought.

"Tell me about your friend," Mantere said, "the one who died, the one whose body you burned."

Myllysilta took over for Millbridge. "He died. He drank himself to death. I didn't need to kill him. I just needed the story of his death to be useful. I had gone to his shack to ask him to do a job for me and found him dead, so I burned down his shack, and every time I was asked about his death, I smiled and said I knew nothing." He laughed. "People became afraid of me, for a while. But they didn't pass on what they thought they knew to their children. And no one ever spoke to Annie about it either."

How odd to think of her when I remember Kari Petterson, first drunk, and then dead, and then ashes from the fire, Millbridge thought.

"Vilho thinks you killed the fellow. Are you saying that he knows only that part of the story?"

"And coughs it up whenever he feels the need. Vilho knows what I want him to know, what everybody knows," Myllysilta said, "and he does what I ask him to do." He paused, then mockingly said, "It is in the stories, you know—not in the truth—that the power lies to change men's lives." He smiled impishly then became serious once more. "Vilho believes what I tell him. Such men are useful."

"Not to a dead man, Antti Myllysilta," Mantere said, "and you, for all your bluster, are surely dying."

"That I am." Millbridge folded his hands on the table and leaned forward. "In dying, a man has to give up much. I will not die forgiven, I know that, but will you, for all my supposed wickedness, agree to keep my past a secret from my son?"

He thought of May, hiding out somewhere, probably still in Toronto, in possession of his true biography. She had not told Owen about it—not yet. And perhaps she never would. But he needed to protect Owen.

He added, "My death is of no concern to me, but his life is. And I think it is of concern to you, too."

"You never speak of your daughter. Why is that?" Mantere asked.

"We are—I do not know the word—*vieraantuneet*."

"Estranged."

He knows English better than I do, Myllysilta thought. "Is that the word? She will have nothing to do with me."

"Why is that?" Mantere seemed genuinely interested.

Again, Myllysilta shrugged.

The steps outside the upper room creaked. Both men kept silent as one of the waitresses came up the stairs.

"Do you men want anything?" she asked, poking her head in at the open door. "Coffee? Pie?"

"Coffee," Myllysilta said. "With cream. My throat is dry. And … do you have lemon pie?" He added his thick Finnish accent; both *th* and *d* had once again become *t*.

"We do."

"Double it up," Mantere said.

"It won't take a minute." The waitress headed back down the stairs.

Mantere waited until he was sure that she was downstairs again. "Did you know that rage makes a man see only what is in front of him?"

Myllysilta leaned forward almost imperceptibly, attentive.

Mantere went on, "When I killed the last of your brothers I felt like I was peering down a tunnel, and the bullets went exactly where I was looking."

"Interesting," Myllysilta said. *Some people think death is like that for the dying,* he thought. "That isn't how it is for me," he said aloud.

"You learned to kill in the war," Mantere said, "but not in rage." It was almost a question.

"No, not in rage. There was no tunnel. I knew exactly what I was doing. And felt almost nothing. A little excitement, perhaps. Sometimes pleasure." He paused for just a second. "But I didn't kill your mother." He remembered the night when he had killed his father with a stone. It had been, in its own way, a pleasure too.

Mantere raised his right hand, his fingers making the sign for *one minute.* They listened to the waitress on the stairs. She entered with two cups of coffee in one hand, two pie plates and a small pitcher of cream in the other, and set them down on the table without spilling anything.

"If I tried to do that," Mantere said to her, "there would be broken china on the stairs and lemon pie from my elbow to my chin."

He speaks to her as if he has known her all his life, Myllysilta thought.

The waitress laughed. "Practice, practice, practice. Sugar's on the table. Enjoy the pie." She went down the stairs and disappeared into the hubbub of the restaurant.

"It is easy for a young man to kill," Myllysilta said, as if the waitress had never brought them lemon pie and coffee.

"Not for most," Mantere said. "Most need to practice."

Myllysilta let a moment pass before he let Millbridge speak. "When I met Annie, my life changed," he said.

"You came to Jesus, did you?" Mantere's voice was wry but not bitter.

"No," Millbridge said, "nothing like that. I walked out of a cold room and into one where a fire was going, there was coffee on the table, and the smell of cinnamon in the air."

"Not lemon?"

Myllysilta sighed, but it was Millbridge who spoke. "No, not lemon. Apple pie is still the best, with lots of cinnamon. But this is not a day for apple pie, nor for Annie."

"Is it a day for truth? Or are you going to tell me once again that you were paid by a man who gave you money for a soldier's boot?"

Myllysilta sent Millbridge away and drummed his fingers. Then, suddenly becoming aware of them at the end of his frog's hand, he stopped and said, "It doesn't really matter, does it? I was paid or I was not. I lie or I tell the truth. All that matters to me, and to you, is that my child will be happy." He splayed his fingers on the table, simultaneously offering his illness and his cards, both laid down. "So will you keep my secret?" he asked.

For a moment, Mantere didn't respond. Then, "Yes."

Myllysilta was taken aback. He had not anticipated that this would be Mantere's reply. What did it mean? What had he not foreseen? What trick had just been played on him?

"But I have one condition," Mantere said. "You must keep it as well. I want you to promise me, on Annie's soul, that you will never confess your secret to your son, never tell it to your daughter. You must bear it to your grave. I am not granting you mercy, Antti Myllysilta. If there is a God, I want you to die unshriven, unforgiven, unable to escape into a merciful death."

Millbridge, for it was he now—not Myllysilta—watched as Mantere took his fork and lifted a small piece of pie to his mouth, savoured it, and swallowed.

Mantere fixed his eyes on Millbridge and said calmly, in words built of ice, "When the gates of Hell gape open, I want the fires to eat you whole. I want to stand over your grave and smell the sulfur and gunpowder rise, reeking, from the soil beneath my feet."

For a full minute, Myllysilta tried to break out of Millbridge and speak, but he could not. Finally, he let Millbridge say, "So be it," and nodded. "You have poetry in you, Jussi. And, for what it is worth—I know it's not much—you also have my word."

He raised the hand that held the fork and its small piece of pie. "Thank you," he said. He put the pie in his mouth and swallowed it. "The pie is very good, don't you think?"

#

When Andrew Millbridge got home, he was exhausted. He spent part of the rest of the day thinking about what the meeting with Jussi Mantere really meant—what it *portended*. Then he lay down on the couch in the living room and fell asleep.

Sometime in the night, he woke to the sound of Wolf scratching on the door. He let the dog in, then went back to sleep.

7 • NIGHTMARE

HIS HANDS, THEIR FINGERTIPS shaped like somewhat flattened snowballs, were cold and numb. He could see that he was holding the horse's reins, but he could not feel his hands. He wanted to tell Marku that he had read Sun Tzu's *The Art of War*, but that would lead to a beating, and it had nothing to do with his fingers except that war is cold.

He woke a little—enough so that he thought to roll over and put both hands under the pillow to let them grow warmer. The dream broke just a little as well, was almost lost, but came back when he put his head on the pillow once more.

Marku, at thirty, the only one who knew the date of his birth, shouted at him: "To hell with *The Art of War!*" as if Antti had spoken the words out loud. The snow was cold.

And now Antti was in the forest, crouching in the snow. His feet were cold and, no, he wasn't there—he was asking Seppo, who was just a little older than he was, if Marku had told him why they were only in the introduction to Tzu's masterpiece, and why they had come to kill Jussi Mantere who was not mentioned in the book that Bertil Granbakken had lent him.

"Because *Jussi* means *Jesus*," Marku said, "and I am *Mark*."

"No," Antti said pointedly. *"Jussi* means *a gift from God."*

"Same thing," Marku said.

"And *Marku* means you are *devoted to the god of war.*"

Antti could feel the cold steel of the sword handle under the drift of snow. He tried to pull the sword out of its sheath, but he could not. Nor could he move.

"Coward," Marku said.

"I honour God," Timo said. *"My* God," he added.

"I am a twin," Tuomas volunteered. *"His* twin," he said, pointing at Timo.

"I am the blacksmith," Seppo said. "*I* bend iron to my will."

"I am a man!" Antti shouted at them. "*I* am a *man!* That should mean something!"

"What was our mother's name?" his brothers shouted in chorus back at him.

"She had no name," Antti said quietly. "She had no name. She was our mother."

His brothers began to laugh at him, the laughter rising until Bertil Granbakken pointed out that Henning Wikström would know what to do ... would take their behavior and make of it a plot-point.

"Söderhjelm!" Antti shouted. "Her name was Söderhjelm!"

He was holding the violin, but its strings were steel—not catgut. Catgut burns, he knew, but steel does not. It rusts like an andiron, too hot for the hand—like the neck of a violin played feverishly.

"Shhh. Don't shout," Annie said. She was smiling at Andy. "May will wake up, and you know what that means," she said.

Standing beside him, she held his hand and then released it and leaned over the crib to touch May on the lips, to feel if she was feverish. Andrew felt her fingertips on his lips.

Andrew tried to explain. "I don't," he said. "I don't ... something. I don't know what to do. Yes ... I don't know what to do. You need to look out the window when you turn. Don't look at the steering wheel ... look out the window."

His father lay dead on the straw in the basement. The box that had killed Annie lay beside him. Andrew rolled over on the bed and looked up through the hole in the ceiling. He could see the stars. The violin was under the bed, and it helped his pillow warm his hands.

He should lay a wine bottle in the straw, beside his father, if he remembered. If he remembered. Söderhjelm—no not that, not him, it was Solbakken.

Karl Solbakken, dead, lay face down in the dry grass on the hillside. The black angel, the Musta Maija, though its granite wings were chipped and broken by bullets, still was reaching down to touch the body.

Antti shot her twice in the back, stole her book, *The Gold Mine*, the one about ... something. Then he scattered the playing cards on the dry grass.

Below the cemetery, the blood that flowed down from the cemetery's banks and into the river turned its waters the red of a rusty nail waiting on a basement shelf.

Behind a tree at the edge of the river a rabbit sat as still as death, keeping its eyes on Antti. Waiting, as Antti had waited the day his brothers died.

Antti, terrified, burst awake. He sat up, breathing heavily. After a moment, he said "Goddamn."

It was dark outside. He turned on the lamp on the night table beside the bed. The clock said it was just a little after three in the morning.

Antti got up and began to dress. He did not want to risk more sleep.

Wolf woke as well, and Antti opened the kitchen door so that the dog could go out.

The air was cool on his face. September approached, and winter would soon be arriving. He had no wish to see another winter or feel the cold wind once more scratching at his throat and taking his breath.

Therefore, he had much to do, and just a week to do it. He began to picture what would happen, the steps he would take.

He sat at the table, waiting for dawn.

8 • THE DEVIL'S VIOLIN

THE SATURDAY BEFORE LABOUR DAY, Andrew Millbridge was nearly ready. At noon he drove to the shoemaker's shop.

He picked up a packet of letters and notes from the front seat beside him. Then, careful to look both ways before crossing the street, he went into the shop.

The shoemaker waited until the sewing machine had stopped before looking up.

Millbridge said, "I have some items I'd like to put in the boot. Do you mind?"

"Not at all." The shoemaker had almost become used to the old Finn; he'd stopped by the shop more than once during the past week.

"I've ten dollars for you, as well. This month's rent for the space." Millbridge handed the money to the shoemaker, then went to the display and dropped the letters and notes into the boot.

On his way to the door, he said, "Thank you." Then he turned back. "Oh, I forgot." He took his wallet from his pocket once more. "I'd like you to stay open on Monday—Labour Day." He took out a five-dollar bill. "That's for your trouble. And we have a deal, remember? Are you clear about what you need to do?"

"Yes, sir." The shoemaker was not clear, exactly, but he knew what he was supposed to do, and he also knew, very well, that he didn't want to know more.

"Good." He touched his hat. "Good day."

The shoemaker, his reflection distorted by the uneven glass of the door's old window, watched him leave. *Good day. Almost like goodbye.* He went back to work.

Millbridge, at his home, loaded his car, moving slowly and carefully. He carried one item at a time, taking breaks even when he didn't need them, ignoring the urgency nipping at his heels.

He slept well Saturday night, tired from the day's labour.

In the afternoon on Sunday, Millbridge drove to Riverside Cemetery. There, when he could see no cars coming from either direction on Oliver Road, he got out of his car. He untied the ropes he'd used to secure a small wooden ladder to the roof, passing the ropes through the partly open back seat windows of the car. *That worked well*, he thought, then he took the two empty dynamite boxes out of the back seat.

Like a lot of people, he knew about the shortcut to the Hanging Tree. He slowly walked the shortcut, carrying one of the dynamite boxes with the coil of rope inside it. He dropped off his first load at the Tree, then went back to the car for the other box. After he had returned from carrying the second load, he sat in the car, resting. A few minutes later he felt strong enough to make the third trip, carrying the ladder, stopping as needed.

At the Hanging Tree—some of the old Finns at the Hoito called it the Last Stop—he sat down on one of the boxes and had a cigarette, his first in thirty-three years. It was one of the old-style unfiltered kind, less expensive and less habit-forming than the new-style longer ones with filters.

It's getting harder and harder to find the old-style cigs, he thought. *People don't want to watch their fingers get yellow from the burning tobacco.*

When the cigarette was too short to hold without burning him, Millbridge butted the cigarette out on the box, then wet his thumb and index finger, pinched off the front of the cigarette to make sure it was out, and flicked it away.

Everything comes to an end, he thought. *Everything.*

He stood and flattened the cigarette pack before flinging it away like a playing card being thrown into a hat. It didn't even come close to the spot he had chosen as a target.

He took a deep breath, then let it out slowly. The last step would be the hardest.

From one of the old Finns that he had met at the Hoito, he had learned, over coffee and *pulla* bread, that there was a way to make a noose that would not cause a man to choke to death. Instead, it would pinch off the carotid arteries, and kill by depriving the brain of blood. No pain, no strangulation, no need to struggle.

It would be fast, like riding a Don, but off into eternity, Myllysilta had thought. He took careful mental notes and made such a noose at home. Now he needed to secure the end of the rope to the branch of the Tree, and then tie the rest of the rope to the trunk. He hoped the rope would be long enough.

He placed the upper part of the ladder against the trunk of the tree. He climbed up, high enough to tie the rope to the branch, but he had to twist his body around in order to reach the part of the branch he needed. He knew the noose must be at least three feet, maybe four, away from the tree's trunk. Otherwise, his body might try to overrule his brain—it might make him swing himself to the trunk and wrap his legs around it so he could call off the hanging.

Also, he was beginning to feel tired—really tired. Not the kind he could sit and wait to recover from, then continue. Instead, it felt like the time just before he had passed out and urinated on the kitchen floor. He let the rope drop to the ground and climbed down the ladder. The alternative now—since the ladder wasn't helpful—was to use the two dynamite boxes as steps. He'd be able to get much further from the trunk than he'd been able to reach from the ladder.

But first, he needed to rest. He hoped he had at least one more round of "exert, rest" left to him.

He sat for almost twenty minutes on one of the boxes and regretted not keeping the cigarettes.

At long last, when he felt part of his strength return, he placed one of the boxes under the correct spot of his chosen branch. It looked strong enough to take his weight without bending too close to the ground. He positioned the box so that when he looped the rope over the branch, it would hang down sufficiently far from the tree's trunk.

Sometimes the body is stronger than the mind.

"It might," he said aloud, "it might try to save itself."

I must be careful with the tree's branch. If the noose is too close to the branch, I might reach up and grasp the branch, pull myself up, and hold on with one hand while I slipped the noose off my neck. Same with the trunk—I might try to brace myself. I can't allow that to happen.

Exactly, Myllysilta whispered.

When Millbridge stepped up on the box, however, he was still too low to reach the branch and attach the rope. He needed to put the second box on top of the first. But would he be able to step up onto the top box, a full two feet? Also, the boxes might wobble, and he might fall. He might break a leg and not be able to get up, or he might break an arm and not be able to tie the rope. So much could go wrong.

It was hard to think. *Mitä tulee, tulee.*

I need to put the top box sideways on the bottom box, he thought. *Ninety degrees to the bottom box. That will make it easier to get up—I can climb up one, then the other. Two little steps instead of one big one. And when I'm on the top box I can easily reach the branch. Then I can put the noose where I want it, and loop the rope around the branch a few times, then tie it securely to the branch so that the rope won't move, and it will be exactly where I need it to be.*

He succeeded. The bottom of the noose dangled just below his chin. *Good*, he thought.

He practiced putting the noose over his head and then tightening the loop so that it wouldn't let him drop through. *Also good.* But now, could he get the noose off without falling? *Careful. Don't lose your balance.*

After much fidgeting, he loosened the rope, then climbed slowly and carefully down again, removed the noose from his neck, then climbed back up onto the top box once more.

This time he managed to get the noose to dangle where it should, then he looped the rope around the branch three times. *In the name of the Father, Son, and Holy Ghost*, he thought.

He climbed carefully down, took the end of the rope and tied it to the trunk of the tree. *And that*, he thought, *is that.* He smiled.

He left the boxes piled on top of each other as they were. After another rest break, he carried the small ladder back to the car, tied it to the roof again, then rested again before driving home.

At home he fell instantly asleep on the living room couch.

#

Millbridge woke just before suppertime. He stretched—not too stiff, not too sore. Slowly, he pushed himself upright. So far, so good.

He made himself a TV dinner. Just as he took his dinner out of the oven, Owen arrived with a paper bag from the bakery.

"Get a dinner for yourself," Millbridge said. "There's lots in the freezer compartment."

"Oh good," Owen said. "I brought buns. Can't go wrong with buns and butter." While his dinner was baking, Owen put the buns onto a plate on the table and retrieved the butter from the fridge. They'd share a knife between them.

When Owen's supper was ready, he brought it to the table.

Andrew was still eating, one slow bite at a time.

"This is nice," his father said as Owen retrieved a bun and broke it into two. "Kind of like the Last Supper."

It was a line that Owen would remember for the rest of his life.

#

Just after midnight on Labour Day, the alarm clock on the night table rang, and Andrew Millbridge stared into the darkness above his bed. In a little over seven hours, the sun would rise. He did not want to see it come up.

He got out of bed, turned on the bedroom light, and checked to make sure the blinds were drawn on the window. They were, so he got dressed. He inspected himself in the mirror.

Clean shirt, clean trousers, shoes shined, he thought. He might need a jacket. The temperature would keep dropping until the sun started to rise. He might appreciate a little more warmth. He went to the kitchen and looked through the kitchen window to see what the outside thermometer said. *Just over fifty.* He would need a jacket. *I can take it off before I get there.*

He put on his jacket and went down into the basement. At the bottom of the stairs he looked around. *What did I come down here for?* He could not remember, so he went upstairs once more.

Flashlight? Yes, but that was in the kitchen drawer, not the basement, Myllysilta pointed out. *The history, perhaps? No,* Myllysilta said, *that's in the book on the living room shelves.* Millbridge thought something about that wasn't quite right, not anymore, but he couldn't remember. He had meant to do something with the book. *But what?*

For the next four hours, he sat in the kitchen, paced in the living room, looked out the windows, and napped in the comfortable living room chair. Sometimes he was Andrew Millbridge; sometimes he was Antti Myllysilta.

At 5 a.m. Millbridge woke with a start and passed a hand over his face. He was still wearing his jacket. He looked at his watch. Time to leave.

First, he locked the front door. Next, he turned off the lights in the living room. He didn't lock the back door, because he couldn't be sure Owen had a key. *No matter.* Outside, at the end of his driveway, he stopped for a moment to think. *The flashlight!* He went back into the house. He found the flashlight in the kitchen.

The whole place is a mess, he thought. *A goddamned mess.* In the kitchen he had to step over some of the remnants of the violin and its case. *When did this happen?*

While you were resting, Antti Myllysilta answered, *I broke it. I stamped on it until it was in pieces, and then I scattered the pieces with my feet.*

Andrew sniffed. Wolf had urinated on it, marked it as a warning to other dogs. The kitchen floor was *his* territory. *Beware of me,* the urine said.

I let Wolf out. He will survive. Andrew had not let Wolf out. Had not thought of Wolf in days. *My mind is....* He didn't remember what he was going to say.

The shoemaker had promised him that he would be in his shop today to greet Mantere if he should come by. Millbridge had put all the letters and messages that he had in the boot, and had paid the shoemaker five dollars to stay open until normal closing time.

He had also made sure that the shoemaker knew where to find the shoe he would leave behind, and he had told him to put it in the display window once he'd found it.

Most of all: under no circumstances was the shoemaker to walk to the Hanging Tree.

Myllysilta's plan, as far as Millbridge could see, was perfect. Jussi Mantere would be, at the very least, implicated in his death—maybe even tried for it. The shoemaker would be interviewed by the police—of that he was certain because ... something to do with the shoe.

So he needed to get to the cemetery. But he could stay on flat ground. He would use the same route he had taken with the children not so long ago.

Just after 5:30 a.m., he left the house, still in a mess. He didn't want to think about that.

An hour later, exhausted, he came to the trail that led to the Hanging Tree. Even along Oliver Road there had been no traffic. Just one car had gone by him as he walked along the last stretch. Labour Day was, after all, a holiday for most people.

At the start of the trail that led to the Tree, he took off his left shoe and sock. Then he flung the shoe across the road, where it landed in the tall grass. He put the sock in his pants pocket.

The shoemaker—cobbler? What was the right word? The cobbler, he decided. *The cobbler would know where to find the shoe. And the cobbler would ... what.*

He couldn't remember. *What was it? The cobbler would take it back to the shop and put it on display. Yes, that was the plan.*

He checked to make sure that he had actually put the sock in his pants pocket. Then, using the flashlight, he walked along the short trail until he came to the Tree. Anyone who saw his body hanging there would think his shoe would be nearby because they would notice that his socks were clean.

And they'd think that ... something. He was tired. More tired than he'd ever been. Unbelievably tired. *They'd think that whoever had possession of the missing shoe was the killer!* Millbridge allowed himself a laugh. The police had their choice of murderer—either the cobbler or Mantere.

All right then, he thought. He took off his jacket and hung it carefully on the broken arm of a nearby scrub cedar.

Labour Day, he thought. *People are going to remember this at the Hoito for a long time.*

"This is the day that Millbridge hanged himself," they'll say. "Back in '55. Remember that?"

No.... "This is the day that Jussi Mantere killed Andrew Millbridge," they'll say, or "Remember when that shoemaker murdered Millbridge?"

So many choices.

He slipped the noose over his head, then tightened it.

He did not know if he had the courage to step off the box.

Should he call it all off?

The box, however, took the decision away from him. He felt a touch of dizziness, had a momentary loss of balance, and the box shot out from under his feet.

He dropped down onto the bottom box, but hit it at an angle. It skittered to the side. The noose tightened immediately, and his feet never touched the ground. They were six inches above it.

The noose, which he had been assured would cut off blood flow to his carotid artery, killing him without making him choke to death, instead tightened on his throat and cut off his supply of air.

Goddamned lying Finlander! he thought. *Goddamned Hoito!* His body began to fight for oxygen. He was choking! *Choking! Goddamn choking!*

Hands! his mind shouted. *Your hands are free! Do something!* He reached over his head, tried to find the branch, but he could not—his body was too low to the ground now. He tried to swing himself back and forth, holding onto the rope just above the noose, but though he could get his body near the tree trunk, could even touch its branches, he was too goddamned tired to hang on.

He tried climbing the rope with his hands, but they kept slipping, stopping only when they slid down onto the noose. He had lost the little grip left to him.

He was choking! He was choking to death!

The noose, this stupid special noose, wasn't special. It just did what all nooses do.

Still, he fought. He tried to get his fingers between the noose and his neck, but the noose was too tight. He tried to turn so that his feet, perhaps, could find the tree, so his legs, perhaps, could encircle the trunk, but he was choking, and he had no strength, no strength!

He couldn't think.

The rope continued to strangle him, holding him by the neck as if he were a violin, the noose the hand of the Master, his father, gripping him by the throat.

He couldn't hold onto the rope any longer. He was nothing now, nothing but the Devil's violin.

Annie! he cried in the voice that had no sound.

But there was no answer.

He felt bathed in golden light, a flash of her smile, her hands, his hands reaching toward hers—but they disappeared. *For a while,* he thought, *for a while I was a good man. Will she let me be with her?*

For a few more seconds, he saw pin-prick flashes of light.

Then his hands dropped to his sides and the world turned white and went away bearing both Millbridge and Myllysilta with it. Their body defecated.

Neither Andrew nor Antti was aware of its last act on earth.

9 • EULOGY

BECAUSE IT WAS LABOUR DAY, Rabbit let himself sleep in until close to noon. Then, after waking, after breakfast—coffee and a two-day old doughnut—he left his shack and went for a walk. He was careful to lock the door.

First, he followed the trail through the woods, then he took the one that ran along the river. It was something he did most Labour Days, unless it was raining, or he was too hung over to think about taking a walk in the woods.

He had a book with him, *The Count of Monte Cristo*, and he was looking forward to reading it at the Last Stop, the Hanging Tree—a place with many names, some serious, some facetious. The police referred to it brusquely as "the usual place." Others saw it as a spot on the banks of the river that flows through Hades, and whose waters make the dead forget their lives on Earth.

Rabbit, however, thought of the tree as a kind of church in the wild—a church whose communicants were primarily labourers, most of whom had ended their lives in despair, and some, perhaps, in hope of a better life on the other side. What was a man's life but a river?

It was a warm day, and he assumed Jimmy and his friends would be playing in the river, somewhere. He couldn't hear them, but he wasn't listening for them, either. When he was at the point where the cemetery proper—the cleared but not mowed part—started, he climbed the riverbank and began walking through the long grass.

He headed toward the part of the cemetery where, as Jimmy once said, "The tombstones start to grow." There, he cut down to the river once more, and in a few minutes, he was nearly at the Tree.

Partly obscured by the trunk of The Hanging Tree, a body twisted slowly in the warm sun.

Rabbit's heart started to pound. He went closer to see if it was someone he knew from the Hemmet or the Hoito or from the apartment building that was usually his winter home. It was none of those—it was Owen Millbridge's father. It was Antti Myllysilta.

Rabbit needed … he needed to tell Jussi, first. Jussi would know what to do. But Jussi would also have questions.

Rabbit began to quickly look around for things he could tell Jussi about. *No left shoe*, the Ivor part of him noted. *He has a clean sock on his foot, but no shoe.* Why would someone throw away the shoe? Millbridge must have had two shoes on, so where was the other one?

Rabbit knew there was a trail that led to Oliver Road. But it was, most of the time, a muddy trail, and the sock was not dirty. So the shoe had to be around, close by somewhere, otherwise the sock on Millbridge's left foot would have been really dirty. Nobody could hop on one foot all the way from the street to the Tree—especially a sick old man.

Rabbit went down the trail that led to Oliver Road. Millbridge would have parked his car close to the beginning of the trail. But at Oliver Road, Rabbit discovered, there was no car. Had Millbridge walked? *Not possible*, he thought. *Not all the way from his house. Wasn't he too frail?*

There was no point in doing any more detective work. *Jussi will know what to do*, Rabbit thought.

He took the shortcut through the cemetery, across what had been Mrs. Toivonen's potato field, and east along the park road that became Montgomery Street. He found Jussi and Viktoria sitting in their back yard. Neither Marilyn nor Owen were around. *Thank God.*

Viktoria noticed the book in Rabbit's hand as he came around the corner of the house, but before she could ask him about the book, he said, "Myllysilta's killed himself. At the Hanging Tree. I saw the body."

"*Gud*," Viktoria said in Swedish. "Oh, my God. Has anyone gone to find Owen and let him know?" she asked without thinking. Of course Rabbit wouldn't talk to someone before coming to tell them.

"No one else knows." Ivor took over from Rabbit. "I go there sometimes. It's a quiet place." He paused. "He wasn't wearing his left shoe."

"No one else knows yet?" Jussi asked. "You're sure?"

"No one," Ivor said.

"One shoe missing?"

"Yes." Rabbit could see that something had crossed Jussi's mind.

Jussi had a knack for seeing through the camouflage. But why did he ask about the shoe?

Jussi turned to Viktoria. "If Marilyn and Owen come back before we do, say nothing to them about this. Tell them I've gone to have a look at the job so I can get the boys organized when we start work again tomorrow."

Viktoria nodded. She understood immediately that Jussi was working from his intuition. She trusted that it would lead him to do the right things, and she would help by doing exactly as he asked.

To Ivor, Jussi said, "There's something not right about this. We need to go look. We'll take the car."

Five minutes later, as they neared Riverside Cemetery, Ivor said, "Park in the cemetery parking lot like visitors do. There is a shortcut we can take, and we won't leave any tracks too close to the road. It's best we don't take the trail, I think."

When they were in the parking lot, Jussi shut off the engine. Ivor got out first and went through the cemetery's gates, Jussi following. They walked a short distance north, past a dozen or so tombstones, then Ivor had them cut west to a spot where a steep bank led down to the river's edge. They scrambled down and then followed the river as it ran south, then turned west.

"A few hundred feet and we're there," Ivor said. A couple of minutes later, they were at the Hanging Tree.

Millbridge, Jussi could see, was dead. The body's feet were inches from touching the ground, and it stank of feces and urine. Ivor pointed. "See, his shoe is gone. I looked around a bit, but it's not here."

Jussi made no move to start his own search for the missing shoe. Instead, he asked, "How did he get here, do you think?"

"Either someone dropped him off at Oliver Road, or else he walked here from his home," Ivor said. "To walk all this way, though—it's a long way for a sick old man to walk."

"I think that's just what he did, though," Jussi said. "He walked here. He lives—lived—on High Street, but if he used the streets along the top of the city, instead of going down the High Street hill and then up the hill on Oliver Road, the walk would be relatively easy, no hills at all, and it wouldn't take much longer than the time it takes Jimmy to go downtown with his friends to see a movie. Forty minutes, maybe. Myllysilta was sick, but if he was determined enough, he could do it."

"You really think he walked?" Ivor wanted to know.

"Yes. Last night, maybe. And if he told no one that he was going to do this, nobody would know about it, nobody would take one of his shoes."

"I don't understand." *I think I do*, Rabbit whispered to Ivor.

Jussi said, "Let's follow the path he used, back to Oliver Road. I think I know where the shoe is."

It took them less than two minutes to get from the Tree to the road. "The shoe," Jussi said, "is going to be right across the road. Wait here."

Yes! Rabbit thought.

Jussi crossed the road while Ivor waited, and a minute later came back, shoe in hand. "Let's get back to the tree before someone comes along," he said. Just as they were about to head back, however, he stopped. He pointed down at the ground. "See the print?"

In the soft soil of the path were footprints—a man's bare left foot, and one step further on, a man's right shoe print.

Ivor shook his head. "He stole his own shoe. He took his sock off, then put the sock back on again before he hanged himself. Anyone coming along the trail from Oliver Road to here, would mess up the evidence."

"Well done, Sherlock," Jussi said. "Arthur Conan Doyle would be proud of you." He slipped the shoe inside his jacket, then he and Ivor followed their original route back to the car.

"Now where?" Ivor wanted to know.

"To the shoemaker's."

"It's Labour Day. He won't be open."

"I'm pretty sure he will," Jussi said. "I think he's expecting us."

A few minutes later, they entered the shop. When the shoemaker saw the shoe in Jussi's hand, he shook his head. "I told him you'd catch on, but he insisted. And, yes, I was supposed to come for the shoe and put it on display. And, yes, I've been amply compensated. The boot, by the way, has something you might be interested in. He told me to tell you."

Ivor went directly to the display in the window and brought back Karl's boot. *The letters*, Rabbit said. *All the letters are in the boot.*

"Letters and notes," he said to Jussi. He pulled one out. It was in Jussi's handwriting. "Yours," he said, and handed the boot, letters and all, to Jussi.

"I liked the old guy, in a way," the shoemaker said to Jussi. "Did he really...?"

Jussi could see that the shoemaker knew at least something of Millbridge's plan—maybe more than just the mechanics of the suicide itself. "Yes," he said. "At the Hanging Tree." He paused. "Do you have a phone?"

The shoemaker shook his head. "Not at the shop. I have one at home, though. Do you want me to call the police?"

"Yes. Just let them know where to find him. You don't need to identify yourself. They have to do this from time to time. They'll take care of things."

A momentary quiet, a silence louder than words arrived and then passed.

"I liked him," the shoemaker said. "But he was a little—you know." He tapped the side of his forehead. "Funny. I never knew his name, though. I don't think he had any family in town. Never mentioned any."

"Probably just as well." Jussi was glad the shoemaker didn't know. He wondered when he'd learn that Owen Millbridge, one of his favourite customers, had lost his father. "I'll keep the shoes, if you don't mind—the one from the display, the one you were sent to find, and the boot as well."

The shoemaker got some large sheets of brown paper and wrapped everything up in a bundle.

In the car, on the way back home, Ivor said, "I don't understand why Myllysilta wanted the shoemaker to fetch the shoe and put it in the window."

Jussi was quiet for a moment, then he said, "Maybe Myllysilta wanted me to think that, despite his confession, he wasn't really the man who shot Karl in the back and took his boot. Maybe he wanted me to think that the man who actually stole the boot is still alive and well and living in Port Arthur. Perhaps he wanted me to spend the rest of my life watching my back and worrying that our family was in danger."

"But why would he do that?"

"Maybe because I killed his brothers. Maybe because I *didn't* kill *him*. Who knows? He could also have been trying to set me up somehow as his murderer. The shoemaker, after all, knew about my letters to Myllysilta, and his to me and Viktoria."

"Myllysilta was crazy."

"Yes," Jussi said. "Yes, he was. Crazy but smart. Trying not to be stuck with the last card. We're all a little scared of that."

"*Musta Maija*," Rabbit said. As a child, he had learned to play the Finnish card game in which there is no winner—just one last loser. For the player who was stuck with the last card, The Musta Maija, it was Death who won—not one of the other cardplayers.

It was a while before Jussi spoke again. "But he loved his son, and so must I. The daughter, too, if she can let me. Who knows what came between them, what he may have told her."

"What he may have *done* to her," Rabbit said. He remembered the incidents in the Finnish Civil War in which he'd been attacked, where he'd lost himself, becoming both Rabbit and Ivor to survive. "In any case, it may be difficult for her," he said, his voice even, unemotional.

#

When Jussi and Ivor got home, Ivor said goodbye, and Jussi watched him walk up the street. Ivor waved before disappearing from sight.

The house was quiet. Viktoria must still be in the back yard, and Owen and Marilyn still at Boulevard Lake.

Before joining Viktoria, Jussi went into his bedroom. Kneeling on the floor, he took a box out of the back of the closet and lifted off the lid. Then he unwrapped the brown paper from the bundle he'd picked up at the shoemaker's shop. It held Karl's boot and the shoe of the Myllysilta brother who'd killed Svensson, the storekeeper back in Gamlaby, so long ago. He put Karl's boot—the one that had been in the window—into the box that held its mate.

He debated a moment. He didn't want Karl's boots to touch the other shoes. He wrapped the two shoes from Svensson's killer in paper and put them into the box. Last, he also folded Myllysilta's shoe in paper, and laid it alongside the others. He sat back on his heels.

He nodded, satisfied. He replaced the lid on the box and put it into the back corner of the closet.

Then he went outside to sit with Viktoria, have a smoke, and wait for Owen and Marilyn to return.

Jussi knew how this would go, how it had gone many times in the past decades, though never about someone so close to his family.

The shoemaker would call the police, who would say that a "routine patrol" had found the body. They would answer, as best they could, any questions that Owen and Marilyn had.

Eventually, Owen would ask, and they would answer, that his father had committed suicide.

And then Jussi and Viktoria would try, as best they could, to offer comfort to Owen and Marilyn.

#

Very few people attended Andrew Millbridge's graveside funeral a week later. Owen had been uncomfortable announcing it publicly, given the nature of the death, but he'd done as expected. He'd put a very brief announcement of death in the newspaper. He'd told people at Millbridge Enterprises.

He'd decided on a graveside service, without clergy. His father wouldn't have wanted any.

Owen's sister, May, refused to attend, and she wouldn't tell Owen why, even though he offered to schedule it at her convenience. Marilyn came, as did Jussi and Viktoria. Jimmy was in school.

Besides them, only two or three older Finns from the Finn Hall, plus Ivor Mantere and his friend, Vilho, came. Owen didn't know Vilho's last name. Both Ivor and Vilho had been drinking a little—not enough to be drunk, nor to lower the solemnity of the service.

The shoemaker was not there. Owen half-expected to see Rufus Karialainen at the service, but he wasn't present. Neither was Dr. Wainwright. He had declined to come. No one from the office—not even Mrs. Vogel—attended. He wondered why but knew he could never ask.

Owen had expected a few phone calls or even cards from people who had read the notice in the *News Chronicle*, but had received none. He realized, with surprise, that he didn't know whether his father would be disappointed or pleased by the silence.

Before the eulogy, Owen made it a point to thank each of the people who were there. In the eulogy, he outlined some of his father's successes, building a company, gifts to the community. He said nothing about his father's physical illness, but focused instead on his father's love of family. He also told the story of his father's discovery of TV dinners. A couple of the older Finns laughed. Owen was grateful for their generosity.

He mentioned that he had found his father's violin broken and lying on the kitchen floor, but he did not elaborate, did not tell them that the body of the violin was in several scattered pieces, or that its strings were still connected to the tailpiece, the bow snapped in two, and that the violin's broken wooden case lay in the middle of the floor, open, stinking of dog urine.

He also did not tell the mourners what he'd found in his father's living room—the dead soldier's framed document, signed by mayor Edward Blaquier just after the end of World War I. It was still on the wall, but now, its frame was askew, the glass broken.

He didn't mention Wolf, sitting outside the back door, waiting to be let in.

The grave already had a tombstone. "Annie Millbridge" it said—not Anne. The years of his mother's birth and death were carved on it. His father's information would be added in a few days.

Owen wondered what his mother might think of having her husband lying beside her for eternity.

Would she feel offended at the manner of his death?

Would she be glad to have him back?

Would she forgive her husband for whatever had come between him and May?

#

That afternoon, when the burial was over, Owen called May to talk about the funeral, as they'd agreed.

At the end of the short conversation, Owen risked a question. "Will you come back now? At least to visit?"

"I—I don't know. It's still too soon to know. Maybe in a month or so. I'll let you know. Love you, bye."

As usual, Owen said goodbye to dead air.

After they hung up, May stayed sitting in her chair, face in her hands. *That's that,* she thought. Then, with a wry smile, what her father would have said: *What is, is.*

She retrieved a thick manila envelope from the shelf of her front closet, where she kept her coats and winter boots. She pulled out the pages she'd taken from the *Suomalaisen Kulttuurin Historia.* Briefly, she wished for a fireplace, but it wasn't necessary. She ripped each page in half, and then half again, and shoved them into the garbage bag that she would put out for Tuesday's pickup. From there, they'd be lost in the detritus of a major urban centre.

She wondered if her father had killed himself because he believed that she would, some day, alert the police to the murders and other crimes he'd committed.

Perhaps, she decided. But she felt no survivor's guilt. At the same time, she felt no duty to the state, no need to explain or reveal what she knew. Perhaps not even to Owen—she wasn't sure. She'd decide that later.

She thought only of this moment. Her father was dead, the man she'd loved, who'd tried to love her, who'd tried to keep her and Owen safe.

And, too, the man she'd feared, once she'd learned of the man he truly had been.

That man was no longer a danger. No longer of importance.

But she cried for the man she'd feared, and for herself, anyway. She cried for the man he'd tried to be. And for Owen.

And she cried for her mother.

PART V

ACCEPTANCE

"What is past is prologue."

Antonio, *The Tempest*, Act II, Scene i
William Shakespeare

MELODIES OF THE FUTURE

OWEN BEGAN WITH THE PAPERWORK—the will and documents that were in the lawyer's care, the material in the filing cabinet in the room that had been his father's office, the contents of his father's safe deposit box at the bank, the boxes of papers that were stored in the basement.

Once those were disposed of to appropriate lawyers and accountants, he took a break—just a quick breather, a few days—before he began the serious work of going through his father's belongings.

He had already adopted Wolf and begun to train him into more civilized behaviour. He had a hope—still unspoken—that Jimmy would help. Someday.

The box with the boot and the shoe was no longer in the basement, though a box with the improbable family history was. He wondered if the secret of his father's suicide lay in those pages. *Probably only the madness*, Owen thought. He had no *real* history with which to replace the fiction—which May still contended it was—so he debated keeping it. *But,* he imagined May saying, *he's dead. Who cares now?*

Owen shrugged and sent his father's writing into the incinerator.

He attended the rounds of meetings to make sense of the items in the will and the disposition of the listed assets. After one of those meetings, Owen had to stop himself from heading to his father's house, to discuss everything with Dad over a TV dinner.

Instead, he let Wolf into his own kitchen. He made a bacon-tomato sandwich, not sharing the bacon. He, like Wolf, was learning some uncomfortable facts. His father had not been especially beloved. He was not remembered fondly. Even over time, no one came forward to pay their respects.

Owen thought of Mozart, buried in a mass grave. His father, at least, had a headstone. He and May could go to a cemetery. He wasn't sure why this comforted him, except that it reminded him that his father was more than the manner of his death or the contents of his will. He slept better that night.

He knew he could ask for help, and he did. When he became intimidated, Marilyn counselled him, frequently, "One step at a time." And he remembered how she, and Jussi and Viktoria, had gone through many losses. Their steadiness helped him.

Occasionally Owen called Mrs. Vogel to get advice about, or an explanation of, something he had found. She even came out of retirement to help out at Millbridge Enterprises for a while.

By early October, Owen felt more confident. The paperwork still seemed endless, but at last, he didn't have to devote *all* his time to it. He could spend a moment or two, here and there, peeping into the near future to make decisions.

Should he keep his father's house, either for May or for himself? For him, selling was an easy choice. He'd never be able to live in it. It wasn't his childhood home, with fond memories. Instead, it was the place where his father's madness had taken hold and sent down roots, where he had planned his suicide, and where he had played the infernal violin.

Looking back, Owen recognized that despite his father's hopes and efforts, the house had never, not even for May, become a real home. It was merely someplace they'd lived. He phoned May.

May answered her phone on the fourth ring. She'd become much more communicative, calling him every couple of days since the funeral.

Owen told her that he was ready to tackle the problem of the house. "Are you sure it's okay with you to sell it?" He knew what she'd say, but he needed to hear her say it. "Have I given you enough time to think about it?"

May's affection was tinged with exasperation. "Owen, just *sell* it, for crying out loud. I don't want to ever have to see the inside of that place again."

"It's a big job." He tried not to sound downcast.

"Okay." May took a breath. "Okay, here's an idea. How about I come up, and we spend as much time as it takes to do what has to be done? I shouldn't make you handle it all by yourself. I can get the time off work. That won't be a problem."

"Are you sure? You just said you don't want to see the house."

"Oh, I don't. It's the last thing I want. But I'm sure you don't want to clear it out either, and it's not fair for you to do all the work. You've asked Mrs. Vogel to help with the business. I can help with the house."

"If you're sure," Owen said. "It would be a huge help. You can stay at my place."

Working one room at a time, Owen and May sorted the contents of the house, leaving some of the goods but discarding its poisonous memories. Owen arranged for a sale of the best contents—furniture, appliances, artwork, tools, books—and scheduled the sale for a week before Halloween, to give them a deadline. And then he ordered a commercial garbage bin to be parked in the driveway, and over a two-week period, they filled it with the remains of his father's life, and some of their own.

The first thing May threw into the bin was the strange Finnish Cultural History with its heart cut out—partly for her own satisfaction, partly so Owen wouldn't handle it and wonder. By the time they were finished, the autumn leaves had turned their last brilliant colours and let go of their branches to drift softly to the ground.

#

When the bin had been carted away, they took a break. Neither wanted to be around for the estate sale itself. May went back to Toronto, as she said, "to clear up a few things, but I'll come back for Halloween. I want to see Jimmy's pilot costume. And I have to make sure you're giving out good treats."

"Great. We should have more paperwork to sign by then," Owen said.

May laughed, as he had intended. "Lighten up, brother." Her laugh came more easily, and she'd lost the aura of fear and worry she'd carried for more than a year.

One Saturday afternoon, Owen phoned Marilyn. "I need to talk to you," he said. "Got a favourite restaurant?"

"You could just come over here," Marilyn said.

"Thank you, but no, this is complicated. I need to talk to you alone."

"How about you just pick me up, then? We'll go for a ride."

"Good idea. I'll see you in about five minutes."

Wolf, sensing that something of interest might be afoot, ran to the car as soon as Owen opened the door to the driveway. Owen let him have the back seat all to himself.

They parked at Boulevard Lake, and Owen turned to Marilyn.

"I found something odd." He smiled without humour. "Well, extra odd." From his shirt pocket, he pulled out and unfolded a piece of paper.

"It's my father's handwriting. The pad was in a kitchen drawer, but this piece of paper was shoved in the back of his top desk drawer."

Marilyn examined it. "It's a diagram—of names?" She shivered.

"Apparently. I know Dad's memory was failing, but I don't know why he drew this. I don't know what to make of it."

In pencil on the sheet, there were names: Mantere, Lassila, Solbakken, and Myllysilta—written in a shaky hand, four times each. Through various circles and arrows and notes, the diagrams seemed to show how the names were linked.

Owen said, "Maybe he was just doodling. Maybe this is some kind of mnemonic device to help him keep stuff straight. I just don't know."

He pointed at the first diagram on the sheet. "I think this means that Jussi Mantere married Viktoria Lassila—no problem there—and had a son named Raimo."

To the right was a barely legible scribble. "This part shows that Viktoria had been married before, to Karl Solbakken, who was killed in 1918."

"But not the first World War," Marilyn said. "It was the Finnish Civil War."

"Right—I remember Jussi mentioning that war when I came to dinner. I'd never heard of it before."

"No one has. Dad—Jussi—told me the story last summer. He fought as well. The war was an awful thing, and its aftermath worse. People still don't talk about it, neither here nor over in Finland, he said." She turned the subject. "Did your father fight in the war?"

"I don't know. He never said. But would he? He never talked about Finland." Owen pointed to another part of the chart. "So after Jussi Mantere came to Canada, Viktoria did, too, and they married here."

"Yes. This makes sense. And this other arrow also says Solbakken?"

"That one's a puzzle, but if read my father's notes correctly, Ivor Mantere is actually Ivor Solbakken. For some reason Ivor felt he had to dump his own name and pick another one—and he picked Jussi's."

Marilyn was quiet for a moment. "Yes, that's true. Jussi told Jimmy the story, and Jimmy, of course, told me. There were three Solbakken brothers—Anders, the oldest, then Karl, then Ivor, whose childhood nickname was Rabbit." She blinked quickly to keep tears at bay.

Owen didn't seem to notice. "Good. It's nice to have confirmation. Now we're at something I don't understand: the name Myllysilta. In Finland, names often have something to do with where the family lived, so I looked up Myllysilta in an atlas. No such place—at least nothing like a town or village. But break the name in two—*Mylly* and *silta*—and it becomes Millbridge."

"Jesus, Owen! So you and May are really Myllysiltas?"

"Maybe, but I don't think so. My father always said we were Niemis, remember? But he gave Millbridge as his name when he arrived in Canada. That became his legal name here. Lots of immigrants did that. But why write Myllysilta? And how is it connected to all these other names—your family's names?"

After another pause, Marilyn said. "I don't know, Owen. Do you want to talk to Jussi about this?"

"Yes." A pause. "No. Yes. I mean, I did. But now, I don't know." Marilyn waited. "Why?"

"Because...." Owen could not continue. *Because I want everything to feel finished, no matter the cost? Because there's a story I think I'm entitled to hear?*

After a moment, Owen said, "You know what? I don't have a reason. Since Dad died, I've felt like Alice in free fall down the rabbit hole. I'm looking at everything around me and waiting for the bottom of the hole to smack the life out of me. I'm—I'm in a world where nothing seems to make sense anymore."

Marilyn sat in silence, waiting for Owen to finish.

He said suddenly, "And that's stupid. Sometimes, the best thing to do is to not ask questions—to stop trying to dig up the whole story, to just shut up and enjoy life. Sometimes no good comes out of knowing something. I'm done with trying to fit puzzle pieces together."

He tore up the paper, saying, "Goodbye Alice, goodbye rabbit hole. May your mysteries rest in peace." He put the pieces in his breast pocket.

Marilyn reached over and took his hand in hers. "Yes," she said, a benediction.

Owen dropped Marilyn off at the Manteres' home and returned to his house on Dufferin Street. He put the scraps of paper directly into the kitchen garbage bin.

Wolf, released from the car, trotted into the back yard to sleep in the sun, near the porch steps. He came in for supper and a few pats on the head, but asked to go out again when night fell. Owen knew he'd spend the crisp night exploring. He hoped Wolf wasn't looking for his father—he knew, or hoped, that Wolf wouldn't find him.

#

When May returned at the end of October, Marilyn booked a few days off. One drizzly day, she borrowed Owen's car and took May out to lunch. On the way, she drove past Big Day Bridal and pointed it out.

"Nice window," May commented. "I'd know to go there even if I weren't a bride but just wanted a fancy dress."

Marilyn said, "So, window displays—is that what you do? Owen never seemed to know, exactly, and I haven't had a chance to ask you."

"Yes, among other things," May said. "I've worked at bookstores, gift shops, hardware stores, restaurants—even a few department stores." She was finding Marilyn easy to talk to. "Not full time. I'd do other things, too, usually whatever the owner or sales staff hated."

"Inventory?" Marilyn laughed, and May joined in.

"Say, I have a question for you." May stared straight ahead, at the expanse of windshield cleared by the wipers, then spotted with raindrops, then cleared again.

"Ask away," Marilyn said. She braced herself for questions about Owen and Jimmy, or perhaps Ivor.

But May had no need to ask about Ivor. She already knew. Instead, she said, "It's about—about your family. Jussi, Viktoria. And mine." May took a breath. "I know things. Some things Owen doesn't know at all. About Dad. And Finland. And even in Canada. They're—not nice."

Marilyn held up her hand to stop her. "And you want to know if you should tell us? Tell Owen?" At May's nod, Marilyn said, "No. Not unless it—it *haunts* you, somehow. If you can forget, I think you should. That's my opinion, of course. You will do what you like."

May said slowly, "I think I can forget. Or if not forget, put it away. My only hesitation was about Owen. What he might need, or want, to know."

"Owen wants to move on, or so he's told me. I strongly recommend just leaving it be. The past is the past, now. We have a future to create."

Marilyn thought then of Raimo, and of Viktoria's first husband, Karl.

It came to her in a flash: *Sometimes honouring someone means letting go to love again.*

"I hoped you'd say that. It feels better," May said. "As Dad would say, 'What is, is.'"

Marilyn smiled. "Viktoria and Jussi would, too."

Marilyn didn't ask whether May would think it was odd for Owen to raise raised Jimmy—who was, after all, another man's son. No relation at all, not really.

If she had, May would have laughed darkly. After the lies her father had told to keep Owen safe while Raimo was not, she'd have said, "It's the absolute *least* we can do."

#

Over the next few months, Owen sold his own home as well as his father's. On Franklin Avenue, he bought a modest place, a storey and a half, about a block from the Mantere's on Montgomery Street.

When he proposed to Marilyn, she accepted, and they were married in the spring of 1956. May and Marilyn's long-time friend Laura were bridesmaids; Jimmy was the best man, Rabbit a groomsman.

May returned to Port Arthur to live, ostensibly to take over Marilyn's job at Big Day after she married Owen, and but truthfully to stay near family. "Now that I have some," she said in an aside to Jimmy.

"We've got lots," he answered.

He was right. A year after the wedding, Abigal May Millbridge was born, Abigail because it meant "my father's delight," and May for her aunt.

Jimmy Mantere had two homes—one that he shared with his parents and Wolf and Abigail, and one that he shared with his grandparents. He scuttled between them at will.

Jimmy and his Aunt May and his Uncle Ivor all watched out for each other, shifting roles as the years passed.

Rabbit, who had been broken by the Finnish Civil War, healed a little more each year, but even to his closest friends—whose numbers steadily grew with time—he never again spoke of Antti Myllysilta or Andrew Millbridge.

He became something of a philosopher. May wrote down a few of his best thoughts. She read this one, his own favourite, to the large group gathered at his funeral a few years later.

"Though honesty is the best policy and experience the best teacher, it is only in our sleep we learn to dream; only in our silences that our spirits learn to heal; and only through our actions that our spirits learn to love."

ACKNOWLEDGMENTS

This novel came into being with the help of many people.

Much of this novel is in conversation with my first novel, *Silences: A Novel of the 1918 Finnish Civil War*. For that book, many generous members of the Scandinavian community throughout Ontario, some of whom are no longer with us, provided invaluable help and support. Many thanks to Kaarina Brooks, Ahti Tolvanen, Elinor Barr, Freda Karioja (one of my elementary school teachers), Donna and Melvin Johnson, Lillian Erickson, Carol Vukovich, Signe Ranta, Beth Boegh, and Gordon Aegard.

I am eternally grateful for the time they spent with me and their interest in helping create fiction with factual roots.

For information about the Finnish Civil War, I also read J. O. Hannula's *Finland's War of Independence* (1939, with excellent battle maps) and Anthony F. Upton's *The Finnish Revolution 1917-1918*, a well-balanced history of the war written in 1980. D. G. Kirby's *Finland and Russia 1808-1920: From Autonomy to Independence,* and the second volume of Väinö Linna's brilliant trilogy, *Under the North Star*, helped me create sensory impressions of the war. Much information about the war is now available online, far more than when *Silences* was first published in 2017.

Evoking Port Arthur, Ontario, from the 1920s through the 1950s was almost as daunting—and every bit as fascinating—as rendering the Finnish Civil War. At the Thunder Bay Public Library's Brodie branch, I read all the microfilm copies of the *Port Arthur News Chronicle* for the summer of 1955, when the story of the Millbridges and the Manteres comes to a head. I dabbled in reports from other years. The library also provided me with a useful map of the Lakehead—one with the old street names from before 1970, when Port Arthur and Fort William amalgamated into Thunder Bay and half the streets in each former city were renamed.

Other important works for the local Canadian sections included *A Century of Sport in the Finnish Community of Thunder Bay*, published by the Northwestern Ontario Sports Hall of Fame and the Thunder Bay Finnish Canadian Historical Society, and Kaarina Brooks's and Raili

Garth's *Trailblazers: The Story of Port Arthur Kansallisseura Loyal Finns in Canada 1926-2002*. Beth Boegh's monograph, *Immanuel Evangelical Lutheran Church 1906-2006*, unlocked a lot of memories.

To help me create the feel of Finland before and during the Civil War, I found *Through Finland in Carts* by Mrs. Alec-Tweedie (Ethel Brilliana Tweedie) very helpful. It is a tourist's record of the sights and sounds of Finland in 1897. Her descriptions of ordinary life in the country and, in the 1913 edition of the work, the political situation were fascinating and incredibly useful.

For *Silences* I created the village of Gamlaby and its environs, as well as the Myllysilta brothers, but Antti's family became more real throughout the writing of this book.

The violin on the cover is Finnish, made in the 1930s, advertised for sale online. It reminds me of a violin my uncle Emil once owned, and what Millbridge tells Rough-house about violin shapes is what I learned when restoring that violin.

Like *Silences, The Devil's Violin* is a work of fiction. I've mentioned a few actual incidents and people, but their characters are fictional. Anyone interested in the real history of Thunder Bay and its people should definitely check out the publications of the Thunder Bay Historical Museum as well as other historical archives.

Speaking of support: I am grateful to the many leaders of the Northwestern Ontario Writers Workshop for their hard work. Their contests, readings, and publications during the past twenty-plus years provided many opportunities for me to create, revise, and share my work.

Author and designer H. Leighton Dickson not only created an amazing cover for *Silences* and this book but has also provided guidance for all our publications. Thank you, Heather!

My son and daughter, Bill and Karen, both read drafts of this novel and provided helpful input and support.

I am also indebted to my wife, Marion Agnew, who is not only an exceptional writer, but a talented editor as well. Her insights and suggestions were invaluable. Thank you, Marion, for your patience with me when I would recite yet another "fascinating" story about the Finnish Civil War.

Roy Blomstrom
Shuniah, Ontario, 2024

ABOUT THE AUTHOR

Roy Blomstrom, born in Port Arthur (now Thunder Bay), Ontario, is the son of Finland-Swede parents who lived through the Finnish Civil War and later emigrated to Canada. He has published poetry, stories, and essays, and his ten-minute plays have been produced in Thunder Bay, in Finland, and at the Brighton Fringe Festival.

He is grateful for support from the Ontario Arts Council for several of his works, including *Silences: A Novel of the 1918 Finnish Civil War* and his speculative fiction multiverse novel, *The Iterations of Caroline*.

He lives and writes in Shuniah, Ontario, Canada, just outside Thunder Bay. It is the territory of the Anishinaabe peoples, especially Fort William First Nation, and Métis peoples.

More information about Roy is available at www.shuniahhousebooks.com and at www.royblomstrom.ca.

www.ingramcontent.com/pod-product-compliance
Lightning Source LLC
Chambersburg PA
CBHW072110020726
47501CB00003B/793